İskender Pala wa … rgraduate degree from the faculty … He received his Doctorate in Otto … from the same university in 1983. His short stories, essays, academic papers and newspaper columns have inspired his readers to see Divan literature in a new light; his Ottoman Literature seminars are widely attended. İskender Pala is revered for his love of Divan poetry. He is the recipient of the Turkish Writer's Association Prize (1989), The Turkish Language Foundation AKDTYK prize (1990) and the Turkish Writer's Association Essay Prize (1996). He was given the title 'The People's Poet' by popular vote in Uşak. His books *Death in Babylon, Love in Istanbul; Katre-i Matem and The King and the Sultan, Od, Mihmandar* and *40 Songs of Nightingale* have won numerous literary awards and enjoy a wide readership. Honoring his success, The Turkish Patent Institute has registered İskender Pala as a brand name. He was granted the 2013 Presidential Culture and Arts Grand Award in literature. İskender Pala is married with three children and teaches at Kültür University.

www.iskenderpala.net

Fulya Vatansever

Fulya Vatansever is an Australian journalist, educator, translator and voice-over artist. Born and raised in Sydney, Australia, she earned a degree in Communications with a specialisation in Journalism from Monash University, a Graduate Diploma of Education from Charles Sturt University, and most recently a Master of Arts in Islamic Studies from the University of New England.

She worked for many years as a teacher, educational leader and public speaker in Melbourne, working both within and outside the classroom to educate and inspire Australians from all walks of life.

In 2007, she was invited to contribute to the Australian Broadcasting Corporation (ABC) publication, *Mosaic: Favourite Prayers and Reflections from Inspiring Australians*.

Fulya has a passion for English literature, cryptic crosswords, and public speaking. Living in Istanbul for the past 5 years, where she worked for a short time as a journalist, she now predominantly continues her work translating and in voice-over.

Her translations to date include a wide repertoire of works from the fields of Sufism and spirituality, Ottoman history and architecture, as well as political science and the media, particularly within the Turkish context.

When she's not translating written text, she's more likely standing in front of a microphone and rendering the printed word into speech.

Publication No. 470
The Complete Works of İskender Pala 66

Death In Babylon Love In Istanbul
Original Title: Babil'de Ölüm İstanbul'da Aşk
İskender Pala

Translated by Fulya Vatansever
Edited by Allegra Mostyn-Owen

Cover Design by Utku Lomlu
Page Layout by Mürüvet Durna

1. Edition: September 2015
ISBN: 978-605-5147-19-8
Certificate No: 10905

KAPI PUBLICATIONS
Ticarethane Sokak No: 15 Cağaloğlu/ISTANBUL
Tel: +90 (212) 513 34 20-21 Fax: +90 (212) 512 33 76
e-mail: bilgi@kapiyayinlari.com
www.kapiyayinlari.com

Printed by Melisa Matbaacılık
Certificate No: 12088
Çiftehavuzlar Yolu Acar Sanayi Sitesi No: 8
Tel: +90 (0212) 674 97 23 Fax: +90 (0212) 674 97 29
KAPI is a trademark of the ALFA Publishing Group.

DEATH IN BABYLON
LOVE IN ISTANBUL

İSKENDER PALA

kapı

An Attempt at the Impossible –Why I wrote *L&M*[*]

If you ask me, a reader who knows nothing of love should not even attempt to read this book. The writer – no matter what his experience or powers of persuasion – cannot convince anyone that his subject matter is remotely interesting if the book is just about the anguish, longing and separation that everyone finds so painful.[†] This much I know.

On that long night during which I recited the poem about Leyla and Mecnun as we sat under the ornamental ceiling of the west room, I kept on repeating to my friends that a story which told only of suffering would prove none too attractive to today's readers.

---

* [Translator's note: The letters L and M are the initials of legendary lovers Leyla and Mecnun. The story originated as a short poem in Arabic which was adapted into Persian and then Turkish.]

† [Translator's note: The letters 'L' and 'M', when pronounced together with their English vocalisation, (i.e. *'el-em'*) form the Turkish word which denotes 'pain' or 'suffering' – author's pun.]

Suffering blends idea with action. It has been with us since time immemorial and so it will continue. One might say it lies somewhere between dream and reality, between literature and history. Extracting an exciting adventure from this appeared to be rather difficult for our day.

But on the following night, I had a dream. Before the window of the Temple of Ishtar overlooking the Ziggurat of Babylon, wise priest Akeldan told me everything, absolutely everything, that had happened in his time. Showing me seven tablets carved in cuneiform script which lay close to beautiful golden temple idols, he declared, "There are just seven secrets for one who knows love."

"Could you transform ore into metal and distil the sea down to a single drop by teaching me these secrets?" I asked him.

"To know is to burn," he responded. "If you want to learn the meaning of love, you must first experience suffering. If you explore Fuzuli's* book on love, you will discover the proper manner and means of doing so." Over the following days, I re-read Fuzuli's book in the light of Akeldan's words. To comprehend what had happened to him, I trawled through historical manuscripts and dressed up the ancient stories of love with my own imaginings. When I beheld a vision of high gates opening onto space, I felt the need to share with the reader my adventures in the corridors of time.

It is surely the reader's final word and not what the author writes first that matters most. This is the unchanging fate of books and their writers. All my toil, this attempt of

---

* [Translator's note: Fuzuli (d. 1556) is regarded as the greatest poet of Turkish literature in general and has always been known primarily as a poet of love. He is the author of *Leyla and Mecnun*, written in the *mesnevi* genre (narrative poetry in rhymed couplets). The work explores the philosophical implications of earthly or metaphorical and divine or true love.]

mine at the impossible, is aimed at having that final word uttered truthfully.

In the east, it was the year of the white dragon. Wafted by the autumn breeze, I dipped my quill into the ruby inkwell and began writing this story. In Fuzuli's verses, a 23,000 year-old mystery became a story of love.

1
The Beginning of the Story – Joy out of first Sorrow

Neither within time am I,
Nor completely outside it.
Whole, in the Unbreakable
flow of a protracted moment

A. H. Tanpınar

Light seeped into the library of the Academy of Sciences. The building looked like an ancient basilica towering over the Tigris River. Each time the library was rocked by cannon fire, his heart felt as though it might stop. It was not so much that he feared being hypnotised by the rhythms of the tambourines beating along the city walls swarming with people; it was rather that he was unnerved by the change overwhelming the city. But he resisted the urge to go outside and close the library gates behind him when the blind hunchback returned with the forbidden volumes in hand.

The librarian had only gone to the vaults to retrieve them after much wheedling and flattery. Fortunately, this aged Assyrian – an expert in Chaldean and Assyrian history – was none too excited by the entrance to Baghdad of Ottoman Sultan Süleyman the Lawgiver*, merely coughing intermittently and murmuring, "What must happen will happen and what is awaited will come. That which is born today will tomorrow certainly die."

Then he asked, "Do you want the volumes, or are you going to go and watch the Sultan's horse parade like one of those date merchants from Basra?"

This proved a truly difficult question for Hilleli Mehmet Efendi, a man in his fifties. Should he watch the Sultan's entrance to the city like most other people? Perhaps the dilemma would not have presented itself had the librarian not prompted him. Now he felt as though the sights heralded by the Sultan's cannon fire were scenes worth witnessing. And yet he yearned for visionary excursions into the realm of the written word among the ruins of the Tower of Babylon where he had lost his childhood sweetheart. For a moment, he thought that the librarian might even hear his racing heartbeat and see the wrinkles that the dilemma between mind and heart etched upon his forehead. "The volumes!" he exclaimed.

"Then study until the sunbeams enter through this window," the librarian instructed, as he turned back with a sure step to close the door from the inside. He placed the binders

---

* [Translator's note: While Sultan Süleyman came to be known in Europe as Süleyman the Magnificent in recognition of his conquests and the awe that visitors felt when they saw the Süleymaniye Mosque, he is recalled in the Muslim world today as Süleyman the Lawgiver (Kanuni) because he was an active legislator during the course of his long reign.]

down on the blanket next to the stove as though he could see. "It is only then that the Sultan's men will be able to come in here and seize control." With these words, he indicated one of the stained glass windows beneath the dome and did not turn his gaze away, as if keeping an eye on where he stepped.

Mehmet Efendi opened the first leather binder excitedly: it resembled the bags carried by horseback riders at the circus. Some vellum scrolls rolled out. These were similar to the scrolls that the early Christian priests who had to leave Jerusalem in the sack of 70 AD placed in great vats, but they were written in a script that Mehmet Efendi did not know.

"I suspect that this blind fellow fetched them from the wrong chest, or else he miscounted the aisle," he said to himself. All the scrolls were of the same kind: upon them were depictions of the crucifix and baby Jesus in his mother Mary's arms. Had Mehmet Efendi known when placing and fastening the scrolls in the leather binders that they held around 100 logia written in Hebrew and Aramaic script by monks living right in the middle of the desert, he would in all likelihood have spent the rest of his life engaged not in medicine or poetry, but in theology. He would have devoted his remaining years to unravelling the mysteries of the land between the two sacred rivers, especially if he had known that he held the parchment describing the fish that Saint Augustine bought from Ostia and that the sentences written upon it were the mystifying verses taken from the Gospel of Saint Thomas...

The second leather binder was filled with folders piled higgledy-piggledy one on top of the other. Within each folder were treatises of 20 or 24 pages sewn together; on some pages were depictions of naked women and men sketched with ochre, as well as drawings concerning human anatomy, diagrams of primitive distilling methods, vessels, carafes and crucibles, a series of medicine bottles, cross-sections of the leaves of various herbs, root fibres, and sketches of diverse birds and insects. This was indeed some of the information he sought. At least the librarian had been right when it came to these.

But it was only when Mehmet Efendi began to read the annotations someone had scribbled in Arabic that he realised he had a treasure in his grasp. "The Treatise of Yellow Fever Ptolemy I Soter Commissioned from the Royal Library of Alexandria," "Ibn Sina's Treatise of Healing On the Life of the Embryo in the Mother's Womb", "Treatise on the Syrups Obtained from Plant Roots in the Serapaeum and Methods of Treatment," "Plato's Treatise on the Spirit and Death". These were the bundles of books taken secretly from the Great Library of Alexandria that the Roman Patriarch and priests had burned exactly a millennium earlier on the pretext of idolatry and paganism. Here at last were the manuscripts of medicine and philosophy that Muslim scientists had later developed.

The last binder contained only two folders. One of these concerned horse domestication and rearing and the ailments and treatments of desert animals and camels; the other related the history of Baghdad and stories of The Forty Thieves and famous caravan robberies. At the end of this was a chapter from the *Arabian Nights*, and all of these were written on Egyptian papyrus.

Since the blind librarian obviously knew the names and locations of every kind of binder by heart, Hilleli Mehmet Efendi was just about to tell him that some of these were not the books requested and that he had likely searched the wrong shelf. But then he pondered that the librarian had removed these binders from the chests with great difficulty. Also, judging by the sounds coming from outside, it was only a short while before the Lawgiver's chief of the palace guard appeared, so he changed his mind.

He re-opened the second binder and began researching ancient methods of medical treatment for the book entitled *Health and Disease* he planned to write in Persian, analysing and copying the diagrams of human anatomy one by one. Supposing the librarian to be listening to his every move and even deliberately coughing when he turned the pages a little roughly, he reckoned the old man more effective at his office than one who kept his eye firmly fixed on the reader. He felt ashamed for having contemplated slipping one of the books under his robe and taking off with it.

The book he coveted bore the most ancient seal of the Royal Library of Alexandria. The seal had been carved upon a clay cylinder and then impressed upon the papyrus with a rolling motion. He could see that it belonged to that first library which had burned to the ground due to Cleopatra's indifference during the uprising which took place when Julius Caesar – he who transformed the Roman state into an empire – had reached Alexandria after pursuing and defeating Pompey. "'Treatise on the Discussions of Philosophers Pythagoras and Thales.' Oh! if only I could read this script!" he sighed. As he turned the pages, he wondered how the book was spared the flames which had forced the history of science to begin afresh. It did not take him long to find the answer.

"This must be one of the 200,000 books that Mark Anthony brought from Pergamon," mused Fuzuli Mehmet Bey. He began to caress the volume like a man touching his delicate loved one, slowly and joyously wiping off the dust of the long majestic ages which outrun mere history, smelling the cover and gazing down upon the pages.

The odes of conquest being proclaimed from all the city's minarets indicated that the Sultan was about to enter the latest addition to his territory. The bell-ringers of the Assyrian and Roman churches also sounded their bells with all their might as though competing with the town criers in jubilation. Everyone, including the Jews of the East Coast, gathered at the squares of the Great Mosque of al-Mansur, of Taq-i Kisra, the Tomb of Zubayda and the Mustansiriya *Medrese* along the Tigris and participated in the exaggerated festivities marking the end of the long and unjust rule of Tahmasp I and the Safavids. It was always the same story: new masters always required the rejection of former rulers and their relentless criticism by their subjects. Those who were natives only yesterday behaved today as though they were entering a newly conquered city. Amassing in throngs in the city's streets and squares, they formed choruses cursing Tahmasp and showering praise upon the Ottoman Sultan as though they had been paying homage to him for years. The real crowds, however, had gathered in the vicinity of what was the centre of Sunni Islam in Shiite Baghdad – the tomb of Abu Hanifa.

From here to the east bank of the Tigris and towards the entrance of the Tabriz Gate, people from all walks of life, including beggars hoping for a share in the gold the Sultan would dispense, lined up in rows and shouted stock slogans, as though reciting prayers. After the formal ceremony, when the Safavid Governor Tekkelu Khan's offered the city to Ibrahim Paşa, the crowds grew enormously and went on celebrating

throughout the night. Most of those who stayed out on the squares until daybreak were desert dwellers, criminals and fugitives prowling the city for plunder and pillage, like wolves after sheep.

The chief janissary held all four gates with a battalion of troops and had criers proclaim a clear message on his behalf, "I will have the head of whosoever removes so much as a stone without my permission." So the low-lifes kept their hands to themselves. You could hear them snarling, their praise for the Lawgiver trailing off.

The date saplings filling the Tigris valley were shaken by the boom of 11 retorts of cannon fire, and the whooping crowds of the city surged once again. The Lawgiver was entering the city. This was something akin to the reunion between the lover and her beloved. The Sultan set off from Kasr-ı Şirin which had, according to legend, been constructed for Şirin by Ferhat the architect. After receiving the citadel keys from Ibrahim Paşa's standard-bearer Cafer Bey and presenting him with 500 gold coins and one fur coat, the Sultan advanced towards the wondrous Aleppo Gate. The gate was rendered still more impressive by its relief carvings of beasts attacking men.

Those who now witnessed the Sultan's assured nobility atop his horse in procession, accompanied by his ceremonial troops – sergeants, dignitaries, infantry officers, footmen and commanders – could easily understand why he was referred to as Süleyman the Magnificent. It was as if this man had been created to combat the Roman gods. Each of the stone cannonballs on either side of the gate, weighing around 163 kilograms apiece, appeared as if it could have been a mace in his hand.

***

The librarian was listening out for the sounds coming from outside as though he could actually see with his ears. As whoops of joy reached the outer courtyard of the Academy Library, he snatched the books from in front of Hilleli Mehmet to lock them back inside the trunks. When he returned, he held a bejewelled dagger with a two-horned, fork-tongued hilt cast in the form of a snake. He unsheathed it from its emerald- and jade-encrusted scabbard and, as though reading the inscription on the blade, he declared, "For those who know how to die, the dagger means life; there are seven true secrets for one who knows love, and one who possesses it gains mastery over the world." He stressed each of the words separately.

"May this dagger be for you a divine trust and secret placed in your possession by God. Guard it well!" Puzzled, Hilleli Mehmet wondered why the receipt of a gift should be kept secret. But then he ruminated over how the exchange of gifts was the oldest tradition hereabouts and so he put another interpretation on this admonition. "I dare say the old man does not want me to come back here again."

The old man stooped, as though projecting his hunch, and pricked up his ears at the sound of approaching footsteps. "Time is running out. When they ask you for the trust, do not place it in the wrong hands. You will most certainly recognise them," he whispered. The fellow had suddenly changed: it was as if he had become a different person and lost his voice. His actions were not those of yesterday's librarian. Beads of sweat broke out on his forehead and his hands were shaking. He removed the ring on his finger with difficulty, opened the hidden compartment under the bezel and, before Hilleli Mehmet's confounded gaze, raised it to his mouth, gulping at the same time.

"The man's a drug addict," Hilleli Mehmet told himself in astonishment; he deduced that he had needed a shot and must just have been blabbering nonsense. Otherwise, it was rather difficult to make sense of what had happened. Sounds from outside indicated that the Lawgiver's soldiers had entered the inner courtyard.

The librarian was very altered and began to touch the objects around him in a strange fashion. He was either looking for something or attempting to identify what his eyes could not see. At one point, he approached Mehmet Efendi and, stroking the dagger once more, said, "Whatever you do, do not forget, there are seven true secrets for one who knows love, and one who possesses it gains mastery over the world." Hilleli Mehmet was familiar with the delirium and confusion of drug addicts, but the old man spoke softly, as though reciting his last will, repeating the same sentence in exactly the same way each time.

"You're a good person," he said, almost as if he were looking straight into his eyes. "Promise me you'll keep the secret, promise you won't place the trust in the wrong hands."

"?!"

The inner door of the library swung open and an officer entered wearing a silver-brocaded kaftan. He was of high rank judging by the way he was issuing orders and had a dark complexion and a short, grizzled beard. "My name is Celalzade Mustafa," he greeted the librarian from the entrance. "I am the Sultan's Chancellor and I have come to take control of all the books and the whole library, old man."

The librarian passed the keys over as he began explaining the book collections and their value. The Great Chancellor charged four soldiers accompanied by one of the officers in command of a small subdivision of janissaries with counting the books. He gave the library keys to his steward and ordered him to guard them. He then examined the book repositories as well as the structure of the building itself. He was just about to leave the chamber when he caught sight of Mehmet Efendi, who was busy gathering the notes he had taken. "And who might you be, Sir?" he asked.

"The poet Fuzuli of Hilla, your humble servant, Sir."

The Great Chancellor was astonished. In an incredulous tone, he recited aloud the verses:

Whoever loves their own self for the sake of the beloved, loves the beloved;
Whoever loves the beloved for the sake of their self, loves their own self.

Then he asked, "And is it you who composes these charming words?" His voice ill-concealed the scorn of disbelief.

"Indeed, Sir, your humble servant."

"So you recite lyric poems and sing of love, is that right?"

"I endeavour to do so, Sir."

Celalzade made him speak while he sized him up. Was this man standing before him really the self-same poet who could recite those lyrics of love? A caravan which had brought a bundle of his poems to Istanbul two years previously had never returned, but those poems were still being recited at every assembly. Was this humble but neatly dressed man that very poet? Could he have been so lucky as to have chanced upon the poet he had hoped to find come what may, on the very day of his entry into Baghdad? Had fate treated him so kindly? All these thoughts crossed his mind as he spoke and, as he heard each answer and responsive recital of verse, he felt childish joy and enthusiasm. In his desire to feel still closer to the poet, his commanding manner of address turned to reverence.

"Come then, great poet!" he finally exclaimed. "Allow us to receive you with open arms. On the day you were born, the hand of fate hung a star over your cradle. If you do not turn your back on the ability that God has conferred upon you, you can be certain that your fame, which has reached the city of Istanbul and the Sultan's own doorstep will one day be known wherever Turks reside."

No couple living close together over 40 years could have been as deeply companionable as these two who now embraced beneath the library's high dome. They took turns reciting couplets and lyrics, chatting as though they had known one another since childhood. There was no lack of respect or affection on either side. Only a sentimental member of the Ottoman Imperial household responsible for the chancery of the Ottoman State, a person of feeling whose emotions were heated by the winds of Mesopotamia, could have shown such friendship. "My dear master," the Great Chancellor said upon taking leave. "Please come and find me in three nights' time, so that Huseyin Baykara's soul may rest in peace." This invitation implied that politics and other matters would be left to one side and only poetry and art would be discussed. And so, the poet Mehmet Fuzuli replied, "The decree is from Your Highness and your wish is my command."

When he left the library, it was one hour after sundown. He squinted as he walked to protect his eyes from the dust sweeping Baghdad's open squares in the evening wind. It had been one of the most intriguing days of his life. The intensity of his emotions stemmed not from the delirium of the crowds celebrating the conquest, but from the odd encounters with the librarian and the official and then the prospect opened by the invitation. He did not know whether to rejoice or feel afraid.

Fuzuli remained troubled: when he had left the librarian in his chamber, the old man had been feverish, but he had spurned Fuzuli's offer to stay and urged him on. But then he was overcome with relief that he had met the man at the head of the Ottoman bureaucracy. What a stroke of good fortune! He could not help thinking about his own hardship. All his expenses and book purchases had left him penniless. But privation mattered little to him compared to the excitement of meeting Anatolian poets!

He examined the dagger with which he had been entrusted and which he had been keeping close under his arm. If the worst came to the worst, he could sell it and perhaps stay on in Baghdad for another few weeks and complete his research. "What a strange fellow the blind librarian was," he thought to himself. "He seemed wise, but maybe it was the drugs that made him speak thus."

His thoughts turned to Celalzade's invitation once more. Poets from Istanbul whom he had once known and whose fame was now widely celebrated would be coming in tandem with the Sultan's army. It was certainly going to be thrilling to meet and talk with them about poetry. Taşlıcalı Yahya, who would later be appointed district governor, Divan transcriber Hayali, janissary from Üsküdar Aşki and many others. He kept reminding himself along the way that he needed to stay in one of the city's cheap lodgings for another few nights.

What fortunate people these Anatolian poets were! They were like tame falcons eating out of the Sultan's munificent hand. Who knows what merry hours they spent at the Baykara parties and what beautiful poetry they recited! He supposed literature to be a way of life for these people. What a wonderful fancy it was for him to imagine sitting at a Baykara assembly in Ali Şir Nevai's quarters in Istanbul!

The first day's victory celebrations were over. So began a night fraught with fear as the people awaited not just the soldiers' intemperance but also police interrogation as well as wholesale looting. Hilleli Mehmet removed his belongings from the inn where he had been staying for two nights to a cubicle in a *medrese* school which had a canteen kitchen. Here he could expect free board and lodging.

If only he did not have to feel the weight of the bejewelled dagger on his chest when he retired at night! He carried a fortune and having the dagger on his person on such a day in his circumstances at the *medrese* could cause a great many problems for him. He would probably be subjected to lengthy questioning.

It was, without doubt, a very beautiful dagger. He delighted in admiring its beauty, likening it to one of the handsome officers of the volunteer vanguard. He felt a constant pang of conscience at selling a gift which clashed with his regret for the books he could not buy if he did not realise the money.

He gazed upon the dagger in the dying light of the candle and sank into reverie, mesmerised by the beauty of its inlay. One moment he considered going to the bazaar and selling it outright, the next he thought of paying a moneylender a few coins to remove the stones. Then he thought he might have a ring set with the largest ruby for the woman waiting for him in Hilla; he toyed with the idea of purchasing books for scientific research, or of having his children's clothes embroidered with the gems. He admired the dagger's beauty anew each time and was afraid of it.

He was struck by the double-horned snake on its pommel – what a strange symbol this was! In symmetrical arrangement was the relief of a hand with outstretched fingers. This did not look to be made of any metal he had ever seen before. It was nothing like steel; nor was it bronze or brass. It was unthinkable that such a fine dagger be wrought of iron. He could not call it gold or silver for its colour was unlike theirs. He wanted to scratch the surface with his pocketknife and later rubbed it with a rasp, but still he could not work it out. It was certainly very hard

Engraved upon the dagger were signs resembling writing. He was well versed in Assyrian script, but this was not Assyrian. When examining the bare, double-edged blade, he almost cut his finger so he immediately re-sheathed and took to inspecting the marks on the hilt. Upon the two finger-width cylindrical handle were engraved filigree divisions in the form of spirals. Each division was superimposed on the other like cartouches with oblique interlacing; letters were inserted into each cartouche and seven big and small rubies reminiscent of rosary beads were set between them. These were shiny and clinked when shaken. Then the seven letters and seven rubies caught his attention and he remembered the words of the old librarian. "There are seven true secrets for one who knows love. One who possesses it gains mastery over the world."

He was puzzled and spent the remainder of the night reflecting on these words, examining the dagger before him. On the dagger's hilt were seven panels, with seven rubies on the uppermost point of each of the seven panels and seven letters scattered at random beneath them. There had to be a connection, but what was it? The librarian had said, "For one who knows love." This, therefore, was related to love. It was Fuzuli himself who possessed more knowledge on love than anyone else. He was so much taken up with it that he had not been able to provide a single answer for what it was.

For years, he had sets its tracks to melody and been nourished by its pangs. He could recognise longing and sorrow wherever he saw it. He had experienced the seven stages of love and had learned the seven wisdoms ardently spoken of by the Sufis.

He repeated the words "love", "seven", "dagger", "ruby" the whole night long. By dint of this incantation he spent the night as though in a state of delirium. He knew his first task the following morning was to go to the library. When he finally fell asleep, the accumulation of an entire civilization collided in his consciousness with the figure seven, but this did not suffice for him to know the secret of seven.

When Fuzuli reached the gate of the Great Chancellor's mansion by the Tigris and began introducing himself to the chief steward, he thought that his heart would stop. He stepped into a hall where dressed silver trays were laid out on long low divans and could not gauge whether the heat he felt emanated from the large brazier at the centre, the excitement surging within him or the congenial countenances smiling upon him.

The hall rang with the song of harp and dulcimer; half of those present stood up when he entered and the other half voiced their separate welcomes by reciting verses from his poetry. When he sat on the cushion to the right of the Chancellor, he felt himself before an examining board. All eyes were upon him.

Tall cupbearers began preparing the table, and formalities gave way to a free and easy conversation about poetry accompanied by the sound of sweet music. Some recited lyric poems, others asked after the meaning of mysteries, while others still explained the teachings of Rumi in the verses of the *Mesnevi*. The music emanating from behind a curtain was occasionally made up of classical Ottoman *Meragi* compositions, or else harmonies to accompany Mevlana Rumi's lyrics.

Following all the debate, quips, banter, stories and laughs, discussion moved to the eternal love binding Leyla and Mecnun. After mutual renderings, Hayali Bey turned to Fuzuli and said, "O precious rose of Baghdad! O eminent master of verbal expression! The story of Leyla, daughter of the desert, and her crazed lover Kays has oft been told by Persian poets. Those relating the tale in Turkish are few and their words are rather feeble. Would you please open this hidden treasure, write a book thereon and bring fresh beauty to this old garden?"

Although Fuzuli left the mansion at dawn feeling drowsy, his host's words were already ringing in his ears.

2
Of Priest Akeldan's Ornament of Wisdom and the mystifying Tale of the Secrets of Space

Behold the land of the Chaldeans; this people was not, till the Assyrian founded it for them that dwell in the wilderness: they set up the towers thereof, they raised up the palaces thereof; and he brought it to ruin.

Isaiah 23:13

The importunate doorkeeper of the Baghdad Academy of Sciences blurted out in astonishment, "Great Sir, it has been but seven days since our venerable librarian – and I can attest to his being a true believer – was discovered poisoned on the evening the Lawgiver's soldiers came to the library. You are thus far the sixth person to inquire after him." If, on the morning he heard these words, Fuzuli had been able to overcome his urge to meet once again with the poets from

Istanbul, he would have returned to Hilla and spent the remainder of his days trying to forget what he had experienced.

But this did not happen. He succumbed to irresistible desires from within and recalled the librarian's clear countenance, his unseeing eyes and his wisdom. They had shared good times or rather, the librarian had been consistently obliging and shown him enough friendship to avoid his feeling home-sick. He had shared his food, offered his coffee and earned his trust through giving voice to his longing for home when they had spoken of wife and children. He knew a great deal and lived in a world with its own kind of nobility. He had refined tastes and loved to treat others. He was most generous considering his meagre wages.

After hearing of the old man's death, Fuzuli weighed up these considerations before deciding to return to his lodgings to re-examine the dagger. For starters, the librarian had not been poisoned as the doorkeeper had said, but had imbibed the poison in his ring. He felt remorse for having naively supposed the man to be on drugs. So why had he taken his own life? If he had nothing against Baghdad's new Ottoman identity, his death was cloaked in mystery. Fuzuli could not help but think that those who had come inquiring after the librarian must be after the dagger. He was overcome by fear. This is perhaps why he felt the need to re-examine that dagger; at least, this is where his thoughts led him.

Now he clasped it in both his hands: it did not look like the simple ram's horn dagger that men of Karbala hung on their sashes to complete their traditional costumes. It was clear that this dagger held antique value: the swordsmiths in these parts no longer forged such weapons. Perhaps it was the work of one of the old swordsmiths who crafted the rare bejewelled item as a gift to ancient Persian shahs. The handiwork and ornament were quite unique. Closer examination of the carved relief on the scabbard revealed it to be a right hand with the little finger and ring finger clenched and the middle fingers joined and extended. He had not noticed this before. What did it symbolise? Could it have been a tribal mark used by the Bedouin Arabs? Or did it signify something? He had never come across such a crest or emblem. These questions applied just as much to the other form on the hilt – the two-horned snake head.

And so began a day which was to pass in fear of a knock at the door. What did fate hold in store for him? Had the old librarian not been so good to him, he would have just said, "To hell with him," and gone his own way. He had a family to look after, research to undertake and books to write all waiting for him in Hilla. "I must find a way of getting rid of this dagger," he kept telling himself, only to recall the librarian's last words, "Protect the trust and do not place it in the wrong hands."

Now he remembered: with these words, the librarian had laid his hand on Fuzuli's shoulder and clenched his fingers together, just like in the carved relief. He inferred that this was a sign of friendship and trust. Then his thoughts turned to how he was meant to fulfil the old fellow's last wish: what had he meant by the seven true secrets?

"What if I were to remove the cabochons from the hilt and bury the dagger in an unknown place? I'd be rid of it and I'd also prevent it from getting into the wrong hands," he pondered. The stones were not fixed in place, but it was not as if they were easy to remove either. He inspected each gem in turn and tried to group them together according to shape, but to no avail. He attempted to lever the bezels with the willow leaf blade he used for cutting paper at home. But he failed to loosen a single setting. Despite their clinking, none could be extracted. "This is very hard cast steel; a lot of water must have been used in making this dagger," Fuzuli said to himself. He squeezed with all his might as he tried to gauge the strength of the settings. Then he placed pressure on all the stones at once between his two palms. The blade detached itself from the dagger's hilt and shot into the wall opposite, making a metallic twanging sound as it did so. Fuzuli dropped his arms in fright and excitement, and mumbled some prayers for protection. He could not remember his heart ever racing in such panic before. He was terrified at the thought that the dagger in his hand was an assassin's weapon rather than some kind of traditional accessory or adornment.

The dagger promised trouble. "Yes, yes, I must get rid of this as soon as possible," he repeated to himself. He did not know what to do. After what seemed a long time, his gaze was drawn to the hilt lying where it had dropped to the ground. From out of its base peeped a soft leather saffian strap which was tan-coloured. It was rolled into a scroll and looked to measure half a cubit in length. The strap was cut diagonally like a longish piece of baklava and had markings identical to those on the dagger's hilt engraved upon it apparently at random. He picked it up with a faint heart and began examining it thoroughly.

"The secret must be written here on the leather," he reckoned to himself as his pulse rate shot up and his hands began to shake. Perhaps he was going to have to consult different libraries once again in order to understand what it all meant. For the time being, he decided to take down a copy of the markings, as if drawing a picture.

"This must be a code," he mumbled as he lifted out some parchment from the bundle where he had stored the conclusions of his research. He laid down the leather strap ready to copy the letters. But what was it that the code unlocked? What did all these numbers and letters mean? He hesitated, overcome by confusion, until he felt his mind grow tired.

If Fuzuli could only have mastered his anxieties, he might have been able to think more clearly. He might then have wound the diagonal strap around the dagger's spiral lines and discovered the great secret of the wise priest Akeldan and the Babylon Society. But regrettably, since he supposed that the dagger would land him in trouble, he chose to bury it beneath the mulberry tree in the courtyard of the *medrese* in the middle of the night. Before doing so, he pieced it back together and re-sheathed it. When it came to the strap, he decided to fasten it like lining to the inner side of his water bottle strap. On the last day of his stay in Baghdad, he planned to bury the parchment on which he had copied the markings beside the body of the librarian, interred in the cemetery outside the city's walls. In this way, he felt he could return the dagger entrusted to him to its rightful owner and banish it from his mind forever.

Hours passed and still he could not overcome his nagging curiosity. What were the letters all about? Ridding himself of the puzzle by burying it would probably leave him devoured by doubt for the rest of his life. Perhaps spending a few extra days in research at the Academy of Sciences library was not such a bad idea after all.

According to the first book he examined, these were letters of the cuneiform script as used by the Chaldeans. The animal motif on the dagger, resembling a two-horned, fork-tongued snake, carried traces of bull and dragon motifs, as well as snake and griffin derivations. The long-necked and large-headed Babylonian dragon Sirrush, with clawed feet and scaly body, represented Marduk, the patron deity of the city of Babylon.

He evaluated the results of his research after several days and sensed that he had begun to open the door to a lost civilisation. He shuddered with dread at the enormity of his task. At the end of the seventh day, he deciphered the letters of the cuneiform script and had two locked chests at the library opened with special permission from the Lawgiver's genuflecting ağa. He handed all his spare change over to a half-deaf Egyptian Copt in his seventies who knew Chaldean in exchange for a translation of what was written on the papyruses from the chests. A long stretch in the flickering candlelight of the dark room lay ahead.

"The Chaldeans lived in the Mesopotamian lands where you now tread, centuries ago. They established the most advanced civilisations of their eras in such cities as Arbela, Nineveh, Cutha, Sippar and Ur and were the first to develop theories of philosophy, units of measurement, geometry and the calendar. It was they who divided the circle into 360 degrees. It was they who invented the true alphabet, which identified sounds with particular signs and set forth the first ever written culture on Earth. Everyone knows that they displayed astonishing feats of science well ahead of their time. They administered their kingdoms in accordance with legal and literary codes of behaviour and spoke in a sophisticated way. But most significant was their breakthroughs in astronomical research."

This was the topic that intrigued Fuzuli the most. According to what the old man read from the papyrus, the Chaldean scholars believed themselves to be living in a realm beneath the Moon, while the seven heavenly bodies in the region above the Moon managed nature.

"Yes, of course," he commented regarding the old man's reference to the Chaldeans' worship of the stars, as with the majority of the atheistic kings of old. "It was natural for them to be affected by the stars which shone in the sky with a light unseen elsewhere. They became preoccupied with some stars seeming brighter and livelier than others. They could only account for this order and grandeur with the idea of a god, so this is precisely what they did. They named every heavenly body that they identified and declared them to be deities, seeing and representing each of them with a different colour." As the Egyptian imparted the knowledge he had been unable to share with anyone for a long time, he felt a sense of self-importance and projected his excitement in his tone: "Samash (the Sun) is gold. Sin (the Moon) is like silver. Nebo (Mercury) is blue, Ishtar (Venus) white, Nergal (Mars) red, Marduk (Jupiter) purple and Ninib (Saturn) is black."

Fuzuli listened with the keenest attention and, as the sentences in the man's hands unravelled, the papyrus scrolls rolled back and the information they divulged reverberated on the lightless walls of the library. According to Chaldean scholars, these deities resembled the features of certain animals and, as they travelled across the sky, they sojourned in divine zodiacs and moved on different days in different ways so as to converse with those in the realm beneath the moon and express themselves to them.

In this way, astronomers took to anticipating and predicting what would happen on Earth and were, for the most part, on the mark. This is why priests were both soothsayers and scientists. When driving away Satan, catching fish in the Tigris or Euphrates, hunting lions, ploughing their fields or making love and war, they invariably acted in the name of these deities. They made figures and idols of solid gold to represent them in their temples and held ceremonies invoking their help. Wearing necklaces of precious stones on feast days and dressing up their idols in silk garments were deemed the greatest form of worship.

There was something else that drew Fuzuli's attention in what the Egyptian translated: everything was explained in terms of the figure seven. Everything in the realm beneath the Moon in which the Chaldeans lived, like the deities in the realm above the Moon, was connected to the number seven. They used to say that the skies were seven in number and that the universe had a structure composed of seven cosmic forms. And in their sermons, they spoke mainly of the seven periods of time to come, each of 10,000 years and of zodiacs pertaining to the gods, and the seven significant prophecies that would be realised in each of these seven periods.

Fuzuli looked at a plan of the seven-storey Great Ziggurat of Babylon on one papyrus. Had he known then that the dagger entrusted to him belonged to this ziggurat, perhaps none of what ensued would have taken place. He merely muttered under his breath, "Clearly, they gave it seven storeys because they had dedicated it to their gods."

The Great Ziggurat was buttressed with the seven columns of wisdom. On the bottom level were seven hidden interconnected divisions. Carved on the last of these was the scene of the sacrificial ceremony of a child. The child appeared to be seven years old and was waiting under the knife surrounded by seven priests, each carrying a candelabrum with seven branches. On seven dishes were mushrooms with seven spots, and beside them were seven goblets, each with seven panels. "I'll wager that the wine within them is also seven years of age," said Fuzuli, unable to stop himself, and the old man gave a roar of laughter.

On another page was a map of Babylonia, watered with the seven streams of the Euphrates. On the fields divided into seven beds stretched out the seven arms of the deity of abundance, Enlil. Subsequent pages of the map recorded that a seven-day fast of thanksgiving was observed every autumn and that the fast needed to be broken with a soup made of seven grains. He also learned that royal palaces and temples were constructed with seven doors.

In another picture was a depiction of the Eucharist. The high priest stretched out his joined hands, and the royal family were shown greeting him and the people by placing their hands upon his. What caught Fuzuli's attention was that the hands of the priest in the middle were shown with the two small fingers closed into the palm in exactly the same way as on the dagger. The liturgical garments worn by the celebrants were also very striking and, judging by the detail, there was great complexity in the ceremonial rites.

For three days, they examined the papyruses in the chests, one by one. The poet did not tell the old man what he sought, nor did the old man ask him anything.

When they came round to reading the last papyrus, Fuzuli thought for a moment that the old man would hear his heart thumping before remembering that, providentially, the fellow was deaf. He felt that what was written here must have something to do with the dagger and the codes.

Yes, indeed: this papyrus contained information pertaining to the Babylon Society. The old Copt started translating: the Babylon Society was comprised of seven scholarly priests who conducted astronomical research. They established a Space Research Centre where they could carry out observations and calculations, and discovered that Earth was spherical and that it revolved around the sun, but they were unable to disclose this to anybody. Nippin, a third-generation descendant of Nebuchadnezzar, was a tyrannical king. The astronomers feared that their discoveries might so startle him as to cost them their lives. They had come up with so many revolutionary theories as a result of their observations: they had, for instance, looked into whether the universe was made up of galaxies and whether intergalactic travel might be possible through black holes given the right speed and conditions. They also considered communication with other worlds and postulated how extra-terrestrial beings might journey to Earth in the future, how the inhabitants of the first planet to conduct such journeys would establish intergalactic dominance, and they investigated methods of self-protection in the event of ill-intent.

They encrypted their findings on seven kiln-fired clay tablets. Little could they have suspected that one of their own would betray the others for petty self-interest and reveal the location of the diagrams hidden in the secret vault of the Temple of Ishtar. Flagrantly disregarding the scientific ethics to which he was apparently committed, the traitor denounced his colleagues' findings as heresies and stripped himself of any claim to wisdom in the process.

As night fell all around, this miserable wretch disclosed to General Nippin that his colleagues' discoveries contravened the laws of Nebuchadnezzar. He claimed their research would lead the people astray and drive them to rebellion.

In response, the decapitated heads of five of the priests were flung to the bottom of the observatory wells. By noon, their bodies had also been buried, but all the technical equipment of these heretics were left perfectly intact.

But one scholar out of the seven priests, Arshiya Akeldan was out of town, having gone to visit his sick mother. He listened aghast as his slave, who ran all the way to catch up with him, explained to him between breaths what had befallen his friends. He was petrified. He considered hiding out for a week and then returning to the city to save the discoveries of the Babylon Society which had cost so much dedication and effort.

Sure enough, Nippin had him declared guilty and, presuming him to have stolen the golden idols in the King's treasury, he succeeded in drawing the wrath of the people against him as well.

The priest hid himself in a vineyard shed where he lived off dried fruit and nuts and hatched his plans. Entering the city in disguise under cover of night, he decided to take all the research equipment along with the golden idols, the findings with the seven tablets showing the positioning of the stars and planets as well as various astronomical discoveries to the Temple of Ishtar at the Great Ziggurat of Babylon. There he closed the marble door from the inside, burying himself together with the secrets of the Babylon Society for future generations to find. His final prayer was for his slave to pass on the Sirrush-headed dagger to good people with scientific acumen so that, when right-minded scholars and rulers emerged in the future, there would be those who could continue the work. The research recorded on the tablets concerning space travel, communication with other worlds or indeed delivery of the world from invasion by ill-intentioned extra-terrestrials could all be paid for with the sacred treasure of the idols.

The old Egyptian declared there were no more writings, but he said there were jottings in Arabic script. Fuzuli's excitement mounted. These were in all likelihood notes made by the blind librarian who wrote in Middle Persian Pahlavi. The old Copt did not know this language.

Fuzuli offered up a prayer for the dead librarian: "May he rest in peace according to his religion." The notes made mention of the Temple of Ishtar and the codes on its gate. Moreover, there were drawings just like the markings on the hilt of the Sirrush-headed dagger, as well as the hand motif with its two clenched fingers. It was clear that, after Akeldan, there had been others who had researched the dagger and recorded their findings on these papyrus documents. Notes had been made about the lock system: when the keys embedded in a marble cartouche like a chessboard were pressed in the form of one letter followed by one number, the door of the temple vault would open automatically.

According to the last sentences, priest Akeldan explained everything to his 13 year-old servant of just two years' standing and then, dividing the code into letters and numbers, marked the letters on the dagger's hilt and the numbers on its strap; then he entrusted the dagger to his servant and drifted off to eternal sleep in the Temple of Ishtar. In order to immortalise his name, he wrote the code letters as A-K-E-L-D-A-N and placed the numbers 6-0-0-3-3-2-0 in between them.

Hilleli Mehmet Fuzuli was able to recognise in these lines the letters and numbers on the dagger he had buried under the mulberry tree at the *medrese* and the saffian strap that came out of its hilt. But he could not gauge how this was to be used on the gate of the Temple of Ishtar, the location of which was also unknown to him.

The code that he did not and would not ever know was actually arranged very simply. Had he been familiar with the lives of seafarers, he would have been able to decipher it. In their secret communications, seafarers of old would write on saffian hides they wound around barrels and then gave to a deckhand to wear as a sash. When the ship docked, the intended recipient would search for a barrel of the same size, and so the code was deciphered by itself. In the event of the letters being scattered erratically on a strap wrapped around a barrel of another size, it would be impossible to make any sense of the code. In this case, Arshiya Akeldan had used the Sirrush-headed dagger's hilt instead of a barrel. He had scratched letters at certain intervals on the dagger's handle, left gaps continuing in spiral form between each two letters and written the numbers with which he wished to fill these gaps on the strap. When the leather strap was wrapped correctly around the dagger's hilt, the sequence would have read A-6-K-0-E-0-L-3-D-3A-2-N-0.

This sequence was the code which had to be keyed in on the cartouche above the Ishtar Temple gate. It only made sense on the dagger's handle. The strap was of no use without the dagger and likewise the dagger without the strap. The code would have been destroyed in the event of any alteration in the hilt's radius or the length of the strap if it had been duplicated. Since Akeldan held the code to be at too great a risk if it remained a simple single-stage code, he had transformed it into a cryptosystem, placing a number in-between each letter, thus introducing a second-level code. The numbers revealed the exact number of times that the letters forming Akeldan's name, written in the Babylonian cuneiform script, needed to be pressed. And this was to continue according to the order of letters or numbers; for instance, the sixth letter after A, then K, then E, and then the third letter following L.

It was apparent that Akeldan's loyal servant had not only kept his master's secret, but had also formed anew a secret seven-member Babylon Society in memory of the scientific path which his master had trodden. Perhaps he himself lived as a scholar who continued this research, or perhaps he lived a worldly life among the king's men. There was no information about him in the texts, but there was a condition concerning membership, according to which those who knew the Society's secret must never number more than seven in any given age. There must have been a very varied membership over the centuries. There would have been statesmen and great scientists, visionaries seeking fame by revealing the astronomical discoveries of earlier Babylonian scholars as well as slaves to ambition seeking worldly power, and members of secret services eager to steer international politics as well as greedy treasure hunters, not to mention amateurs and adventurers. No matter the circumstances, only the Great Master Marduk of the seven society members was to have possession of the dagger, but he did not have the authority to dismantle it or reveal its secret to others. According to one of the Society's sacred tenets, he who dismantled the dagger and wrapped the strap around its hilt incurred the wrath of the gods and died foaming at the mouth like a rabid dog.

Fuzuli read further: the Society was to assemble in secret every seven years and assess the state of scientific advance, debating whether or not to reveal the secrets of the Chaldean researchers. Moreover, on every seventh full moon of the year, Master Marduk was to send a message of greetings to his fellow members by means of seven carrier pigeons. This allowed him to monitor their lifelines and, if one had died, he was to be kept informed of any new appointments.

Fuzuli pondered the situation. "At the Society's last meeting, the Assyrian must have tested the characters of each of the members and concluded that they sought treasure over science. Why else would he have taken his own life?" He was quick to find confirmation for his theory. Here was a memo noting that, throughout the last meeting a Berber scholar and an Austrian merchant had spoken more of funding than research, that they began talking money before even discussing the facts. "That's why," mused Fuzuli, "the blind librarian preferred to present me with the dagger that day rather than handing it over to them."

He returned to his cubicle at the *medrese* and his thoughts became still clearer. By the end of a sleepless night, he had come to understand that the first members of the Babylon Society had left no clue concerning the leather strap hidden in the dagger. They probably suspected that anyone dismantling the weapon would find it. If the person dismantling the dagger were purely after treasure, then they would not be interested in the strap and would not jeopardise the scientific studies that were more precious to them than gold and emeralds. But if the person dismantling the dagger were in pursuit of knowledge, then they would need a cipher to read the letters on the hilt. If they were in search of a cipher, they would surely find it. As a further test for those deciphering the code – whether motivated by pursuit of treasure or knowledge – the founder members had played a trick on their future colleagues by introducing the second-tier cryptosystem.

In any given era, those who make history never outnumber the seven members of the Babylon Society. There was no need for more as the world was deemed small even for seven people.

3
A small Strawberry by the Tigris was I
I became Mecnun and found Life again

A caravan on the path of isolation, in fear of peril
Mecnun and I, in turn, stand sentinel

Fuzuli

I grew as a strawberry on the cool banks of the Tigris. During the last flood, the gardens and vineyards of the desert dwellers were ruined, but I was late to turn green and then I reddened early in the strong sunshine. One day, a black-browed, jet-eyed Arab maiden picked me with her delicate fingers and placed me in her basket. My stalk and leaf came too. I hoped to touch her scarlet lips. In fact, just as she drew me close... It was not to be... It could not have been... I could not be. I was left incomplete, in pieces.

Her name was Leyla; she plucked me away and tossed me into a cauldron, without pity. My juices stewed and seethed along with date-palm leaves and desert thorns. I fell apart and was crushed. I burned alongside an unripe date: we were companions in this inferno, but that was no consolation! I hoped for rosy lips, but thorns pierced my heart instead.

Was I burning because of the fire or out of love? I could not tell. That most beautiful maiden poured my love-filled being into a vessel, and had me trampled upon by children. Water once made me bud and moonbeams brought me colour. Now I dried in the sun and was severed from my soul My every fibre was mixed with the date: we shared the same fate between the marble board and the rolling press. We were woven together with thorns. As my colour faded, I could blame nobody for the thorns piercing my soul.

It was a few days later that my wounds began to heal and my boiling blisters began to dry. Leyla's hands were patting me, like compassionate physicians stroking the heads of melancholics. That day, I loved Leyla. All was bathed in red light reflected off the Tigris. I tasted the delight of love as her delicate hands played over me. She had pulled me away from her lips, but I was enveloped by their colour in between her henna-dyed fingers. It was almost as though the most magnificent heart of a lover ever to leave its mark on history were beating at her touch. I was being made into fine parchment on the surface, and the hands stroking me were insensible to the stirring within.

It was as if the very elixir of life drawn from my embrace with the green date in the cauldron had permeated my being. Was I dying or returning to life? I could not tell. I was at the crossroads of being and seemed to be breathing.

I wished Leyla's hands would hold me and never let me go. I harboured feelings. I could have burned for eternity with the warmth of her hands and gone wherever she took me. I was, but I could not make out what I was.

I resembled organisms unable to complete their development or infants placed in incubators, yet I was growing rapidly. My first nursemaid was my first love. Leyla! What a great guide she was for me. Oh! If only you knew what it was like to listen to Leyla's songs on starry desert nights... Her breath was like the sound of the scorching wind; for me, it was life itself.

Humid nights following scorching days found me intoxicated with the most profound pleasure. I do not remember properly, but others now called me paper and spoke of buying and selling me as a scroll. If only they could put a name to that thing I felt when Leyla touched me! Those blissful days passed by without my knowing how many times the thing I had only just begun to explore had enveloped my heart in a kind of fog, giving me a measure of myself, and leaving me feeling somehow completed.

I felt this even more strongly in the songs whispered in the desolation and depths of the desert during the warm nights that flowed into the little mud hut through Leyla's window. Tears streamed from Leyla's eyes each time she heard the bells of the faraway caravans, and the crickets chirping upon the thistles which merged into the dense desert silence. I too, became tearful. I harboured hatred towards the desert's ruthlessness to which she listened for nights on end, alert to the slightest sound coming from the horizon on which her gaze was fixed.

As new scrolls piled up on the shelves each day, I sensed the growing sadness in her voice. I thought I understood the adventures recounted by the lyric poems and odes she recited. Back then, I could not communicate that I had understood. I knew, but I could not make this known. I wanted it to be noticed that I had noticed, but it was not to be. Leyla did not notice me. In her eyes, I was a piece of parchment. I wondered if all the other scrolls felt as I did, if they understood Leyla's pain.

I was to learn later that what I experienced during those days was what is known as the "Soul of Things": in the Orient, "observing things and events" was deemed one and the same as seeing truth and reality. Accordingly, everything with existence has a spirit, a life. Just like humans or animals, plants and even seemingly inanimate things each lead a particular life: Earth breathes as a whole, living and letting others live. There is life in soil, water, fire and air and, indeed, life itself is made up of these components. I was the son of soil and water, who had breathed fire and taken nourishment from cool breezes. It was as though my existence were kneaded into being with knowledge. I knew, I knew with the consciousness of knowing that I knew; I knew, felt, beheld a great many things – Leyla, the desert, the Tigris, the bells of the caravans, the desert thistles, the leaves of the date palms, the roar of lions and the braying of donkeys.

That day, the shelf on which I lay overflowed with parchments. Leyla grabbed me, stretched me across her lap and, with a carbonised twig from the hearth, she wrote "Kays" on me. "Kays," she repeated several times over. "My beloved, we put the sheep out to pasture together and what beautiful days those were! Many a springtime has come and gone, lovers have united, but you have not returned. The rains have fallen for the eighth time upon the valleys. You said that you would come at the first rains, but you did not come. Would that we had never grown up, Kays! Would that our lambs had never grown, O disloyal beloved!" She raised me to her lips, and kissed the place where she had written Kays' name in charcoal... It was as though my heart thumped. "Kays shall be your name," she declared as she held me up to the sun filtering though the window, and she kissed me once again where she had written my name, right on my heart.

That night, I was intoxicated by the imprint of her lips. Her kisses penetrated my innermost depths. I wanted to be not Kays' name, but Kays himself. I wanted her to call out to Kays and kiss me again and again.

I felt her warm touch until morning. She had embraced me, placed me upon her heart and gone to sleep in this manner. It was a magnificent night. In the morning, there was a bittersweet taste upon her lips and the salt of her living breath was on me. It was the first and last night that I would remain between her hand and her heart, without stirring.

She had loved me too, such that she stroked my tender body on the morning left over from our dreams. Then she washed away my name with the two teardrops that fell from her eyes, so that her father would not see. Those letters now turned into a smoke-coloured stain: *qaf, ya* and *sad*. They no longer read "Kays", but had separated, smeared and been obliterated.

What of the charcoal mark? She had given me the name Kays like a hidden watermark. I loved this name. This name became my name, and I swore an oath that I would carry Kays' destiny along with his name. A mad love settled in my heart in the same way as the name etched on my bosom.

At daybreak, a caravan passed close to the hut in which we shared that blissful night. These were merchants travelling from the Hijaz to Baghdad who stopped over every season to collect the Tigris parchments.

The scrolls on the shelves were evened out and rolled up, one by one. When my turn came, Leyla kissed me again on the place where she had written my name. Staining it with her tears, she whispered, "O beloved to whom I have devoted my life! I hope that this paper reaches you and that, once you have opened the eye of your heart, you will read your own name and understand the greatness of my love!"

Between my pages she secreted three long strands of her dark hair, a pinch of black cumin and some lotus leaves so that her father would not find them. She entrusted her love to me and left me her scent. As though knowing that I understood, she whispered sweet nothings to me. "I love you, do not forget!" she declared, and kissed me for the last time.

As I squashed against the bundles that Leyla had packed with her gentle hands, it seemed a pity that she could not detect my screams. I was learning the pain of first separation and first sorrow on this journey. Within me I carried the leaves of love and longing.

The first separation and first sorrow... Would I ever return? Could I ever return? Why hadn't Leyla lifted the strawberry to her lips instead of tossing me into the cauldron? I accepted that I would be sold, even if I could not know to whom and for what reason I was to be sold. Perhaps I was to be passed around from hand to hand. Perhaps my colour would be smeared in all directions across book pages. Would I ever again feel the hand of my beloved, she whom I dreamt of night and day? I wondered what part of me was to live on in which book. With what writing was my being, scattered sheaf by sheaf, to be composed and compiled? I knew not.

What I did know was that I was ready for the sharp reed nibs to scrape my bosom and make my heart bleed. Scribes would crudely carve their words upon me without feeling the extent to which I hurt. Maybe they would draw indecent pictures or list legends one-by-one, unnecessarily.

I wondered if lines of love would also be inscribed on my surface. According to what the caravan leader explained to his friend, mainly sacred texts were written on paper in

Baghdad. Would there be a single line of consolation in those books to relieve me from my sorrow?

When I was sold to the merchant from Hilla, nobody asked me the reason for this transaction. I was the one who was traded, whereas the seller and buyer were worlds apart. This was my fate after all. Who cared what I wanted? As I journeyed towards Hilla on the pack mule, I wished so much to be nothing, I hoped for complete annihilation. I felt like imploring the hungry lions on the lookout for any opportunity to attack the mule in whose saddlebag I travelled. The sword on the merchant's belt as well as the bow to which he clung, and even the dog which accompanied us along the way, seemed my enemies.

When we reached an oasis, I wished that snakes or scorpions would bite the merchant. I thought of staying in Leyla's lands and merging with the sands lashed by the winds. But it was my fate to be immobile: I could want, but not do. Then I understood that I would always be at the mercy of others.

No one would hear my screams, no one would ask me what I wanted. Who could know better than me, what an unbearable burden was existence? From this day on, everyone would be making decisions concerning me regardless of my feelings. They could do to me what they wished and I was to wait obediently throughout my passive life. Perhaps I was to be sold for a high price and serve notables and scholars, but my reputation, how I was esteemed, was to be determined by lines written upon me. I was now a slave. I told myself this truth repeatedly throughout the journey. "I should at least be of service to good masters and remain in the company of the beautiful," I tried to reconcile myself.

And I, Kays, lover of the rare lotus of the desert, prayed for days and nights on end, that Leyla would be written on me.

4

My first Love and first Sorrow
Love is the Cure for my Affliction: Her Name is Leyla

I have a capacity to love exceeding that of Mecnun.
I am the true lover, Mecnun carries just the name.

Fuzuli

Upon Fuzuli's return to Hilla from Baghdad, the memory of his exchanges with Anatolian poets lingered with him. He delighted in the thought of the nine silver coins he was to receive in return for the ode he presented to the Sultan. At the same time, he was home-sick for the family he had left behind three months previously, and the gravity of what he had learned about the Babylon Society weighed on his spirit. At least he would no longer feel his inner demons attacking him every time he reached for the strap on his water flask. Thanks to those nine silver coins, he could enjoy a more comfortable life. He hoped to devote more time to science and poetry and aimed to add new works in Turkish to his books in Arabic and Persian.

As the number of visitors at his *medrese* cubicle in Baghdad increased, he imagined he had brought upon himself the curse of the dagger. There would be no use explaining the situation to the sultan's men and he might be placed in even greater danger if one of them were a member of the Babylon Society. He decided to feign ignorance and surrender the dagger if necessary.

He now wondered whether the dagger could have fallen into the hands of scholars or treasure hunters. The people who paid him frequent visits threatening and intimidating him were actually part of a courier service and none had made mention of the hidden section of the dagger, or the leather strap with which he had fashioned a lining for the strap of his own flask.

Fuzuli decided it was his duty to visit the librarian's grave during his last days in Baghdad. He was astounded by what awaited him. Here was a grand marble sarcophagus. Clearly, the old Assyrian had had it prepared before his death and someone had fulfilled his last wishes and put the stone in place before the soil on the grave had even settled.

At first he did not know how he was to pray beside the grave. He examined the carved figures, reliefs and decorations on the sides of the sarcophagus, on the headstone and at its foot. He found what he sought on the inch-thick marble cover. As soon as he saw the Sirrush-headed dagger design, he prayed. "I will protect your secret, old man. Sleep well in your grave and may you rest in accord with your religion."

When he returned to his room, he set about memorising the Ottoman Turkish counterparts of the Chaldean letters on the reverse side of the flask strap because of the vow he had taken at the old man's grave.

Nevertheless, just three months after his family welcomed him home, his Baghdad adventures were well and truly erased from his mind. For the first time, he placed an order with some of Hilla's merchants for a bundle of *abadi* paper from Baghdad and some European vellum, in return for two barren ewes. This was paper he had not been able to buy during his time in Baghdad due to lack of funds. On the precious parchment he would pen the story Hayali Bey had encouraged him to write on that unforgettable night with the poets of Istanbul.

Already, he felt like a student about to sit for examination. "If you would please write in Turkish the story of daughter of the desert Leyla and her crazed lover Kays." Hayali Bey had asked him to open up this hidden treasure, bringing fresh beauty to this old garden; in so doing, he had expressed his confidence in the poet and paid him a great compliment.

Fuzuli was filled with apprehension at the thought of this difficult undertaking. He wandered about in a state of pensive reflection. His mind was busy at each moment with a new storyline. He sought and found copies of all the Leyla and Mecnun variants written by Persian and Turkish poets. Whether he liked or disliked them, he nonetheless read each version again and again.

Each of the poets had his own distinctive method: some summarised the events while drawing out the descriptions and some did not explain anything save events and incidents. A prosaic articulation stood out in the poetry of some while others were able to convey ultimate beauty. He understood once more the importance of what was called method.

"I must relate neither events nor descriptions. I must speak of love, only love," he told himself.

When the paper reached him, he felt ready for the task at hand. First, he prepared a special starch called *ahar* with egg white and cornflour. In the windowless study at the centre of his low-ceilinged mud-brick house, he placed marble weights at the corners of the parchments he spread out so as to render them even.

Then, using a sponge, he applied the *ahar* primer with a custard-like consistency. He did it slowly and gradually so that it would be fully absorbed. He applied the *ahar* twice to both sides of the paper, dried the sheets, re-bundled and stretched them, placed heavy stones upon them, only to re-apply the *ahar* coating and dry them once again. As he rolled the polished cylindrical stones in order to level down the coating and buff the pages, he could not have known, of course, that every page beneath his hands felt pain and suffered. The beauty which would appear on those surfaces could only come at the cost of uniting writing with suffering.

Fuzuli opened another unprepared bundle from among the rest and stepped back in wonder, gaping at the black cumin seeds and lotus leaves strewn across the floor. A pleasant aroma spread across the room. This was like the fragrance of the Babylonian deity Enlil, who rubbed his body every day with essence of lotus from the banks of the River Nile. Picking up the black cumin seeds one by one, Fuzuli felt something snag his finger: three strands of hair, dark as the musk of the land of the Hittites, they diffused an intoxicating scent.

The form of Leyla, daughter of the desert suddenly appeared to his mind's eye. Somewhere deep in his heart, he felt a sharp twinge. He tried to build a mental picture of the maiden whose tale he was engaged in composing. He imagined personalities for her, came up with various identities, dressed her, made her walk and talk, and then combined them in an attempt to understand the person whose story he would tell. Now the beautiful girl had truly come to life in his imagination. It was only then that he decided this was the beauty he had sought for days. But he could never know that the Leyla he visualised slightly really did evoke Leyla, the legendary beauty who collected strawberries on the banks of the Tigris. Neither when writing his tale, nor later, when speaking of Leyla... He would always insist that the Leyla he visualised was a heroine of his own fancy whereas she really was the lotus-scented girl from the Tigris.

A long time later, he rubbed the three strands of hair between two fingers, took a closer look at them and tried to imagine the woman to whom they might belong. He also tried to extract from the lotus fragrance, the noble and delicate sense of smell of whoever owned these strands of hair.

It never occurred to Fuzuli that the origin of the hair in his grasp – to him a mystery – was known to the paper before him. As for me, I waited forever in the hope that he would think of me, discover me and address me directly. Merely feeling the knot of love between the charcoal stain on my bosom and the cumin seeds in his palm was not enough for me. A little later, he lifted me up, wanting to get a closer look at the paper which had concealed the hair in his hand. He held me up to the light for a while, looking at my fibrous veins, and then carefully examined the mark of Leyla's lips between his fingers.

"There must be a memory hidden here. I wonder whose it is," he mused as he set me to one side for the frontispiece.

Then he placed me carefully on the top shelf in the corner. Now, I could easily observe all the goings-on.

Once he had applied the *ahar*, Hilleli Fuzuli took a deep breath. He was considering writing the first verses today. While reviewing once again his plan for the composition, a vision of the blind librarian suddenly came to him. "There are seven true secrets for one who knows love. One who possesses these gains mastery over the world."

This was a decisive moment. He would conceal the code which he had been unable to decipher in the book he was going to write. "For one who knows love," the librarian had said. In that case, the couplets in which he would embed the cipher should speak of love. "Seven true secrets..." he had said. Then these had to be as hidden as secrets. Love and secrets... The librarian would not have brought these together in vain. Moreover, the juxtaposition of love and secrecy would not attract notice. "True love is that which lies hidden," he said to himself. He did not omit to congratulate himself for coming up with the formulation.

Now, he needed to bring together the letters of the name AKELDAN on the dagger's hilt with the numbers copied onto his flask strap lining. Before him were seven letters and seven numbers. He needed to disperse these among the seven couplets in which he would relate the tale of *L&M*. All well, but which couplets would these seven be?

He finally made up his mind after spending hours in thought and vowed he would never speak of the matter to anyone. Dipping his quill in the inkpot, he embarked on the story of Leyla, daughter of the desert and her crazed lover Kays.

❦❦❦

I was now restless with the frustration of not being able to tell anyone that I was the lover who bore Leyla's love. While Fuzuli's hands folded and cut me into sheets of the same size, I expressed no complaint at being unable to voice my screams to the high heavens. I had learned too well in my time with Fuzuli that love meant suffering. I knew also that a slave's anguish was that much greater. And pain brought spiritual maturity. Besides, it was I who had wished for love to be written on my bosom and my prayers were being answered. I had fallen into the hands of a poet whose voice reverberated in every place frequented by Turks.

What he would now write upon me was to place me in high esteem. Of course it hurt when he perforated my bosom with a needle and sewed my skin, page by page, with silk thread. But when I became a book ready to be written on, and especially when a poet like Fuzuli began to form his verses upon me, I felt utter joy and forgot all that pain that I had endured.

When Fuzuli spoke of love, he always mentioned pain, suffering, separation, burning and disintegration. He referred to separation of love as a torment (*azab*) and then related its being derived from the trilateral root '-dh'b, which comes to mean "pleasure". That is to say, there was a pleasure in the pain of love and love could not be savoured without an appreciation of anguish and affliction. I, who carried the tale of the greatest lover that history could ever know, was assuredly to suffer as much pain as Kays and exist in his being through suffering. It is because I knew this that I decided to endure patiently every pain and not complain of love.

What beautiful words were the words penned by my master Fuzuli! What is more, the tale being written upon my bosom fell from the lips of Kays himself. "My Lord, render me intimate with the affliction of love. Sever not my soul from love for but a moment."

Fuzuli was composing a tale of love on my pages and he called me a book. This was a talc comprised of verses which formed a necklace, strung pearl by pearl across my pages. I was like a groom in preparation. These beautiful words were worth all the pain that I suffered. As though he knew my entreaty, Fuzuli had written at one point, "The universe is connected through and through with a single strand of your hair, O universal beauty named Leyla!"

This was the story of Leyla and Kays, first cousins from the Banu 'Amir tribe. The poem became even more beautiful as the quill filled with more ink. As the quill advanced, the letters intertwined in a fever of love. Fuzuli resembled a lover who had only just met the beautiful daughter of his teacher and addressed his sweetheart thus, "Apple of my eye, my darling, my master, my beloved, O esteemed ruler of my heart!"

Everything this man knew of love flowed forth from his pen with the lucidity of raindrops. The deep, associative verses, the thousand and one states and the philosophical solution of love. He called love "ivy". Moreover, his choice for the word for 'love' in Turkish literally meant a kind of ivy. This ivy climbs up great sycamores and cypresses and cleaves to them just as love takes over and smothers gallants and tall beauties. Eventually the ivy dries out the tree it envelops and, while the tree may look lush and fine on the outside, it will rot and collapse inwardly. He strung his words together whilst looking out at the ivy which had clambered up and stifled the beautiful date palm in his garden. As he wrote each verse, he looked once more at the date adorned like a bride; the tree was already beginning to wither and tears welled up in his eyes.

"Kays," he said to himself. "He withered away like this sapling when the ivy enveloped him." O Leyla! She fared no better than Kays either. When writing their story, he could not decide whose love was superior. Yes, Kays had lost his mind and become known as Mecnun, the Madman, but he had acquired worldwide fame. Such was his madness that it made thousands of others seem sane. He had gone mad, but all the sane throughout the ages envied this madness. On the other hand, there was Leyla, whom tradition prevented from speaking of her love. She felt shame in expressing her love and was held captive by tradition. Mecnun could voice his love, but hers remained hidden in her heart. The lover who keeps their love secret is certainly superior to one who discloses it. One who kept their suffering to themselves and who did not disturb the beloved was assuredly superior. Had not the Assyrian librarian said, "Love and secret"? Was he to understand that, from Arshiya Akeldan onwards, love and secrecy suited each other like milk and sugar? The wise priests of the Babylon Society had made love inextricable from secrecy.

According to Fuzuli's version, Kays and Leyla's love began when they were at school together, before Leyla's breasts had even budded. Before long, their love became known and Leyla's mother removed her from school and locked her in the house, while the pain of separation sent Kays to the desert, where he lost his mind. People began referring to him as Mecnun, meaning one who is crazed, and the magnificent love of these two culminated in death. Unable to find unity in this world, Leyla and Mecnun were locked together in close embrace in the same grave.

Days passed, and the tale began to fall into place. Events unfolded rapidly over the pages and the years slipped by. Scenes were narrated with tragic and lyric elements such as to bring tears to every reader's eye. As the events neared their climax or rather, as Leyla was entombed and Mecnun followed to embrace her, Fuzuli's excitement increased. The words were flowing gracefully and would be successfully delivered at the request of his most refined peers. But mine was the real excitement as I felt those poems filling my bosom. My excitement did not stem from any curiosity as to the tale's conclusion: it was due to the frequent mention of Leyla's name. Each mention made me experience anew my life on the banks of the Tigris: it was as if I could smell the scent of her hair as I did that last night when she had fallen asleep with her hand on my chest.

This Fuzuli was a master, and that was that. He drew such a likeness between Leyla – whom he referred to as the member of the Banu 'Amir experiencing love – and the beloved I left on the banks of the Tigris that I almost thought he was trying to humour me. I thought I could hear and feel Kays' love as if it were my own, as if it were me uttering the words of love in the story. Sometimes, it even got to the point where

I cried out silently as though Fuzuli could hear my voice. If any verses seemed inappropriate, I would flutter the page with a view to splattering the ink so that the letters would distort. I wanted Fuzuli to erase them with his moistened little finger, scratch them from my bosom and replace them with more beautiful and accurate words instead. That way, the verses would relate the story of this Kays and not Kays of the Banu 'Amir.

As the story unfolded and the reality of the couple's love for each other emerged, so my feelings increased as well. I had come to accept my lot as a slave. Being a slave to my master Fuzuli's elevated words was preferable to being master in an assembly of dunces. Even if no one else perceived it, I began to see myself as a master in my own right, in this case the master of lovers. When Fuzuli wrote, "I have a potential for love beyond even that of Mecnun; I am the true lover, but Mecnun has all the fame," I responded, "No! It is I whose love is greater than that of Mecnun and I am the true lover!"

Irrespective of what people called me – parchment, scroll, paper, book – I was the hero of this tale of suffering and I felt Leyla's love within me. Perhaps I was a servant in the eyes of others – this was unlikely to change. Others might buy, give, sell, throw, conserve or locate me against my will and never ask me what I wanted. But I would still feel Leyla's love within me and I would forever be her suffering lover. I was a slave, but a magnificent one – an enigmatic slave who loved and carried within himself his beloved.

As the verses were arranged on my pages, my splendour increased. Love made me undergo a form of transformation. My love, which had started at Leyla's desert-scented bosom, was finding completion. This lay behind the occasional pang of envy for the Kays of the story which made me want to chase him away. Surely I was also entitled to act like Mecnun! I did not think that anyone could love Leyla more than me and if perchance there was one such, I reckoned my malediction would send him to his grave. Just like the curse my brother-in-fate in the story called down upon his rival Ibn Salam.

As my master Fuzuli versified the words, they found harmony: expression became music and rhythm ensured fluency and full engagement. During this time, Leyla had matured and become a matchless beauty. I felt like plaiting her hair or kissing her lips as she slept. It was an unbearable ordeal. Every page wherein Leyla's name was mentioned caused my heart to pace. I felt her near me, at my side, or embracing me tightly. On some days, the Leyla with whom the Kays in the tale could not unite, slept in my arms, and on other days, the Leyla inside me flew away. Weeping upon the pages which told of her sorrow, forever fell upon me.

It was 58 days since Fuzuli had begun writing the poem. On this day, Leyla was to take her leave of the pilgrims' caravan. She would turn to the wilderness in search of the madman of the desert Mecnun. Tossing the reins of her camel around her neck, she would address her beast. "O friendly companion! You know my desire, but I do not know the way. You are now my guide, go now and find Kays for me." The camel would keep wandering along until he found him sitting amongst wild animals. My master Fuzuli had begun to relate the story from this scene on most vividly: my excitement increased with every syllable.

For a time, the two lovers reproach each other and test each other's faithfulness. Or rather, Leyla constantly tries to gauge the depth and authenticity of Mecnun's love. But Mecnun fails to appreciate Leyla's entreaty. She tells him, "O loyal lover! I have come! Your Leyla has come, the beloved you have been awaiting for years on end," but he responds as though it is not Leyla he loves, but love itself. "Leyla, if I am me, who are you? If you are you, then who am I?"

Fuzuli wrote this couplet to illustrate that Mecnun had become one with Leyla in the desert: he felt her altogether within him, he lived with her in spirit year in, year out, and so he wanted to express the transcendence in his feeling. So filled with Leyla was Mecnun that he deemed Leyla's "I have come," as dualistic; he viewed losing his essence and entering into the service of another as a base form of love. "O beloved!" he responds. "For quite some time now, I have been you and you me. We are a single spirit in two bodies, two almonds in a single shell. Thus, your producing a duality by saying you and me does not befit our love!"

This couplet became strangely manifest in me and, from that point on, I sprang to life like a true lover. I kept repeating to myself, "O Kays, if I am truly me, then who are you? If you are Kays, then who am I?" At that moment, there no longer remained any separation and otherness between Kays and me.

My master Fuzuli never knew that this couplet, which rang in his ears for days, *was* the love that I incessantly repeated, the lamentation that I forever wanted to shout out loud. He thought that the voice which said, "If I am me, then what are you, O Leyla? And if you are you, then what am I, O peerless beauty?" came from the Unseen. But in fact this couplet was nothing other than the words I proclaimed a little louder each time, with which I completed my selfhood and identity, and which I considered to be my faith and belief.

I, the downcast strawberry of the Tigris, had now become Kays, Mecnun. I was to live on this paper until the tale had been told and was to taste love with all its sorrow and suffering. The Leyla in the story was now the slim-fingered, dark-eyed, dark-haired beloved I left behind on the banks of the river Tigris. As a piece of paper, I was incomplete; I became complete only with the words of Leyla. I died and was revived; I slept and was awoken.

I felt myself so altered as to be capable of conversing with my master Fuzuli had I so wished. I saw and felt his hand, his fingers and the ink spreading from the nib of his pen; I could read his thoughts and understand his speech. When he slept, I waited by his bedside like a slave. When he left the house, I awaited his return on the shelf. When his children came beside him, I felt his fatherly compassion. When he wrote poems by candlelight night after night, I could read his mind and even his dreams. I could not fathom exactly what had happened to me, but I could see with the eye of my spirit and perceive through the language of my innate disposition. I experienced the same time period, in another dimension, as that described by the poet depicting me. I clung to my Leyla like tulle and took it upon myself to protect her. This is why I saw myself as a slave and Fuzuli as my master. Even if my master remained perpetually ignorant of the feelings of his servant, this was how it was, as servants typically just overhear conversation and have no right to express an opinion. I could see, feel and confirm by peeking out from between the book's pages, and this was indeed the order of things. If I was to swear like the Kays in the story to find

Leyla, supposing that I possessed all of these qualities for her sake, I had to meditate for days on end and then I would come to understand that love was greater than everything else. Yes, I was to become Kays and find Leyla. This is why I had been torn from the Tigris and thrown into a cauldron. What was more, I was duty-bound to express my gratitude to my master who had given me identity and character.

My will was not my own, but I trusted that my road would one day lead to Leyla. For this I prayed without cessation. To live for Leyla and to annihilate my existence for her sake, just like Kays... To find that desert beauty whose lips I desired since the day I was plucked from my root. If I was to be annihilated, to be annihilated in her... And, in this way, to give my master's sorrowful tale a happy ending. I had sprouted by Leyla's side and now I wanted to wither away in her hands.

The sun had risen exactly 73 times since Fuzuli had first dipped his quill in the inkwell to write out the title of his tale in dark ink on the first page of his notebook, where the charcoal stain was, right on Kays' watermark washed by her tears, in the place where Leyla's lips left their imprint.

He picked up the book in his hands with all the joy of a father who receives the news of a baby boy after having had three daughters. He ran his fingers over each corner as though stroking and caressing it. Eventually he re-read the title he had taken pains to write in *ta'lik* calligraphic script: *Book of Leyla and Mecnun*. The love of the ill-fated, jet-eyed, black-haired daughter of the desert merged with the dark and beautiful letters.

As I lay drunk with Leyla's love, the Babylon Society's secret was transposed among the dark letters. It was as if the secret had drifted into a tranquil sleep where it would remain eternally hidden. My master Fuzuli inscribed the numerals on the strap lining of his flask into the couplet sequence numbers. He interspersed the words "love" and "secret", drawing from the number seven and its multiples in precisely the same way as the Babylonians. Accordingly, when the number of the couplets in which the words "love" and "secret" both occurred was identified and each was divided by the number seven, the result revealed the cipher. Here was the key to unlocking the secrets of the Babylon Society's space research and their treasures.

My master Fuzuli was a very intelligent man no doubt. At what point the numbers entrusted to me would be discovered, and who would hunt me down for my secret, I could not know. I did find it slightly strange that in amongst the beauty and perfection of my love was concealed a mysterious adventure. My life was in the hands of others. I had to wait, keep waiting and then I would see. I was to experience love in the same way as eminent poets of refined cultures and yet I would have to keep going without feeling crushed by the burden I carried, without allowing myself to feel trampled. This was my fate.

Two years had passed since my master Fuzuli moved from Hilla to Karbala with his wife and children. Whilst enjoying the most fortunate days of his life, he made small corrections to my couplets and distributed them to those wanting to copy them. He made additions or deletions to my couplets and inserted the changed sheets between my pages so that the line numbers in my duplicates would be different to mine though the copyists changed the line numbers anyway, numbering them as if on a whim. Still, my master Fuzuli did not want to overlook any possibility. He thus managed to protect the secret of the Babylon Society and so honour his promise to the Assyrian librarian.

My master's life in Karbala passed in quiet and indeed idyllic fashion. In fact, he had earned this reward long before. His son Fazli studied at the Karbala *medrese* and, just like his father, spent his youth writing poetry. He had married off one daughter to one of the descendants of the Prophet Muhammad's grandson Husayn.

The Sultan's governor Ayas Mehmet Paşa would regularly send gifts to Fuzuli in an attempt to persuade him to settle in Baghdad. My master responded to the invitations with odes full of praise, but he could not bring himself to go to Baghdad and place himself under the protection of the governor, living off his generosity and hospitality. He considered the frequent removal from office of Baghdad governors and their relocation elsewhere. Who would governor Ayas Paşa's replacement be and what would he be like? Would Fuzuli get on with him and would he take kindly to poetry and the arts?

There were a great many more questions running through his mind in relation to any move to Baghdad. Most important amongst them was the harm that might befall his family from treasure hunters seeking the golden idols of the Babylon Society if his presence were known. All these reasons forced him to decline Ayas Paşa's offer. Instead, he saw fit to send me rather than the usual laudatory odes. Back in those days, I had no garment to wear. Upon me was inscribed *Book of Leyla and Mecnun*, but I could not yet be regarded as a neat, compact book. I was worn without having been used, old without having lived. My surface was still being punctured by silk thread and needles and I felt pain. In particular, the scribe who had made a copy of me the year previously had used me most roughly and had even spilled coffee on me. My master had had to pull me apart and put me back together again in order to treat my scars and tighten my shrivelled hands. Once more, he pricked me with the needle and bound me with thread. Lastly, he wrapped me in a layer of cowhide and in the flickering candlelight, he read and re-read certain sections far into the night, making changes as he went along. Some of these changes were made for the purpose of putting three of the couplets containing the Babylon Society cipher back into their original positions. In the final quarter of the night, as his wearied eyes were closing, he pressed me against his chest and sighed deeply. That night, I saw him sink into the happiest sleep of his life...

This was the first and last night I listened to my master's heartbeat to my heart's content and felt his closeness. I did not know whether he saw Leyla in his dreams, but I felt that Leyla was in his heart. Did my master and I love the same beauty? Was I betraying him? Did I need to feel ashamed of myself? Would he have felt shame before his wife who was sleeping in the next room?

I wept till morning, listening at times to his heart and at times to my own. Perhaps it was impending separation from my master that caused me to weep. Was I ever going to see my master again? And more importantly, how was I to live without my tender-hearted guardian who invested me with the imperial crown of a mysterious world?

I am Mecnun, the slave living in the verses of my master Hilleli Mehmet Fuzuli... I was a strawberry and they threw me into a cauldron, then sold me as paper in the market. My fibres made two sheaves; I was bartered for two sheep at Baghdad bazaar and knew myself to be the slave of the lyric poet from Hilla. I came to know love in his house, then became accustomed to anguish, and studied Leyla, year in year out, in the school of love. I was written and became a book; I began to talk, spoke and became speech.

I am Kays, the magnificent slave! And my queen is Leyla...

5
How the Snow was bloodied and my Heart was torn out for the first Time

O Naili! Is not the gradual approach of night
Worth the worlds of anguish of waiting?

I left the saddlebag of the administrative official collecting Karbala's annual tax and was received by Ayas Mehmet Paşa. He kissed me and raised me to his forehead, just like my master and, as the last beams of sun lit up the domes of Baghdad – the city of fairy tales – he began to read the beginning of my story. I gauged the excitement he felt before this detailed and poetic narration of the *L&M*, a story which he had first heard from his mother as a folktale, from the way he held me in his hands.

When I saw two teardrops trickle down his cheeks as he was reading the section where Kays seeks different ways of reuniting with Leyla, I understood that he too had once lost his heart to a secret love. Who knows how many nights had passed in reverie? He did not even hear the servant who came in to change the brazier which had burned right down. As he neared the end of my story, the wind picked up and the dawn call to prayer recited by the two callers from the A'zamiyya minarets could be heard. He threw his marten fur over his shoulders and made his way to the residence's living quarters. He was already making plans for presenting me to the Sultan as a gift. "If I send this magnificent work and remind him of my existence, maybe he will consider assigning me the post of Chancellor in the future," he thought to himself.

A few days later, the Paşa summoned the obsequious military commander of the procession that Basran ruler Emir Rashid was sending forth to the Sultan to proclaim his subservience to the Ottoman state and to present the keys of the city along with a great many other gifts. "Now look here," said the Paşa, assuming an authoritative tone. "I have appointed to your service 50 guardsmen from my elite janissary corps. Take this book along with all the gifts to be presented to our Sultan to Istanbul and convey it to Kara Piri at the Covered Bazaar. It is incumbent upon you to protect the gifts, but know that it is my command that you deliver the book to its rightful destination. Now make haste and do not squander the gifts or my men in this harsh winter weather. God speed!"

When we set off, I carried in my bosom my master's lyric verses of love and a memorandum addressed to Kara Piri:

Following the Salutation,

My companion in plight, fellow-traveller, my brother Kara Piri, I convey to you the gazals of my master Fuzuli along with one stanza from his L&M verse composition.

Deliver the gazals to Zati of Balıkesir and Hayali Mehmet Bey. The mesnevi is for the Sultan, our master. However, it is incumbent upon you to find master craftsmen to decorate its empty pages with miniatures and gilding. You should then have a bookbinder make a bejewelled leather binding so it can finally be presented in the proper manner to the Sultan.

Your childhood friend Ayas Mehmet

As we advanced, the cold increased in intensity. Everything went smoothly except that the horses' trappings and the riders' kaftans were soaked until we arrived at Diyarbakır, the *sanjak* capital of the province of Amid. The fortress commander had the Sincariye *medrese* prepared for our lodging and I rested here for two days, packed in a trunk. I needed to rest because, during our journey over peaks and ranges on the back of a mule and tied to a bag, I was exhausted by the maddening rattle of tombac bowls, basins inlaid with silver, pedestal candleholders, spoon and scoop sets and plates, and I could not bear to see their dull faces any more. I needed to wrap my loosened cover around my waist and lie motionless for a long period. Moreover, throughout the journey, I was bothered that the head of the aides-de-camp had not packed me in the trunk with the fabrics, silk embroideries and satin, or even deemed me fit for back-saddles, along with horsewhips, harnesses, sandals, boots and waistcloths.

Caravans usually transported *gazals*, *kasides* and *mesnevi* poetry over these lands packed inside velvet-lined chests made of cypress and even Sindiyan oak and inlaid with pure ebony and red coral. None was presumably treated like a slave, unlike me, imprisoned in my four-square wooden crate. Apparently, I was locked up in this trunk so that if perchance anyone came looking for me, they would not be able to find me. At least that is what I thought. At any rate, I suppose I had to endure all this to realise that travelling has intrinsic disadvantages.

We left Diyarbakır in the last days of the famous "Old Woman's Cold". Our first stopover was on the foothills of Mount Karacadağ. The wind seemed as though it was about to blow away the mules along with all their loads. Tents could not stand up to this storm; the trunks were offloaded and lined up like bricks to form a low wall. I was in the last trunk and was being lowered to the ground when the lid suddenly broke open. I spilled out across the snow accompanied by the smash of dishes and cutlery. I heard the voice of the senior aide-de-camp scolding the guardsmen and suddenly found myself in his hands.

Fortunately the snow had only come into contact with one of my pages and I had scraped through this terrible accident with just two lines of my text smudged. I could not make out whether the senior aide-de-camp had placed me on his own back-saddle rather than again imprisoning me in the crate so that he could read me during the humdrum journey, or to avoid the dread of dropping me once more in the snow. He was a soldier who always obeyed orders to the letter. In all his years of military service he had always preferred to carry out commands instead of coming up with any initiative of his own. As a result, he was always quite clumsy when it came to finding solutions. The simplest things could strike him as very complicated because his intellectual powers of thought and foresight were not developed. Like a great many soldiers, he became puzzled and lost when he presumed to do something on his own, and so he would set out to apply his artillery before his reason.

When the day's weariness seemed to darken even the snow, the guardsmen were ordered to unpack the bales. They made short work of rearranging the low wall of bales and then they lit fires in groups around it. The tents and military cloaks which had been packed on the backs of the mules were spread out across the ground in two layers and the few dry tree trunks which could be found, branches and all, were placed upon them. The brimless calpac fox fur hats, the sheepskins and the buffalo-hide sandals worn by the guardsmen were soaked through: the men walked heavily and the cold gnawed at their bones. In an effort to keep warm, some sat and rubbed their feet and some rested their toes against the mules' hindquarters, wrapping their heels with the animals' tails. Others found relief by winding with ropes the trunks of the pine trees which served as refuge for the beasts. They found shelter using the warm bodies of their horses as shields and, as they had become familiar with each other over the years, they slept huddled up together.

Night fell and the blizzard became fiercer. The fires lit by the guardsmen were extinguished one by one. The watchmen were numbed by the sharp frost and extreme exhaustion; they reached the point where their eyelids were gummed together and their blood was about to freeze over. Just as every man opted to fend for himself, the howling of wolves and the noise of jackals and hyenas began to make themselves heard from a distance. The mules and horses grew more restless.

Knowing full well what it meant to be left without a horse on these mountains, the soldiers whose lives were spent on horseback valued the welfare of their horses just as much as their own. So the guardsmen who were woken by the watchmen tied the feet of their horses together to stop them fleeing. The dense trees and the snowstorm made it very difficult to see anything.

Past midnight, one of the watchmen was breathing onto his palms as he made his rounds. He snapped to attention to listen to the sound of the darkness. He sensed danger in the air. For a moment, he caught the murmur of squirrels and turtledoves. "I wonder if they are scared of something," he muttered to himself. He reflected that he was in a region where imitating animal sounds was a common way of communicating. He started listening even more carefully and quietly called out to the other watchman. Horror lay ahead! His comrade sprawled lifeless on the ground. "We've been raided," he was about to shout when the cold blade of a dagger pressed into his throat. His final vision was of the son he had left behind when the boy was but two years-old. "O

Loooord!" he spluttered and his last cry shattered the darkness.

The place was suddenly filled with warriors at each others' throats. Following a short scuffle, both sides recognised one another. Friend and foe became apparent, swords were drawn and guns were lowered. Close to 10 corpses lay between the two sides and the large heavy-set men reminiscent of old mountain dwellers waited for the order to attack. They looked at each other like demons startled by incantation.

The arrivals were followers of the former Bey of Erciş, who had fallen out with the palace because of Georgian judge Mavrol Han's daughter Perihan. Following Perihan's betrayal, the former Bey had expressed his sorrow with the words, "One who heeds the advice of his wife out of regard for his wife becomes far worse off than her." So he and his men had joined the *Celali* rebellions against the Ottoman state. They had no idea about the convoy they raided except that, having seen it leave Diyarbakır, they had set their hearts on the horses and clothing and had followed in pursuit. Had they known that they would encounter the Basran treasury on its way to the Ottoman capital, they would undoubtedly have come with a much larger group and set up an ambush at the foot of one of the steep escarpments ahead. Only one person among them knew what he was after and he preferred to observe rather than fight.

The silence was broken by the rebel chief known as the Little Persian who, judging by his speech, was a vassal of Shah Isma'il. This man was a tyrannical brigand, the kind who could find dough in a house with no flour or milk in a house with no cow. Whilst appearing loyal to the Bey of Erciş, he would treacherously send all his booty to Iran.

He was a Shah-loving Ağa who would travel hither and thither making fried pastry *lokma* without changing his clothes or sandals for days on end, masquerading as an Ottoman soldier and raiding villages in order to maintain the unruly bandits he gathered around him and, in so doing, increase the prestige of his Bey. Once, when he was deployed near Karacadağ, he was caught in very fierce storms at the coldest time of winter with over 18 inches of snow on the ground. The hands and feet of his men began to freeze so he raided the closest village, ejected everyone from their homes, installed his men therein and attempted to treat their frostbite by sawing off their arms. The villagers reached their limit when he threw out a woman and her baby with nowhere else to go, but this only spurred him into ordering the deaths of all the men. The women he shared out with his own band of bounders. Having lost all semblance of reputation and honour amongst friend and foe alike, he took to being a bandit in earnest. Murders, raids, pillage, thieving... He was now someone from whom every kind of evil was expected. It was as though all compassion had been removed from his heart and replaced with violence. There was no-one else who took as much pleasure from torture, torment and tyranny. Even his own men could not trust him. They followed him through fear or self-interest. There was none left who did not know that he had burnt the barns and empty storehouses in the last village purely for the sake of warming his fingertips. He was now on the scene again having sighted the caravan which he assumed was easy pickings. In his deep bass, he recited a quatrain:

A rooster for the scrambler
A packhorse for the scuffler
A camel for the squatter
Give me an 'Abbasi!

The 'Abbasi he demanded was the name of the official silver coin in circulation in those parts. This signified he was asking nicely for the trunks. But Emir Rashid's Adjutant was no stranger to his manner of poetically articulating his demands. In an effort to display self-confidence and spur on his men, he retorted obstinately:

I am to earn and make do
Collect it and pay tribute
In heaps and piles to you
Not on your life, you rascal!

This refusal was sufficient to set the çakaralmaz guns blazing on both sides. Whoever had seen around 30 men come crashing down to the ground could not have borne the sight. What is more, behind every tree there lay another gun waiting in ambush. Amidst the wild neighs and cries of the horses and mules, it was not clear who shot or swung a sword at whom.

Only one person, avoiding combat and watching the combat from behind a thick pine trunk at a distance, could see all the actors and tried to follow every step of the battle. He was here not to fight and collect spoils, but to enter the presence of his master from whom he received orders, and he conducted himself with the pride of one having duly fulfilled his duty. As the hours passed, the calls of battle faded and the cries of death multiplied. Towards daybreak, the wolves – which had been attracted by the smell of blood – encircled us and whatever corpse there was had been pulled to shreds. As the poor horses in their roped-off shelter were tied together at the bridle, they could not escape attack by the wolves and most cried out in terrible pain as they died.

Daylight filtered through the needles of the fir trees and pines and began to sparkle upon the white snow. Mustafa of Alacaat, a private with the cavalry division, looked down from the tree from which he was about to fall. As the sounds deadened during the night and the howling of the wolves came closer, he had climbed a tree and waited between two of its branches. From where he perched, he could see that the wolves came one or two at a time and left after eating their fill. When the wolves seemed to finish feasting on his friends or horses, he would observe the arrival of the jackals. He called out, screamed and tried to throw snow at them by shaking the branches of the tree, but he could not scare away any of them. In any case, before long, he became exhausted and lost consciousness in-between freezing over and fainting. Now, when he opened his eyes, he tried to remember what had happened and surveyed the scene. Yes, he had escaped, he was still alive. But what did that matter when all his companions were dead?

The hungry wolves and jackals had gone. He came down slowly from the tree and began to search for something to wear and a dressing for his wound. Suddenly, he thought he saw one of the bodies moving. This was Gökçe Ali, a janissary from the 3rd regiment, a man with whom he had broken bread. He had fainted from loss of blood after sustaining an injury to the arm. A tree trunk had fallen onto him and his exposed feet had been covered by the carcass of a dog, so the wolves had not got to him.

Mustafa rushed to his side, rolled the trunk and tried to turn the injured man onto his back. He was busy with Gökçe Ali's heavy body, when he was suddenly startled by a monstrous-looking man he took for one of the Little Persian's cohorts wielding a sword before him. "Evidently, he hid in a tree like me," he thought and tried to counter the parries with a handy branch. But the man turned out to be strong and soon he was holding the sword to his neck. "Give me the book or say your last prayer!" he ordered. No one but me could have understood Mustafa's astonishment. The poor man knew nothing of me or of the goings-on concerning me. With expressionless eyes, he looked at the man hulking over him.

"The book!" he insisted, indicating my master Fuzuli's flask strap in his hand. "The book written by the owner of this strap! Give me the book! I've been searching the trunks and your men since dawn. You must know where it's hidden! The book!"

Even while Mustafa stared in bewilderment at the strap the man swung at him and asked, "Which book?" he knew that his attacker would not know which book it was. He thought he might gain time and cause the man to withdraw the pressure from his neck if he stalled him with some hollow responses. Surely, this was what clinging to dear life meant. This is what it was to struggle for just one minute's grace. I watched them and kept an eye on my master Fuzuli's flask strap at the same time. It was the real thing. Had something happened to my master? How had this man gained possession of the strap? Who was he? Was he from the Babylon Society or was he a treasure hunter? Why was he behaving so barbarously and how could he be so ruthless? Was he any different from the wolves which had no regard for the lives of others? Despair drove the cowering man to beg for mercy, but it was not enough to stop his attacker.

Just as the dagger was about to slash Mustafa's throat, something completely unexpected happened and a gunshot rang out. Mustafa thought he had died as the weight collapsed on his chest and he felt the blood in his veins draining. But he was conscious! It was not he who had died. He threw off the dead weight and took measure.

The commotion had roused Gökçe Ali and, on seeing his friend's predicament, he had summoned all his strength and fired off his çakaralmaz. He was well aware that his friend knew nothing of the book in question. At the fiercest point of the previous night's battle, his genuflecting ağa had approached him. "O brother Gökçe," he implored, "Your mission is to convey this book to Istanbul. This matters more than the treasures we carry and even all our lives." Gökçe Ali had then placed me in his bosom and that was how he came to be shot. You see, I owe it to Gökçe Ali and this Turkman gallant that my text emerged unscathed: no sheaves were scattered and I was not torn to pieces in the thick of battle.

All night long, as he felt cold, I too felt cold. I prayed for him not to freeze as he lay there unconscious and I prayed he would stop bleeding. What had happened gave me a sense of self-worth. Now I knew there were people after me.

Carrying out the Assyrian librarian's last wishes, my master Fuzuli had encrypted the code in the Sirrush-headed dagger's hilt into my story. After burying the dagger beneath the mulberry tree in Baghdad and whilst later removing it and handing it over to the dark-faced men who came for it, Fuzuli assumed that he had freed himself of all trouble. But clearly the lining of his water bottle strap was enough to land me in it. So long as the strap and the dagger were not brought together, the secret of the Babylon Society could not be deciphered, that much I knew. But, you see, the strap had already fallen into the wrong hands. This is precisely why I was left wondering whether my master had been harmed in any way. The question tore at my heart and even now, I am deeply saddened each time I think about it...

The two friends, Mustafa of Alacaat and Gökçe Ali, surveyed the scene amidst the peeping glances of jackals and foxes. There were corpses everywhere. The snow had continued falling throughout the night and covered some of the bodies as well as the Basran treasures. The corpses chewed by jackals were unrecognisable. None of their other fellow travellers had survived. They immediately lit a fire and warded off the wild animals beginning to approach them. They also found something to eat, cooked it and put on warm clothing.

Towards noon, they felt more energetic. Gökçe's arm had also stopped bleeding. They opened one of the treasure chests. Each removed a bejewelled dagger and three emeralds, locked the chest again and concealed the trunks that remained uncovered under snow. They saddled two out of the four horses which had survived. They did not neglect to kill off the wounded horses, wearied after struggling all through the night, so they would not fall prey to wolves. Mustafa was to return to Diyarbakır to inform the governor of what had happened, while Gökçe Ali would go forth to Istanbul to report to the appropriate authority, and then convey me to Kara Piri in the Covered Bazaar. They did not have time to bury the bodies, so they sought forgiveness from the souls of their departed friends and bid them adieu.

I was now travelling to Istanbul on the back of Gökçe Ali's saddle. Within me was Leyla's love. I carried a letter and my master Fuzuli's gazals. Hidden in my story was the code leading to the Babylon Society's stash of space secrets. Should the opportunity ever arise, I would one day return and seek my dark-eyed love. Who knows, perhaps fate would also lead her to the land of the Sultan and we would meet somewhere. That is, if the Babylon Society did not find me before I found her.

Leylaaaaaaaaa!

6
How we scaled Mountains without being seen, and endured Hell and High Water to reach Istanbul

This city of Istanbul that is without peer or price
For its single stone may the land of Persia be sacrificed
Nedim

Gökçe Ali rode for days on end through forests, over ploughed fields and across barren valleys, without knowing the way or running into bandits. He followed the barking of dogs echoing down from snow-capped mountains and stormy peaks; he scented out the smokey smell of cattle dung in the hope of finding human settlement close by. He ate porcupine and rabbit as he went and drank melted snow from thc mountains. When night fell, he hid me in his bosom and by day I travelled on the back of his saddle. He did not know how to read. "What is a book other than a burden for a cavalryman?" he asked himself at one point. But he was not

a man to betray another's trust and felt himself obliged to fulfil the last will of the obsequious ağa appointed by the Paşa.

He skirted cities and towns, but never mixed with the people. On the eighth day, he drank a hot soup for the first time near Sivrihisar, on a table set in a garden away from others in a Bektaşi Sufi lodge where he slept on a soft mattress. He related what had befallen him to the *baba-dede* before whom he appeared the following day, though he did make a few changes to his story. He made no mention of the fact that he had me hidden in his bosom.

Revived by the hot soup and soft bed, he donated his horse to the lodge and set off once again. This time, he was a Sufi of the Kalenderi order and completed his journey in exactly 11 days. He embarked for Istanbul at Üsküdar and, as the rowing boat steered its way between the large waves and neared the city walls, he slowly removed the bejewelled dagger, with which I had slept back to back throughout the journey, as well as me, in a manner such as not to attract the attention of the boatman or the other passengers. He behaved like a merchant about his daily business.

He placed the dagger diagonally in his waist belt. He checked the emeralds one by one – the first he hid in his robe, the second in the toe of his rawhide sandal and the third in his armlet containing Qur'anic verses. His heart was now at ease. Beyond lay the safe city of Istanbul. The people called it Darüleman or "Land of Peace". There could be no lawlessness here.

I saw the sea for the first time that day. I was struck by how the city within the walls extended from the point where the waters of the Bosphorus flowed into the Sea of Marmara all the way to the Golden Horn. The Bosphorus was several times wider than my native Tigris and the city shimmered with towers, obelisks, monuments and minarets appearing here and there amidst green woods. There were overlapping wooden houses on the slopes overlooking the Golden Horn. The city's districts appeared as clusters extending their arms to one another through vineyards and gardens, looking a little like glittering lovers standing back-to-back or shoulder-to-shoulder.

When we entered through Bahçekapı, the sixteenth gate and third in terms of size, I came upon a city filled with anxiety and dread. The people, who had woken a week previously to screams in the city squares or else to fists beating against doors, took to the streets, aghast at what they thought was the end of the world. In nearby villages and towns, everyone witnessed a Judgement Day rehearsal, hour after hour. The sky caught fire and the stars were falling to the ground. Women screaming, "Our gardens are filled with stars!" had seen balls of fire the size of the full moon falling on rooftops and roads. There were even those who counted 250,000 stars till day dawned once more.

The following day, in anticipation of Doomsday, everyone was restless and repentant, and no one slept properly for two nights in a row. Some alarmists stirred up the masses with warnings that stones were raining down from the heavens and the city's order was turned upside-down.

The mosques filled up while the brothels, secluded at the foot of the city walls, were pelted with stones and the coffeehouses, Persian tobacco shops and taverns were demolished. It was the self-same men who had intoxicated themselves and bedded the prostitutes the previous night who wrought the destruction. On the previous day, a whore had been battered to death in the middle of the street. The poor woman was cut to pieces and her body parts nailed to the city's columns, fountains and plane tree trunks as a lesson to others.

The people's anger towards the palace came across in their language. Everyone spoke of how rulers left affairs of state to the direction of women, how corruption was manifest everywhere, how goods were sold for more than their worth, how people rebelled, how stones had rained down from above in retribution and how lessons needed to be learned. Some recovered quickly from the effects of this frightful night and began to return to their usual mundane struggles.

The road forked at the city gate. The way leading to the heart of the Ottoman state, the Topkapı Palace, was paved in stone and people gathered at the entrance where soldiers from the gardener corps stood guard, waiting for the Chief Astronomer to return from the palace. The sounds of street pedlars and the town crier advertising the books in his basket were drowned out by the din of the crowds. Each person had his own theory. Each asked the other the questions he would a little later direct to the Chief Astronomer and ran his own commentaries. Alas, all these people wanted to learn not what the stones were, but what they portended. Like the cardinals who blamed the comet which appeared at the time of the Fall of Constantinople, the Chief Astronomer was now expected to interpret these star showers as ominous.

"If only the Chief Astronomer knew what the sage Akeldan knew," I reflected. "He could advise that this was a meteor shower and that the Lord favoured us with such firework displays every 30 years. There is no cause for fear, but I dare say the poor soul is himself as scared as the people."

The dirt road which Gökçe Ali took led to the city centre and we passed houses on both sides, the Covered Bazaar, the Grand Bazaar and the Old Palace, ultimately arriving at Etmeydanı, where his janissary friends were stationed. I could sense that Gökçe Ali's spirits lifted as memories of military expeditions, battles, blood and violence faded, and I heard the peaceful beating of his heart as his thoughts turned to the serenity of life in Istanbul. A freshness and vivacity quickened his step. He considered that the city he had not seen for three years had not changed much. However, as he approached the barracks, he saw a construction site in the meadow adjoining the Meşini Mosque and the Byzantine aqueduct, where he was occasionally wont to go out for drill together with his former fellows from the regiment. Seeing the foundation diggers, carpenters, stonecutters, metal-workers, sand carriers and lime burners hard at work aroused his curiosity.

"Presumably," he thought, "These are the foundations of the complex Süleyman the Magnificent will build in memory of his dear Şehzade." He was to learn much later that, in this place, Chief Imperial Architect Sinan planned to bring together for the first time mosque, *medrese*, mausoleum, soup kitchen, caravanserai, primary school, timekeeper's clock room and public fountain. The plans had already been drawn up. "More power to your elbow, Master Sinan!" he said to himself.

We arrived at the door of the barracks and one of the guardsmen poked fun at Gökçe Ali's dervish garb. "What is it, sage? Have you lost your way to the Sufi lodge?" Gökçe Ali responded by opening his coarse woollen cloak and showing his tattoo. This was the mark of a wolf identical to the emblem on the regimental standard and it ensured that he was admitted immediately.

He sought out his former comrades in arms and caught up with their news. Then he went up to see the regiment chief and related to him everything that had happened to him. He presented the dagger and emeralds and so they set off together to the Palace to report on the adventure.

I remained in barracks that day. In all conscience, after seeing this magnificent city, I did not know if I was up to seeing the Topkapı Palace that was considered to be its heart. Besides, it seemed I would be spending entertaining days in barracks; everything was so alien and interesting to me...

When Gökçe Ali handed me over to Kara Piri at the Covered Bazaar, it was a Tuesday. He was a dark swarthy man of medium height and clear countenance. After reading Ayas Paşa's letter, he cast an eye over the gazals which were written on separate pages, folded them and slipped them under his robe. As he was going home that night, he sent his steward to the market, instructing him to buy dried fruit and nuts, snacks and seasonal fruits. This was for my benefit since from then until Friday, my pages were read out aloud from beginning to end in Kara Piri's house in Yedikule by a veteran tutor.

Those most affected most by the tragic tale of love were the youngest son and daughter of marriageable age as well as the slave girl Dilşeker. When I first saw Dilşeker, I thought my master Fuzuli must have written his verses with this girl in mind. The pages turned one by one and Kara Piri's stout wife kept letting her head slump down on the divan for a nap, but Dilşeker and the daughter were entranced. As the section about Leyla and Kays' reunion in the desert was being read, I saw that scene in all its realistic detail from behind Dilşeker's veil, reflected on the teardrop on her eyelash. There was perhaps an attachment between Dilşeker and me dating back to time immemorial. My heart was thirsty for love and perhaps it had languished beside hers when our share of spirits was being meted out in the pre-eternal assembly. Perhaps it was decided then that my lot would consist only of love, pain and rapture and my book of destiny was filled with these.

On the page which set off Dilşeker's tears was a miniature sketch which bore the trace of my master Fuzuli's quill pen. At that very moment, I saw myself among the miniature's blurred lines meeting with Leyla in the desert. My body was half-naked and around me sat wolf and lamb, lion and gazelle, eagle and pigeon, spellbound by love. Leyla extended her hand. "O one familiar to savages and strange to me! O cure of my affliction, ruler of my heart! Do you not recognise me, your Leyla? Or have you forgotten that you and I were little together, we went to school together, loved and were loved together? We were two spirits in one body, two almonds in a single shell."

Yes, yes, my master Fuzuli had attempted to depict me here. How fitting everything in this scene was for what I felt. Towards the end of the tale, I saw once more that the spirit hidden within me until now belonged to Kays. How else, whilst my three-thousandth couplet was being recited, could I have seen the Leyla sitting by my grave with her former freshness? The vision of the girl on the banks of the Tigris who had not deemed me worthy of her lips was before me no more. Here was Leyla before me. Leyla, the ill-fated daughter of Mehdi from the Banu 'Amir. And I, son of Mülevvah, was the madman who took to the desert for Leyla. Yet I am Mecnun, my master Fuzuli's slave. And the secret of the Babylon Society is the window of my world of feeling facing life. The secret that makes me sought twice over...

The night my story came to an end in Kara Piri's house, Dilşeker fell ill. The young daughter of the house did not shy away from revealing the tears she shed in secret. I knew that when she said her sorrow was for Leyla, it was a lie. She wept for the love of the coltish lad who had secretly held her hand at the market two months before. The fire of longing that seared her burnt me up inside and reminded me of my Leyla.

"I ought not be making beauties weep," I pondered. I did not want my path to Leyla to be all tears. Was I going to hold myself responsible for the tears of others as much as for my own, for the longing of others as much as for my own?

And there was another dimension. If those who had read my verses had known that they could not hide from me that which they supposed to keep hidden from others, I wondered which feelings they would have confided in me. If they only knew that I involuntarily observed their private lives... They merely read my cover, looked at my pages, saw what I looked like on the surface. But I knew their inner worlds as much as their outer and could feel the warmth in their hearts. This caused me great pain, as their moments of joy were outnumbered by their times of sorrow and their sadness was greater than their happiness. On the face of it, virtually all were happy, but deep inside lay sorrow. "Are people always like this?" I asked. "I wonder if the beloved Leyla I left on the banks of the Tigris was so full of sorrow." My faculties were not as developed back then: I tried to gauge people's personalities solely from the warmth of their fingertips.

I understood for the very first time at Kara Piri's house what a great burden it was to know the intimate lives of others. The household behaved as though I was not there; they acted as though their careless attitudes were commonplace. Their behaviour and thoughts when they were alone caused me to feel like I had stolen their honour. For instance, the fact that Kara Piri's daughter did not even feel the need to turn around while putting on her nightgown drove me crazy. I wanted to be felt, noticed, addressed. It was to be regretted that on the night I was alone with Kara Piri's love-struck daughter, I wanted to behave in a manner befitting my master Fuzuli. I shut my eyes tight, but could not stop myself looking at the beauty undressing before me.

We left Istanbul, passing talismanic pillars inherited from Byzantium and mosques converted from churches as well as statues of Venus, Apollo and other nude deities that Ibrahim Paşa had his men transport on gun carriages on their triumphal return from the Vienna Expedition, before he fell from grace. Ibrahim Paşa had positioned them among the ruins of the Byzantine hippodrome in front of his resplendent palace. It was as if these were virgin sinners who had been petrified so that their descendants would see their shame and take heed. But fate decreed their separation from their descendants. They were themselves thrown into a situation so abominable as to bring out a cold sweat in any onlooker.

I was held in the hand that Kara Piri rested against his lined kaftan. Next to us was a slant-eyed merchant who imported paper, spices and silk from Hoten; this man who, judging from what he said, was visiting Istanbul for the first time, was a very curious character. At one point, I was even under the mistaken impression that he was one of the members of the Babylon Society. He wanted to get to know the city and asked about everything he saw. I realised that the obelisks attracted his attention most. Kara Piri explained, as though exasperated by his questions: "Almost all these pillars were left over from the Byzantines. The people used to believe that each of them possessed its own magic. According to beliefs handed down from antiquity to the Middle Ages, some of these pillars protected the city against earthquakes and some against fire. They were erected with the incantations of monks and commissioned by the Emperors themselves. Nowadays, erecting magic pillars when cities are being founded or repaired is commonplace everywhere.

There are many of these in Istanbul. This monument was erected in front of the old palace during the reign of Constantine. It is constructed out of a thousand slabs of white marble: each side was decorated with figures of soldiers and a fairy-faced virgin statue was placed on the top. This is the most famous of all the obelisks. When this virgin cried out and summoned all the birds, some of the birds died and fell to the ground due to the scramble in the sky and the people jostled for these, in order to eat them for healing, like sacred food.

On the site of this pillar in Tavukpazarı there used to be a column of solid red marble. This was erected as a talisman in the repairs carried out after a devastating earthquake. There used to be a carving of a starling on the capital back then. After the earthquake caused it to fall, it was repaired with hoops of metal, and came to be known as Çemberli Taş, the Hooped Stone."

Kara Piri took a break to rest his throat. Again he was assailed by questions. He spoke, paused again and then resumed. "The six marble columns in the walls were dedicated to six sages. It was believed that the one with a bronze statue of a common fly made a constant buzzing sound and kept mosquitoes away from Istanbul. The one with the wolf motif on top was supposed to mean that flocks of sheep on the city's outskirts could make do without shepherds. The column with the statue of the two lovers locked in a tight embrace was supposed to improve the relationships of those experiencing marital discord. There are even some who still believe this," Kara Piri said, shaking his head and hand in a manner indicating his own lack of faith in superstition.

He noticed that they were nearing the Bazaar and was delighted that his job as a tour guide was coming to an end. With a final effort, he shared what he knew with the merchant. "A talisman can be found in Istanbul for epidemics, fire, enemy attack, preservation of morality and, in short, for every imaginable thing. The people remember that, only 12 years ago, after a janissary commander struck the head of one of the snakes on the twisted column with a three-headed dragon motif – which apparently protects Istanbul from snakes, scorpions and other vermin – thugs in the

Greek and Armenian districts wrought destruction, claiming that snakes were infesting the city. The ensuing unrest was barely contained by the Sultan's men. So the real reason why the public did not take kindly to the statues that Ibrahim Paşa brought to Istanbul was this restiveness."

Together with the merchant, I listened to all that Kara Piri explained as if it were a fairy tale. Eventually, we left behind Ibrahim Paşa's grand palace which he had perhaps built on that scale in order to spite the Sultan, and so we reached the Bazaar. Comprised of a fairly wide courtyard surrounded on all sides by small shops with eaved frontages, the Bazaar functioned like the bands of artisans who were called to military duty when going on campaign. According to Kara Piri, the most important specialist bazaar in Istanbul was this one, which included paper traders, binders, paper marbling specialists, miniaturists, gilders, inkwell manufacturers, silversmiths and silver embroiderers and sellers of silk thread and needles from the Imperial company. It worked as a guild and was affiliated with the official in charge of stationers. We passed a shop displaying papyrus, parchments, Baghdad, Peking and Vienna paper bundled into separate baskets awaiting customers and entered the shop of Rüstem Ağa who was to meet with the merchant accompanying us.

This old man, one of the imperial court stewards, made different kinds of clocks of all sizes, carriage clocks and musical clocks. Customers came to him from all over the world and commissioned custom-made clocks, or purchased one of the clocks lining the walls, handing it to a porter to carry. Rüstem Ağa was known to employ around 100 craftsmen and apprentices in his workshop. His success in making clocks was ascribed to the way he used magpie gut for his timepieces which he tore out from the magpies with his own hands.

It struck me then that the foul-smelling strings left to dry in front of his shop were actually bird intestine smeared with chemicals to suppress offensive odours.

Leaving behind the head-spinning clock pendulums, we entered into the shop where illustrators seated upon cir cular cushions painted on the pages resting against sloped stands. I sensed that this was my new home, or that I would be staying here for a few weeks at any rate. In the middle of the shop stood a round bench covered in ceramic cups filled with paints of diverse colours. There were also wire combs, sand-filled bowls, glasses half-filled with water holding fine-tipped paintbrushes, as well as burnishers, rulers for drawing straight lines, penknives and cutters.

These fresh-faced men seated around the bench received day wages for the series of drawings they produced once every three months; they also illustrated books to order. Once in a while, they produced very special illustrations and presented these to their most esteemed customers. In the absence of their masters, they drew secret delight in drawing lascivious images for sexual compendia, or *Bahname*, and other sexually explicit books.

Many of them eventually lost their eyesight for the sake of their art, generally living out their last days dependent on the charity of others. To console themselves, they related to each other how well their masters, who had lost their eyesight before them, could depict famous scenes by heart.

I scanned the illustrations in front of these men. On their faces glowed the projection onto their souls of the beautiful images they produced. Suddenly they all stood up and greeted the elderly man who had walked through the door.

This was Nasuh Efendi who was considered to be their master. Thanks to his proficiency in cudgel-fighting while in the Sultan's army and his impressive brute force, they called him master Matrakçı Nasuh. He was the head painter of the imperial painting studio. My master Fuzuli had made frequent mention of him and would speak of their acquaintance. Apparently he too had been present during the Sultan's capture of Baghdad and had even produced miniatures of the places he had visited, including an image of my master's hometown of Hilla. They shared a mutual acquaintance in Kara Piri and had decided two days previously to meet at this time, in Nakkaş Haydar's shop.

Master Nasuh said that he was most curious about me and wanted Kara Piri to show me to him. And indeed, just as soon as he took hold of me, he kissed and smelled me and spoke at length of my master Fuzuli. He read verses from a few pages and expressed his amazement. Then he instructed Haydar Usta: "O valiant one! You among us most appreciate the value of poetry. I present to you my master Fuzuli's work *L&M*. May you take pains with it and beautify it."

In response, my entire being shook as though buffeted by a fierce wind. Momentarily, I wished to shout, "Yes, this is me and this is my story!" I pondered what a pleasant home this bazaar and this studio would make for me and delighted in the thought. "A home in which I can live peacefully until the Last Day!" I thought to myself. I, Mecnun, prince of Mulawwah from the Banu 'Amir, whose fate has been written with sorrow. The slave of my master Fuzuli, who lives in his book. And you, where are you, O Leylaaaa?

7
How I awoke in Workshops devoted to Beauty and was painted in Colours of Distinction

The fabric of mastery is sold in the markets of this city
This bazaar of wisdom is the wellspring of scholars' knowledge.

Nedim

Nakkaş Haydar Ağa, one of the senior apprentices of Master Nasuh, had a true taste for poetry. I could sense this from his ever-increasing delight and from the pacing of his heart as my master's verses were read out. Now and then, as he hummed verses to himself, it was as if he strove to match the poems he wrote under his pen name Nigari to my master's verses; he would then recite couplets to his junior craftsmen and add his own commentary.

He explained what kind of illustrations were to be drawn where in the course of my story and which materials were to be used. In order to separate the sections left blank in-between chapters and not lose the supporting footnotes, he attempted to memorise my story or else sought codes in the meanings of these couplets. I came to understand that Master Haydar was aware of the Babylon Society. This was why he quickly copied the couplets off the pages he distributed for illustration. If there was indeed a change in order or binding or if, by accident, a page went missing, then he did not want to get himself into hot water and show negligence in his duty towards the Babylon Society.

From the night my pages were separated from my battered binding and handed out according to the mastery of the senior apprentices, Master Haydar set about reading me, starting with my very first couplet. At times, he was left full of admiration for the gazals written in Fuzuli's nom de plume and felt regret that they did not carry his own pen name; sometimes he sought a sign pertaining to Arshiya Akeldan and at other times he tried to find clues from the progression of events in my narrative.

Each time he checked the craftsmen drawing the scenes relevant to my tale on the white spaces of my pages, he surveyed my master Fuzuli's sketches again. Thus, while checking that the miniatures being drawn were relevant to my story, he took pains to ensure that my master Fuzuli's drawings were preserved with all their essentials. For the first time, his craftsmen felt suffocated by this degree of supervision; they felt distrusted and the rumour began to circulate that their master was not himself.

As pieces of me were taken away, I wondered about the illustrations. I wondered how people imagined me and how much these artists could know me. They were going to draw pictures befitting my Master's narration, this was certain, but to what extent were they going to be able to make me resemble me? I was impatient to see.

The craftsmen determined the scenes they had mastered through repeated sketches and re-examined the relevant miniatures from the work *Nizami Hamsesi* sitting on the shelf. They studied the illustrations contained therein. However, my master Fuzuli had left spaces for illustrations to scenes which were not even pictured in other *mesnevis* so it was hard to determine my state of mind in those chapters. Amongst these were the scenes where I gave away all my garments and precious stones to rescue the fawn that had fallen into a trap, or where I had myself tied in chains and then went to Leyla's village and where we later fainted after seeing one another.

On the other hand, the craftsmen were exacting in their depictions of many other scenes. Here was Leyla's birth and the festivities that ensued, here we were sitting side by side amidst our classmates, here were my friends taking me to the wilderness after Leyla was removed from school. Further drawings chronicled my father finding me in the desert and begging me to return home, representatives going to Leyla's tent, asking for her hand in marriage on my behalf and being turned down by my uncle. "No daughter of mine will marry a madman," he had said. Then I was shown being taken to the Ka'ba in the hope that I would come to my senses: I had laid my head at its sacred entrance and entreated God with the words, "O Lord, increase my love." I was shown being taken to the desert again on my return and befriending wild animals. Then Ibn Salam was depicted catching sight of Leyla and becoming captivated by her. After their wedding, gallant Nawfal was shown gathering his forces and fighting against my uncle's army to take Leyla back for me. Leyla was shown pretending to grieve upon Ibn Salam's death as she wept with longing, then coming to find me sitting amongst the beasts in the desert. The last scenes showed her dictating her last will to her mother and dying and me then receiving news of her death, throwing myself on her grave and perishing on the spot.

As each painting was finished, master Haydar would check it carefully. Whilst assessing the colour contrast and play of pattern, he was also trying to discern any mysteries reaching him from the Assyrian librarian at the Baghdad Academy of Sciences. He wanted to understand how Fuzuli's memories from his days in Baghdad were projected in this book.

I came to realise that he knew nothing of me as yet. For example, he was unaware of the Babylon Society's ciphers and the fact that these had to be sought among my couplets. All that he did was dwell on the paintings; as if confounded by a treasure map, he seemed to expect a miracle that would reveal to him the location of the Temple of Ishtar and open its door. His attitude eased my anxiety, if only a little. That is to say, the Babylon Society clearly lacked any information regarding my composition, and they did not know about the dagger or the coded leather strap. If they had known of these, Nakkaş Haydar would have paid very close attention to my poetry rather than my illustrations just as soon as he had possession of me.

Nakkaş Haydar had two students called Osman and Pervane who promised artfulness in their every manner. Whilst painting with the brushes they made from the hair taken from the nape of the Ardabil cat, those hairs were reduced to a single strand in their hands, so that the line became thinner and thinner and was reduced to sheer imagination.

When obtaining colours from natural ochres and from cochineal and indigo compounds mixed with alcohol and other chemicals in correct proportion, they displayed such skill that people would visit the studio just to watch them at work, sometimes staying for hours at a time. It was these two colours that represented me best and the face of Mecnun which resembled me most among all the depictions throughout the tale was that in the scene of me draped over Leyla's grave as drawn by *kalfa* Osman.

I must say that I had a great many visitors in Nakkaş Haydar's studio. These were people who knew nothing of the Babylon Society nor anything like it, but wanted purely to see me on the basis of concern for art and a love of poetry. Among these, I can list mufti Lütfi Efendi who barely managed to carry his hunch back as he leaned down on his walking stick. He had headed the special scientific commission when Christopher Columbus came to Istanbul seeking a patron for his sea explorations, saying to Ottoman Sultan Bayezid II, "Give me ships and I shall give you a new world." The Sultan ordered, "May the words of this unbeliever be investigated!" and mufti Lütfi Efendi had recommended rejection. "Could there ever be a new world at the End of Time?" he had asked. Other distinguished visitors were the Austrian diplomat Baron de Busbecq who sent back trunkfuls of books and a tulip bulb during his posting, some librarians who placed special orders for the private books of the Paşas, *mullahs* with a keen interest in reading and a great many others besides. These were the finest people of Istanbul, city of wisdom and craftsmanship, who found great pleasure taking small breaks between my pages.

❦❦❦

There are six people from among my visitors that I must mention, as failure to do so would lead to your being unable to grasp my significance within this city. First of all came Satılmış Efendi who had started off as a saddler's apprentice in Balıkesir and then come to a *medrese* in Istanbul where he discovered an inclination to poetry. From the rule of Sultan Selim I onwards, he held an esteemed place among Istanbul's cognoscenti. People called him Satı Bey and he had a shop in the courtyard of Bayezid Mosque. There is no one who does not know that the poets of the age as well as all manner of enthusiasts frequented this place, recited poetry and sought the literary opinion of the owner. I over-estimated him so much that, when a short, slim, sparsely-bearded man of a certain age appeared before me, I exclaimed inwardly, "It cannot be! This little man cannot be the great poet Zati Efendi!" But it was indeed he. Here was the famed poet standing before me. What is more, I knew that as he scanned my story, he was thinking to himself, "Oh if only it had been me who wrote these verses!"

Three of my other visitors were still pursuing their tertiary studies at the Fatih *medrese* and their common attribute was there sensibility towards history and literature. I learnt from their conversations that one was Abdulbaki, son of the Fatih Mosque's *muezzin*, another was Ali who had come from Gallipoli, and the third was Sadettin Mullah. From the reverence they showed towards me and all the words of praise they uttered about my master Fuzuli, I made out that they were promising students of science and literature and that, providing the winds of fate did not change, they would make great men in the future.

The other two visitors I wish to mention were Hayali Bey by whom I was treated with the greatest respect, and Aşık Çelebi who had taken it upon himself to write the life stories of the poets. Hayali Bey read me page by page while sharing his thoughts with master Nakkaş Haydar. At one point, master Nakkaş Haydar took out from his bosom the gazals that I had brought with me as my master's gift, and recited in sequence the poems that he himself had written in the same rhyme and meter. He called these his imitations and wept.

As for Aşık Çelebi, he kept calculating how he might obtain more information concerning my master's life and how and in what style he would include these details in his work. When I came across this pleasant-faced man, I wished so much that I could speak. At no other time have I wished so ardently to have the faculty of speech. Just think, if I could have related my knowledge and memories of my master Fuzuli, what a magnificent chapter these would have made for Aşık Çelebi's biography and what beautiful paintings it would have inspired. Perhaps he would then have penned a work in its own right, based upon my account, and would have introduced my master Fuzuli to all Turkish provinces. My inability to speak on that day caused me to reflect anew upon the great influence of my master who had conferred such prestige upon me and this grieved me. Somewhere deep inside, I felt pain that I had not been able to thank him properly. I was to feel the same anguish years later when I received the news that he had died. I was never able to repay him for all that he had done. All those reading my verses would always remember him and speak of his goodness, but because of him, I would remain forever confined to living under the burden of exalting the love of the desert beauty. Others would see in me a splendid love story, but I would love vicariously.

Even now, I remained a slave deep down, my master Fuzuli's slave, but I was received like a king wherever I went. *"I am a slave like a sovereign, a magnificent beggar."* I think my master had uttered that famous verse not for himself, but for me.

When I was taken for binding to Nakkaş Haydar of Üsküdar's house, I trembled at the sound of a guillotine falling from on high upon a book laid out as if for torture. Everything in this place was like the instruments of torture in the dungeons of Babylon. The punishments meted out on Arshiya Akeldan's former colleagues were carried out using contraptions resembling those found here. I considered how the Babylon Society and the thieves hunting the golden statues were no strangers to these instruments and I shuddered. Here, before my very eyes, they pierced skins with awls, cut hide with arbelos, squeezed cardboard beneath heavy marble slabs, sewed paper with silk thread and screwed in brass rosettes and corner moulds, leaving them in place for days on end.

Although the same instruments were used and the same tasks undertaken, there was a vast difference between the imperial workshop and the dungeon. One encouraged the pursuit of beauty as a manifestation of the aesthetic dimension of human creation, while in the other, inhumanity ruled supreme. An arbelos or a needle might occasion objects of beauty here and cause anguish there. Where knives might hack away at beauty here, they caused blood to spurt from beautiful necks there. Those using hooks might in one place be termed executioners while here they were known as artists. I pondered how human beings gained meaning through intention and forethought. That is to say, human beings can be good or bad, beautiful or repugnant according to their intentions and their manner of looking at objects. Those who sold their souls to the devil and those who devoted them to the All-Merciful were separated by this thin line. Some made use of their time, while others squandered it; some gave meaning to life through goodness and others worshipped evil.

My spirit had been nourished by all the beautiful paintings at the imperial workshop but now I felt suddenly chilled. I decided this was a test and that I needed to discipline my spirit. Powerless and desperate, I was to endure everything that came my way. And this is what happened. First, they sewed my sheets together after continuously compressing them and I could not voice my lamentation to a single soul. Subsequently, they subjected me to torture, lowering the guillotine down on me and making me feel as though they were ripping out my nails. My screams were enough to wake the dead, but those at the binder's paid no heed. They tied me with cardboard dipped in marbling troughs and inside an envelope flap they prepared a gold star rosette upon textured leather. None of my convulsions helped. Finally, after applying varnish to my binding, they pressed weights upon me and left me in a dark trunk. I could not make myself heard and even lost my voice completely. This torment lasted for exactly three days. I could only endure it by repeating Leyla's name. Throughout, I treasured her love in my heart, her picture in my bosom and her image by my side. In all other respects, I had ceased to be me. I had lost myself.

Nakkaş Haydar, who produced the most beautiful drawings of the Imperial bookbinders' guild, lifted me out into daylight. As he was wiping off the dirt and dust with his linen rag, it occurred to me to take a look at my new appearance. O my God! Was this me? I was now a slave in princely garments. The charming men of this city of wisdom had conferred this finery and projected my inner beauty onto my face. I looked like a prince donning a kaftan inlaid with gold.

I realised at that moment why they called this place a bazaar. A corset fastened my waist, there was kohl around my eyes, blusher on my cheeks and my locks were combed into place. It was as though I had been readied for the nuptial chamber. My torments and my three-day confinement in that dungeon in the name of beauty gave me self-confidence in my new appearance. I wanted so much for Leyla to be by my side, to embrace her once again.

Leyla! I am afraid that my will is not my own. I cannot seek you out. He who takes me, despatches me, sells me and buys me is another. I cannot come to you so have me brought to you! I cannot have myself sold to you so you be the one who buys me!

8
How a vagrant *Abdal* pursued me and thousands of Thoughts assailed me

So enraptured am I that I perceive not what is the world.
Who am I, who is the cupbearer, what is the wine?

Fuzuli

As I walked through the gate of the Topkapı Palace, seven pigeons took flight from Nakkaş Haydar's binding workshop. These were the seven homing pigeons conveying small notes to the members of the Babylon Society in different parts of the world. Master Nakkaş Haydar had written, "A bride can be protected from the evil eye only in a palace and can live eternally therein." At the same time, two male pigeons had taken off from the Bektaşi Sufi lodge at Ahırkapı and returned one hour later with a third pigeon, one of Nakkaş Haydar's females.

The Bektaşi Sufi lodge was established to provide work and quarters to vagrant *abdal*s and itinerant dervishes of the Kalenderi Sufi order serving Shah Isma'il's intelligence service. It was hidden in an apple orchard right by the palace. I learnt about it when Nakkaş Haydar heard of it by chance in the workshop of master Ahmet who bound me.

On one of the days when my body writhed in pain, one such vagrant Sufi arrived, saying that he sought new books to read. He wore a halberd in his waistband, a rosary on his arm and a ring on his ear; on his chest and biceps were tattoos of Ali's sword and beneath his cloak he wore only a sash and a knee-length skirt.

He removed his turban of the Malami Sufi order from his shaved head and drank his tea after mixing in the contents of the box of opiates he hid in his sash. Nakkaş Haydar noticed a metal band around the man's exposed penis. "So you have tied the bird to the snare, Baba sage!" he jested. "It keeps taking flight, you see!" came the reply.

The vagrant dervish entered into conversation and described at length the places he had visited, the people he had met, the extraordinary events he had witnessed. He also spoke of state politics. Master Ahmet realised from the very beginning that the dervish had come with a particular objective and that is why he had summoned Nakkaş Haydar. Nakkaş Haydar decided that it was odd for an *abdal* dervish to be so literate and profess so many profound ideas. He weighed up the discussion, made some mental notes and prepared to put someone on his tail. He tried to prompt him saying, "One who travels often knows much more than one who reads widely. Let us hear all about it, O sage." The dervish explained only what he wanted to explain and failed to give worthwhile answers to any of Haydar's questions.

According to his own account, his name was Musa. He travelled to Iran and Turan to spread the love of Fadlullah al-Hurufi, the secret of Hallaj al-Mansur and the teachings of the poet Nasimi. He was travelling from Baghdad towards the Balkans and hoped to show the people the true path. Wherever his knee-length coat collapsed for the night was his resting place. He contented himself with whatever fell into the beggar's cup at his waist, drinking water from brooks and streams and gathering his provisions from trees. He crossed hill and dale and travelled in the path of Truth.

Musa said that he had spent the previous month in a Bektaşi Sufi lodge in Sivrihisar. I realised then that we had both come from the same place and began to suspect he was following Gökçe Ali's trail. I was now going to listen to him very carefully too. Like master Haydar, I did not believe that he came to find new books. My suspicions were justified by what Musa later divulged. This man was a spy of Shah Isma'il who had been pursuing me from Baghdad. I could see that Nakkaş Haydar thought on the same lines as me from the way in which he gave the impression of continuing his own work while listening intently to Musa. Haydar removed a gazelle skin from the trough and placed it under the marble which had flattened my pages to drain the water away. I could no longer see them but could hear every word perfectly. "Sage," said Nakkaş Haydar, "Now, pray tell about ancient civilisations and historical matters."

Abdal Musa was a very cunning man. He understood immediately what kinds of things were being probed with such a question. He had hoped to find what he was looking for if he could only convince Nakkaş Haydar. He started with the Crusades, thinking that it would be an easy way into the subject. He explained at length how all the knights of Christendom abandoned their castles, fields and wives to reach Jerusalem in throngs from across land and sea for the Church-steered holy war. He related how the armoured horses and knights devastated the places through which they travelled like plagues of locusts, but when they reached the holy land it was their turn to endure terrible pain and suffering at the hands of the Muslims, who had no other protection than their own flesh and bone. He spoke of the ruthlessness of those never-ending wars, how the stench of burnt human flesh in forests onto which fireballs and poisonous arrows had rained drove away even the ravenous wolves and hungry dogs. He compared the virtues of Saladin and Richard and, after describing the struggle between the Cross and the Crescent, he asserted that the deep wounds made by these wars still remained raw. "Now let me tell you another story, master Haydar," he resumed. I felt like replying, "Here we go, now spill the beans!"

"On the fourth of these Crusades, Pope Innocent secretly gave a dagger to Hungarian King András asking that, after Jerusalem's capture, he should bring it into contact with Jesus' crib and then exchange it with a dagger in the Temple of Solomon. This dagger was a cursed dagger from the Babylonian era, bearing a twin-horned dragon head upon its hilt." After Musa uttered this sentence, I felt something breaking inside me, as I realised that he was referring to the Sirrush-headed dagger that my master Fuzuli had buried beneath the mulberry tree in the *medrese* courtyard.

Musa resumed excitedly. "Apparently this dagger brings death to whoever takes possession of it. The Pope wanted to bind its curse until the end of time by having it placed in the Temple of Solomon. András eventually chose seven men from his army. Conferring upon them the rank of 'Knights of the Universe', he presented each of them with a gift of steel mesh armour for themselves and their horses. Entrusting the dagger to the most dauntless among them, he bade the others to protect him and despatched them all into Ayyubid bastions under various identities and guises. They spoke in the same accents as our raiding forces, observed the commandments of Islam and gathered logistic and strategic intelligence from Saladin's men at the same time.

However, on the third day, Saladin issued an imperial order, promising that anyone who brought him the head of a military spy would receive a bay horse. Three of the knights fled in fear of their lives and, when the remaining four saw them fleeing, they were overcome by panic, were caught and immediately killed on the battlefield. In the turmoil, some fellows removed the heads of a couple of Crusaders who had died two days earlier and presented them to Saladin as though they were the heads of the fleeing spies and thus received a reward. The number of those killed as spies over the following days reached 32."

After topping up Musa's tea, Nakkaş Haydar steered the story towards the subject which interested him. "So what happened to the dagger?"

"What do you expect? Its curse continued from that day forth. It was last with a blind librarian during our Sultan's – may he live long! – conquest of Baghdad. The man apparently committed suicide and it was never seen again. It is said that the dagger's curse was later transferred to a book."

Nakkaş Haydar hooted with laughter. "By God, seeing as I am still alive, this cursed book of yours has not yet come to us," but it occurred to me that the secret I carried might indeed be a curse. I had left corpses behind me in every place I had been. All those who possessed me came face to face with death... Still, I did not feel myself to be cursed. However, it became clear from Nakkaş Haydar and *abdal* Musa's conversation that not only scholars but thieves too would be looking for me from now on.

Which member of the Babylon Society had chosen gold over science and disclosed Akeldan's secret to those unworthy of it? Which man had confounded good and evil and sold his soul like a spy playing both sides? Yes, knowledge meant danger, but scholars were the most highly esteemed of people. What could those mastering knowledge have to do with gold? Even if knowledge and wealth could come together, knowledge and greed would still clash constantly. "May they be the target of poisoned arrows," I prayed.

They spoke of other topics and books until dusk. Just as Musa was saying farewell and was about to leave, he extended his beggar's cup to Nakkaş Haydar. Haydar dropped inside a biscuit and a miniature for him to sell, then showed him to the door. He intended to track Musa's movements. Just as soon as the so-called dervish had walked out of the eastern door of the bazaar, his tail started following him.

On the following day, Nakkaş Haydar speeded up the work he was doing on me and this troubled me. Perhaps he believed that I was cursed and wanted to get rid of me.

He realised that the man who had followed Gökçe Ali all the way to master Ahmet's binding workshop was not a Malami follower or a Kalenderi dervish, but on the contrary was a gangster hunting down the treasures of Babylon. He suspected Musa of being one of the so-called friends of the Shah but, then again, he reminded himself, "Shah Isma'il has spies everywhere," and did not dwell on the thought for long.

Nakkaş Haydar now decided that it fell to him to protect the secrets of the Babylon Society from thieves and vowed to himself to do so. Suspecting that I would not be safe in the workshop, he tried to find a way of securing me against danger. He decided that the safest route was to finish off the binding and deliver me to the palace as soon as possible. Surely the Bektaşi Sufi lodge in Ahırkapı could not reach as far as the palace. And besides, in a few days, it would be possible to inform on this lodge to the palace gardener and circulate the fact that it harboured friends of the Shah who worked as his spies.

He spent the whole afternoon trying to come up with solutions, though he did also manage to call on one of his relatives employed in the palace secret service known as the Three Crescents. He learned that some officers in command of a division of janissaries formed a gang which secretly observed the Bosphorus maritime traffic and recorded the flags and regimental standards of passing vessels. The lodge communicated with French vessels using the signal flags raised on its roof, relaying certain information to them. The lodge employed around 20 intelligence officers in Istanbul disguised as dervishes and had established a porters' guild at Galata as a means of support. The guild brought in revenue as well as information on loading and unloading operations. Upon the arrival of illicit cargo, members of the gang would go down to the shore dressed in porters' garb. They also enjoyed security by virtue of their status in the janissary corps.

When he learned all this, Nakkaş Haydar resolved that conveying me to the palace without delay would be the best course. He reckoned that I would be logged under the books of the Sultan's Treasury anyway and would be kept under lock and key whilst I remained at the palace. When the time came to reveal the secrets of the doors of the world which open onto space, ever-accelerating scientific advancement would have rendered it safe to transport me from the Imperial Treasury to the Sultan. Nakkaş Haydar supposed that the Babylon Society would re-form in Istanbul given his belief that his city stood at the centre of the civilised world. Could any other state be superior to the Ottoman? Could any surpass it in science? Were not the numbers of sages and scholars who had previously served the Cross and were now serving the Crescent increasing since Istanbul's conquest? It was highly likely that most of the Babylon Society members would be living in these lands! If only these thieves were no more!

***

When I entered the Palace, beautiful as a bride, the note that Nakkaş Haydar sent out with the pigeons had caused me to believe that I would live there until sage Akeldan's secret came to be revealed. Would the Palace give me peace or sorrow? I knew not. Would it be easy or difficult for me to seek my Leyla? I knew not. Would I possess power here or have to acquiesce? I did not know this either. What I did know was the excitement I felt as I took in the magnificence of the Lawgiver's sable-lined chamber. I too was fit for palaces having been beautified so much that I outweighed all the gems and jewels of the slave markets in the covered bazaar. I was oblivious as to whether my embellishment had been ordered by the Babylon Society so as to protect me or whether master Ahmet Usta was responsible in a bid to attain the Sultan's favour, or indeed whether I owed it to Nakkaş Haydar.

All I knew was that I missed Leyla.

Leyla! Free me from those who placed curses on me in your absence!

9
How I merged with a Walnut in Gülhane and embraced a Mingrelian Leyla

The lover is at times in union, at times in separation...
This is the world: sometimes mourning, sometimes elated.

Baki

I embraced her as Leyla. Her hair was like daylight. Those who looked at her might have commented, "This girl carries the sun upon her head." Her eyes were clear blue. Those who saw her would have thought, "The sky has descended to Earth!" Her face was lit up like a morning garden in Eastern climes and on it could be read the colours of Anatolian fables of old. Were she to walk, green meadows would spring up beneath her feet. Her heart was pure and radiant.

The bitterly cold winter night was shaken by the rage of the rain and a howling south-westerly and I let myself be warmed by her breath searing my face. I was taken and I burned. The bird-like weight of her delicate head and the amber perfume of her henna-dyed hair made my insides swoon and enraptured my mind. We enjoyed the late hours of the night in the hollow of the centuries-old walnut tree which only had a few dry branches left. Only the two of us could fit in our niche. Listening to the mournful melody of the rain dripping from the leaves of the ivy wrapped around the great trunk and suffocating it with love, I could feel the way she drew in freedom deeply. Her white skin trembled with the consternation and excitement of contravening the laws of the sovereign and the jealousy-laden instructions of his wife. She was wet through, the pain in her foot worsened and the cold seeping into her marrow numbed her mind, giving her nightmares between sleep and wakefulness. And yet she was happy. She felt pain like a first-time mother. Unable to budge, with one hand resting upon me and the other on her belly, she tried to survive.

When she jumped onto the branch of the noble walnut tree from the high walls of the palace, taking advantage of the reverse patrol of the soldier from the gardener's corps who guarded the palace walls by making use of flashes of lightning, her four-month old son was in her womb and in her bundle was me. However, the walnut branch on which she relied remained faithful to the laws of the palace and betrayed her. Her weight made it snap. How I wished I had two hands with which to support my Leyla as she fell to the ground.

I found my Leyla in a fragile spirit and, that night, embraced her delicate frame as if she were my Leyla. "Rukal," the Sultan had called her when he first embraced her. "You have filled my nights with delight. May your name be Şebsafa, my Night-Delight."

Rukal had been sold to the Ottoman palace four years previously and upon her entering, she was told: "Being a slave here is being a master, as one who cannot be cultivated here can learn refinement nowhere else. Here, learning is music, painting, literature, history and geography." Her attention was engaged.

Slave traders had abducted her from Mingrelia in Georgia and had brought her to Istanbul. When she was bought from the Yedikule slave market and given as a concubine to the palace, she was a maiden of 16 who addressed the full moon saying, "Either you rise or I will!" All the beauty of her race was in her face, her chest, her waist and her legs. Fate had ensnared her as she herself set out to trap wildcat, fox, prairie chicken and marten among the boxwood, juniper and cypress of the Caucasus. Neither tamarind nor pomegranate sherbets, neither soft toffee nor halva could make her forget the taste of the spring waters, honey and walnuts of those sombre mountains.

Locked in a tight embrace in the hollow of the walnut tree in Gülhane, we listened to the sound of the rain and thought of days gone by. She had four and I 40 years' worth of memories between these walls. Between these walls, which I had entered as though never to leave, were our sorrows and our joys. Our joys, sorrows, laughter and tears had stayed there.

Was it a good idea for us to run away from the palace? Had she acted wisely in taking me with her? What would befall us outside and what had fate decreed for us? Were our loves to increase or be lost? Had we hidden here to rise again or die? Were we going to laugh or cry? We knew not. Our dreams and memories were confounded. Two tear-drops fell from Rukal's eyes onto my cover. Two tears blended with bitter smiles. I read the entire life adventure of this fresh bride in those two tears; I saw all the hopes out of which her love was knotted and, as my heart burned once again, I loved her as I did my Leyla.

In the first days of her arrival in the harem – by which time I was already acquainted with every inch of the interior of these magnificent walls – she kept on seeing her father, a church bell-ringer in her dreams. She spoke in her mother tongue and sang a folk song in the tones of her soft and plaintive voice:

A fad passes, not love -
My destiny is another.
Ah! I have wandered in sorrow -
Bad news is said to travel fast.
Nani na didou nana nanina

Her voice echoed off the desolate stone walls. It was not a consolation but a torment and, every time she climbed into bed, she repeated like a prayer the chorus, "*Nani na didou...*" She would wake from her nightmares gasping for breath. She always felt her soul to be cold whether she was walking through the wooded garden with its marble paths, or sitting beneath the lofty domes as candlelight flickered behind sturdy doors, or absorbing the colours of spring in the garden during the Newruz festival and celebrating with sweets wrapped in ribbons. This life, that had started out with fear for the black rage of the Chief Eunuch donning a glittering floor-length dress, the most important figure in the garden, perhaps even the whole palace, appeared to her as surreal. She kept waiting to wake up from this dream. As time passed, she began to accept the realities. The friendship of Russian and Martinican concubines also brought consolation. They related similar stories and endeavoured to reassure one another. They split their bread together, and shared their sweets and pastries, joys and dreams. The only thing they did not share was their perfume. They were reluctant to divulge the secret of the essence they applied to their bodies and necks in order to guard their chance of prosperity. Or perhaps it was so that the Sultan could distinguish them according to their scents. And, in a manner most intriguing, these young women were always heroines of a separate story.

During the time of the Lawgiver, life here was entirely different. Everything changed in the reign of Selim. However, Sultan Murat who then governed the Ottoman Palace, seemed to have reversed the rules. Over the previous decade, palace life had suddenly degenerated. Assemblies of the Imperial Council, official meetings, decisions of war, international relations, diplomacy and the reception of envoys were all dominated by the changed harem hierarchy.

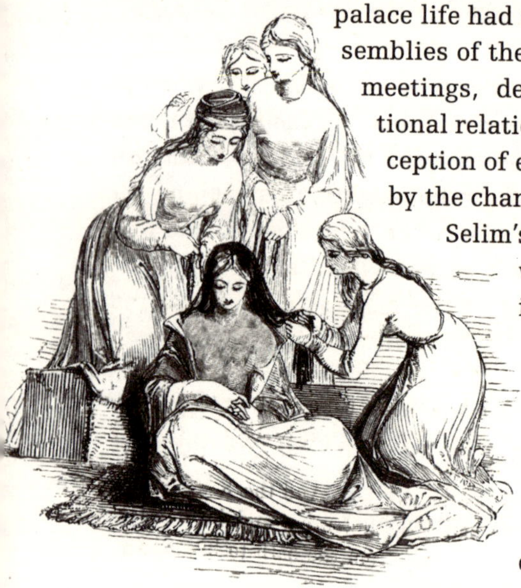

Selim's son Murat had three wives. The eldest organised everything in the imperial harem and made every arrangement that would be pleasing to the Sultan with a view to retaining his interest. She stimulated the Sultan's curiosity for strange tales and appeared to imprison him in his room virtually every night with public storytellers and jesters. *Kadın*, the Turkish word for woman, means "one who governs and commands" in Old Turkish and in this palace where Hürrem presided, the word had deep resonance.

On the face of it Sultan Murat reigned over the vast lands left by his father and grandfather but he did not lead his army on a single military campaign. He chose the path of trying to dominate his empire from the corridors and high-domed halls of the palace. The tales of heroism and buffoonery related by his storyteller Tifli consoled him and screened him from his own weakness.

One day, Rukal was presented to the Sultan. She was barely 17 years-old when they massaged her tender skin at the hamam with a coarse glove and then applied perfume and dyed her hands with henna. Preparing her for marriage was one of the 200 slaves that Hızır Hayrettin Reis had bought off Genoese pirates and presented as a gift to the Lawgiver. She was known as Şebperi, meaning night fairy, but her real name was Speranza. Şebperi dressed the girl in a silk evening gown which left the declivity between her collar bones uncovered, rubbed her neck with essences from Mingrelia and whispered advice as to how she should behave.

Under the spiteful and envious gaze of the senior consort, Rukal slipped like a houri into Sultan Murat's chamber. She stepped through the door excitedly as though entering a fairy tale. She walked slowly and silently, like a feather falling to the ground. Like every woman in the imperial harem, her intention was to keep frequenting this chamber and eventually to become senior consort. This hope gave her pause for breath between those thick walls. Seeing as she would never be able to leave, she ought to at least get noticed, rather than being passed over as merely ordinary. Rukal had received a good education and knew how to read. She had developed her knowledge of music from the days when she sang in her father's church; she also played the harp and wrote poetry. It was her belief that a woman only felt beautiful in the company of a man and that life continued through the union of a sexuality that was split into two at creation.

Rukal's romanticism was stronger than her femininity. She preferred acting in character to heeding Speranza's whispered advice and saw fit to present to the Sultan her heart ahead of her body. She knew that the Sultan wrote amatory gazals under the pen name Muradi and would appreciate such conduct. If poetry was to be their shared interest, then why should they not love each other? Rukal soon captured the Sultan's heart. She offered him stories told in her homeland, read from her new poems and sang songs in foreign tongues. She discovered the tender heart beneath the grand veneer and won his sympathy not through feminine wiles, but with her silver tongue. Poetry was their meeting point.

As the days slipped by, Rukal noticed that she had been rejected by all her former friends. When she realised that she was pregnant, she could not find a single woman among her old friends with whom to share her happiness. The Sultan's love and her own jubilation at carrying his child meant she brushed this aside at first, thankful that her consolation was greater than her grief. However, with each passing day, everything began to turn on its head and jealousies merged with enmities and words with lies. When she was not with the Sultan, she retired to her cell where, in an effort to dispel her vexation, she would play her harp, hum melodies and read books of poetry, but she became increasingly lonely.

Having become the palace favourite, there was nothing further to divert her in the great palace. What a great contradiction this was! The loneliness she felt after pulling away from or being cast out by her rivals was unbearable.

Should the price for bringing a prince into the world be so high? And what if the baby was a girl?

***

I, Mecnun, slave to my master Fuzuli, came to know Rukal during that time. The Sultan gave me to her so as to divert and amuse her. She dried the black monogram on the edge of my first page with fine sand she sprinkled from her writing set, touched the mark with the tips of her fingers and kissed me. This was my third kiss, placed on the self-same spot touched by the lips of my Leyla down by the Tigris, and then once more by the lips of my master Fuzuli.

Our friendship began suddenly. It was the evening of the day when jealousies had been transmitted to the Sultan in the guise of unmasking traitors. I heard it whispered in the palace corridors that Rukal intended to avenge her captivity by bestowing a Christian prince on the Ottoman throne. Before falling asleep to the sound of her heartbeat, I had revealed to her the deepest meanings of my verses, the most enigmatic elements of all my being, hoping thus to lift her spirits which had been dulled by sadness. The tale of love that my master Fuzuli had composed for me shook her for the first time that night. She thought about Leyla and suffered agony as she imagined herself in Leyla's position. How could I have been happy when Leyla was in pain, when I was bent on being the most magnificent Mecnun of all time? That night, I opened my heart and read hers and felt that she was aware of my existence. She was the first to address me directly and speak to me. She related all her secrets, one by one, and muttered all my verses individually. That night, we found solace in reading each other and embraced one another. It was a magnificent night and a magnificent love!

⁂

It had been almost a month since Rukal had last seen the Sultan. By lavishing gifts upon the storytellers, the senior consort and chief eunuch were succeeding in putting him to sleep to the sound of those stories he loved so dearly. When he inquired after Rukal, they told him that she was ill. Two days before she had tried jumping from the palace walls, the senior consort came into Rukal's room and announced that the crib she had ordered would no longer be made and that the midwife would attend to the matter three days thence in the hamam.

Rukal dreamt of rain in the trunk of the old walnut tree: she felt as happy as though she were rocking the cradle of the baby in her belly. When morning came, the girl of fairy tales did not see the silver-coloured strands that appeared in her hair like daylight. Only I understood that this was her atonement for the happiness she felt about the baby she carried.

10
How my Story was dedicated to Sultans and my special Honour lasted 40 Years

To the bounties of the world we prefer our bread and water.
To the mansions of others we prefer our own derelict corner.

Bakı

As Rukal slept in the hollow of the walnut tree, resting her hand against my chest, I felt for an instant like climbing to the longest branch and viewing afresh the 40 years spent inside the walls. Easy to say – exactly 40 years. I had first entered into the presence of the Lawgiver not as my master Fuzuli's slave, but with the magnificence of an envoy sent to alleviate the anguish of a father whose inner world was shattered after the loss of his son Prince Mehmet. How many times had his heart been scorched with the pain of losing a child! How many times had I fulfilled my duty as an envoy of solace!

The Lawgiver had loved me dearly and had favoured me. 20 years passed in his imperial harem: half of my life in the palace. During the other half, I found myself in the seat of honour especially during the concubines' musical performances or in the eunuch barracks during the day. Virtually everyone placed me on a pedestal. There were many times when I was entranced by a vision of the daughter of the desert Leyla whilst the different rhythms of the *makam*s *suznak*, *zirefkend*, *nihavend*, *ruhavi* and *hicaz* were being played. I savoured the delights intoxicating my reason in the Sultan's poetry assemblies. In the Palace School where music was taught according to the *Sofyan* Ottoman rhythm, I was studied by the bright students and oscillated between happiness and sorrow when listening to the *devşirme* children's recollections of their homelands.

I remember the times I allowed myself to be caught up by the rhythms and felt like dancing to the sounds of the kemenche, şeştar, *santur*, *mıskal* and reed flute. I realise now that I did not truly appreciate my happiness back then. In this palace, music and poetry were like two halves of one apple. There was great subtlety in the small concerts that the concubines responsible for daily tasks around the palace organised for themselves. What beautiful words I learned between these walls! Epigrams of such refinement as to make one both laugh and weep at the same time. I experienced moments when amusement mixed with world politics in the council of conversations that the Sultan organised after every victory and news of conquest. I learned during the reign of the Lawgiver exactly what kind of power was conferred and to whom by sounds of festivity coming from outside the palace. After all, who can describe the joy of sharing in the jubilation of a ruler who makes his people happy?

My 40 years slipped by between banquets and battles unique to the palace. Banquets and battles: what sultans carried in their genes, what they had brought with them all the way from Central Asia – like their Turkishness, their notion of race and philosophy of life... Making merry to celebrate triumph or thirsting after victory to heighten enjoyment. Victory and diversion were the main pastimes of the palace and they were always accompanied by sophisticated discussion and music. Then there were the long winter nights of recitation and conversation where poetry prevailed. Now and then, I had the great honour of being read from my first couplet to my last. My love story affected virtually everyone here. I reckoned my master Fuzuli could enter Paradise many times over purely thanks to the prayers said for him from this palace.

Dar saadet was Istanbul's most exquisite sobriquet and came to mean the "door of bliss". Any skilful person could attain bliss in the streets of this city where wisdom was on sale. During the time of the Lawgiver when the happiness of the common people was reflected by the stability of the state, I lived a life without fear or worry, protected from every harmful idea and action. I had even forgotten about the men from the Babylon Society or the treasure hunters who would hunt me down.

Sultan Mehmed the Conqueror built a residence in this most exceptional corner of old Constantinople called Zeytinlik because of the groves of olives covering it. The buildings which emerged upon the tree-covered hill that formed a headland projecting into the sea did not look like a palace at all. People nonetheless referred to it deferentially as the New Palace. Later, in the Tulip Era, it became known as the Topkapı Palace and the land was referred to as Seraglio Point. The buildings were fewer and the garden was smaller back

then; what is more, Mehmed II did not fell a single tree during the works. This was why architects found it difficult to locate the boundaries when drafting the plans.

On that first day I entered the palace's Courtyard of Processions from the *Bab-i Humayun* on the side of Ayasofya, ribbons were strung from tree to tree and men from different regiments of the imperial cavalry were making merry at tables laden with various foods. Apparently, two days previously, Hürrem had given birth to a prince they named Cihangir.

I entered through the middle gate where the white eunuchs were stationed and reached the chamber of petitions. I remember the Lawgiver recalling my master Fuzuli, to whom he had assigned a salary of nine silver coins in Baghdad, and speaking of him warmly.

In the days and years I spent living as a palace insider, I observed how this centre of power expanded with new structures day after day. How it burgeoned over time! Years passed in-between kitchens, ovens, the armoury square, the fish house, the boathouse, the domed chamber in the second courtyard of the palace, the basketmakers' pavilion and other pavilions besides. They allocated me to the Imperial Treasury and my actual place of residence was a trunk in the room housing bejewelled weapons, jewels sent as gifts by other states and valuable treasures brought as war booty.

But the number of times I spent the night in my own trunk were few indeed. I spent long winter nights and hot summer afternoons occasionally in the Sultan's hall, sometimes in a concubine's room and every so often in the cell of a palace official. The feelings, thoughts, aspirations, joys and sorrows of each were different. And yet it appeared as though a spirit of rivalry had penetrated the walls of the palace. Here were more sorrows than joys. When the Lawgiver and his son Selim were away from the palace on expedition, this friction had the potential of turning into design and intrigue. This was why I sometimes imagined life would be happier outside.

During the reigns of the three sovereigns which I experienced in my stay here, I came to understand how a great empire is administered and what a great responsibility its leader must shoulder. I realised that, after the Lawgiver, what is called the state consisted merely of a palace and that these now grim-feeling walls provoked a sense of awe amongst people and other nations. This is why I have always wanted to ask those looking from the outside who are curious about life inside, "For how many days would you wish to live here?" I am of the belief that, since the Lawgiver's death, the number giving a favourable response would be few indeed.

I wonder exactly how long those looking from the outside and envying palace life would endure the cold winds blowing through these chilly corridors. Even so, there is still something appealing about this palace that adorns the dreams of people from all over the Muslim and Christian worlds to the point of becoming tragic ambitions in some cases. Some fancied taking possession of this palace, some of dominating it and some of spending a single night here. No matter how dilapidated this palace was to become, this would always hold true.

The glow off the snow reflected on Rukal's ruby red cheeks where all her hopes accumulated whilst we sat in the crevice of the walnut just big enough for the two of us. I pondered all that my 40-year sojourn in the palace had taken from me.

So many people had touched my body, so many had stroked my face that, from time to time, I recalled likening myself to the secret agent floozies plying their trade at the foot of the city walls. My dress was somewhat sullied, my colour scuffed; the depictions of the Leyla I had left behind in Mesopotamia were compromised and the sanctity of my first love felt violated.

There were many nights when I cried in despair that even our most private communications were public, but no one could hear my lamentation, even in this palace that was the house of bliss. While I felt my spirit to be getting younger and younger in the hearts of those reading my master's verses, it was wearing away, becoming withered and sullied by those eyeing the illustrations wherein Leyla and I were depicted side-by-side. All the hearts feeling my noble love that was to take my beloved and me to the grave, all the tears of pity which were shed for us ruined my pages, causing dark patches to spread throughout my script. On many occasions I wept inwardly along with those who made my most intimate adventures a little more legendary with each passing day. There were times when I might notice some concubine bite her lip in grief and even feel a secret lust as she surveyed the pages portraying my meeting with Leyla in the tent, or our embrace in the countryside. Then my heart would bleed and my tears turn cold. I could not bear our hidden communion to be looked at lasciviously and I still cannot bear it. If they wanted to look at erotic images, then they could send for a *bahname* from the palace library. I wanted my love to remain pure. But perhaps this was the price I had to pay for learning all the secrets of the people of the palace and of course for seeing them naked.

I will never forget the times I flowed from the tongue to the hearts of those sitting knee to knee on starry summer nights, listening to the sounds of cicadas, squirrels and night owls in Zeytinlik. What happy nights they were! Now and again I slept in the Sultan's mother's hand, at times in Gülbahar's bosom and sometimes in Dilefruz's hair. I delighted in the nights I remained awake listening to the tales of sweethearts left back home recounted by the Haseki Ağa Uruzbay, the commander of the Solak Guard Toraman Ağa, the imperial court steward Beşir Çelebi and the Chief Surgeon Mehmet Ağa. Private Yamalı Mustafa, who served in the imperial kitchen always looked out for me.

The Lawgiver's reign was drawing to an end. On long winter nights, after the doors to the harem and privy chamber were closed and most officials had retired to sleep, Yamalı Mustafa would tirelessly read sections from my pages to janissaries and other bachelors of the palace to remind them of the feelings of love and attachment which lay within them. He received their gratitude in return. He had learned how to read as a child from a master confectioner from Damascus under whom he had worked as an apprentice. On such poetry-filled nights, he would often lay on feasts for his listeners. He would take ingredients that could be served as *meze* from the storeroom without the knowledge of the commissioner of the imperial kitchen and sneak some of Prince Selim's wine, giving a few sips to each man. But what surprised me most about these nights was that these men, who during the day aroused feelings of longing, envy and perhaps even a little fear thanks to their splendid apparel and the awe they inspired, actually wept like children in private. Each had a Leyla whom they had left in faraway lands with a bleeding heart, and I sometimes felt myself luckier than them.

Rukal placed her frost-numbed hands against her chest and sank into a dream. She imagined herself in her old home in the Caucasus Mountains, in the fables she missed and memorised. "What have I experienced in my time in the palace that has affected me so much as to earn a permanent place in my memory?" I wondered to myself.

I tried to recall everything and, as my adventures flashed before my eyes, I was able to capture a few scenes. I remembered the chief eunuchs who examined me every seven years to check that my binding and pages were still intact and they appeared to me followed by two different female silhouettes. I realised the former were members of the Babylon Society passing the secret flag from hand to hand, while the latter were the fortunate women who had lived in the palace during the Lawgiver's reign.

There were most certainly Babylon Society members in the palace in every period and not a soul but me knew it. Their mission consisted merely in checking that I was safe and secure. I suspect that they could not obtain the knowledge required to probe the secret I carried and were afraid of the Lawgiver's judgement. Ultimately, when Hürrem's arms began to reach in all directions and the Sultan's authority started dwindling, I would be spirited away to hidden cells where I would spend the night. But in all that time, the Babylon Society only directed three pairs of eyes at most to examining me. These eyes scanned my verses not to gain hold of a certain secret, but for the inner peace to be had observing a ritual in memory of great Marduk. Nearly all the members of the Babylon Society possessed a child-like ingenuity: they believed that the state of scientific advance was not then sufficient to conduct astronomical research. They judged it necessary to keep the secret of the Society hidden.

Only one from among them, the last – Sudanese Abdüsselam Ağa – understood both what love was and also how to read. Whenever he was able to take me to his room, he would peruse my pages by candlelight until dawn, checking and rechecking all the couplets in which my master Fuzuli spoke of love, reckoning them up through the *ebjed* numerological system associating numbers with letters in the alphabet, recording them in a notebook and then hiding away his findings. I do not know with whom he later shared his intelligence, but I was certain that he conveyed the information to someone from outside the palace.

Only once, around a year previously, had he hidden me against his bosom and taken me to a house adjacent to Kocamustafapaşa Mosque, where he showed me to a person I could not recognise. The man had a Greek accent and wore scholarly clothing. "If you want to solve the riddle of this book, you must interpret the couplets in which the word love is mentioned," he had advised. I was shaken by a sense of betrayal for the very first time. I wondered how I would feel if my master Fuzuli's secret was disclosed. Would I have betrayed the trust placed in me? For several days, I wished my binding would fall apart and my pages drop out. This was akin to wishing myself a cripple.

The man in scholarly guise made a suggestion. "Let us copy the couplets making mention of love at once, translate them into the alphabet on the obelisk at Atmeydanı and look into them." Beneath this man's cloak, dangling from his neck, I spotted a medal in the form of a sun disk sacred to the Asur culture. On one side of the talisman I glimpsed writing in cuneiform script and on the reverse the image of the famous King Nebuchadnezzar of the 4,000 year-old Chaldean civilisation which flourished between Baghdad and Mosul. Superimposed was the mythical Sirrush head.

That night, Abdüsselam Ağa read while this dark man wrote, and together they compiled a list of the 66 couplets in which the word love was mentioned. Fortunately, they copied these not in the sequence relating the story of Leyla and me, but in their own particular order.

Right then, as I clambered over the palace walls in Rukal's bundle, I wished I could see just how sorry Abdüsselam Ağa was at losing me. I was curious to know with whom he was corresponding and in which direction the pigeons with gilded nose-rings were flying. Underlying my great love for Rukal may have been my desire to escape and the restlessness of my adventure-loving spirit. I did not know if I would be as safe where Rukal took me as I was in the palace, but one thing was for certain: I escaped from someone who was very close to deciphering my secret.

Perhaps I was wrong to have felt exhilarated. I could not distinguish between the Babylon Society members who were concerned with intergalactic travel and black holes as much as the notion of the Earth being round on the one hand, and those hunting the sacred treasures of Babylon on the other.

My anxiety was due to my growing awareness that I would be threatened if my secret were discovered. I was alarmed by the growing numbers of sinister types who followed me and collected my copies, subjecting any of the copies of *L&M* that they found to minute scrutiny. They were gathering up all my brethren in an effort to find me. I was as certain as I was of Leyla's love that being confronted by the different couplet sequences and page sizes in all my duplicates sent them mad. They would have been exasperated that their calculations gave a different result each time. I was sure they were reduced to uttering profanities, arguing and squabbling. If they got hold of me, they could cross-check their calculations.

They set about examining each new copy they found, hoping to find my exact copy each time. But before long, owing to the different scripts the calligraphers used – *nesih, ta'lik, rika* amongst others – as well as the sheer number of couplets and the fact that scribes had sometimes changed the order of certain couplets at will, they were overwhelmed by confusion and decided to re-examine their mission. Only I possessed the ability to solve the puzzle as I was written by my master Fuzuli himself and he had concealed the cipher of the Temple of Ishtar among my couplets. Whether a person sought the Babylon Society's supreme scientific truth, or hankered after the golden statues, they had to find me. They would soon realise it was impossible to embark on this journey just by looking at the copies which shared my name, *L&M*.

Over the last years, anyone who could read the hieroglyphics on the obelisk at Atmeydanı became, for me, a potential member of the Babylon Society. I knew that the number of people who spent hours studying *L&M* and these obelisks was increasing. Fortunately, in a great many of my copies, the pages were not in the same order as in my story and the position of the couplets, titles and other sequences had been modified. The secret of the Babylon Society lay within me and those wanting it would never give up the chase. My master Fuzuli embedded 14 words laden with love in seven of his couplets on love and arranged them in the same order as the numbers on the temple door. I could now comprehend how clever he had been. "This would not even have occurred to Satan," I said to myself.

In the night we spent at Kocamustafapaşa, Abdüsselam Ağa laid great stress on one couplet. "It seems impossible to decipher this code without knowing the philosophy of love." Then he asked, "Sir, have you ever been in love? Do you know what a malady and cure it is? Look at what the poet says:

Raised was the veil of the hidden lover
Love became the companion of censure.

He means to say that, when the veil of the bride of mystery is lifted, love and censure speak the same language. What the poet here refers to as 'the veil of the bride of mystery' is in my opinion the lost cipher of the Temple of Ishtar. In order to find this, we need to know the connection between the words 'love' and 'censure'. I have been in love; I know the censure of the people. It is not religions which have forbidden love: we have forbidden it to ourselves for some reason. The history of Christianity was shaken for centuries with the scandal of love. The Inquisition accused its victims of falling in love and burnt them to cleanse their souls of the devil. Muslims too regard love as shame and reproach those who fall in love. All that exists for them is metaphorical love. What evil, do you think, can there be in two hearts or let us say, two bodies, loving one another?

Only metaphorical love, love for the Creator is perpetually praised. Poets also toe this line. Now, in Istanbul, everyone who speaks of love seems busy trying to establish a mystical sheath for the proverbial stolen minaret.* Poets composing eulogies are applauded, whilst those who are actually in love are censured. Love and censure constitute an ancient Eastern combination. The true lover must first free himself of reason and must bring his heart to the fore. If the mind holds sway over the person, the road to exaltation through love is closed.

Reason directs a man to show interest in the world, to form connections with beings other than the beloved, and to attach importance to these. But when the lover attaches importance to the slightest thing other than the beloved, he cannot attain true love. This is why Sufis annihilate first their carnal selves and lovers their minds. The lover must be censured in order to achieve annihilation of reason and the carnal self, because what weighs most on the human ego is censure. The Malami Sufis, the people of blame, aspire to be censured purely for this reason, that is, with a view to being freed of their ego in the form of carnal desire. Their behaviour and mode of dress attract censure. People condemn them and cast them out, and so they share their loneliness with their Lord and turn to the true Beloved. In exactly the same way, lovers are censured by those without a capacity for love. The irrational behaviour of lovers, the way they go mad because of love and act on the basis of feelings rather than reason, the way their attitudes change compound the condemnation of others. This is what

* [Translator's note: Alludes to a famous Turkish proverb, "*Minareyi çalan kılıfını hazırlar*," which literally means, "One who steals the minaret will already have the sack in which to hide it." This is used to refer to a person's taking precaution not to be caught when intending to commit any kind of trespass. In this case, it is the poets' attempt to establish a mystical pretext on which to base their 'offense']

happens to the Kays in this story: he loses his mind when he falls in love with Leyla! He goes crazy, takes to the desert and lives as a mountain madman! Remember how they refuse to give Leyla to him because they disapprove? This is just how the Malami notion works. A person is elevated spiritually by means of reproach. Thus Kays attained great spiritual stations by losing his mind. His was a madness that was greater than thousands of minds."

As Abdüsselam Ağa developed his idea, I came to know myself anew and felt a hidden reverence for this person who explained the greatness of my love. At the same time I regretted how he had cracked the clue to the first cipher. I marvelled at how this black eunuch, who would have been castrated in his youth, knew so much about love. Which concubine did he yearn and burn for? After his lengthy exposition, I felt pleasure but I realised there was still much I needed to learn in order to complete myself.

Thanks to his understanding of love, Abdüsselam Ağa was the first to discover my cipher. The couplet which he had read out was the key to my master Fuzuli's secret. He had identified it correctly and its order in the sequence was 617. This was the number which indicated the first button on the cipher grid that had to be pressed to unlock the gate of the Tower of Babylon. Up until this point, Abdüsselam Ağa was accurate in his thinking and was on the right track, but then he stumbled. He began puzzling over the numerological counterparts for the words love and censure appearing in the couplet instead of the particular line number for each one. "The numerological value of love is 470, while that of censure is 511. But what is the connection between them?" He racked his brains for hours.

At the call to morning prayer, he finally rested his aching head upon the pillow in exhaustion. I realised once more how intelligent my master Fuzuli had been. In an age when numerological *ebced* calculations were fashionable, he had decided to encrypt his message without using *ebced* and no one thought that it could be so simple. My master had chosen to hide what had to remain hidden by setting it forth and keeping it in plain sight: no one who sought what was hidden would look at what was evident.

Moreover, he had preferred making those seeking the cipher divide the couplet line number by seven to obtain the remainder, instead of making them calculate at length the words within the couplet. The total of the figures making up 617 was 6+1+7=14 and its remainder, after being divided by 7, was 0. Thus, the second digit that would unlock the key to the ancient tablets and the idols that Akeldan had buried in the vaults of the Temple of Ishtar was this "0". But everyone looking for love and secrecy among my verses encountered further walls as they sought to derive philosophical solutions from the Babylonians and made new calculations on the basis of the words they found.

If Rukal had known that I was wanted by the Babylon Society, would she have taken me with her, watered my love with her tears and blended it with her love? I cannot tell. For the present, we had left behind the Babylon Society along with the palace and its residents. In Rukal's arms I formulated plans for seeking out Leyla and dreamt of finding her.

On this night, in the hollow of the old walnut tree, accompanied by the sound of rain and wind, I slept my most enchanted sleep. I lay covered by Rukal's hair, just as I had done with Leyla... Was it Rukal or Leyla who was my beloved? I knew not... Love transformed together with me, as did my beloved...

11

Of the Sultan's magnificent Tale and the cheerful Song of the Russian Belle

There is nothing as prized by the people as the state
Nor a state in the world as precious as good health.

Muhibbi (Sultan Süleyman the Lawgiver)

I have said that I would remember two women other than Rukal once I was beyond the palace walls. When I think of one, I am always saddened, and I am happy when I think of the other. I still feel the same way. It is as though, if I were to turn one of these women inside-out, then the other would appear. One was at the pinnacle of her glory and possessed the power of turning everything she touched into gold, but her ambitions forever deprived her of the happiness she deserved. The other languished at the very bottom, but her pure heart enabled her to live in bliss. The material wealth of one left her spirit hungry, while the other's generosity invested her with material things. The name of one was Hürrem while the other was Tuti.

After I was beautified in the covered bazaar and sent to the Ottoman palace, Hürrem was at the peak of her intelligence and feminine charm. She was already in her forties, but hers was a personality which inspired respect. She was a sultana to the core. Pens and words would not suffice to describe her. It is said that the greater the praise, the greater the truth. Not a single day passed without mention of her name amongst the women of the palace. Whenever I left the vault on borrowed nights in the harem, I would always listen to tales and gossip about her.

If the talk was to be believed, her name was Roxelana. Early on, after being plucked out of Russia, she learned such palace rituals as how to walk, speak, flatter and greet in the Lawgiver's palace. Then she was employed in daily palace work and the concubines called her Ruşen. Just like Rukal, her simple life was spent dreaming about her homeland and entertaining visions of the future.

One autumn day, her friends bathed her. They sang songs, perfumed her, combed her hair, dressed her in silk and presented her to the Lawgiver. When she entered the magnificent Sultan's chamber with all the sensibility and sensuousness of her Slavic race, she pondered the fact she need never again leave this room to see all life's colours, collect all its lights and listen to all its melodies. That night, she played chess with the Sultan and they spoke at length. Her objective was to leave the Sultan thirsty for her in the desert of love and she succeeded in her aim. She indulged the Sultan's poetic disposition with words, filled his spirit with fond memories and recited poetry he could savour.

Before long, the Sultan, just like the Russian girl, would wait impatiently for the next night and those to follow. Roxelana was not a great beauty but she doted on the Sultan enough to make him forget time. When she entered, the Sultan's eyes would sparkle and he found respite from his loneliness at the apex of the state. She was able to express her feelings to him through poetry and readily assumed the role of immortal lover. Roxelana brought plurality to the Sultan's singularity and brought him down to a level of humanity from the quasi-divinity that others ascribed to him. One night, the Sultan professed his love for her.

Is it love that has placed the chain of woe around my neck
Oft parading and pillorying me like Mecnun?

She felt this to be the beginning of a completely different fairy tale and surrendered herself to it. She giggled loudly in the presence of the Sultan even though it contravened Mehmed the Conqueror's rules. She felt a secret pleasure in making the small dome of the bedroom reverberate with her coquettish and vivacious laughs. Her voice tinkled like crystal candelabras on the walls. From that day on, the magnificent Lawgiver called her Hürrem, the cheerful or laughing one.

Hürrem was now the name of the woman who was to change the course of Ottoman history and she felt delight at being united with a state rather than a man. Naturally, she felt herself to be nothing without the Lawgiver, Süleyman the Magnificent. On that day she began to genuinely love the Sultan also. She gave birth to a child each year, as a fruit of their long nights of love. Mehmet, Cihangir, Selim, Bayezid and Kamilla or Mihrimah. Over the course of these years, she estranged the Sultan from the other woman Gülbahar, of whom she was perennially jealous, and closed off paths to his acquiring new favourites.

Throughout those years, the Sultan dedicated countless poems to her. This was how I became acquainted with Hürrem. One night, as dawn broke, the Sultan presented me to her along with silk overblouses as gifts so that I might surprise her with a *gazal* he had just written.

I saw Hürrem's first joy when she read that letter placed in between my pages. In the poem, written on silk paper whose fibre had been mixed with musk, Roxelana's beauty was measured against the cities which inhabited the Lawgiver's memories and dreams. She shone like a sun rising over all of them.

> *My Istanbul, my Karaman, my Anatolia through and through...*
> *My Bedahsan, my Kipchak, my Baghdad, my Khorasan.*

Hürrem, her spirit caressed with poems laden with love and her heart nourished by the feelings of the magnificent Sultan, tasted her first anguish with the death of her eldest son Mehmet. Mehmet would have sat upon the Ottoman throne as a ruler carrying Slavic blood. But Hürrem was in great haste over the construction of the Şehzade Complex that Gökçe Ali had seen on the day I first came to Istanbul. She kept sending gifts to Chief Architect Master Sinan which carried implicit ultimatums because she did not want to divert the Sultan's attention away from her children. More than a mother, she became a warrior fighting a tactical war. She believed she needed to sever the attachment that the people and the nobility felt for Mustafa, the princeling son of her ruthless rival Gülbahar.

Roxelana even ran the risk of crossing swords with her own son-in-law, Vizier Ibrahim Paşa. She made an agreement with him in the name of the Babylon Society and united on a common objective. But, upon the Sultan's return from the Baghdad expedition, she tried to persuade him to have his childhood friend and son-in-law Ibrahim strangled. Her ambitions grew along with the Sultan's advancing age and she used love games to manipulate him and have him amend certain laws. All these exertions were directed to this end. It was regrettable that her beloved prince Mehmet had died since the next in line, Cihangir, though very intelligent, was crippled and epileptic. Selim and Bayezid were growing, but the former became addicted to alcohol and became known as "the Drunk", while the latter enraged his father with his stubbornness.

In contrast, Gülbahar's Mustafa acquired fame as the rightful heir to the throne. Grand Vizier Ibrahim was also disposed to use his influence in favour of Mustafa. Worse still, he harboured other plans for the future of the Babylon Society. Previously, they had both agreed to implement the ideals of the Babylon Society by promoting them in Ottoman dealings with other world states. However, when they fell out over who was to accede to the throne, their interests and authority over the Babylon Society also began to clash. This proved the fateful juncture for Ibrahim: by command of the Sultan who always believed Hürrem's intrigues, Ibrahim died at the hands of mute executioners. I saw her delight the night he was executed. She was in as much peace as a Babylonian priest after making a sacrifice to Marduk. It was in honour of this sacrifice, I suspect, that she read my entire narrative from beginning to end, bringing my face up towards the flickering candle flame. Towards daybreak, she reached the death scene, remembered her son Mehmet and wept.

Roxelana now needed a faithful servant to replace Ibrahim. And she was quick in finding one. This was none other than Rüstem, protagonist of the famous story of the louse. She calculated she could grant him the vacant Babylon Society seat, complete the membership and implement their joint interests more effectively. These were years conducive to the establishment and promotion of small states in the Mediterranean. She thought about an island state in which the Babylon Society could operate in future. She supposed that if she could marry Rüstem off to a princess, she could make him her slave. The exuberant palace belle Mihrimah had turned into an all-out beauty so Hürrem decided to give Rüstem her daughter Mihrimah.

The reason Rüstem was associated with lice was as follows: physicians of the day used lice to diagnose leprosy. They would decide whether a person suspected of infection was indeed a leper by checking to see if he had lice. Those who opposed the promotion through marriage of Diyarbakir Governor Rüstem declared that he was a leper. Hürrem found a way around this by secretly sending one of the palace physicians to Diyarbakır to check Rüstem Paşa's clothing. Fortune was on his side: the two lice found on Rüstem's clothing were brought to Istanbul amidst cries of victory and a wedding feast was held.

The new bridegroom burned with ambition for wealth and power, just like Ibrahim before him. One by one, the righteous barriers of his conscience was broken down. But whilst Ibrahim had been forced into servitude, Rüstem was more than willing. Ibrahim was a favourite while Rüstem was a slave. Ibrahim seemed to be created for history, while Rüstem was a mere footnote. Like every other slave, he was outwardly faithful, but was actually always open to compromise.

When Rüstem married Mihrimah, one of the poets of the day composed a couplet under an assumed name. This couplet was recited discreetly everywhere from spit-and-sawdust pubs to coffee houses, from janissary get-togethers to formal assemblies in the palace, provoking laughter wherever it was heard.

If in luck and good fortune a person is to be
Even the louse in their own house would not go amiss.

In other words, when one hits a lucky streak, even a louse can bring good fortune. This couplet accompanied Rüstem for the rest of his life and whenever historians made mention of him, they always referred to this amusing anecdote.

Mihrimah meant "sun and moon" and in the mind of this graceful woman shone the sun and in her heart the moon. Poor Mihrimah, that ravishing beauty, led a harrowing life with a lousy man and even came to resemble him every now and then. With one notable difference: so as to screen her unhappiness, she devoted herself to charity and good works, constructing mosques and public fountains. Only then did the people see her smiling.

Hürrem corresponded in the name of the Babylon Society with notables in other nations. She would try to direct the Sultan seated upon the throne of her possessions and her heart in accordance with their guidance. At the same time, she began slowly shaping the destiny of Prince Mustafa. She showed great talent for intrigue and forged letters to sow discord between father and son. After hundreds of decisions and reversals, she caused the Lawgiver to have his beloved son – whom he treasured as his own life – strangled in Konya, in the vicinity of Ereğli. When she sent news of Mustafa's execution to one of the ships docked at Karaköy, she felt like a Babylonian goddess who had offered her second sacrifice to Nebo. For as long as I can remember, she would isolate herself from the common people. Those wanting to approach her would get a sense of this and always shied away from her.

What they call the world comes and then it goes. Just like everyone else, Hürrem too bid farewell to the world with all its lustre and loneliness, its sorrow and joy, its light and darkness. She had the Süleymaniye Complex built on the most exclusive property overlooking the Golden Horn and behind the Old Palace, with a view to it standing as the symbol of the Lawgiver's reign. She also wanted to immortalise her own name. In this same year, whilst gazing upon these stone monuments rising among the wooden structures of the city, she had also personally chosen the place for her eternal rest. The Magnificent Sultan regarded Hürrem, the woman whom he considered as magnificent as himself, as belonging to this complex despite all her foreign-ness, her contradictions and incomprehensible ideas. When the shrewdest queen mother that the Ottoman palace had ever seen breathed her last, she was buried near the Lawgiver from whom she wanted to flee and by whom she wanted to be captured. They were as close as to render the fragrance of the rose springing up between them sufficient for both of them... But, nonetheless, she remained all alone... That was how master Sinan had designed her tomb...

If the Lawgiver, whose reign lasted for 46 years, had been aware of the Babylon Society, would he still have wanted to embrace the woman he nursed and cherished in his bosom for all those years? Would he have chosen to have himself buried so close to her and have a special law enacted for her? Perhaps it was the nobility of the women they both loved that caused Kays and the Sultan to resemble one another. When Leyla died, Kays threw himself on the soil still fresh with the smell of death and beseeched God to take his life also. When I look back after all this time, I see them both as magnificent people. One was called magnificent for his sultanate, the other for his love. One was Süleyman the Magnificent, Sultan of both Roxelana and the people; the other was Mecnun Kays, slave of Leyla and her nomadic household. What one exhausted in his sultanate the other enhanced in his madness. One lives in time with the name of magnificent, while the other gives time a magnificent name. And I, carrying the soul of the second in my verses and his love in my heart, embraced Rukal as Leyla.

12
How the Poet saw Tuti at the Blue Angel and his mournful Elegy for the Sultan's Death

When all of a sudden the parrot and
the crow are thrust together,
Is it not strange that 'tis again
the crow who complains?
Nev'i

You probably recall my mentioning a Mahmut Abdülbaki Efendi who waited upon me one week before Nakkaş Haydar Nigari and the Shah-loving Musa asked each other about the secrets of the Babylon Society. They spoke to each other in symbols in master Ahmet's workshop at the covered bazaar when I was about to be subjected to the marble torture of the binders. He was the youth who, along with his classmate, was left in utter astonishment on hearing my master Fuzuli's verses. When I ran into him again, I encountered a mature young man and poet who was always envied at recitations and assemblies. The fame of his Sümbül Kasidesi or "Kaside on the Hyacinth," which he had written in honour of his teacher Karamanlı Mehmet Efendi around the time he had completed his studies at the *medrese*, had even reached my ears on one of the evenings I spent with Gülbahar.

The short and carefree Istanbul poems he penned back then were repeated in soft whispers around the palace. It became fashionable to read from his poems at divan meetings, Baykara assemblies, even the odd rose council. I know this because I listened to his poetry most in my time at the palace. I can honestly say that everyone from the greatest to the humblest would mumble his verses or recite them out loud. During the reign of the Lawgiver, I saw Mahmut Abdülbaki, or Baki Efendi's fame increase with every passing day and even spill over beyond the boundaries of the empire. He became pre-eminent thanks to the native voice that permeated his verses and so, after my master Fuzuli, the capital of Eastern poetry moved to Istanbul. I do not know how influential the Sultan's praise was, but Baki Efendi's gazals were heard in every place, from Istanbul's promenades to its taverns. One might hear them in Sufi lodges, councils of wisdom, palace and villas, along the street, aboard boats, in the home, atop oxcarts – in short, everywhere. His were the most beautiful poems I ever heard after those of my master Fuzuli. There were even times when his poetry recitals were more melodic than my master's. I wanted my lyric couplets to be filled with his proverbially impassioned language. I think that I was even a little jealous. The versatility he demonstrated in his odes has never been repeated in any of Istanbul's poetry markets.

While the Lawgiver was having the Süleymaniye Complex constructed, Baki Efendi was assistant to religious scholar Kadızade Şemsettin Efendi. It was during that year that Baki Efendi and the Sultan, who was also a poet, began to recite short *nazire*s or parallel poems repeating the rhythm of those of the other. At that time, it was customary for artists to enjoy the favour of the Sultan or members of the nobility.

A few poets, artists and craftsmen could be found in the social circles of nearly every Sultan and Paşa. They sought out talent and always distributed honoraria for the works they produced, which they referred to as *caize*. In this way, the artist avoided financial hardship and art found state support. Although this practice was an Eastern tradition, it passed to Western lands after the Middle Ages and gave rise to the knightly circles which formed around the nobility. Of all the people he patronised, the one the Lawgiver esteemed most was this young poet whom he named "Sultan of the Poets".

In return for patronage, the poets would name their supporters in some of their poems. The main reason why the Sultan sponsored Baki Efendi was so that his name would be immortalised in the poet's verses. He also appointed him site manager to the building works of the Süleymaniye Complex to cement their relationship.

This job served as an eye-opener for Baki Efendi. He watched for months on end the hypnotising aesthetic that master Sinan produced by placing certain stones side-by-side or on top of one another. He tried to achieve with words what Sinan achieved with stone, developing his own style by hiding layers of meaning within one another when placing them side-by-side or one on top of the other. So he made poems with words paralleling the monuments of his stone master. Sinan was his example and he responded to his every drinking fountain with a couplet, his every public water fountain with a stanza, his every bridge with a gazal, his every hamam with a quatrain, his every mosque with an ode. Both formed their divans – one with stone and marble and the other with syllables and words. Throughout all those years, Baki thought that whatever he was to do, he could never write as magnificent a tribute as the Süleymaniye. Master Sinan was always a step ahead. It was a pity that fate was to make him recite this poem much later when his great patron died, amidst sorrows and tears, in the form of a *terkibibent* poem, the stanzas of which are connected by the refrain, which is an elegy for the Lawgiver.

⁂

It was the 6th of May, the day of the Hidrellez Festival which heralded the spring. The Lawgiver was to set sail on the Bosphorus with his richly decorated galley Blue Angel. This galley was constructed of rosewood, sandalwood, agarwood and juniper and was festooned with trappings. The *Bostanci Ağa*, or commander of the Imperial guards who was also steersman of the Sultan's barge, had made the necessary preparations for the cruise: now the galley, onto which a procession of 50 people including palace dignitaries and harem residents was to embark, moored with its stern secured to the pier facing the Garden Gate near the Golden Horn. State officials not from the palace as well as the string ensemble players waited to join the party having taken their places ashore according to their rank.

That day, as a member of the palace household, I planned to make the most of this magnificent procession which I was seeing for the first time from between the silver-braid embroidery of an ornamental leather bag inlaid with pearl. I too had taken my place in the cortege, hung from the naked shoulder of one of the Imperial guard soldiers which bore the tattoo of a snake. I was heading towards the shore observing very carefully all that was going on. Were it not for the Imperial guard's smell of sweat...

It was as if all the well-known faces steering world affairs were there. The Şeyhülislam, the senior judge, the viziers, boon-companions of the Sultan, gentlemen-in-waiting, marshals of the procession with their gleaming kaftans and plumed brooches of pheasant and peacock feathers attached to their turbans, formed a fabulous procession. I understood then why the Lawgiver was referred to as the Magnificent in entertainment as well as on the battlefields. The Blue Angel had 25 double seats; 200 oarsmen donning white boleros gripped the oars in fours, waiting with eyes fixed firmly on their toes while the head oarsman held fast to the sail, watching over them.

When the rhythmic clip-clop of the pacing horses with their bejewelled harnesses and silver horseshoes could be heard on the stony pavement of the Garden Gate, the expectant party lined up on both sides of the path and waited for the Imperial procession to pass. In the lead was the Commander of the Janissaries, followed by the Sultan's son-in-law Ibrahim Paşa, then Şeyhülislam Kemalpaşazade followed by the Lawgiver's bay advancing from the ranks of bodyguard footmen and infantry officers. Walking behind them was the chief eunuch and then the Sultan's womenfolk, female slaves carrying parcels together with the harem company. Bringing up the rear was a dwarfish clown seated backwards on a Cyprus donkey. He stuck his tongue out at those left behind and poked fun at them. Had the Sultan been aware of his antics, he would certainly have had him mounted on a wild mule with one foot tied to a stirrup. He would have had a dreadful ride instead of his easy amble on the donkey.

The Lawgiver passed between the people gathered on both sides of the path to greet him and it was not until he reached the pavilion section of the galley that those in the front row raised their heads. Those applauding him at the back were watched by the ceremonial guard who made way for the Sultan by lifting their staffs. Officials of the first and highest grade in the state bureaucracy then began to board the galley one or two at a time.

As the harem community began making their way carefully along the wooden pier extending towards the galley, it all happened. Sudden chaos and the sound of screaming women. The Imperial guard and I were walking behind the harem cortege. Next to us was Mevlevi Çelebi Hüsamettin Efendi and the Sultan's foster brother Şeyh Yahya Efendi. I knew that the Çelebi had been on my tail for quite some time now and no one other than me saw him forcefully stick an awl into the leg of the horse belonging to the janissary commander who was charged with protecting the harem cortege.

His was a very intricate plan. Hüsamettin was to cause the janissary commander – himself Bektaşi – who had slowed down the construction of the Mevlevihane at Yenikapı – to fall off his horse and out of favour with the Sultan at the same time. With his other hand, he grabbed me and threw me onto the back of his saddle. If he had had the opportunity, he would perhaps have wandered through my verses for a few days. Like all members of the Babylon Society, he too was a very intelligent man. After all, who could have become suspicious after the tumult caused by startling one horse? Furthermore, everything happening on shore seemed designed to alarm the horses: the sounds of bells and drums, the turbulence of waves, the screams of seagulls and a huge crowd of people bedecked in multi-coloured finery.

Çelebi's efforts to procure me proved vain. But by rearing up at the harem residents about to board the galley, the startled horse's behaviour paved the way for an auspicious event. Just as one of the concubines was running to avoid being crushed or alternatively falling into the sea, she risked slipping between the galley and the seawall. A turbaned

Efendi from one of the learned institutions was waiting with his head bowed. He was a man in his thirties and, in a reflex action, he grabbed her by the wrist and then held her waist to save her from falling. The rest of the screams were reserved for this dark and weak looking teacher with a crooked nose who had taken this concubine into his arms. The inconceivable had happened: an unrelated stranger had touched a *cariye* of the harem and, not only that, he had held her in his arms.

When both the woman and her rescuer overcame their respective shock and recovered themselves, they were shaken by the thought of the punishment customarily meted out for such familiarity. The concubine fainted then and there. The young teacher fell down on one knee, locked his hands in the twisted guardrails of the galley and extended his neck.

The Lawgiver indicated the physician and the midwife should bring the concubine back to her senses. He then summoned the Şeyhülislam and they whispered between themselves. Life had all but stopped on board and on shore. Then the concubine's face was washed with rosewater and she was brought round with the smell of camphor and taken aboard the Blue Angel. The Sultan subsequently came all the way to the seawall. Warmly taking the young teacher – who was still awaiting the order for his execution – by the hand, he led him onto the galley. "Grieve not, dear Mullah," he said. "I have bestowed this lady upon you as your wife!" Then the Sultan addressed Şeyhülislam Kemalpaşazade, the head of the Ottoman religious hierarchy. "Efendi hoca, have you ever performed a marriage ceremony before so many witnesses?" he asked.

The concubine's name was Tuti, which means "Parrot". By a strange twist of fate, the man who saved Tuti Hanım from falling into the sea was known as Crow Baki. This was the poet Mahmut Abdülbaki Efendi who had called upon me during my stay at master Ahmet's workshop. He was the most exceptional poet writing in Istanbul Turkish.

❦❦❦

The most commonly told story of the Hidrellez cruise that day was that of "The Crow and the Parrot" in the book entitled *Gülistan*. This is how it went. They put a crow and a parrot in the same cage and the parrot began to complain, "My Lord, what sin have I committed that when I could have been chewing on candy in front of a mirror, I have ended up in the same cage as this crow with ungracious demeanour, foul habits and hideous apparel?" And the crow was praying, "O Exalted Creator! What unpropitious fate is this that when I could be strutting with my fellow crows along a rickety wall, I have been forced to live with this conceited egotist?"

Years went by and Baki Efendi wrote his most beautiful poems inspired by Tuti Hanım. The gentle dreams and love of life in his poetry were reflected from the lucid countenance of this noble concubine onto the pages of his notebook. She was the one to hear a great number of his poems for the first time and she was the first to hear a great many beautiful poems. On Tuti's shoulders were heaped Baki's poems, Istanbul's tears and its happiness. This carefree, brash and witty writer of spirited scenes and lively assemblies who could easily express all that occurred to his heart, transformed love into an exalted experience of civilisation and spoke of it thanks to Tuti Hanım. Instead of the abstract thoughts and distant dreams kneaded by my master Fuzuli, Baki brought to life in his poems the springtime and winter of Istanbul, as well as a love for its moonlight. Love, nature and wine turned into delicate pleasure in his verses and poetry offered his language harmony and fluidity.

Baki reminded me of my master Fuzuli. In the gatherings where I was present, his poems were most often recited and he was the most popular subject of rumour. Shortly thereafter, he became a man defeated by ambition. Two years later, Tuti left him and set off on her greatest journey. A year after that, he was discharged from the office of Supreme Judge of Anatolia. And then, he and his old friend Sunullah Efendi were left fighting a cold war over the post of Şeyhülislam. His two sons from Tuti were then adolescent.

No one had ever seen Baki Efendi weep as much as he did on the day of the Lawgiver's death. His famed elegy *"Kanuni Mersiyesi"*, one of the monuments of Turkish poetry, reduced to tears all those who read it, no doubt because he wrote it with that eternal anguish preying on his mind. Even once the Magnificent Sultan's grandson sat upon his throne, when so many years had passed, the eyes of whosoever read the elegy still welled up with tears.

Tears well in the people's eyes when they look to the sun
'Tis no wonder, for they recall that sun-faced Sultan.

What he means is, when the masses look up at the sun, tears fill their eyes and of course, this is to be expected, as they remember that Sultan whose face was like the sun.

Had Fuzuli not have been my master, than I would have wanted to refer to Baki as my master and this would have suited him greatly. What a tremendous blessing it would have been for me to listen to my tale with Leyla from a native of Istanbul after having heard it from a native of Hilla! Both of them dreamt radiant dreams while stringing together their beautiful verses and they left behind a pleasant sound on this terrestrial dome. Their words were captivating and luminous. They were like the sun and like the moon. Like illumination, like divine light... When the fire of my master's love like light of day was removed, Baki's luminous nights began. Just like how the moon rises in spring, right when the sun goes down...

13
This Chapter is a Statement on the Legend of the Walnut Tree

Wisdom in our day lies in seeking wealth like Qarun.
In search of the morsel Luqman is all but forgotten...
Nabi

On the morning after my heartbeat combined with Rukal's in the hollow of the walnut tree, we woke with the recitation of the Call to Prayer coming from the minarets of Ayasofya. I could see from the way her face tautened in pain that the fracture in her ankle had gone cold and her agony had begun to penetrate her lungs. I even saw her feel with her swollen fingers at one point and heard her moan deeply. She did not want to make a sound. After all, this place was considered part of the outer garden and being caught here meant a gruesome end.

In the morning light, we made out indistinct sounds. Candlelight filtered from the adjacent *Kozbekçileri* dormitory. When Rukal raised her head to take a quick look around, two soldiers carrying ewers were making for the washing area just 10 steps beyond the tree trunk in which we were hiding. Judging from their white undergarments and their speech, they had just woken.

In the palace, I had seen one of them giving a basket of walnuts to the Treasurer. On his head was a cone-shaped hat made of camel hair felt and as pointed as the Egyptian pyramids. I had heard they were called the Girls' Guardians.

Chroniclers report that one night, a few months after Mehmed the Conqueror had this palace constructed, one of the concubines in the palace had attempted to escape for whatever unknown reason, just like Rukal. She had jumped over what was then a lower wall, when a poor dervish saw her and rushed to her aid. Hiding her in the hollow of the walnut tree right next to the palace gate, he sent word to the Ağa of the Gate of Happiness and ensured that she returned safely. When the dervish's faithful gesture was made known to the Sultan, he was summoned to his presence and asked what he desired. He requested that a shelter be built beside this walnut to enable him to earn his keep and perform his remembrance of God without difficulty and that a job be assigned for him therein. The Sultan had a shelter named *K*ızbekçileri built here and entrusted its administration to the dervish. He also assigned 40 guards to his service to see to the security of the palace garden. These men, considered the first conscious Turkish environmentalists, were the 40 who came from the Boyabat, Kargı and Elus precincts. They planted pear, apricot and mulberry trees among the garden's sycamores, as well as grape vines and new walnut saplings. Making various molasses from the yellow, purple, white and black varieties of mulberry, they also used to prepare unfermented grape juice and offer it to the Sultan. As the generations changed over time and the dervishes gave way to insincere types who were only after money, the grape vines and mulberry trees died away and only the walnut trees remained. As walnuts were then called "*koz*", the people came to refer to the soldiers on duty here as "*kozbekçileri*" instead of "*kızbekçileri*". The tree that sheltered us from the rain that night was the oldest walnut in the garden, the very one which that dervish had planted with his own hands.

The two *kozbekçi* guardsmen returned to their dormitory and Rukal realised she had to get away at once, before the sky turned brighter. She pressed her parcel right against her bosom, tucked the hem of her skirt into her waist and stuck her head out of the hollow to listen to the sounds of daybreak. She had taken her first step when she toppled over, writhing in pain. The fracture in her ankle had cooled through the night so she could feel the pain right from the tips of her toes. Rukal's momentary moan was followed by the sound of a wet stick being stuck in the mud. The dim light was shattered by an impertinent cry. "Who's there?"

This was the voice of Patlak Memi, a bulky *kozbekçi* soldier who was urinating against the trunk of the nearest sycamore. Before long, he was standing right above us. Patlak Memi was a man whose cheekbones seemed to pop out of his frightful face. His eyes were like two deep wells in the whites of which the eyeballs had fallen like dark splotches. With his big head atop his monstrous body, he appeared to us at that moment like a shockingly hideous creature. As he tied up his drawstring with one hand and felt for his sabre with the other, he began talking.

The words poured out of his mouth any old way as he swore indistinctly. It was as though he were speaking with difficulty, having been dulled by the languor of the night before. "And who are you?" he challenged Rukal with flashing eyes. His hands moved constantly and the thoughts in his head alternated between seizing her like a criminal or showing the respect due to a palace resident. As he looked at Rukal and saw the pain in her face, I realised that he wanted to feel sorry for her and then, on noticing her beauty, he began to admire her as a woman. Stuttering for a while, he began posing questions, attempting to learn why Rukal was there and what had befallen her. He was at ease seeing that the pain in her ankle stopped her from attempting escape. He even began to make advances to her in his own way.

"Does this man want to shield Rukal, take her under his protection or embrace her wet body?" I asked myself. Patlak Memi had understood at first glance that Rukal was a resident of the palace from her clothing. He began to devise 1,001 plans in his head. His ever-increasing nervousness and jittery manner indicated that he wished he had never set eyes on her as the woman before him was as dangerous as molten gold. She could have burnt anyone who touched her. Forget speaking with a woman of the palace, even looking at her face would spark hundreds of questions. Where on earth had this woman come from now? And how beautiful she was!

14
How I opened my Eyes in the Darkness and fled from my Destiny to my Despair

I cannot express my suffering at the hands of fate
For its very mention is a kind of suffering.
Tarihçi Raşid

The other face of the city was not at all as Rukal imagined. Life on the streets onto which she had secretly looked from the little window of her room was very different once outside the palace. It was evidently harder. The tinkling of grazing herds outside the walls mixed with the sounds of stray dogs and children playing, occasionally disrupted by the boisterous cry of the street-hawker selling yoghurt. "Yoghuuurrrrt milk creeeeam!"

We realised long afterwards that we were in a room of an inn overlooking the barracks of the customs officials at the Yedikule gate. The gate of the city walls in which those coming and going were checked and monitored throughout the day was closed for the call to evening prayer. The drawbridge suspended over the water canal was raised ceremonially with a great screech of the windlass. Every so often, a funeral procession took a corpse to the cemetery outside the walls and sometimes a straw wagon or an ox-driven cart laden with vegetables was allowed entry after being checked. At noon, the snarls and shrieks of a cat and dog chase were followed by the calls of a passing street vendor with cow and sheep livers hanging off a pole across his shoulders.

At night, the patrol sounds of the guards at the wall gates could be heard. The silence was filled at regular intervals with the exclamations, "God is One, God is One," giving the impression that they were proclaimed each time with a different pitch and tone. The words were repeated in succession, as though chasing one another, by all the gate's guardsmen all around the whole city.

The last rays of the sun poured into the city over the walls and melted in the emptiness. People headed for home with quick strides, panicked by the approaching curfew. The streets suddenly grew quiet.

The door of the inn where Rukal and I lodged faced the back street and had been closed earlier than usual. The more stringent checks and controls carried out by the guards throughout the day did not go unnoticed. It was certain that something was happening on the streets which we did not know about. Poor Rukal was beginning her third gloomy and sleepless night on the stone floor of the room, which was furnished only with a small couch. She limped back and forth between the window and the door on her aching foot, listening at the door, watching the window and with 1,001 thoughts racing through her mind. The water jug at the door was empty and there was no food left other than a crust of dry loaf.

The wind had intensified and blew inside, whistling between the window frames. The mosque's evening congregation dispersed, the streets were enveloped in a deathly silence and the Patlak Memi that Rukal was expecting still had not come. Exhaustion and hunger made her head spin. Her foot had been bandaged by a bone-setting matron the day we got there, but her pain was still worsening. The fuel in the oil lamp was about to run out. In the middle of the night, there were two short and two long raps at the door. Rukal was about to faint with exhaustion. She gathered her strength and listened. When the same code was repeated, she slowly lifted the latch. In the dim light of the corridor, a small man slipped inside. "Have no fear, sister. Get ready quietly, we have to go."

This was not Patlak Memi, but he had called her "sister". This indicated that he was appraised of all that had happened and knew who she was. Rukal had come to this place disguised as a man, with a fake moustache and beard so that even the innkeeper did not realise his lodger was female. "Grab your bundle and let's get out of here before the stinging scorpions hunt us down," instructed the man. His words pierced her to the core. She was desperate and felt that she had to do whatever she was told. She wore a robe resembling the cloak of an imam from the Ja'fari School and they tiptoed down the corridor. She thought her heart would not be able to bear the excitement and fear. The man left all her questions unanswered, and kept repeating, "I'll tell you on the way."

When they reached the back door, the man rummaged for a purse he carried in his leather bag and handed it to the innkeeper. The latch opened for them and they stepped out onto the street. The sounds of dogs barking blended with the noise of the front door being smashed in.

The wind licking their faces knew everything. All that had happened was at least as violent as this wind.

16 secret service agents were present at the secret sitting that the Commander of the Imperial Guards held in the barracks of the Old Palace Halberdiers. On the second day after Rukal's disappearance had been noticed, the incident caused a huge fuss. To begin with, the Chief Eunuch of Sultan Murat III was discharged from office and handed over to the executioner. The commander of the Imperial guards was warned, "Our concubine or your head!" and given three days to find her.

The *bostancıağa* responsible for the protection of the palace dressed two of his men in burqas and charged them with listening out for gossip among neighbourhood women, sending one to the slave market and the other to the mosques where sermons for women were preached. He instructed them to wander through the districts of Samatya and Cibali to survey the insalubrious houses on the doors of which hung drums, as well as the indigo-painted residences in Fener functioning as hideouts for outlaws. He sent his two most promising agents to check Istanbul's inns where they were to interrogate the boatmen conveying travellers to Üsküdar. He also stationed three of his men disguised as beggars at the ports. On the same day, he sent two women disguised as peddlers to visit the brothels under the city walls. The Ağa did not neglect to form a team of one-armed and otherwise crippled men in the role of blind beggars and mendicant Kalenderi dervishes, sending them out onto the city's streets to regroup again at dusk. That day, beggars, tailors, jewellers at the covered bazaar and chamberlains of bachelor barracks appeared before the *bostancıağa,* one by one, and were secretly informed of the situation. They were told that the person for whom they were searching at the behest of the state was a concubine and they were to undertake their investigations in confidence. The night prayer curfew stopped the people going out onto the unlit streets and facilitated the *bostancıağa*'s mission. He could send out his men who carried special permits stamped with three crescents in red ink wherever he wanted. When Rukal and I left through the back door of the inn at Yedikule, I was mistaken in thinking that those beating down the door were from the Babylon Society. They had to have been the *bostancıağa*'s men.

Meanwhile, the mother of the reigning Sultan wasted no time in meeting secretly with the janissary commander and commanding that the scarlet woman be found immediately. What needed to be done had to be done. Needless to say, the first thing the janissary commander did was to summon the *bostancıağa* to his presence and demand that he be immediately informed of any developments.

***

After we spent the night in the trunk of the walnut tree, Patlak Memi, the *kozbekçi* who found us, first thought of turning this beautiful woman over to the palace, just like the kind-hearted dervish who founded their brotherhood and was their spiritual guide would have done. However, he was also afraid that he would be asked hundreds of questions. But he was unable to resist the charm of the emerald ring on Rukal's finger. "To hell with the founder!" he said and kept us hidden in the tree hollow for a whole day. He even brought a bowl of hot soup and some tail fat to use as a dressing for Rukal's foot.

Volunteering to keep guard the following night, he risked everything by bringing Rukal some men's clothing with a tall padded *barata* hat for her head and a fake moustache and beard for her face. He paid no attention to her pain as he supported her through Istanbul's muddy side streets to Aksaray, sweating profusely all the while. They mounted the horses he had procured that day and paced across empty meadows, from the Kocamustafapaşa coastal road, through the Samatya Armenian neighbourhood, finally reaching the bachelor barracks at Yedikule.

On the way, he mentioned a friend of his who would take her all the way to Mingrelia; she would first go to Alanya by boat whence she would travel to her family home with the help of a slave trader whose address he would provide. He would write a letter addressed to his friend who would then attend to her in Alanya. If all went according to plan, she would be reunited with her mother two months thence and raise the baby prince in her own home.

Rukal would determine the reward for his kindness after returning to her homeland. And what was more, he implied, when word of the escape got out, Rukal would be in a better position to appraise how to return the favour. She would decide what gift to make him at a future date.

They arrived at the inn when the evening prayer was being called. Patlak Memi summoned a female bone-setter and bandaged Rukal's foot. Like every man who displays kindness and magnanimity, he too experienced the inner peace which comes of having another believe in him. He said to Rukal, "I'm going to head off on the quiet and continue my guard. I'll be back tomorrow, knocking at the door with two short and two long intervals. Make sure you don't communicate with anyone else!" he ordered, trying indirectly to assert his claim to her.

Patlak Memi rushed from the inn that night as though in flight and Rukal tasted for the first time the anguish of being left all alone. She tried to console herself by embracing me. I was her diversion, her joy, her sorrow, her hope and her dream.

It was a breathless escape. They rested for a few minutes beneath the wall of the Greek church adjoining the Topkapı walls and the man re-bandaged Rukal's foot. Her pain was getting worse. "I am Memi's colleague," he announced. "They call me Alapaça Temür. In two days' time, I will get you on a galley headed for Antalya. For now, we are headed for my sister's house at Fener. There, they will apply a dressing to your foot. Oh! And before I forget, I have a letter in my sash. For the family in Alanya. I'll give you the letter when we get to the port and you'll give me your L&M book."

Rukal was not in a position to think or to object. How could she possibly have known that her fate and mine were one? She only prayed inwardly. She beseeched God to protect her from this unknown man doing her any harm. She was well aware that she could do nothing but resign herself to all that befell her. At one point, it occurred to her to check her bundle. Her fingers touched me and her tension eased a little.

At that moment she was struck by doubt. "So how does this man know that I have L&M?" She had borrowed me from the Chief Eunuch two days before fleeing from the palace. "If Alapaça knows about L&M, this means that he is in correspondence with the Chief Eunuch. So my escape from the palace must be known about and therefore he may be one of the Sultan's men charged with taking me back. If I go back, I can tell my Sultan about all that has happened to me and about the baby I carry. But if this man is connected to the senior consort, this means that I am going to my death." The ifs kept multiplying in her mind. If the possibilities concerning me and the Babylon Society were added in, the picture became even more complicated. I calculated that the men in pursuit of us were undoubtedly from the Babylon Society.

Even if the Sultan was aware of the escape, he would suppose that the concubine had betrayed him. With his male pride mortally offended, he would be prepared to sacrifice her and order her death. How was he to know that she carried a male heir in her womb and that she planned the escape in order for the baby to survive? The Sultan was at the apex of the empire and would not be aware of petty intrigues. He certainly did not know about the Babylon Society. The existence of this secret society would have been unfathomable to him. He had storytellers and they told tales to entertain him. Since his administrators portrayed everything as rosy, he imagined there to be no problems in his territories.

The man accompanying us demonstrated the truth of what I had surmised, even though I kept trying to dismiss it. The Babylon Society no longer considered it suitable that I should reside at the palace as the palace had failed to protect me and even an innocent concubine with no specific purpose had succeeded in plucking me out from there. The Babylon Society could not run such a risk again. This man who said that he was taking Rukal to the port was definitely one of the Society's hired extras and who knows where he would take me and what he would do to Rukal? I trembled, not from the cold, but from the chill I felt at the prospect.

Rukal and I... We were helpless in Istanbul's shady outer neighbourhoods. Our will was not our own – others were now making decisions concerning us and putting them into practice. Helplessness increased the burden on her shoulders and my soul fell prey to nightmares.

The poor concubine mumbled to herself some of the couplets remaining in her mind from the *gazal* she had read the night before. Whilst seeking solace in my lines, she had vexed the sleep fairy, and tearfully entreated God for Him to make the Sultan aware of her tribulations. The bite that she took from the hard biscuit the man had given her became lodged in her throat. As she gulped down water from Temür's flask to help her swallow the morsel, she beat her hand against her chest. After a few slight blows, she stopped choking. The amulet her father had hung around her neck in church while reciting prayers when she was a child came into her hand.

"Oh father," she said, heaving a heavy sigh. "Beloved father, what an unlucky daughter you have!" She had kept this amulet for years as the only memento of her distant girlhood. It was her most cherished possession and recalled Mingrelia at each and every touch. She was at ease as long as it hung on her chest. Her father's image appeared before her eye. She wanted to believe that the prayer he had said for her had not worn off and that this Christian amulet written in Cyrillic letters still protected her. Perhaps now she was in greatest need of its protection so she squeezed it tight. Later she touched something else that would protect her and it brought her a little relief. She felt the three diamonds she had received on a joyous night in return for three poems she had read to the Sultan and which, on the night of her escape, she had hidden inside the amulet. She had packed them in with cotton wool so they would not be noticed.

She had taken the precaution of removing the amulet's silver casing to avoid others coveting it. She had then wrapped the triangular pendant with cloth dipped in beeswax and hung it around her neck with cheap string. The amulet and its contents were her material and spiritual life insurance and she clung onto life as she clutched it in her hand.

After resting for a while in a secluded section of the church wall, Alapaça Temür unfolded two sets of female garments out of his leather bag. These were loose tops and trousers of black cloth. He took one set for himself and passed the other to Rukal. Then he turned his back and I saw the familiar strap around his waist as he removed his clothing. Everything fell into place and I shuddered. This was my master Fuzuli's flask strap and it was obvious that Alapaça was not wearing it by accident. I wished I had the strength to tell Rukal, "This man is after me, not you!"

A cloud of sorrow fell over me.

Rukal removed her men's clothes along with her fake beard and moustache and hid them in the bushes by the wall. We set off and I examined the streets one by one in an effort to ascertain where we were being taken. Behind us, we could hear the barking of the janissary sniffer dogs, specially trained in tracing scents and trails.

I was determining Rukal's fate and Alapaça minc. Those coming from behind were forever condemned to remain in the background. Knowledge meant power and the sultanate was governed by power. I had begun to feel the Babylon Society's power.

A sudden thought occurred to Rukal. "What a formidable city is Istanbul beyond my master Murat's palace!" she announced.

I, my master Fuzuli's slave, was accustomed to the scent of roses and the sounds of nightingales in the palace. The thorns outside had already started making me bleed. I could not make the sound of my helplessness heard by another living soul when my Leyla was in agony...

15
How a Pearl was thrown into the Sea and my Love was sold to the Pope

'Tis that fairy's promise to appear in my dream one night.
Due to my jubilation I have not slept a wink in years!
Zati

I, my master Fuzuli's slave, did not know where I was going and where I was being taken in the hull of a galleon. I was grappling with death. It had been three days since the beginning of the journey and, as time went by, I was becoming more confused and more nauseous. I was afraid of not being able to carry the burden of the love in my story. I was afraid of being accused of treason. I was afraid of squandering sage Akeldan's secret. I was afraid the treasures unknown to anyone save the Babylon Society would be forgotten for all eternity and the doors opening onto space would remain forever closed. I was locked in a trunk and, as time passed, the dangers surrounding me were growing in number. Here, I had two important enemies: the saltwater and the unruly rats.

The sadness of leaving Istanbul, the land of happiness, pained me deeply. I heard when the seamen were talking that we had reached the end of September according to the Julian calendar. According to the *firman* published by the one on whom God had bestowed the Earthly Caliphate, all Muslims were to start fasting that day. The crescent moon must have been sighted! I thought to myself.

But I did not have too much time to think here. I was like the listless inmates locked in the Yedikule dungeons. I had stopped. I was waiting. I was waiting for all that was to happen. At times I said, "What is to be will be," and thus tried to console myself; at others I cried, "What is to be should not be thus," and fell into despair. I was thinking about the new moon of Ramadan. My master sometimes referred to it as the beloved's brow and sometimes as the lover's niche. "For what is a crescent compared with the full moon?" How strange people are: they await not completeness but incompleteness and when they see once again the ever-diminishing crescent, they start to fast, hold their festivities, begin their month and their new year.

Neither the captain of our ship, nor the pirates who suddenly turned wild and rebellious and ditched their humanity knew that the storms in the open seas of the Mediterranean would be this fierce or its waves this violent. As for me, I was getting to know what the open sea was like for the very first time...

There were around 200 armed guards and 43 crew members on board. One of the stores was filled with barrels and kegs. These were the amphorae used to carry olive oil, wine, sesame and rosewater. While waiting for my turn at the dock,

I imagined being placed in one of the upper stores, where I saw the sailors packing the luxury goods with a fear-driven uneasy discipline. There was fabric from Aleppo, bejewelled weapons, Istanbul-made bows and arrows, saffian harnesses, Caucasian furs, tooled jewellery from the Istanbul covered bazaar, whips made at the *arasta* complex, percussion and stringed *saz* instruments and silver cutlery sets. While waiting, I had seen parrots from the Far East in cages being lowered into the hold, along with parakeets, staked Arabian horses and different species of dog and greyhound. I could not have known of course, that these animals would be made to scare and bait each other for entertainment on our voyage.

Now the sounds of the parrots became so confused, one could not make out what they were saying. In fact, these were not so much sounds as discordant resonance: an excess of noise like the clamour of the workers building the Tower of Babylon. One would not encounter such a din even in great halls where everyone spoke but nobody understood. Evidently the crashing of the waves against the ship was driving the animals mad. The trunk holding me was stacked amidst stamping horses and dogs which alternated their barks and snarls with rhythmic insomnia. The parrots forgot all the words they had learned and shrieked for all the world to hear. I am afraid to say that no souls other than the captain and the helmsman were aware of my existence. They were just as oblivious to the diamonds and gold scratching the surface of my skin as were the waves beating against the sides of our galleon.

Upon leaving behind the Sultaniye and Kilitbahir fortresses overlooking the Dardenelles, the captain dropped the signal and dressing flags and hoisted the skull and crossbones. The crew swapped their equipment and uniforms, and preparations were made for sailing across the open seas in accordance with pirate practice. Out came the weapons while the masthead lamps were covered with felt and great effort was expended in preparing the vessel for escape or pursuit. I could make all this out from the hurried steps of the sailors and by listening to their foul and agitated speech.

When it had sailed into inland seas flying commercial flags and registered its consignment on entry into the port of Istanbul, this galleon had been carrying wine to be sold to the non-Muslims in Galata and cooking oil to be sold at Balkapanı. The owners were a Jewish family from Seville and had fled the Inquisition during the reign of Sultan Bayezid. They had sought refuge in Istanbul and the great-grandfather, Yasef Nasi, attained an important position in the palace serving as advisor to Sultan II. The family's younger generations took up posts as translators and physicians and so maintained their close connections with the palace.

One branch of the Nasi family was in Italy, while another settled in France. All of them were engaged in maritime commerce and obtained commercial agencies in various cit ies. However, like all pirates, their profit was subject to the vagaries of the wind, sea and other pirate ships. At times, they made great gains, but there were also times when they did not receive news from their ships for months on end and occasionally, their ships were taken by other pirates. About 50 years earlier, the elders of the Nasi family had calculated that this maritime trade was well beyond the commercial risks that a Jewish family could stand and decided to seek an alternative living. Using the galleons that were outwardly engaged in legitimate commerce, they had succeeded in forming an international intelligence network.

Now the Nasis bought and sold information across the Mediterranean, exploiting the rivalries between the great powers. Mastery kept changing hands: in the name of the Cross, dominance shifted between the Kingdom of Spain, the Republic of Venice, the Papacy in Rome, the Republic of Genoa, and the Kingdoms of England and France. Under the Crescent, different Ottoman states came to the fore. The intellectual climate shifted according to who was in charge.

From time to time, the Nasi family triggered speculation by releasing counterfeit metal currency and by circulating the thaler known as Levantine gold, Indian gold, as well as

Persian and Abbasid gold on the markets. Sometimes they hoarded money, giving rise to inflation and facilitating cheap acquisitions.

The stimulants, and the drug-filled jars and bottles that they conveyed were as effective as the Nasis' purses in the business of intelligence gathering. All the galleons were built with secret closets for gold and contraband. A high-ranking official from the family lived in every state: every king or sultan was acquainted with someone from the family and paid them trunk-loads of money in return for the information they collected about other countries for their own self-interest. Yasef Nasi's dynasty enjoyed functioning as a very well-structured family business and not one member fell prey to the ambition of earning more than the other.

Sometimes they would live out their lives without meeting any relatives but they still bought and sold secret documents confident of their blood line in distant places. There was a Nasi resident in every great power, ready to exchange precious information. The secret they treasured most was Yasef's instruction to conceal the fact that they were related. On no account were they to appear acquainted unless their lives were at stake. In this way, the states buying intelligence were faced with individuals rather than a family network, with single agents instead of an organization. This ruled out the possibility that kinship might be used for leverage by other states or in attempts to purchase spies. Even the Knights Templar – who steered the secret connection between the Crusaders and the Papacy – did not operate with such dedication as the Nasi family, and preferred to save their own skins rather than those of distant relatives they had never met.

I would not have wished to set off on a journey across the Mediterranean in a trunk. In particular, I would never have travelled in a trunk lined with zinc to make it water-tight in which I felt suffocated. Nor would I have chosen to be dropped through a hidden door in the bottom deck and placed in the hull where I was deafened by the noises of horses and parrots, when I could have been lulled by the romantic sound of the waves instead. In the trunk were the three holy crosses taken from Cyprus and a small golden statue of the goddess Isis procured cheaply from the gypsies in Alexandria to be presented to the Pope. There were also reports to be presented to the King of France concerning Ottoman dominance in the Eastern Mediterranean and the Maghreb, a copy of a document outlining the Sultan's thoughts on Mediterranean policy, copies of feasibility reports regarding a canal project in the Suez connecting the Mediterranean and the Red Sea, and a political report detailing how the Black Sea and Sea of Marmara Canal Project between the River Sakarya, Lake Sapanca and the Gulf of Izmit – for which excavations had already begun – could be stalled. On top of these, translations of the *Arabian Nights*, *Tutiname* and *Panchatantra* filled with miniatures to be presented as gifts to the cardinals and copies of the divans of the Ottoman sultans for the purpose of character analysis, scientific works influencing the Eastern sciences, master copies of each of the books taught in Ottoman *medrese*s written by famous scribes and bound in gold, works of history and medicine in ancient Greek, Syriac, Latin and Arabic, a book of herbal medicine and finally a few diamonds and ruby brooches, necklaces, aigrettes and daggers inlaid in jewels, were my fellow travellers.

I had entered this trunk that had been ripped open with the ferocity of a violent south-westerly and which was later frequented by on board rats the size of cats, completely by chance. At least this is what I thought. As I said, a person has a lot of time to think in such a place.

Poor Rukal, the downtrodden damsel I embraced as Leyla... How distant her memory had become. It was as though ages had elapsed. I missed her greatly. I missed also the hours I spent in the shabby suburbs of Istanbul where I tried to find solace in the longing I felt for her warm embrace each night I spent without her. I thought of the day I waited next to the furnace of a hamam to be handed over to the head of the Babylon Society, while she oscillated between hope and fear in the house to which Alapaça Temür took us. I thought of the time a Cretan sailor tried to drag her into his bed and how she had fought back as a matter of honour. It was my desire that I should never be parted from her. I laid claim to her and, if I was so able, I wanted to protect her. I understood that day that the only difference between my objective and my anguish was a mere sequence of letters.

Poor Rukal, she woke that morning with the anguish of a pregnant woman whom another had tried to violate, with blood dripping from the hem of her skirt. As this was a frequent occurrence in this house, the madam in charge immediately summoned a reliable midwife who lived in Balat and had her do what was necessary. When Rukal regained consciousness, the midwife, who had become so expert in women's complaints that she was a complete substitute for the Greek physicians from Galata, greeted her with the words, "You have miscarried, dear girl. You must rest for a few days."

Rukal's baby, for whom she had risked her very life, was a mere embryo suspended in a bloody mass in a rusting washbowl. It was taken to the base of a wall in an unknown cemetery and dumped there, amidst the barking of hungry dogs. Rukal wanted to die. I witnessed her pray for death with her entire being. I saw what anger really was and felt very afraid.

Needless to say, Alapaça was not Patlak Memi's friend. He was one of *bostancıağa*'s spies who had learned of the story of the Babylon Society and was on the trail of the treasure. On the second day of the investigation into Rukal's disappearance, he had questioned Patlak Memi's fellow guardsmen. Once Patlak Memi left his watch, Alapaça stopped him, locked him in a cell, tied his hands and feet, plucked out his nose hairs one by one and subjected him to prolonged torture. In the end, he broke all his resistance as well as his capacity to think.

To make him talk, Alapaça made him swallow nails attached to string. Patlak Memi vacillated between life and death as Alapaça wrenched the nails out and lacerated his oesophagus. Patlak Memi revealed himself unworthy when desperation drove him to divulge what he knew. When Alapaça hung him and thereby silenced him forever so that he would not tell others what he had told him, Patlak Memi was still begging for mercy and hurling expletives at Rukal, cursing the day that he had set eyes on her.

Alapaça lost no time nor did he tell anyone of his plans. He reached the inn at Yedikule where he kidnapped Rukal and me just ahead of the *bostancıağa*'s men. The brothel where he then took us was managed by a madam with whom he was in partnership. He assigned some of his company of bodyguards to look after the clientele and protect the brothel with their own lives, and paid them in female flesh.

Alapaça redrew to his own ends Rukal's plan of escape that he had learned from Patlak Memi. He met with the captain of the Genoese galleon at Karaköy and told him of the ravishing beauty whom he would bring two days later when the ship was about to weigh anchor. He received three bags of Genoese gold in advance. What he did not know, however, was that Rukal carried the Sultan's baby in her womb. Her miscarriage sent him into a panic and prompted him to seek solace at one of Galata's taverns. But he drank so much that he collapsed in a barrel and failed to attend the nightly meeting of the *bostancıağa*. The *bostancıağa* expected all the spies he had sent out onto Istanbul's streets to report back to him so, when Alapaça did not make his appearance, he grew suspicious and sent an agent after him.

Alapaça was under observation when he reached the brothel the following evening. The spy did not suspect anything amiss on seeing two women leave arm-in-arm from the establishment and waited for quite some time at his post. When he realised his mistake, he traced the women's footprints in the muddy streets all the way to the pier and noticed that one set was much bigger than a woman's. The bird had flown! He hired a caique immediately and set off for the port.

At the port, the spy tracked down the man who worked as a look-out for the secret service. He dispatched him as a messenger to the *bostancıağa* and set the port clerks to work checking the galleon's paperwork. Meanwhile, Rukal was about to set foot aboard. She carried nothing but a small bundle in which I was wrapped among her clothing. One hand remained locked on the amulet, moist from the beads of sweat on her pert breasts. My forlorn Rukal, my Leyla knew neither where she was headed nor what was to befall her. The only thing she knew, or wanted to know was that she never again needed to fear the *bostancıağa*. Everything had faded into insignificance for her. She had lost the Sultan for whom she had struggled to survive and his heir whom she had nurtured in her belly. She hoped to find consolation through me until we reached Mingrelia and prayed that she would not lose the gems in her amulet along the way.

As soon as she stepped onto the deck, some of the deck hands approached her importunately in the dim lamplight. In a language she did not understand, they demanded she pay entrance duty. She thought they were after passage money and it sent her into a flap as she believed she had already paid. "O God!" she cried, "What else have You in store for me?"

Rukal had no silver coins left in her purse but she still reached hopefully for the sash around her waist. When she discovered it gone, she panicked. I sensed how she hesitated as to whether she would hand me over or the amulet around her neck, and I loved her for weighing me up against the diamonds.

Her hands were shaking and she felt cold and afraid. Her head had started spinning and she was weak from loss of blood. Her knees gave way and her bundle fell onto the deck. Until then, nobody was aware of my existence. Perhaps the man who was following Alapaça... I fell onto the deck straight onto one of my corners and my tailband was about to tear. I felt hurt for the first time. Was this hurt due to my fall or my separation from her? I could not make it out, but I really was in a lot of pain.

Rukal had collapsed onto her knees. Now she tried to get up despite the pain in her broken ankle. She scooped me up off the deck and, rubbing my back cover for the last time, handed me over to the brigands demanding payment. The taller of these rough-looking men laughed out loud at

Rukal's weakness, perhaps out of jealousy for her beauty since his teeth were completely blackened by tobacco. He wanted to take her arm while the others were still insisting on payment.

When Rukal gave me to them, I tasted the agony of separation. Separation from Rukal was going to be difficult, incredibly difficult. Was it possible for Kays to be separated from Leyla a second time? Could the spirit of a Kays separating from his second Leyla bear such pain? If he was to endure it, if separation was to be destiny, was the Kays of the Tigris riverbanks or the Kays of the Najd desert going to envy me? As these thoughts tormented me, I crashed down onto the deck again. This time, I was thrown down in rage and came loose whilst my pins pierced my parchment.

"Gold!" the men were shouting, "We want gold!" I cannot say that I was in any less pain than before. I surmised that this was what was termed persistence, adaptation, habituation. This is what suffering for the beloved was about! Poor helpless Rukal! She would not leave me spreadeagled on the deck so, ignoring the fracture in her ankle, she threw herself on the wet planks in such a way that she fell flat on her face. When she tried to get up, she noticed that her right index finger was bleeding. Had the captain not seen what had taken place, the sailors would perhaps have manhandled her, seeking their payment through assault and molestation. She would have had to extract her sole capital from the amulet she carried despite the pain in her finger.

The men scattered at the captain's command and he ordered her to be locked in the galleon's only cabin. The pain in Rukal's hand accompanied that in her foot. In the dim light of the tallow candle, she saw that her finger was still bleeding and that a single drop of blood had dripped on me.

She was devastated. It had fallen on the clearest section of the page on my marbled bookplate, which was embellished with patterns resembling river stones. The spot lay adjacent to the letter *alif,* the first letter of the alphabet which she had written in black after returning from the Sultan's side one night. The drop of blood was shaped like a ring, so it resembled a poppy with its leaves removed, more like a peony. Rukal's heart sank. She wanted to complete the drawing. She spilt another three drops of blood right beside the straight black *alif* stalk and a red poppy blossomed in all its beauty in the midst of this sorrowful sunset. This was exactly the same place where the Leyla I left on the Tigris had first written the name Kays when I was still parchment and where she had later kissed me and then wiped the mark she made. I felt as though I was about to lose myself. How could Rukal have known? How could she have found the very place touched by Leyla's lips? It was as though she had discovered my love. Ah! if only I could have whispered into her ear right then that, since the day my love discovered her, I had waited to be discovered thus! My happiness transposed my sanguine memories onto a poppy and sent my heart soaring. My two beloveds, Leyla and Rukal, had met upon a poppy and their lips had kissed the same point on my cheek. I was never able to understand whether I loved Leyla or Rukal more, or whose memory I cherished more. As Leyla became Rukal, I realised that I did not want to know the answer.

Some time later, the captain sought permission to enter the cabin. Rukal was sitting with her head lowered. Resting his head against the porthole, the captain asked her whether she liked to read without ever looking at her face. The words slipped out of his mouth unwittingly in his astonishment at seeing a book in a woman's hands. Rukal nodded as she tried to hide her tears. Taking one last look at the colours of the poppy that was almost dry, she said, "I like poetry," and pointed at me.

"Can I keep it awhile, my lady? I can hide it on board for you and after I read it, we can even debate the contents!" These words earned Rukal's trust. The captain grabbed me and took me to his cabin without waiting for her response, let alone her permission.

The captain summoned two secret agents who knew different languages and asked them what they made of me. After they had read out my title, the *Book of Leyla and Mecnun,* written on my cover and pointed out the seal of the palace library, he returned to the cabin to question Rukal. He suspected that I was from the palace and probably thought Rukal was the sultan's property also.

He was an intelligent man, the captain. If what he presumed was correct, then he should have realised that the transaction he made concerning Rukal was very stupid. In actual fact, when he learned the truth of the matter from Rukal, he wanted to send word to the palace immediately, but surmised from the noise outside that the coast guard's longboat was pulling up alongside the ship.

The following morning, as the sun rose above the hills of Üsküdar, the galleon raised anchor and set off from port. When we passed between Sarayburnu and the Maiden's Tower, I heard Rukal's last scream. After the three janissary officers who boarded the ship to interrogate her had obtained the information they needed and heard all about her sorry adventures, they had taken her out onto the deck for fresh air and supposedly left her alone. But the ship's crew decided there and then on a new maritime procedure to prevent her from falling overboard and chained a cannonball weighing 50 *okka*s to her ankle.

Rukal leaned on the guardrail and gazed at the pier. She marvelled at the Topkapı Palace where she had left the man she loved and realised that she was seeing the place in which she had lived for years for the first time from the sea. The smoke rising from the chimneys clouded her eyes with sadness. But her sadness did not last long and, at a stroke, she fell into the void. The chain of the guardrail was still in her hand as her last shriek reverberated from Topkapı's walls and the ball around her ankle pulled her swiftly to the bottom of the Bosphorus.

As it turned out, the *bostancıağa* had already informed the janissary commander that he had picked up Rukal's trail. After issuing instructions that he would take care of the matter personally, he sent three of his officers to deal with her, while keeping the other men and spies away from the galleon.

Whilst two of the officers were questioning Rukal, the third, who was expert in engineering conspiracies, loosened the links of one of the guardrails and placed a cannonball weighing 50 *okka*s right in front of it. The cannonball was positioned so that it was inclined towards the sea, a short wedge was placed in front of it to serve as a brake and a hidden fishing line tied to the wedge was lowered all the way to the bottom deck. A rapid pull on this line would set the cannonball in motion and loosen the guardrail. All that remained was for the victim to be stationed in place and the signal to be given when she held onto the guardrail. The fabricated maritime law was of course part of the conspiracy.

The following day, messengers despatched two separate letters through the Imperial Gate. Both were marked "Confidential". The first read,

"Illustrious, exalted, excellent, your Majesty, my Master,

Your humble servant by the name of Rukal, seeking refuge in a three-deck galleon of the infidel Genoese wine freighters, met her end in the early dawn of yesterday in the deep waters of the Sea of Marmara. May God have mercy on her soul. Patlak Memi from among the Kozbekçi guard, your humble janissary's servant Alapaça Temür and a guardsman from the aforementioned galleon were found to have played a part in the escape and were immediately executed. The rest is left to the decree of Your Royal Highness.

Your servant, Ali, on 13 Rabiülahir, Year 999

The second letter was not as detailed and there was no name in the signature section. The mother of a prince, the Haseki Sultan read it and tore it up.

"We have dropped the pearl in the sea!"

At that point, as I listened to the sound of the waves while I beat my head against the sides of the trunk in which I was imprisoned due to the violent south-westerly, I let my thoughts wander. It occurred to me that if, after Rukal's death, the janissary commander had not anchored the ship off Sarayburnu and had not taken me from the captain, I would have undertaken this journey years before and would have travelled across the Sultaniye fortress then. My tail-band had loosened with the humidity and I had been jostled by rough hands. I was at the centre of dispute between those who sold their lives for gold in pursuit of the Babylonian treasures and those who sought scientific truth. The bounty-hunters offered me a life in Istanbul's dens, while the latter offered me its refined suburbs. The destitution of the first seemed to be a consequence of the affluence of the second.

Looking back, I realised that I had never before experienced magnificence so interwoven with squalor and had never seen such deceitful thieves. Those seeking scientific truth and those pursuing the golden idols committed ruthless murders and saw themselves as justified. One lot did it to protect humanity, the other to protect themselves. It was difficult to determine whose objective was more innocent, who was more justified. All this relentless hunting and intrigue has made me forget the number of eyes which I have seen lose their lustre as they searched for ciphers, charts and treasure maps in my pages. But I could make one distinction: thieves were the ones who possessed my master Fuzuli's flask strap, while those with the dagger were scholars. I was always praying that the Assyrian librarian's lost dagger would never be found and, if it was found, that it would not fall into the hands of the thieves. They thought the lines on the strap were a map and they read the hieroglyphics as directions. They were concerned for the most part with my miniatures and looked for similar images among my illustrations. However, the Babylon Society members were focused on my poems and tried to decipher the meanings between the couplets. I gauged from the attention I received from the people in whose hands I ended up whether they were Society members or treasure hunters that were slaves to ambition. What stung most was that nobody attached importance to me for my own sake. The Babylon Society wanted to imprison and protect me and make decisions concerning me in their septennial meetings. The treasure hunters wanted to tear me to bits even before seven minutes was up.

Both sets of people came from worlds different to mine. I remained a stranger to them and increasingly forgot time. I lost my resolve to find my Leyla and felt myself withdrawing from the delightful gardens of poetry. If, one day, Leyla turns up of her own accord, I may now be in a position to tell her:

If I am me, then who are you, O love?
And if you are you, then who is poor I?

When describing Kays' encounter with Leyla in the desert, it was as though my master Fuzuli was depicting my present plight, illuminating the years that the Mecnun of that era spent in the wilderness, describing my path to my contemporary madness. I was in the phase of moving beyond Leyla to existence. There was no longer any difference between the Mecnun in my master's story and me: separateness and otherness had been annihilated. I never abandoned hope, not for an instant. My Leyla was the sorrowful girl of the Tigris, my Leyla was the ill-fated desert beauty in my master Fuzuli's tale and my Leyla was Rukal. I was gripped by nightmares in which love held sway over the other and I could not decide which love I preferred. But I had not lost hope. My dreams and reveries were all mine and I had all the inspiration I needed in my verses.

I passed the night dreaming hopefully that someone else would come to me, to read me and speak of my mysteries. It was 10 years since the death of the Lawgiver. These were the days when Sokollu Mehmet Paşa dominated the capital and his sympathisers formed a network in every corner of the land where he promoted a *devşirme* recruitment policy all around.*

We were in the mansion belonging to Sokollu's chamberlain, Hüsrev Paşa, in Üsküdar. Then he entered: Feridun Bey. He had the face of a friend and apparently penned prose. He was newly wed with Ayşe Sultan, daughter of Rüstem and Mihrimah. His familiarity with love and devotion was evident in his every aspect and manner. As soon as he took hold of me, I could feel his heart pace and throb. The first thing he examined, stroking it with his fingertips and later seeming to inhale its scent, was the peony on the frontispiece. The man was drawn to the image of the peony etched in Rukal's blood over my name which the Leyla I had left on the Tigris had written in charcoal... My most prized treasure! Yes, this man knew love.

He skimmed rapidly through my pages, reading with the corner of his eyes. Beyond mere reading, he looked as if he was seeking something that he already knew by heart. I realised that my copies were multiplying in Anatolia and Istanbul and that anyone who read my tale wanted to read it again. On snowy nights after days of fasting, people gathered in village rooms, mansions and coffeehouses to listen to my story. They would weep and at the same time apply my lessons to the cultivation of their children. I addressed their very hearts. And I addressed them with the richness of a civilisation made of hearts.

As Feridun Bey flicked through my pages, he benefited from the advantages of personal experience. Just as he knew

* [Translator's note: The Ottoman practice of training Christian boys between the ages of 8 and 15 for posts in the Palace, the administration or the military.]

what he was looking for, he was also able to fathom what he found. Finally, he read with fresh fervour:

Pray, mother, what is the meaning of love?
Do render this hidden arcanum known.

He had chosen correctly. My master Fuzuli had placed one cipher of the secret that the Assyrian librarian entrusted to him in the number of this couplet: 688. It was the phrase, "hidden arcanum," which attracted Feridun Bey's attention. He was aware of the need to underscore the fact that love was a hidden mystery. It was obvious that he had read all Fuzuli's works. He seemed to know in advance how Fuzuli would express something and why he expressed it. A reader is able to know how their favourite poet would think when they have read all their verses. I gauged this from the explanations he gave to the Babylon Society members listening to him. He knew precisely my master Fuzuli's thoughts on love and said, "According to master Fuzuli, the lover is a moth. He says,

'In the same way that a moth seeks to burn itself in the fire,
the lover too must throw himself into love and burn thus.'

Of importance here is not the beloved, but love itself. His connection with love is consolidated not because love embellishes and beautifies poetry but, on the contrary, because it is a mirror in which he sees the meaning of existence. A light, a colour, a thrill is the meaning of love for him; making life liveable is possible only with love. To his mind, one can only fall in love with a beloved precisely because of love; the rest consists of empty talk and delusion. The identity of the beloved, whether spiritual like the Sufis, or sensuous like the minstrels, is of no consequence. For his own love, he creates his abstract beloved in his mind, and tailors her so that her soul is patterned from love while she is clothed in the fabric of beauty. So beautified does the beauty become in his verses that every lover finds therein their own beloved beauty and feels the pain, separation and longing of their own love experience. He describes the pain and anguish of love incessantly. He searches for separation, affliction and sorrow in his every verse and rejects union, joy and happiness, seeing them as simple. He believes that the human being matures and becomes exalted with suffering and himself feels a different pleasure in suffering. I suspect this is not too difficult for a person whose being has been kneaded with love. He reigns with love in a world to which he has come for love...

Fuzuli says: *'God, with His Exalted and Infinite Power created from clay beauties whose cheeks are like poppies and breasts like white roses. In order for this beauty to be appreciated and loved, He placed the fire of love in the hearts of lovers. God wills that these hearts suffer and are saddened, and He grants the lovers He creates, the strength to endure the grief of their beauties. Given that He has created beauty and the hearts which love beauty, there is no cause for astonishment that He should allow them to experience the Fire while still in this world.'*

This process that Fuzuli envisions is in fact a test of servitude; if the lover is successful at this point, he can progress from the fire of love to the paradise of ultimate union. However, in order to enter paradise, purification through burning is first required. Love is such a fire that it cleanses spirits from thousands of impurities. In his view, the burning flames of love elevate the lover and increase his rank.

Being successful in love and earning the favour and love of the beloved requires the fire to burn deep. The more the lover burns, the more he matures in love, and the remedy for all afflictions is love, while beyond is a great void...

Again he says: *'I have a potential for love far beyond even that of Mecnun; I am the true lover, but Mecnun has all the fame.'* Love is the same in every epoch. Throughout time, lovers have always passed on the baton to one another. The laws left from Adam and Eve still apply to this race. Ferhat, Kerem, Vamik, Salaman and Romeo stand out in this list of honour. Now, gentlemen, let us address the question of how many servants are fated to live a life for the sake of this ideal. This is precisely why Fuzuli is the lover of true love. *'I have set a table of poetry for the people of the world,'* he says in one of his poems and continues, *'All manner of bounties on that table have diverse tastes. Whether the visitor calling on me is Turk, Arab, or Persian, never will I be ashamed. For that is the degree to which my table is complete. Whosoever wishes can come and eat whatsoever they wish; this blessing will not wane.'* His is a generosity befitting the lands of Mesopotamia and the sages of Babylon, a magnanimity bequeathed by Arshiya Akeldan and a lofty cultural banquet inspired by the accumulation of countless successive civilisations. When reflected in poetry, it relays the most refined words of an entire poetic tradition and all those words are completed in love. *'Verse without knowledge is like a wall with no foundation,'* he says, adding, *'And a wall without foundation is doomed to untimely ruin.'* This is why he was proficient in many of the sciences. He learned the positive sciences such as logic, geometry, astronomy and medicine as well as the religious sciences: Qur'anic commentary, *hadith*, classical theology and jurisprudence among them. In spite of this, he esteems love above knowledge and prefers the heart to the mind.

Perhaps dear friends, perhaps no Turkish poet has spoken of love as sincerely and with as much fervour, excitement, delicacy and wholeheartedness as he. He removes love from mere carnal pleasure and elevates it to the Divine. By ascribing all his transcendental thoughts to love and expressing this in an aesthetic format acceptable to all humanity, while also embodying the premise of beauty kneaded by Plato centuries earlier in a form appropriate to his time, he certainly deserves to be remembered among the greatest poets."

Everyone listened intently to Feridun Bey's excited disquisition. Everyone affirmed their praise for my master Fuzuli, ascribing as much sanctity to him as to me. It was as if they were about to announce in the name of the Babylon Society that my master Fuzuli was as much a sage as was Akeldan. I sensed this from the way they began to show greater respect when handling me.

It was as if I wanted Feridun Bey to read all my couplets that night, to discover all my secrets and dig out all my treasures. I saw just how much I had missed hearing poetic conversations about love and I came to realise how long I had been kept away from poets. I wanted them to take me to places where love was like rain that poured from the skies, where the mainspring of time was wound up with love and love was given as alms.

I wanted to be kneaded with love and wearied by it. I wanted to be a dervish of love collapsing with exhaustion at the completion of his ritual. I wanted all my rituals to consist of spinning in the circle of love. I wanted to long for Leyla so that my separation from her seared my heart to such an extent that the skies ignited with the sparks of my lament. This is what my master Fuzuli said in any case. I wanted to shake the water from my eyes to extinguish the fire of love raging within me. But my fire had burgeoned and my tears were not enough to put it out. On the contrary, they inflamed it further. As the flames increased, my eyes shed more tears and, as more water fell, the flames became even more intense. With this vicious cycle, both water and fire were growing in my love. I thought that the day would come when my tears would choke me. I was like a candle. At my head was the fire of love, tears were in my eyes and my body kept melting away – my thread of life was burning all the time. I came within a hair's breadth of drowning in my tears.

I realised how much I yearned for love and for Leyla on the night I met Feridun Bey. Poor Feridun Bey, what a wonderful owner he would have made for me... We could have conversed about love and wept. Clearly, he too had been gripped by the ivy of a secret love and his sycamore-like body had begun to sustain inner injury. But the day after I learned his thoughts on love to the very last syllable, his naked body was found with his eyes gouged out by the fish, washed ashore near Zindankapısı. Those that found him even invented the tale that, to prove his love for a Greek beauty from Cibali, he had first scarred his chest with a dagger and then driven his short sword into his stomach. He had let himself sink into the waters of the Golden Horn and, what is more, the Greek girl had not even lifted a finger for him. I learned the truth of the matter when the other members of the Society were talking amongst themselves. The thieves after the golden idols of Babylon had intercepted him, taken him first to an inn, seated him naked upon a board designed for torture and, after forcing him to relate everything he knew, had thrust his sword into his belly and thrown his body into the Golden Horn just as the cocks were crowing.

After all the intrigues, murders and wasted lives, I saw that my spirit had as good as forgotten love and that I was even becoming accustomed to violence. This made me exceedingly uneasy. Besides, my body was under ferocious attack from the rats ripping me to pieces aboard the pirate ship, my pages were blistering and aching with the humidity, my forehead was injured by crashing against the sides of the trunk. In the midst of my pain, I was not even worried about what would befall me in foreign lands where I was not even understood. I tried to console myself with the thought, "A change is better than a holiday."

Leaving Istanbul revived the feelings I had when fleeing from Leyla's nomadic village into the wilderness. If forgetting one's memories is an impossibility, then being forgotten in memories becomes destiny. I had already lived this destiny once and by this stage, I did not conserve a single tangible memory of Leyla. But Rukal had left me a gift whose value would increase as it remained on earth and she headed for death. Do you think that the mark of the peony which she sketched in scarlet blood from her bleeding finger as an eternal reminder which she then kissed, is an insignificant thing for me? I would not change it for all the treasures in the world. I would not change this flower, which blossomed on that soot stain touched by the lips and washed with the tears of the Leyla I left on the Tigris, for all the world's bounty. Leyla had given it to me and now only the one who gave Leyla could take it away. This peony gave me life, gave me beauty, gave me love. I understood that all those I loved were always going to kiss me in the same way, right on my cheek. I saw that the lip imprints would always be made one on top of the other and I was forever to feel that bitter-sweet taste of salt.

The rains misted up life in Istanbul over all the years that passed apart from Rukal. The winters yielded to storms and the springs were damp with sorrow. The seasons fell upon my peony like a kiss, spreading the ink from the flower stalk, rounding the shape and spilling over the sides to form capil lary lines on the blood-red leaves and causing the peony to droop. This was a true portrait of my love's torment.

This transformation made me realise that Rukal had loved me greatly, perhaps as much as Leyla. Perhaps she had become Leyla. I remember her tears falling down on me during the nights she read my tale. My misgiving gave way to feelings of faithfulness.

That peony, the tulip of the mountains, bears a great mountain within itself. That mountain, whether branded by the scalding summer or freshened by the spring rain, will burn for eternity in my bosom. Rukal was seared by a dewdrop on the night she slept while embracing me in the trunk of the walnut. A bolt of lightning struck the tree that night, descending its branches in zigzags and burning the dewdrop. The dewdrop fell from Rukal's eye to her ruby cheek and from there to the poppy bud, and her bosom was left scorched for all eternity. Neither the love of Narcissus of Greek myth who was punished with lightning, nor the love of the lightning which fell onto the dewdrop waiting on the bosom of the Turkish tulip, could have transfixed such a delicate leaf. The peony that Rukal drew upon my forehead was the very cheek that was transfixed just like a glowing ember and onto which she placed me like a beauty spot.

And I, my master Fuzuli's slave Kays, will be kissing anew Rukal's beauty spot on her ruby-red cheek with every glance at the depiction of this flower on my bosom. Rukal, how much I loved you, how much I loved you as Leyla, O Rukal, if only you knew! Rukal, however much I praise your beauty, that is the extent to which I will speak the truth... Believe me, O peony of the Caucasus! You were the beloved I left at the Tigris. Your lips merged with hers.

Was it because Rukal was unable to become a bride that she loved the poppy so and, now, as I continue my existence, she will continue to be here with me in this image of the poppy. My heart throbs right where your lips touched, O Rukal! The poppy of the Caucasus...

16
How My Name was changed in the Vatican and how the 1,000th Year came to My Rescue

Friends are heartless, the world ruthless,
time without peace,
Trouble abounds, no one befriends you, the
foe is strong, fortune weak.

Fuzuli

I was tired of counting the years. I was very tired. The unsettling adventure of 16 years reeking of humidity and gunpowder spent on the sea was swathed in fog, banished to an ever more distant place in my memory. If I do not explain this now, I will never again be able to recall how I was disfigured by the cannonballs of the Genoese pirates between Crete and Malta, nor the pain of the nails in the belt into which I was squeezed so that I could be abducted from the patrol vessel of the Commander in Chief of the Navy, Murat Reis the Elder, off the Morean shores. I am even about to forget the deaths of the sailors smashed up by the cannonballs hitting the galleon onto which I was smuggled during the voyage undertaken under different flags and sometimes with no light at all.

These were truly very difficult days for me. I was stale, alienated, flaccid. When the bilge water reached my feet, I was freed from the assaults of the rats but could not cope with the moisture that caused my stitching to rot, spoiled the aesthetic of my script and, most importantly, ruined the red peony and frontispiece with the mark of Leyla's lips.

I had assumed that my journey would end in Venice, city of festivals, luxury and intrigue. Instead we were headed for Rome, with its villas, statues and priests, due to the ongoing wars on the Dalmatian coast. The captain was especially keen to avoid the dangers of Veglia Island and the port of Segna.

He knew that the district governor of Bosnia, Telli Hasan Paşa and his men together with Murat Reis the Elder and his sailors had taken possession of these areas. This was the reason why, off the waters of Ragusa, he issued the astounding command to turn eight degrees to starboard. Three nights later, we docked at Ancona. It took us two days to get from there to the Vatican, under the protection of guards and soldiers.

It was here that I became aware of being truly a slave. No longer was I the magnificent slave of my master Fuzuli. I was perhaps a pitiable slave to be bought and sold by shady types at slave markets. No place and nothing here resembled the life to which I had become accustomed. My experiences in Ottoman lands began to seem like a dream to me. The Vatican, famous for its halls, dungeons and priests, dissolved life away with an utterly different climate. There was no soul here to listen to me in the elaborate halls embellished by Raphael. I decided that my days here were going to pass in silence, listening to everyone and everything. I could hear people and understand them not from their lips but from their hearts. Bearing witness to their true identities and their true thoughts pleased me greatly. Bearing witness meant knowing. However, knowing people's hearts is a heavy burden... This is because knowledge could at times be as deadly as are weapons of war. None could stomach knowledge other than those with an affinity for the beyond. People always sided with power but they kept hidden what lay in their hearts. After having begun to bear witness, it seemed as if I had taken over from others the heavy burden of constantly living unlike their own selves, with a view to knowing the unknown, solving the unsolvable and surmounting the insurmountable. I recognised, knew and remained silent. Seeing winners losing, the destruction of the destroyers and the death of those who were born, I kept silent. I could better see and understand that my master Fuzuli's words proved right: knowledge was held captive to gossip, whatever there was existed only in love, heart came ahead of mind, the heart reigned supreme over reason and still I remained silent. I remained persistently silent, knowing that people's hearts were in the hands of God.

We lived for a long time in a palace whose high windows looked on St. Peter's Basilica and the Pope's gardens extending behind. This was the heart of Rome, the theocratic state under the rule of Habsburg Spain. All around were traces of the Renaissance, Michelangelo's art and Machiavelli's philosophy. The Pope kamat the head of the Catholic Church possesses two important attributes: he is the highest judicial authority and he is infallible in matters of religion. Papal superiority and infallibility placed the Vatican at a distinct advantage as against the Protestant powers. The fiscal crisis which had begun 20 years earlier violently shook the republics of Genoa and Venice as well as the kingdoms of Naples and Sicily, but in Rome the depreciation of Ottoman silver remained in the range of 20 per cent and gold around 10 per cent. The Vatican's coins were as thin as almond leaves and light as dewdrops. They were equal in value to the silver coins of other states which resembled cows' eyes, and seven coins were equivalent to one Ottoman *akçe*.

When I was brought before Pope Julius IV, I was the first to be lifted out of the trunk in which I had spent my journey. I was spread on a table in the centre of a hall aglow with the mid-afternoon sunlight. Yasef Levi's brother and the ship's captain arranged the items in the trunk on the table with painstaking care, one by one. They introduced us in turn to the College of Cardinals. After the silver dinner services and the bejewelled weapons, it was time for the papers and written treasures. Since the cardinals used Latin as the language of science, the books on medicine and pharmacy that were written in Latin were passed around first. This was a land in which human beings were brought together by territory, and science was monopolised by the Papacy. Those who copied, distributed and wrote the books in their workshops, to which the church vestibules led, were exclusively clergy. Thought and writing was a lofty privilege not to be left to the masses. Artists were valued and esteemed as an expression of church power. Like the artists and poets of the sultans, painters and sculptors were patronised and supported. Popes prided themselves on the decorators, painters and sculptors whom they called to their palaces so as to leave their mark on history with their splendour.

Yasef Levi and the captain were rewarded for delivering the precious books and feted with a formal dinner. Afterwards, they knelt before the Pope and a special order of chivalry was pinned to their shoulders. They were also each promised a bonus of 50 bags filled with gold to be collected from the Vatican bursar. After kissing the Pope's staff they walked towards the door of a large hall. The captain mentally calculated the gold that he was to receive as he admired the frescoes adorning the ceilings and walls by Botticelli and Michelangelo.

It was only after the great doors of the hall were closed by the armed guards that the Pope and cardinals gathered around the table and set about examining the bindings, illustrations and documents which comprised my companions in fate. From the outside, it might easily have been assumed that they were interested not in the subject matter hidden within the volumes, but in the papers and pictures of which they were made. Only the Pope proved himself a true bibliophile, as he endeavoured to learn straight away what each book was about.

They examined the books in Latin and deliberated upon them. No one had touched me yet. As the day drew to an end, the cardinals gathered under the gilded crucifix at the eastern end of the hall, knelt down and began singing in chorus. Their voices grew louder and louder. This was the first time

I had ever seen prayers performed by joining the palms at face level. Long after, the pealing of bells pervaded the air and filled the twilight descending on the people beyond the windows of the palace, on all the city's houses and churches.

Three months earlier, the Pope had decreed that the bells be rung three times each day. They called this "the Turkish bell". After the Uskok pirates of the Dalmatian shores kept attacking Ottoman ships and were eventually fed up with constantly being defeated, they appealed to the Pope for a solution. Now, when the people heard the bells ringing three times daily, all the Catholics of the Adriatic coast took to praying that God would vanquish the Turks.

The last book the Pope examined that night was me. He did not understand my language, but I could tell from his looks and the beating of his heart that he was struck by the beauty of my writing as well as my miniatures. He knew that I was a book of lyric poetry and spoke of love. Had he realised that I bore witness to his desire to remember the Tuscan girl with whom he had fallen in love before taking his vows, he would most certainly have blushed with shame. The trembling sorrow of his heart stirred me. He had seen her first and hundreds of times thereafter in the gardens of Florence. But he had never been able to speak to her and declare his love. If he had done so, he would probably not have become Pope. Likely he would be carving wood in his father's workshop, living out his days without denying himself any of life's pleasures. Perhaps he would have taken her blonde locks in his hands and smelt them, kissed her on the forehead when she gave him a child and brought home something for her every evening. Even when empty-handed, his heart would have been full.

He had never forgotten those blue eyes, which had caused him to feel something warm in his heart when he first saw them. It became clear from his heartbeat that, despite the long interval that had elapsed since then, he was still waiting hopelessly for the moment when his soul, split between himself and a woman, would be united.

Love occupied his soul itself and neither decreased nor increased with the passage of time. Throughout all these years he had often wondered whether or not the girl loved him also. Could she have thought of him in this way, if only once? If so – and this is what he believed – then he knew that they would meet again in the house of the Blessed Virgin Mary in Paradise. He often gave sermons on the subject of love, partly to keep this belief alive. "Love is the combination of the fragments of souls divided between various creatures," he would say.

Unlike magnets, in love, likes attract and opposites repel and the same holds true between souls, he would say. In his view, it was impossible for two people whose innate characteristics did not exhibit affinity or likeness to love one another; attachment and love increased proportionally to similarity. If he was thinking about her now, this meant that there were most certainly times when she thought of him also.

The Pope joined his hands over my flower just as Rukal had done on the rainy night she hid in the walnut tree and, as he tried to picture the present-day appearance of the first and last woman he had ever loved, he was overcome by sleep.

His first task the following day was to order the young priest serving him to summon a translator who spoke my language. Towards noon, a priest in his sixties entered the Pope's presence carrying a pen-case and inkwell in his girdle and paper in his hands. He was a Venetian by the name of Antonio who had been captured during a voyage to Malta he had undertaken as a child with his seafaring father. He was taken to Ottoman lands after a battle with the ships commanded by Barbaros Hızır Hayrettin Reis. He had been presented to the palace of Sultan Bayezid in Istanbul as a gift and had impressed those around him with his intelligence. As a result, he was sent to the Enderun School to receive a palace education. Antonio was renamed Orhan and became one of the court interpreters. When he reached the age of 30, he had left the palace to study medicine at Galata. Subsequently, he had gone to a Genoese school in Malta to specialise and there he learned that some of the most important medical sources were stored in the Vatican library. He moved there and, tying a girdle around his waist, reverted to his former religion and entered the service of the church.

Antonio now directed the studies in the Papacy concerning Ottoman matters. He was in charge of the Ottoman library collection and claimed to be the great-great-uncle of Sultan Murat's Venetian consort, Safiye Sultan.

Antonio received me with the warmth of an old friend. It seems that his tutor Hasan Ağa at the Enderun frequently told the tale of L&M and he in turn fell into a reverie tinged with the sadness of being unable to find a Leyla of his own.

"Most Holy Father," he began, keeping his head lowered reverentially. "This book relates a love story like that of Romeo and Juliet. Its title is the *Book of Leyla and Mecnun*, in other words, the story of Leyla and the Madman." He indicated my first page. "Everyone in the Orient, young and old, men and women, knows this tale. A great many poets have written and re-written this story in many different languages. This manuscript is from the pen of Fuzuli of Baghdad. Upon it is the palace seal belonging to the library of Sultan Murat himself. I do not know how it was removed from there and how it reached you, but it contains very valuable writings and magnificent miniatures."

"Read some of it to me, Antonio," commanded Pope Julius.

Antonio began. He summarised some of the couplets describing my childhood schooldays when Leyla and I had started loving one another. They discussed my story for close on two hours, with Antonio showing the miniatures to the Pope as they went along, and they took great pity on me. What affected the Pope most was my encounter with Leyla in the desert when I found her living in my own inner world. His Holiness was no stranger to such feeling. He attached importance to man's ability to find what he seeks within his own self. He expounded on this frequently in his sermons and spoke of the need to emphasise love.

"Fuzuli's poetry is as beautiful as Signorelli's frescoes," said Pope Julius after listening for some time.

"We have very few poets of our own who can describe so well what I have heard." He waved his hand in the air mournfully, as though drawing an ellipse, and squinted. As the last rays of the sun filtered through the window and dissolved against the walls of the hall, he continued as though remembering a far off land. "I daresay, Eastern peoples convey their emotions through sound, while we convey them better through colour. Protect this book well and show its miniatures one by one to the masters in our workshops for them to examine."

I was registered in the Pope's personal library as *Leyla and the Lunatic* whereas they should have logged me as *Leyla and the Madman*. At least this is how I would have wanted it to be. Lunacy implied being affected with madness, whilst I preferred madness to lunacy as the term mad described an insane lover more closely.

My physician Antonio had a high opinion of me and attended to my pains and treated them. He was careful with my appearance and aesthetics, talking to me from time to time, remembering certain scenes from his life as he paused between my couplets, and reliving them. He was my new master. For about five years, I went like a slave wherever he took me and rushed to his service each time. I did not know what was happening in the Ottoman lands at this time. What I did know was that Rukal's memory became slightly more faded in my mind each time and that my Leyla began to dissolve my soul with all the magnificence of her love. Previously, I had embraced Rukal as Leyla and now Leyla was smiling at me with Rukal's clear countenance. How terrible loneliness is, especially loneliness in foreign lands where no one speaks your tongue. Was it Leyla Rukal or the dark-haired girl on the banks of the Tigris whose hand I smelt? I confused the two. I demonstrated all the force of my love through silence and thus tried to protect it. By bearing witness, I saved my love from being forgotten and was able to pluck something from every object I saw and every incident I heard. There were even days when I withdrew from the library and from Antonio and consoled myself with colour.

In those years, there were four great painters in the service of Pope Julius IV: Caravaggio, Annibale Carracci, Rubens and the German Elsheimer. I visited the studios of each of these painters and saw how they treated their students and how some of them curried favour with fatuous noblemen. I watched how they educated their pupils, how they explained the correct way of looking at things when approaching colour. Just like Eastern mystics, they spoke of objects and things as having a soul, and how the beholder had to be cognisant of this.

I bore witness and learned how to be silent, how to watch and how to observe. Observation was wonderful. I watched with amazement the way in which colours spread, not on a tiny page like the miniatures on my pages, but across easels, canvases and walls extending for many metres. I was rather amused at how everything that exists in nature, and I mean everything, was portrayed without being changed or stylised, but exactly as it was. Sometimes I could gauge whether one artist had painted a portrait with greater success than another, and sometimes I would compare and contrast a still life with a seascape. "If only Rubens had been in Istanbul and had painted a portrait of Rukal on one of my pages," I used to say. "And if only her face resembled Leyla's, then my longing would not have grown so great." And then I repeated, "If only..."

I might have found entertainment in the world of colours except that I felt so far from home and hardly anybody knew my language. And Rukal was not beside me, nor Leyla, the dark-haired, jet-eyed girl of the Tigris. I missed her so much. I knew not who the 'her' was, but I missed her greatly...

I grew weary of seeing the priests in their dark robes consulting the gloomy library space. I found relief in roaming through the painters' world and became enraptured by the harmony of colours. Father Antonio would sometimes leave me in the artists' studios so they could steal ideas from my miniatures and use them to paint the walls of palaces and villas. I would travel with the great masters to magnificent houses in the countryside. I could not help but observe the idyllic life that the artists pursued. These artists seemed to me to be slightly strange. Perhaps it was the artistic sensibility, but I still had difficulty making sense of their attitudes. Or rather, it was as though they derived some kind of pleasure from astonishing me. Their beloveds were not like Leyla, for instance. They painted the women they loved in a bawdy manner and had no qualms about treating all the women they encountered as their lovers. Here, men and women were very comfortable in their interactions and did not hesitate to drop a curtsy or a compliment and speak of mutual love at the first encounter. The church did not tolerate such behaviour and people did not find the opportunity to understand the nature of love nor its philosophy from acting as if they were in love with each another. There was one among them in particular who was a great womaniser. I will keep his name to myself. He could not resist declaring his love to noblewomen when painting their portraits. It was not as if some ladies did not scold him – Antonella Layla was one of these – but it was known that he generally seduced aristocratic ladies so that he could portray them in lubricious poses. What is more, he even doubled his fee when presenting to their husbands paintings showing them in lewd positions. The man's indiscretions reached Pope Julius in the form of rumour, but the Pope chose to ignore them because he valued his art and also because he did not receive any complaints from the noblemen. When he once invited the man to confess his sins, the artist related one of these episodes in detail and angered the Pope. But, in general the literate public was tolerant, considering libertinism intrinsic to poetry.

This is why the painter had memorised a great deal of poetry. When painting pictures of half-naked women, he could recite verses describing their breasts, hips and slender waists. Nevertheless, one day when spring-kissed branches filled the gardens of the Vatican with the colour of white lilies, he found himself reciting long stanzas in a lush valley and secretly shedding tears for the loneliness he felt within.

During the years of my stay in Rome, I saw that poetry without rhyme was recited freely and that it was highly valued by the aristocracy. But in Istanbul, words only had worth if they rhymed, and words without metre were not even called poetry. As a result, all great utterances were framed in a poetic format.

Here they had a written genre they referred to as the novel. The loves that Oriental poets related in their *mesnevis* were here written as novels without rhyme or meter, like books of science. The novel demonstrated a lack of privacy whereby the roofs of houses were lifted off and the reader was led right inside bedrooms. Poetry is the form that ascribes all sensation to the heart and so it has kept its nobility. The novel is disclosure, while poetry is a wound and exposing wounds only increases pain. Where my master Fuzuli comes from, what is romanticised is either a tale of love or else the life of a hero. Both kinds of subject matter contain many lessons for the reader.

For me, the novel was a diversion for the bourgeois. While the poem describes the ideal, the novel reflects what is ordinary. The novel can offer much to a society shaken by class conflict, but why should there be any need for the novel in a state which has solved all its problems? Poetry sufficed. A poet in Istanbul could cram all the emotions of an entire novel in a single couplet which would still enable the reader to experience all of these emotions through the window opened between two verses.

What might be reduced to a couplet in Istanbul could be presented in volumes here. Here the word was uttered as mere talk, there it became eloquent speech. Here expanding and there abridging was important.

Rome also taught me the legend of Romulus and Remus – the twin sons of princess Silvia and the god Mars. The story of Romulus and Remus was repeated at temples and theatres as well as circuses, public baths and market-places. Silvia reminded me of Rukal, so I was particularly attached to this legend. In the story, Amulius usurps Silvia's place on the throne. She strives to protect her babies, just like Rukal. She weeps like Leyla and sets them adrift on the river Tiber. Hearing the cries of the drifting twins, a she-wolf finds them and suckles them. Rome is the city founded by these two children and history without Rome is unimaginable.

Of course I also learned that Rome had evolved a particular form of government based on ancient Greek models and had later adopted the religion of Christ. It was the epicentre of a once great empire. The benefits and the burden of administration were felt by all its inhabitants.

Rome represented the white race and its dominion spread from Spain to Egypt, from the Baltic to Asia Minor and Mesopotamia. Over hundreds of years, Rome absorbed hundreds of states into her territories. The Ottoman State now occupies many of Rome's former lands and it dawned on me then that this was why Anatolia was referred to as "*Diyar-ı Rum*" or Land of the Romans and the sultan was called "*Hakan-ı Rum*", Ruler of the Romans. It seemed relatively easy to assess the strength of sovereigns here, whereas to me, each of the Sultans was a state unto himself.

I also came to associate Rome with dungeons and leprosy. Many of those imprisoned were Muslim sailors captured in the Mediterranean. Prisoners could never expect to die quickly or painlessly. Priests and their henchmen discovered special techniques to ensure they suffered so much agony that their souls would be cleansed; if the wretches lost consciousness, they would be revived by physicians and subjected to further torture. Here instruments had been devised to fold victims in two and three and to break all their bones, starting with their back. Everybody has heard of the St Andrew cross onto which prisoners were spread-eagled. Iron maidens, spiked ankle cuffs, razor-sharp spears, hooks for carving flesh from bone and clamps for crushing skulls and many other types of torture device was to be found here...

Prisoners died here on their torture blocks at every hour of the day. At night, I would be awoken by the cries of inmates and mistake them for the wailing of babes. The screams of prisoners as their iron shoes were screwed ever tighter sometimes reached far into the buildings. One could then see priests smirking with satisfaction. The screams coming from outside the city walls and the agony of the starved lepers would descend like soot through the chimneys of the city's houses and fall into its pots and pans.

Villagers bringing flour, honey and milk to market might stop to listen to the forced confessions of women and men whose reported intimacies made them slaver at the mouth. They would watch the condemned being burnt alive as their souls were cleansed from sin. I myself saw many sinners tied to crosses and planted upon piles of logs. There were also hundreds of captives who had their ears and noses sliced off because they would not reject Islam. They too faced the stake. On one occasion, the weather was windless and close and the stench of burnt flesh hung over the city for days so that people could neither eat nor drink.

Rome was a separate civilisation for me, with its good and bad. I tried to pass the time feeling the joy of colour until, one day, all the paintings clouded over. I found the Babylon Society by my side.

I liked the painter Elsheimer from the first day I saw him. But in time this fondness gave way to anger. From the very beginning, he was interested not in my miniatures, like the others, but in my couplets. I learned during my second winter in Rome why he had begun learning Turkish and the reason behind his increased attention to me. He now knew the Ottoman alphabet and could understand my language.

One evening, with the public execution of 11 prisoners following what seemed like crazy festivities in the city square, I felt him shudder as he took me home instead of returning me to the library. Then I realised what lay ahead. No one can imagine what I felt upon seeing the image of the Tower of Babel that he had painted across the entire wall of his house together with the dagger my master Fuzuli had buried beneath a mulberry in Baghdad.

Could this house and this city be the new headquarters of the Babylon Society? If so, then the hill upon which the Society's observatory would be built had to be somewhere nearby. Maybe the seven members of the society met here every seven years. If they did indeed meet here, then what did they discuss? Why had the Society members still not removed the tablets from where they were buried and resumed their scientific studies? What harm did they see in this? Did they think that scientific progress had not advanced enough? If that was the case, what were the real responsibilities of the seven people who were the members of the Society? What did they seek when establishing kingdoms and condemning certain nations to ruin in some places or re-ordering the world's political balance? Considering that all of them were in positions of great power, why did they sometimes choose to travel disguised as beggars or merchants? What did it signify when they were grand viziers or kings?

As I pondered all these questions, I lost all the assurance I had previously derived from thinking that the dagger was still buried in Baghdad. Now I felt like a lost child.

Maybe the Society had found the dagger long before, but since they did not possess the saffian strap on which the numbers and letters were written, they were reduced to deriving the secret signs amidst my pages. This meant that if the Babylon Society members ever managed to determine the couplets pointing to the cipher, they would tear me to shreds or perhaps burn me and scatter my ashes so that I would never fall into the hands of others. But why was I in Rome rather than Istanbul? Why had the Society removed to papal territory instead of staying in my homeland? Was Istanbul no longer ahead in science and economics? The suspicion occurred to me for the very first time.

Three men were seated around a set of silver candelabra. Having greeted one another by placing their hands, with two fingers clenched, upon each other, they were burning incense with a ceremonial air and offering prayers. Strange to say, when they began to examine my pages with excitement, I felt myself ready for a new adventure.

As far as I could make out from their discussions, it had been very hard for them to follow my track. For years, they had sought means of smuggling me out of the Ottoman palace. They had made plan after plan to protect me from the ploys of the treasure hunters inhabiting Istanbul's out skirts and had shed blood, their own blood for my sake. Fate had now brought me to their table. They raised their glasses to celebrate the occasion and seemed overcome with elation. They set about examining me from cover to cover, acting with utmost caution and discretion so as to avoid notice whilst they searched for the numbers forming the cipher.

The connoisseur evaluating the information before them was an Austrian merchant. "Our task is a difficult one!" he began in his deep baritone. "If the poet Fuzuli knew the secret from the master librarian, then he would definitely have written it somewhere in this book. We have examined all the books he wrote after this and have not come up with anything. In terms of its method of narration and style, this book cannot be differentiated from the hundreds of copies made by practically anyone who could read and write. In that case, poet Fuzuli must have encrypted a cipher somewhere within this book itself."

"Let's have a look at all its pages," said the Venetian physician. "What if it was written using invisible ink as a watermark?" Bringing three large candelabra to where they were seated, they held my leaves up to the light one by one and analysed them. They could not see Leyla's lip marks but they did discern some letters they likened to the Chaldean alphabet scratched with a willow leaf blade. Had they known that my paper was coated in *ahar*, then they would not have gone to so much effort. They could have erased my paint, colour and ink from whichever section they wanted by wetting their little fingers. They decided it was pointless to subject my paper to further analysis and turned to the poppy Rukal had left on my bosom just before she died. If they had heard my cry when they crudely dampened a soiled rag and began ruining my flower, they would have realised that the bigoted massacre they had perpetrated was not worth all the treasures of the world, much less of Babylon. I realised that their dark ignorance came from iconoclasm. Those who once destroyed church icons must have been comparable zealots. Rukal's blood began to spread across the page with the rubbing of the wet rag and I thought that I was going to die. Whilst watching helplessly, I felt like embracing the memory of the woman I loved. I wanted to drift off into eternal sleep, never to wake up...

When they had finished picking apart, mishandling, pinching and squeezing me, and were still clueless, they began reading. Elsheimer summarised his findings.

"According to the reports of the meetings prior to the six rites in Istanbul" – by rite he meant the meeting that was held every seven years – "our predecessors supposed that the strap to be wrapped around the dagger's hilt did not represent actual numbers and letters. Since Fuzuli recorded the hieroglyphs as though he was drawing and the master saddler later embossing these upon the belt without taking pains with his work, the marks forming the letters allowed for different readings.

The parchment that was the actual strap is, as we all know, long gone. The sole solution is to determine the numbers hidden within this book. According to what we have established at previous meetings, Fuzuli encrypted the cipher in the couplets wherein the word love is mentioned. There is no special reason for this, other than the personal significance the poet places on love.

Perhaps this is because the master librarian told him that there were seven true secrets for the one who knows love. The specific word love is mentioned in 66 couplets in this book. When the numerological value of this number is calculated using the Arabic script in the manner employed by Eastern mystics, it is equivalent to the word 'Allah'.

Previous investigations have shown that common code words are not placed in all the couplets on love, while couplets containing such words as *secret*, *hidden*, *concealed* and *news* need to be given greater attention. It appears that Eastern masters before us deliberated a lot on love. However, Orientals do not realise that we now understand love. They have a complex culture of love. This is why we must begin this task by attempting to understand love like them. They approach love from several aspects: metaphorical, divine, esoteric and sensual. The love that the poet of Hilla esteems, however, flows in a platonic stream. There is also an Oriental concept called *gönül*. It denotes what we refer to as heart, but is something entirely distinct. More that an object, it is an attitude, an abstraction rather then anything tangible. It appears impossible to accurately describe such love except amongst the followers of Muhammad. They do not describe it either, but live it, as love becomes manifest in the inner soul, and rises and sets in the inner soul. The love and sensual relations we know of in Europe are merely one version of Eastern love, its basest version even. Beyond this, there are seven layers of love.

Love is such a sickness that the stricken derive pleasure from it and do not seek to be saved or cured. It creates such anguish that the loved one desires more and the lover never wants to heal. The sufferer does not seek deliverance. This kind of love is what makes seemingly difficult things easy. It alters innate temperaments and natural inclinations. There, the word 'lover' is an adjective and 'beloved' a noun. Knowing the name of the beloved is sufficient to both love and give one's life for its sake. The lover is forever nourished by the pains of longing, sorrow and separation suffered for the sake of the beloved. He cannot find peace without pain, without sleepless nights. Hence, in the East, lovers are known as the shepherds of the stars. Their eyelids instruct the clouds, their eyes become projected onto the seas. They give their lives for their beloved and wish to be revived only to give their lives once again. They do not want partners in love and have no equal when it comes to ruthlessness towards their rivals. In this regard, the destruction of cities aside, they can bring ruin to ruins over again. They have such people of love among them that these individuals incessantly add new interpretations to the views of such famous Sufis as Ibn 'Arabi and Rumi. They seem to multiply love by degrees, as though wanting to produce a separate work from their every sentence.

As their love increases, their ever more exaggerated feelings are transcribed. Whole volumes and libraries of knowledge on love have been produced in the East. If they had spent all that effort on medicine rather than on trying to define love, they might even have found a cure for death."

Elsheimer could undoubtedly have explained a great deal more to his friends. They listened to him intently. Until then, they had never imagined that love could be this profound. But Elsheimer had undertaken extensive study of the subject because he believed the Babylon Society ciphers were somehow hidden in love. He was right in this too.

"Our predecessors, who examined the book from beginning to end, stressed these two couplets," he said, indicating the pages in question. "The first of these is the couplet describing how the love of Kays and Leyla first emerges while they are still at school, where it remains secret.

Raised was the veil of the hidden lover
Love became the companion of censure.

The other couplet runs thus:

Pray, mother, what is the meaning of love?
Do render this hidden arcanum known.

This couplet follows Leyla's response to her mother's rebuke for loving Kays. Leyla's words are, 'I know not that secret love, what thing it is, but tell me so that I may know whether that in which I find myself is love or not.'

Now, the common characteristic of these couplets is the allusion to secrecy and love. That is, the idea of concealment has been emphasised. I suspect that while the poet was apparently juxtaposing love and concealment to indicate that love needed to be hidden, he actually aimed to show that he had hidden the secret here."

"In that case," interjected the Austrian merchant with excitement, "Let us search for other terms pertaining to concealment in the couplets which speak of love."

At that moment, I thought my day had come. This was exactly what my master Fuzuli had formulated. The thought of using the words concerning concealment as his cipher had occurred to him when he separated the dagger and the papyrus strip and hid them in separate places. In the past, other members of the Babylon Society had identified these verses without singling out their significance. They had just puzzled over the calculation of their numerological values. Now, as they reflected on the words denoting concealment, these men had come a step closer to my secret.

Elsheimer began to re-read the book in great haste from the beginning. "Yes! Here is one more," he exclaimed, jumping up from his seat and reading out aloud.

Where there is love, there is no secret
One within love cannot come to rest.

The term for concealment here was "secret" and, once more, I shuddered. This couplet was my 607th couplet and the first of the ciphers was derived from this number. Previously, code-breaking members had overlooked this and had set to work on couplet numbered 617, the second cipher. Who would ever have thought of going back?

Elsheimer was a very intelligent man. His logic and political understanding were equal to his art. He was well-versed in the philosophy of history as well as in politics. With his qualities, he could even be the grand master of the Babylon Society and re-establish the research committee. Like all other members, he was ready to sacrifice himself for the Society's lofty ideals. He produced research drawings and astronomical plans quite apart from his paintings. In memory of Arshiya Akeldan, he felt obliged to protect and regulate the Earth and cosmos. There was no doubt that he would have sought love and mystery among my couplets when retiring to his mansion that night, and that he would have succeeded in decoding the cipher which had remained a puzzle since Fuzuli had set it. But his servant knocked on his door at the most exhausting hour of the night when insomnia is most unbearable, only to announce that His Holiness had fallen ill. An attendant bearing the consul's summons was waiting at the door. From the front courtyard could be heard the whinnying of horses and the sound of a stable boy trying to hush them so as not to wake all the residents.

"Did he have to choose this time of night?" Elsheimer grumbled and inwardly cursed the Pope. He handed me over to his Austrian colleague with the following instruction.

"Hide this volume and retire to rest, dear friend. When I return, all will be revealed!"

But Elsheimer was only able to return exactly three days later. The ceremonial garment he wore when going to call upon the dying Pope was soon caked in mud and blood and torn all over. I have no doubt that he was never able to forget the horror he felt the moment he entered. Everything that breathed – the cat and parrots included – had been hacked to shreds and force fed to the others. Parts of their corpses were scattered around the rooms. The intruders who had burst in while he was away had entertained themselves by laughing at the screams of the women and children whom they had locked in one room. Having forced the Austrian merchant and Venetian physician to talk, they had killed them and then looted all the gold and silver.

I learned much later that, from that day on, Elsheimer poured all his pain and suffering into his paintings. He hired Rome's three most formidable knights to help him find and punish the treasure hunters who had seized me from my hiding place. He captured all the boorish outlaws, one by one, had their bodies pulled to pieces in the dark of night, but was never able to find me again. As it turned out, the thieves handed me over to Father Giovanni that night, one of the Cardinal's private secretaries. Not even my former physician Antonio knew that I had been imprisoned in his cubicle until the day of my departure from Rome.

As I awaited my fate, all I heard was Giovanni's constant refrain. "What a marvellous plan it was! But I shouldn't have rushed! I should have taken into account that it would take Elsheimer a long time to decipher the codes."

I can say that the most exciting of my days in Rome in the following years passed watching the Ottoman galleys and galleons coming and going off the coast. This city took my Leyla from me, but gave me a world that I would never have known in return.

The day of the official opening of the Quirinal Palace marked exactly five years since my arrival in the Vatican. That day, the rulers of all the Catholic states were in attendance and Pope Julius wanted to promote Father Giovanni to the post of chamberlain. I left the priest's room for the first and last time the following day. The priest wished to present a gift to the Pope in return for the great honour bestowed upon him, and thought that this needed to be me. But what he did not know was that the Pope had seen me before and had even had some of my couplets recited to him.

While celebrations were being held as magnificent as any Rome had ever seen, Giovanni the priest was beheaded in a vault. Rome made merry that day and the next and the streets were pungent with the smell of aniseed. The people found so many crazy amusements for themselves that they forgot their three daily prayers.

The Pope and consul members felt unsettled when the bell-ringers forgot to yank their heavy ropes. I was present in the hall where they met to formulate an emergency action plan for Rome's future. This was the hall where I had met with Pope Julius IV on the first day I was brought to the Vatican by Yasef Navi, when I had spent the night in his compassionate arms. St. Peter's Basilica could be seen from the window and the affluence of the Habsburgs spread from the ceilings and walls in the form of colour. The majority of those present thought that the splendour which drew my attention was about to come to an end. Rome was doomed and had lost its former strength.

The rising star belonged to the Turks and today, beneath this gorgeous ceiling, the Ottoman threat needed attention. I gauged from the discussions that Rome was mired in problems, one of which was the direction of relations with Istanbul. As a mark of good will, they decided to send envoys to the Sultan for the thousandth year of the Hijri calendar which began when the Prophet Muhammad left the city of Mecca for Medina. After all, the mother of Sultan Mehmet III, Safiye Sultan, was felt to be sympathetic to the Christian cause. Just then, Pope Julius remembered me and ordered me to be taken as part of the tribute. Safiye Sultan and perhaps her son Mehmet knew my verses and would be pleased.

I did not know whether the excitement inside me was due to the thought of returning to my homeland or the joy of reuniting with Leyla's memory, but I was never as happy as I felt that night. I had come to Rome in a poor state and living in this climate where I was not understood had wearied me further. I had learned that silence and observation were virtues, that witnessing increased reality and knowledge exacerbated pain, but I had suffered much longing, much anguish, much torment. What had I missed in Istanbul? Would there be something other than bitter memories awaiting me? Of course not. But there was Istanbul.

I could not decide whether what drew me to Istanbul was Leyla's love or my destiny. Happy 1,000th Year!

17
Was this the Union of one Drop with the Sea or a Pirate Battle in the Mediterranean?

It is not easy to discern the stationary from the moving,
The seafarer supposes the seashore to walk.

Koca Ragıp Paşa

Watching a ship glide past when gazing at the shore is like delving into a mystery and becoming lost. In this season the Mediterranean was increasingly petulant. Alternating between still waters and howling south-westerlies and north-easterlies, no sea could have been as enigmatic as this. I gazed in admiration at the waves because I was going to Istanbul, indulging in idle reverie and daydreams. It has been close to two days since the journey began. We had left Messina and Sicily behind.

Our galleon, bedecked in decorative flags, was protected by a flotilla of oared galleys and cargo boats arrayed in crane wing formation. We felt secure from attack by crusader pirates because the ship was the Pope's private vessel and we also felt safe from Turkish attack as we carried a letter of friendship and gifts for the Sultan. But Barbary pirates had also appeared in the Mediterranean of late and, on top of that, the seamen spoke of attacks by the Knights of Malta. We passed Malta unscathed. In any event, every ship may pose a threat and when the identity of a vessel is authenticated, it is either too late or else the language spoken from the gun deck at close range comes to the rescue and the ship is freed.

The big fish eat the small fish. It has been thus for centuries. A great many pirate ships sail under false colours and it is only after exchanging signals and assessing whether or not the message is understood that it becomes clear if they are friend or foe. A vessel that is close enough to read signal flags poses great danger in any case.

I was with my friend Antonio, who had been appointed special envoy by the Pope. Like me, he was in a flutter about seeing Istanbul once again after all these years. He harboured in his heart the bitter-sweet taste of his days in the palace and the Enderun imperial inner palace school. He was filled with memories of his youth and hoped to meet old friends.

As for me, I was bereft of even the slightest hope. My memories lay in the city where I was headed, but my loved ones were no longer there. Would my destiny and dreams coincide or would they collide? I knew not. I fell into reverie, rocked by the sea in the smaller of the two cabins on the galleon's poop where the navigation equipment and maps were stored. Antonio was taken up with vomiting everything in his stomach into the shaving bowl to which he was firmly attached. Next to us was the deckhouse and in front a small space allocated to the helmsman. The look-out on the main mast changed every four hours. When the wind was too intense and the rain lashed down, a trained monkey took the place of the look-out. I was utterly amazed by how these monkeys peered into the distance, shielding their foreheads with their hands, and the sounds they made upon sighting ship or land.

In the navigation cabin, on the shelf above the small chair, which could only just accommodate one tallish man bending his knees, were rolled up maps, and on the chest to the side were astrolabes, compasses, coal and steel rods, sextant and quadrants. The quadrants and astrolabes, in particular, determined our bearings and route in accordance with the positioning of the stars.

Antonio was taking medicine of chamomile root for his seasickness. Whenever he came to himself, he pored over maps. He looked at the geographical guide that Ptolemy wrote in Ancient Greek in the 1380s, the world atlas that Battista Agnese had prepared for the Pope 12 years previously, the Turkish maps the Knights of Rhodes took as booty when they captured Barbaros Hızır Hayrettin Reis' brother Oruç, various maps of the world as well as smaller atlases. He examined illustrations of Mediterranean ports seized from pirate ships, large-scaled maps produced by Arab seamen, drawings indicating ports and lighthouses, code charts of the signals enabling maritime communication. In short, he studied everything in the cabin. This quantity of maps was not normally carried on board every ship as most captains know how to draw maps and navigate from compasses. "I wonder," I said to myself as I saw this wealth of maps, "If there is a copy of Piri Reis' map of the Atlantic Ocean among these."

Yesterday Antonio spent the whole day trying to memorise the alphabetic counterparts of the triangular, square and rectangular signal flags on the code charts. He wanted to understand the messages sent from ship to ship so he could be sure the captain was navigating faithfully. Antonio had developed such an interest in nautical matters that I kept hoping in vain that he would succumb to romantic sensitivity when, like yesterday, he gazed upon the white foamed waves in the night-time and read from my master Fuzuli's verses the scene where Leyla talks to the moon of her love. He studied maritime law in between his spells of nausea while I daydreamt.

As for the seamen, they seemed totally unconcerned by us. Were it not for the sailors bringing provisions and the shipmaster who visited to take one of the maps or navigational instruments and replace it with another, then one might have assumed that they had forgotten us. Fortunately, I was entertained by the sight of the look-out monkeys being flung about rhythmically in the crow's nest; I wondered at their long arms hanging down before them and how they kept watch by shielding their eyes with their hands.

Antonio examined each of the illustrations on the maps indicating land masses. He spent hours poring over pictures of flags and people, looked at mythological symbols, regional boundaries and areas of sovereignty and the symbols representing different lands. He studied the pictures of dark-skinned men in Africa extending their heads out of tents pitched by mountain ranges, surrounded by wandering lions and slumbering monkeys. He looked at fortresses in Anatolia with men in janissary uniform carrying green flags. He saw pictures of camels in Egypt and around the Red Sea, castles in Spain and France, large crosses, cedar trees. He spent most of his time studying the two elements that remained unchanged on all these maps and illustrations on vellum: these were the compass rose and lines drawn on the neck section of the leather, and the images revealing the religion of the author. Needless to say, maps with depictions of Mary and Jesus were drawn by Christians and those with crescents and Qur'anic verses were by Muslims. If Antonio had been aware of the Babylon Society and if he had known about the golden statues of the Babylonian deities, the Sirrush-headed dagger on one of the maps would definitely have attracted his notice. He would then have ceased studying the other maps and focused entirely on solving the riddles on this deer hide. He might even have deciphered the cuneiform script beneath the map, which read, "Protect this in the name of Arshiya Akeldan!" I understood once again that what was destiny for me was ignorance for others.

I thought about how ungenerous life aboard a foreign galleon was. Here, even words are very stark. Sailors here do not show their love and sorrow like on the ships of the

Orient. And yet so many things occur to the heart at sea. It becomes possible to enter a fairy tale or pass into a land of happiness through the fortieth door when watching the moonlight twinkle on the sea. One can delve into dreams accompanied by the fierce or unruly, placid or caressing sounds of waves. What I would have given to explain all this to Antonio, to remind him again of my adventure with Leyla and even enable him to form a friendship with the warm air of desert nights and the lucent waters of these seas.

I was going to Istanbul, but I realised that I was not happy on this journey. I suddenly felt myself in a strange country far from home. It was as if I was overwhelmed by unease following the sun setting on the horizon and rapidly sinking into the sea. I was going to the palace once again, this was true, but Rukal and my other loved ones were no longer there. Perhaps I would regain my standing with the Sultan and vizier and other illustrious members of the court. Perhaps I could continue seeking my Leyla if the name of my master Fuzuli was still remembered, but I felt a burning anguish in my bosom. This was the pain of separation... Separation, whether from Leyla or Rukal, remained unclear. Life was like a sad dream on a rainy afternoon. The full moon appeared and disappeared amidst leaden clouds and the wind increased in strength. The sounds of the sea were like poetry. Dawn approached and we neared Modon in the Pelopponese...

"First oarsmen, prepare to give way!" commanded Captain Jacopo Maggiolo and the monkey standing sentinel began screaming wildly. The masthead lights of three ships had appeared and disappeared off Modon. These ought to have been Maltese galleons. It seemed likely they had followed them out of sight, carefully controlling their speed and course in the waters off Malta. Night attack with no illumination was one of the preferred methods of the Knights of Saint John though it was considered the greatest ignominy by most pirates.

Antonio went up to the deckhouse to be near the captain. The Knights of Saint John inhabited the island of Malta as a church community and were feared as the most savage pirate fleet. Seafarers in these waters had been terrorised by them for 50 years. They would set up garrisons on islands to perform missionary activity and hold maritime trade to ransom to support their colonial settlements. They put Muslim prisoners to the sword and sold Christian captives into slavery to bring in an income for the church. They established a maritime college in Malta and enjoyed dominance in the Mediterranean after Barbarossa. The only adversaries they shied away from were the ships of Sultan Mehmet's Commander in Chief of the Navy, Murat Reis the Elder. They would attack any vessels apart from these for booty, regardless of whom they belonged to.

They had received intelligence that the papacy was sending tribute to the sultan in celebration of Islam's 1,000th jubilee. As usual, they disguised their ships as Arab carracks, hauled down their flags, hoisted Portuguese colours in their place and bore down on Maggiolo's galleon.

Maggiolo wanted to gain time by sailing with the wind behind him so he waited for daybreak. He could have tried signalling to explain that he sailed with a sacred purpose. After all, the journey did have a sacred objective for the papacy. By presenting these gifts, the Pope sought to maintain peace with the Ottomans and, perhaps by taking advantage of Safiye Sultan's native allegiances, ensure the release of 500 prisoners from Ottoman prisons. As tribute, he was sending his personal three-decked galleon. On board were various species of horse, specially trained falcons, gazelles adorned with anklets, mature silver-collared greyhounds, and 20 damsels along with 20 young men to present them. When they appeared before the Sultan, they were due to bear trays laden with gifts: I would be reunited with my old friends upon one of these trays.

Captain Maggiolo did not want to put these gifts at risk or involve the galleon in a skirmish. In consequence, he decided the galleon would continue on its course for Coron and the escort ships would stop the knights or hold them off. As the day began to brighten, we could see the three papal ships and two Maltese vessels burning in our wake. The Modon villagers had gathered on shore to watch. The screams of those clutching at floating timbers could be heard. The sole Maltese vessel left unscathed was busy gathering the wounded.

Just as Maggiolo took a deep breath and shouted with joy that the remaining ship was in no position to attack on its own, the real threat revealed itself. The knights had more in store. Just as they had planned, Maggiolo steered his ship into the waters off Coron. Now, he was unprotected and helpless in the face of the 13-vessel Malta fleet. We floated all but stationary between the red hats.

Together, Maggiolo and Antonio made the joint decision to surrender. They would avoid conflict and when their vessels were hauled in to Malta, they would explain the situation to the cardinal and try to save themselves.

Instead of turning back to Malta, Maggiolo's ship advanced towards Crete, surrounded by its new cortege. Darkness approached and the Morea peninsula could no longer be seen. I do not remember what happened that night. I remember only the darkness of night pierced by Murat Reis the Elder's cry, "Attack the infidel! Forward! Come on, my wolves!" It was hell on the sea. I do not know how much time passed: I was oblivious to what had happened and what was going to happen. I let myself go in the midst of war whilst embracing the vision of Leyla...

18
How old Memories were kindled and my Heart burned 1,000 times in a single Moment

Those who took a piece of love from my beloved and gave it to me, then in return, took my soul and gave it to the beloved.

İzzet

Under cover of the grey clouds, Murat Reis had sent out the burning caicques to set fire to the ships of the Knights of Malta. "For God we vow to fight for the faith!" he had urged his men. Maggiolo was left with no room for manoeuvre except to take evasive action to avoid catching fire. Afterwards, we apparently reached Istanbul towed by the Ottoman fleet. Even nine shots of cannon fire which tore the sides of the ship in the waters off Sarayburnu were not enough to wake me. The brass astrolabe had fallen on me and I had lost my senses.

I began to regain consciousness as my pages started disintegrating and I was revived by the smell of my old memories. Yes, I recognised this garden – I had spent 40 years behind these stone walls. I came to myself again in my old home, feeling the wind of the stone pavement. It took me back to the cool banks of the Tigris and I wept. I was in the Sultan's presence and as the military band played in his honour, I was gnawed by the pain of the pivot nail of the astrolabe, which had fallen on top of me and pierced my skin.

No one but me saw Sultan Mehmet's eyes well up with tears as he kissed the picture of the peony on my bosom. Nobody else heard him whisper in a plaintive yet manly tone, "Rukal, if only you had known how much my father loved you! And I know the truth – they killed you!" The Sultan believed that those who had killed Rukal had been prompted by jealousy. As he held me, he did not know about the Babylon Society or how what had befallen Rukal was in part my fault. If he had done, he would have received me very differently. He would not have spared a bitter smile as he kissed the ring on his finger. I was happy when I saw the diamond on this ring: it was one of the three diamonds that Rukal carried in her talisman the day she fell overboard. "So my dear Rukal's body did not remain in the sea," I thought to myself with relief.

I loved receiving both the Sultan's kisses and did not feel jealous of Rukal for the peony or the diamond. These were the fifth lip imprints to join those of the Leyla that I had left on the riverbanks of the Tigris. Five partners felt love through the image of the peony that Rukal had drawn with her blood, yet there could be no partners in love. Was it at all possible for the lover to share their beloved? Was there room for two loves in one heart? Two guests did not behove such a house.

I reflected that these people, who were to each other unknown – Leyla, my master Fuzuli, Rukal, the Lawgiver and Sultan Mehmet – were all devotees of the heart who truly understood love. The image of the peony had turned into kisses of love warming my forehead like sunshine. After a long interval, the Sultan turned away from memories of time long past. His gaze wandered among the imperial scribes and settled on a pale-faced old man. "Mehmet Bey! My namesake!" he called to him. "You once presented us with an illuminated *mesnevi*. Allow us now to offer to you a Leyla & Mecnun *mesnevi*. My forebear Sultan Süleyman formerly gave this

volume to his concubine by the name of Rukal. We thought that we had lost it, while it appears that it was busy travelling across sea and land. It is now back in our keeping, but it is not proper for one whose privilege in our palace has been severed once to enter our private sphere once more. Take it and invoke blessings and prayers as you read, both for the poet Fuzuli and for our household."

It was only that day that I learned that it was traditional for one who has left the palace for whatever reason to be denied re-entry again. I cannot say that I was not upset by this. Still, after my five-year stint in cities where no one but Antonio could speak my language, my spirits lifted at being presented to Hakani Mehmet Bey who was known for his unique poetical sensibility. My last memory pertaining to the palace was of the Sultan's mother, Valide Safiye Sultan. She watched the Pope's tribute being presented to the Sultan, and embraced one of the young girls presented to her as a gift. When leaving the Sultan's presence, perhaps she was thinking of the childhood she had passed in Corfu and the name she carried back then, Baffo. Clenching the three fingers of her right hand – to whom she was gesturing I could not tell – she renewed her allegiance to the Babylon Society. Her son had shown great delicacy in inviting her to the reception ceremony of the Venetian ambassadors who came to offer their friendship. But he had not presumed that she would leave the Council chamber with tears in her eyes.

It was like being born again when the 1,000th year jubilee celebrations began.

There were naval celebrations along the water's edge. The festivities that were to last 40 days and 40 nights in honour of the princes' circumcision ceremonies had begun. My sole objective for the time being was to visit the walnut tree in which I had spent the night with Rukal and to relive those mournful hours. I am afraid to say that no one took me there and my longing was like a knot twisting in my bosom.

Hakani Mehmet Bey was a gentleman of the Imperial Divan in the complete sense of the word and a true Ottoman poet. He was charged with taking the minutes at Divan meetings where all kinds of administrative and political issues were discussed. I cannot say that he had much time remaining to recline on the cushions of his own home, but he had compiled his own collection of poetry. There were times when he wrote *gazals* on the pages of his collection which were almost as beautiful as those of my master Fuzuli. He was said to have been, at one time, as mad as he was brilliant at writing poems. Everybody who mentioned him cited this for some reason. Until about two years previously, he lived in lodgings allocated to imperial scribes near Edirnekapısı. After he wrote his distinguished Hilye-i Saadet wherein he described the spiritual and physical beauty of the Prophet Muhammad, our Sultan wanted to reward him with honoraria. However he deemed such a fine work as having a value beyond all price and turned to his viziers. "What then, may it be inquired, is he in need of? May this be granted to him!"

The viziers held a council and questioned the poet. "Ask of us whatever you wish!" they said. And what did he reply? "Forgive me, but I will seek the honoraria for this book in the Hereafter from our Master Muhammad himself. Anything I receive in this world I will consider a paltry price indeed!" Insistence was of no avail and a cabinet crisis erupted in the palace as they pressed him anxiously to ask for something. "How will we inform the Sultan? It is the Sultan's decree, it cannot be declined!" they said. Mehmet Bey was adamant; he wanted nothing whilst the viziers demanded he ask for something and were about to subject the poor man to a beating.

"Everyone might as well be contented," he conceded. "I have grown rather old and if he must confer upon me his favour, then it is true I suffer great difficulty when going to my home in the rain and mud. Let me be granted permission to ride a horse." "It is done," they responded. "We will purchase a horse for you immediately!" Only this time, the Commander of the Janissaries raised an objection saying, "The rank and credentials of those who may travel within the city walls on horseback are set. This is the order of things and protecting this tradition is incumbent upon us. Such a break with tradition cannot be allowed!" Now a second crisis erupted, this time about protocol. In the end, a house was purchased for Mehmet Bey on the rise leading from Sirkeci to Cıgaloğlu Sinan Paşa Pavilion, and his belongings in Edirnekapısı were moved there within two days. As a result, all the viziers heaved sighs of relief and informed the Sultan that his decree had been fulfilled. Whoever makes mention of Hakani Bey nowadays refers to this strange episode.

Mehmet Bey was very pleased to have received me as a present. When giving thanks to the Sultan, he related that he had previously read from the Persian *mesnevi* of Genceli Nizami, which told my tale, as well as another manuscript version. He would be honoured to possess a manuscript like me that was gilded, contained miniatures and bore the palace seal. He took me home and celebrated by treating his household to special *hulva* sweets. Then he set to repairing my damaged binding and my head and tailbands that had been pushed out of place.

The Bahçekapısı and Imperial Palace could be seen from Mehmet Bey's house. I found the city much altered. To start with, there was the new mosque and complex that the Sultan's mother had commissioned near Bahçekapısı. One of the minarets of Ayasofya was also under repair.

I spent many poetic years in Hakani Bey's house. As I listened to conversations on poetry lasting until the early hours and shared in the refined company of his fellow poets, soaking up the jokes when he entertained at home or welcomed wealthy guests to Ramadan iftar dinners, I recalled my old palace days. Watching the workers at the Yeni Cami, the New Mosque and at Ayasofya during the day and drifting off into reverie at night entertained me a good deal.

But my happiest hours in this house were spent musing dreamily as I looked out of the south-facing windows of the drawing room onto the outermost branches of the walnut tree in which I had spent the night with Rukal. I had often wondered whether the trunk of the tree in which we had hidden was still standing in the same way. Regrettably, there was nobody who took me there. The house had a maidservant called Dilbeste. Now and then, she reminded me of the beloved, the desert girl Leyla I left at the Tigris. I felt a strange pleasure on the nights when I delved into her auburn hair, her peachy skin and jet black eyes. She was 20 years-old at most. She had fallen in love with the gardener of the mansion next door to Ayas Paşa, but could in no way communicate her love for him. I knew that the young gardener loved her also, but due to his fear of the future, he would stop himself from looking at her despite the fact that he had the opportunity to do so when he came to the house every so often to deliver gifts sent to Mehmet Bey's children. His inner pain increased. But integrity was the greatest reference that servants could receive. Who knows how many lovers spent their lives without so much as winking at each other, merely indulging in idle fantasy?

During my time in Mehmet Bey's house, I did not see any members of the Babylon Society or any treasure hunters. I sometimes tried to reassure myself with the thought that they had lost my trail and were still plotting in the mistaken belief that I was in the palace, but I could not convince myself. It did not seem plausible that not a single one of these very powerful seven members of a society which could access even the most secret societies of governments the world over was not here in the Ottoman state.

As the days flew by in Mehmet Bey's house, I did not become booty for thieves on a dark night or end up in the dingy back rooms of dirty pubs. I did not enter church vestibules adorned with silver candelabra for a quite a long time and I never went to Galata. Hakani Bey steered clear of gatherings in which alcohol was consumed and this no doubt played its part. Even during the 1,000th jubilee processions of guilds and corporations where public order largely broke down, I did not spot the bejewelled dagger I had last encountered in Rome nor my master Fuzuli's flask strap. Nevertheless, I was afraid and perturbed on a number of occasions. The first of these involved a Roman villager who drew my attention among the believers who filled Atmeydanı after the celebration commemorating the birthday of the Prophet on the first day of the Ayasofya festivities.

This shady man following Hakani Bey was a masterly pickpocket who could steal the kohl from a man's eyes and the words from his lips. Until he changed course and decided to seek out a more well-heeled victim after realising that the old man he followed probably carried no more than a few coppers in his purse, I experienced moments of real dread. The man prodded the pennies in the purse, but failed to detect the gold hidden in my bosom.

A beggar who frequently came to our door gave me my second fright. He kept asking if there were any old books in the house and whether the master of the house, being an educated man, would donate any books as he loved to read. "He's probably trying to get information about the kinds of books kept in the house," I remember thinking. But he stopped coming after a few times. Once, a man stopped us at the Zindanarkası cemetery on Kasımpaşa's Sadabad road. His every manner betrayed drug abuse. Unsheathing his yataghan short sword amidst the deserted cypress groves and tumbling graves, he addressed Mehmet Bey. "Give it up, old man!" That day, Mehmet Bey had gone to visit the cemetery and, taking me with him, had wanted to read some *mesnevi* couplets beneath the cypresses along the ridges of Aynalıkavak at the tranquil hour when the afternoon sun sparkles on the Golden Horn.

The grave with a flowered tombstone that he went to visit was about to fall into ruin from neglect. This was the grave of the mother of a young man called Meyyitzade, to whom Hakani Bey gave lessons in Persian and prosody. Hakani Bey ascribed saintly attributes to this woman and he would visit her grave every now and then to recite the opening chapter of the Qur'an for her soul.

According to what he explained to his friends, at the time when the Ottomans fought on the Eğri front 17 years previously, there was among them a cavalryman in his forties whose temples were already streaked with grey. His mind turned frequently to Istanbul and he could not stop thinking about his wife, a fresh bride of just six months, and their unborn child. When joining the military campaign, he had nobody to whom he could entrust them and so, having said, "The decree is the Sultan's," he performed two units of the traveller's prayer, and beseeched God as follows:

"O Lord, my state is known to You. I have a feeling that my wife will give birth before my return from this campaign. I thus entrust my child to You."

But the soldier was mistaken. As soon as he left, the young woman fell ill and she died four months later, without having given birth. The villagers brought her to this cemetery and buried her in a corner. But remarkably, her unborn child was still alive. It was born a few days after she was interred and miraculously crawled to its mother's breast and started suckling.

How the infant found milk from the breast of a dead woman, suckled to its fill and survived in a dark world oscillating between sleep and crying astonished me also, to be honest. What is to be will be, it is said. Around one week after the burial, the imperial army returned from the Eğri Campaign. The returning cavalryman reached his home in next to no time, but it was all to no avail. The door was like a wall. When he learned of his wife's death, he was incredulous and kept repeating, "It cannot be! I entrusted my child to God! He would surely have protected my trust!"

His neighbours eventually showed him his wife's grave. That stalwart gallant with his fine moustache flung himself over the fresh grave and began weeping and lamenting. After a while, he was much altered. He stopped crying and laid his ear against the soil. What on Earth was that? The sound of a voice! What is more, it was nothing other than the innocent cries of a babe. He bounded up and yelled out to those nearby, "Bring me a spade and shovel! My child is alive down there!"

His neighbours scrambled to fetch him a gravedigger's shovel and the grave was immediately opened. An incredible sight met their eyes. A baby boy clinging to the decomposing body of his mother and suckling from her right breast. The astonishing thing was that while the colour and shape of the mother's body had altered and her hands and feet had begun to turn the colour of mint stalk, her right breast remained completely preserved. They took the infant and closed the grave once again.

The cavalryman, the woman's widower, had died two years earlier and Hakani Bey had taken upon himself the care and education of this child. He was an intelligent child with a clear countenance. I do not know his real name, but everyone called him Meyyitzade, meaning son of the deceased. Every so often, Meyyitzade demonstrated the respect and reverence he felt towards his mother's memory by breaking down in tears. I too witnessed this. On one particular occasion, Hakani Bey even said to him, "Look here, dear boy! May they bury you with your mother once again, upon your death, and may they carve a *kallavi* turban instead of flowers on your tombstone." It was implicit from this sentiment and prayer that he meant, "May you be a vizier in the future," as *kallavi* turbans would only be sculpted on the gravestones of viziers.

The hours passed and the twilight, which arrived even earlier in the dark shadows of the cypresses, spread a gloom around the graveyard. Hakani Bey responded to the statement, "Give it up, old man," by removing the purse he carried under his waistband. But the man held the yataghan to his neck. "More! I told you to give it *all* up!" This implied the ring on his finger, the diamond on his armlet and the bejewelled dagger hidden in his bosom, among other things.

When Hakani Bey gave these up one by one, I shuddered, thinking, "Here we go again! My dark days are starting once again. This wastrel is after me!" I thought. The man stripped Mehmet Bey down to his underwear, like one of the city's vagrants, forcing him to remove everything. He measured Mehmet Bey's flat shoes against his own feet, tossed on his woven vest from Bursa and wrapped his crepe shawl around his waist. When it came to his undershirt, the thief even made fun of the buttons. "So why doesn't a fellow like you get buttons made of mother of pearl on his shirts?" When his headgear was taken, Mehmet Bey said, "Ağa, leave me the kaftan at least, so that I can go home. Don't humiliate me!" The thief was no longer indifferent: first he laughed and then he said, "You're right, man! If your wife sees you like this, she'll think that you've come back from a night on the town. And your kaftan is no good to me anyway. If I wear it, I can't wear your reputation and, if I sell it, they'll get hold of me." He then separated the kaftan made of Damascus velvet from the other items of clothing. I was hidden in its lining. When he felt a weight in the kaftan, he stuck his dirty hand in the lining and said, laughing, "Here it is! This is what I've been looking for!" He began flicking through my pages. I will never ever forget that moment and the smell of that man's sweaty body. Within a matter of minutes, I became as tattered as though I had been at war for 100 years. He looked at my pictures, ogled the scene of my meeting with Leyla in the wilderness and dropped vulgar hints. "One of the treasure hunters!" I had only just begun to think when I felt my pages strewn about and flying like a compass rose. It turns out that the rogue was one of the outlaw dockyard drunkards and was making fun of us when he saw the book. When I struck Hakani Bey's face, I thought that my tailband would fall to pieces once more and that I would go under the knife again. I shuddered with pain at the thought.

Both of us returned home that night in a wretched state and Hakani Bey never again went to visit the grave of Meyyitzade's mother. By a strange twist of fate, about one month later, we saw the same dockworker this time seated backwards on a donkey belonging to Tavukpazarı's chief of police with a heavy log befitting the seriousness of his crime tied to his back. The town crier holding the donkey's reins was yelling: "Hear ye! Hear ye! Pay heed and draw a lesson from the predicament of this hell's bandit known as Cennetoğlu☞ who stole clothing from the temperate steam room of Akbıyık Hamam!"

Years passed in Hakani Bey's house. Bitter-sweet memories... I knew that somebody out there knew that I was here. But Mehmet Bey never realised that he was regarded as an innkeeper who served as my caretaker until the day came when I would be seized. He loved me dearly and I must say that I loved him dearly too. I was by his side as he breathed his last and even heard him say whilst smiling, "Faithful friends! What beautiful gardens these gardens of Paradise are!" I thus believed that the felicitous *hilye*, or Prophetic Portrait, brought him happiness in two abodes, and was overjoyed.

Days filled with poetry and love passed in Hakani Bey's house. However, throughout all those years I could not find my Leyla. I could not find a single trace of her but, every time I looked through the south-facing windows of the living room, with each quivering of the leaves of the walnut tree in the snow and the spring, in the summer and the dry cold, I could hear Rukal's voice trembling like a timid gazelle. I forgot about the Babylon Society and the treasure hunters, burned and became scorched by memories of love and lost my way. What beautiful days they were...

19
How Günter Kafir deceived Atai and Endless Longing burnt my Insides

Neither astronomer nor timekeeper can know the night most long
Ask the grief-stricken how many hours are the night!

Sabit

Everyone calls him Nev'izade. He is the son of Nevi'i Yahya Efendi who reached acclaim during the Lawgiver's reign for his poetry. His name, in fact, is Ata' Allah. Poetry, gilding, miniatures, science and Sufism are among his fields of interest. Owing to his ability, he was promoted to university assistant at just 18 years of age. With the backing of Şeyhülislam Yahya Efendi, who became the subject of gossip for ruling that tobacco smoking was not religiously prohibited, he had begun to teach in the Canbaziye *medrese*. When he came to the house to prepare the accounts for Mehmet Bey's estate, they presented me to him as a reward for his services. Two autumns have passed since the start of our friendship. He would meet with such poetry-loving friends as Ganizade Nadiri and Azmizade Haleti in his home in Sarıgüzel and they would talk about aesthetics, Sufism and the fine arts, frequently remembering my master Fuzuli with gratitude all the while and reading and memorising couplets from my pages. His was an enlightened, witty and jocular personality. He had been afflicted with the compulsion to read any book on which he could lay hands. He was in trouble of late with his weight and drank teas brewed with chamomile, fennel, Persian iris and absinthe; he also took frequent walks to the villages surrounding this city he loved so much, going as far afield as Çamlıca, Çırpıcı Çayırı and Küçüksu.

Atai Efendi's highest ambition was to write five separate *mesnevis* and thus compile his *Hamse*, or Quintet. He had already determined their titles: *The Book of the Cupbearer*, *The Breath of the Flowers*, *The Discourse of the Virgins*, *The Seven Courses* and *The Beauty in the Meaning of Precepts*. He had even prepared sketches for the illuminations he was going to place in these books and had secreted them in the hidden compartment of his trunk without even showing them to his wife.

Just as evening was falling a few days before the end of the fast, there was a knock at his door. Two janissary soldiers stood there holding a man by the arms. When Atai Efendi and this man dressed as a foreigner saw each other, the same look of astonishment was visible on both their faces. How closely their mouths, noses and big brown eyes above high cheekbones resembled each other. If a beard and moustache were affixed on the new arrival, he could have passed himself off as the resident; if the resident's beard and moustache were shaved off, he could have been the new arrival. The uniformed soldiers looked at one another in astonishment and stammered as though they were mocking him. "Apparently this foreigner is a relative of yours," they said to his amazement.

That night, they became acquainted with one another by candlelight until dawn, and told each other their stories. According to the mutually confirmed and completed sections of the two stories, Atai Efendi's great-grandfather Hacı Kemal Efendi had come from Ankara and settled in Malkara. He had a son by the name of Nasuh and had two grandchildren named Ali and Irza – which was actually Rıza. Of these, Ali entered the Halveti Sufi order and later became its head. Atai's grandfather was this Şeyh. As for Irza, it is said that around the time he enrolled in the cavalry of the province of Anadolu, he was taken prisoner by the unbelievers in the Lawgiver's German Campaign. Irza's tale, which was embroidered from hearsay and became the stuff of legend, was told frequently.

Now, the man standing before him and resembling him so closely, said that he was that Irza Efendi's grandson, that he came to Istanbul to seek his relatives as well as to conduct studies on Eastern folktales and then to write a book complete with illustrations. He was thankful at having found his cousin at last. I sensed something was amiss in this visit and that the souls of these two men, outwardly so similar, were not remotely alike. I watched carefully as this man, who attempted to act sincerely as he spoke, touched Atai Efendi as a sign of familiarity. He tried to increase his charm by emphasising his words with light contact and warming the air with the occasional witticism. But I saw these gestures were devoid of sincerity and instead denoted the behaviour of a trained secret agent who strove to make himself accepted by feigning foreignness. I did not have to wait long to see that I was not mistaken. At a point where he placed his hand on Atai Efendi's shoulder, I noticed that his ring finger and little finger were clasped into the palm of his hand. This was exactly the way Babylon Society members greeted Marduk. I had heard from Elsheimer in Rome, before his house was raided, that Chaldean spirits greeted foreigners in this way during the ritual for the moon god Sin and that they sought to leave an unseen impact on them.

According to Günter – and that is what he claimed his name to be – they were cousins though Atai Efendi had difficulty believing this. While finding an unknown foreigner coming to his home and claiming kinship somewhat exciting, he was also suspicious. However, acting with an earnestness beyond that of a cousin and more like a brother, Günter awoke his affection.

Günter related that, when his great uncle Irza Efendi was captured after the town of Liriz fell to the Germans, he was bought by the eldest of Ferdinand's interpreters and scribes, Sir David. Irza, the young, dark and handsome man faithfully served his master and thus earned the trust and affection of this elderly Jew with his good character. His good looks also won him the Jew's daughter. Before long, a wedding was held and not long after the celebrations, Günter's father Shimon Hasan was born.

There were many believable aspects to Günter's story, but if a sceptical mind had reviewed just a few elements, it would have been immediately apparent that the Babylon Society had conducted some rather lengthy and thorough preparations prior to sending him here. He had been taught Turkish to take advantage of his likeness to Atai Efendi, briefed about the structure and social life of the Ottoman state and schooled in the unwritten customs of Istanbul.

Following a few days' familiarity, Günter felt at liberty to pose his question. "Do you have the L&M *mesnevi*? The book written by Hilleli Mehmet Fuzuli?"

"I am currently reading the work of this master and admiring it very much," replied Atai, picking me off the shelf and stroking me as he did so. "This is the most beautiful tale of suffering written to date," he added. If Atai Efendi could have felt Günter's pulse, he would have definitely realised that Günter was about to faint the moment that he laid eyes on me. His hands shook when he touched my saffian binding. Who knows just how long he had waited for this and what hopes and dreams he had built up? Swiftly turning my pages, he stopped when he came to my miniatures and was as delighted as a child in a sweet shop. I could not at first understand why he looked at my pictures rather than my script. It was as though he was hoping to discover a treasure map among those pictures.

I could not decide from his behaviour whether he was one of the bounty hunters or a member of the Babylon Society. "Perhaps," I said to myself, "he grew tired of analysing the couplets and turned instead to searching for new ciphers among my illustrations – though it does seem a remote possibility." Only ignorant treasure hunters worked with maps and embedded maps in pictures so they would not be noticed. If this was the case, then Günter was after both the golden idols and the scientific tablets. Maybe he was seeking the gold for himself and the tablets in the name of the Babylon Society.

"I have been researching these miniatures on behalf of the Charles V Foundation of the Dresden Royal Art Workshop for the past five years and have conducted studies on the similarities between painting and miniature," he explained. He spoke in detail about painting, perspective and the tridimensionality of colour.

Atai Efendi did not have much else to do in the winter months other than teaching at the *medrese*, reading books and writing poetry. He and Günter spoke at length over the following days. Throughout the festivities marking the end of Ramadan, he introduced him to other relatives who came to visit. The way Günter pronounced Turkish and his patchy knowledge of the language which, he claimed, came from learning from his grandfather, made all the children laugh. The youngest boy, the house jester who impressed everyone with his sense of humour, had given Günter a nickname, just as he had for a great many others: he called him Günter Kafir or Günter the Unbeliever. He called him this partly because Günter had made him look uglier than his brother in a painting. Günter painted very well and the children took great pleasure in placing the paintings that he produced on palm-sized paper beside mirrors and looking at themselves. They competed with one another in this game and wanted him to produce a new painting of them every day. Günter was bored of this after a few times, but he did not object. He reckoned that his comfort depended on getting along well with the children of the house so, despite his weariness, he went on sketching, over and over, the noses, chins, ears and lips that he had now memorised. He even sought means of turning this into entertainment by sketching the children's portraits with his eyes closed. Astoundingly, he succeeded in this too. He could produce portraits of the three children in less time and with a closer likeness with each passing day.

It had been almost two months since Günter Kafir had arrived in Istanbul. He spent all his time sketching copies of my miniatures or else travelling the city and drawing maps. Among my miniatures, he studied the scene where, after I fainted in front of Leyla's tent, she laid my head on her lap and rubbed my face with rosewater. He copied it over and over again. This scene had a distinctive geography. There were tents, trees, a stream, mountains in the distance and the like, and Günter Kafir was looking for a map. He was adept at transforming my miniatures into actual, real-world locations. In his own pictures, he depicted the external world in the way in which he saw it, and he concealed these pictures from everyone, keeping them rolled up in his bosom.

Günter Kafir and Atai Efendi spoke frequently of painting, Istanbul's archaeology and the drawing techniques employed in my miniatures. One night, Atai Efendi let slip that he painted miniatures in secret. Günter Kafir immediately insisted that they work on paintings together. In this way, he could share techniques whilst Atai would teach him the subtleties of miniature. Naturally, his aim was to detect the map he supposed to be located in my miniatures. He said that the artistic flair they both showed was the product of the genes they inherited from their common ancestor Nasuh Efendi.

"Heaven forbid!" exclaimed Atai Efendi. "What value can there be in the exact imitation of nature when compared with spiritual pleasures and desires? Isn't an artist one who describes what he wants to see rather then what he actually sees, after all?" He was adamant in his defence of the art of miniature as against painting.

"Success is possible through likeness to God's creation," Günter replied. "The artist is an artist only to the degree that he is able to imitate God," summoning up all his expertise in ascribing partners to God. The debate was renewed whenever the topic of painting and miniatures arose. Atai defended the notion that what is called art needed to be sought outside what exists in nature. He said that what exists in nature can only be the handiwork of God and that imitating God's handiwork amounted to associating partners with Him. This was why stylisation was the basis of art in the works of Oriental masters.

Günter countered that Oriental drawings – which he saw as the distortion of space, likeness or dimension – made for unsatisfactory art. The artist should seek perfection and aim to capture God's perfect creation in the form of a portrait or a landscape. In contrast, Atai argued that true perfection could only be found in what came from the soul, so resemblance was actually to be found in abstraction. The two simply could not agree.

To Atai's mind, his cousin's obsession with using perspective was one day assuredly going to spell trouble for them in Muslim Istanbul, but they would have to wait and see. He even stipulated on this account that Günter not mention art outside the house. "If only he would run out of paper, then we'd be free of this painting nonsense," he would repeat to himself.

***

Günter Kafir forced Atai Efendi to study my miniatures with him in the flickering candlelight of long nights. The first pages they examined included the scene describing the day that Leyla and I first saw one another at school. Günter Kafir said that, according to the verse, the school should have been shown as a tent, whereas it was depicted as an Ottoman building made of stone. He said he had never seen a tent made with ceramic tiles or windows of *kündekari* woodwork; he also added said that he was surprised to see wooden floorboards and questioned whether the illustration could have been altered. Atai observed that although the story might take place in the Najd desert, the narrator – by whom he meant my master Fuzuli – or the illustrator would have adapted it in line with where he lived. This was quite natural, he said, explaining that love and art were always perceived in the same way in the East. "Just you wait," he said. "Further on, you will see rivers flowing and drooping willows!"

Günter indicated the single row of girls and single row of boys seated in formation, in front of the teacher's small lectern with Leyla and I at the very front. He wanted to know about the patterns on the floor and questioned whether there was a particular wisdom behind lining up the children thus. Then he turned to the colours of our clothes, the redness of the feet of the child in the foreground who had been beaten with a wooden spoon, the way in which the children held the books and, most importantly, the whys and wherefores of the way Leyla and I looked at one another intently. Perhaps he thought that he could discover the Babylon Society's codes herein but it was clear from everything about him that he sought a clue hidden somewhere on the page. Unfortunately Atai Efendi did not sense this. If I had been able to, I would have turned all of Atai Efendi's explanations upside-down and made Günter quite confused, but...

They discussed my miniatures for several nights on end, repeatedly re-reading and re-interpreting the couplets describing those scenes. With each reading, I felt my heartache deepen a little more. I also felt a sense of shame that my love for Leyla was being treated as if it were common to all. Günter Kafir viewed my illustrations with a cultural degeneracy far removed from understanding of my love and he had no respect for the privacy of my love. As for Atai, he said not what he felt, but what he knew, in his concern to answer Günter's questions. My master Fuzuli had written L&M not to be known, but to be felt and would have wanted it to be read from the standpoint of suffering.

I felt a shot of pain each time Günter Kafir pressed Atai Efendi to talk as if I had been wounded again. They examined one by one the drawings pertaining to my early youth. They looked at the scene where my late father asked for Leyla's hand in marriage on my behalf, the scene of my conversation with lions and gazelles in the wilderness, the day I was taken to the Ka'ba to turn to God in entreaty. They studied how Leyla and I were depicted alone together in scorching foreign lands and the moment when I finally covered Leyla's grave and sacrificed my body. Günter produced paintings and symmetrical drawings from his observations. Atai Efendi kept repeating that he had difficulty understanding him and that he could not make sense of his drawings. In fact, he was very curious indeed as to how Günter would relate these in the book that he said he was going to write but, for whatever reason, he never sensed that Günter might have any ulterior motive. Had he known that after those long nights of debate, Günter would retire to his room and attempt to render their findings in illustration by means of which he hoped to find the path to the golden idols, he would surely not have been at ease.

Atai Efendi did not concern himself with how this distant relative, to whom he had allocated the ceremonial section of his mansion, spent the day at home when he went off to school to teach, or what Günter did when he went out. In response to occasional trivial questions like, "So what did you get up to today, brother?" posed purely for the sake of form, Günter would relate how he had gone to one of Galata's synagogues for worship, had made some Jewish friends and spent time with them, and had thus assuaged his homesickness. One day Atai Efendi casually asked Günter to introduce him to some of his friends. Günter Kafir was delighted with the idea so they made plans; of course, he insisted he wanted to take me along.

A northeasterly knocking the fishing boats against one another greeted us as we left the city walls from Bahçekapısı. When we advanced from between the gardens and arrived at maritime customs, we exchanged greetings with the viziers who attended Imperial Council meetings as well as the Chief Eunuch, a soldier of the Imperial guard, some marble masons, carpenters and the Chief Imperial Architect who was supervising the construction of Safiye Sultan's New Mosque set amidst these gardens. Günter quickened his pace as though not wanting to be seen by them, prompting Atai Efendi to tease him. "Fear not, brother! Our dignitaries do not eat the flesh of foreigners," he joked, indicating his clothes. But Günter's fear did not stem from the difference of his clothing but from being addressed by the soldier of the Imperial guard.

We boarded a bumboat and, as we headed towards Galata, Günter Kafir said that he wanted to shed tears and repent at one of the synagogues because he could not stop himself from painting on the Sabbath. Atai Efendi wanted to climb up the Genoese tower at Galata to admire the view over the city if there should be time left after meeting with Günter's friends.

"In your opinion," asked Günter Kafir, "How many days would Istanbul's conquest have been delayed had the Emperor Constantine not built the walls of the Golden Horn in single thickness when he always had the city's outer walls built in double thickness?" Atai responded that he had never considered or been curious about the matter before, but for the first time he questioned whether this man really was his relative.

They could not see far around because of the sailboats and galleons on the Golden Horn as well as the European vessels crowding the port for months on end because they could not obtain the required internal passes due to customs fraud. What is more, filling the entrance of the Golden Horn to greet the passage of the imperial galley named *The White Gull*, which had only just been released from drydock, so that the Sultan could visit the Prophet's Companion Ayyub al-Ansari later that day, were several gondola-like rowing boats, some seven-oared vessels and caiques belonging to palace dignitaries and officials. The Sultan's galley was the very picture of sovereignty: by the time its milk white awning and matching paintwork could be seen at the tip of the Golden Horn, our bumboat had already reached Karaköy.

If someone could have read Günter Kafir's mind, he would have learned that he was quivering with excitement at seeing the Sultan for the first time, even if from a distance, and was awed by all the pomp and splendour. The presence of the Sultan made him believe that palace detectives and secret service men must also surely be nearby.

The afternoon sun had begun to lick the Istanbul horizon when the two cousins passed the Armenian monastery near Sulumanastır. Laboriously, they climbed up the ice and mud-covered hill, all the way up to the Gothic-style synagogue right beside the Galata Tower. Two monks suddenly lunged at them, presuming them to be strangers and Günter Kafir was sent sprawling across the ice so that his velvet-lined marten fur became caked in mud. Günter Kafir uttered a series of obscenities while Atai Efendi released a deep belly laugh. Curious heads popped out from the windows of neighbouring houses and local children joined in the merriment.

They arrived exhausted at the door of the synagogue. Günter Kafir began directing certain questions to the steward in a language Atai did not understand. The man's answers seemed to anger him as the conversation dragged on and his gestures expressed his bad temper.

"If only I had learned the language of the non-Muslims as I learned Arabic and Persian!" sighed Atai Efendi regretfully. In fact, Günter's anger was completely for show. He had no friends or acquaintances hereabouts and I was well aware that he had bribed this steward with a few Genoese gold coins to get him to play a part. Their argument was sheer mummery.

Eventually, Günter turned to Atai saying, "The wife of a congregation member has died and they have all gone to the funeral." He apologised that no meeting would take place and swore convincingly. "The old hag found the right day to die!"

Not appearing, frankly speaking, too upset about this, Atai Efendi said, "Then I'm going up the tower. See you at home tonight." He was not that curious about Günter's friends; he merely wanted to test whether or not he had been telling the truth and was convinced by observing the row with the steward. Günter felt reassured that he had successfully deceived his cousin and now he planned to kill two birds with one stone. "I'll join you!" he announced. Thus he managed to climb the Galata Tower at a time when foreigners were normally barred from doing so due to a recent murder. Atai Efendi's protests were in vain. "Look, brother!" he said. "A man sometimes needs time to himself. Right now I just want to go to the top and admire Istanbul to my heart's content accompanied by the couplets of L&M." But there was no escaping Günter Kafir's persistence. "Very good, very good!" he said in his broken Turkish, "I also draws picture!"

As they climbed the inner spiral staircase of the Galata Tower, having greased the palms of the fire wardens at the door, they again argued at length on the subject of pictures. As they neared the top terrace, they saw the windows and positions of the cabinets in which Chief Astronomer Takiyyüddin Mehmet had at one time placed his observational apparatus. Before building a new observatory at Tophane at a cost of 10,000 gold coins, Takiyyüddin had taken his measurements here: his was the world's third observatory after those of Arshiya Akeldan and Ali Kuşçu.

I never met with Takiyyüddin. This is why I always wondered whether he was one of the members of the Babylon Society. If he was indeed a member, then he had to have been aware that he was the only man who understood their work with real scientific insight. When Kadızade Mehmet Semsettin ordered the observatory demolished on the grounds that attempting to learn the future by attaining the secrets of astronomy would be inauspicious for the state, this must not only have injured his spirit, but his bones must also have turned in his grave. That is why I was as upset for Takiyyüddin as I was angry with Kadızade. What torment it was for a man of knowledge to live amongst the ignorant.

When I arrived at the top of the tower, I have to say that I was astonished by the scene that I beheld. Istanbul's vegetation, lush and green in spring, was now covered in snow and the city walls separated the blue sea from the white ground like a true map of the world. Facing us stood a paradise encircled by walls; the inner gardens were several times the size of neighbourhoods.

Should he rejoice or dance? Günter Kafir did not know what to do with himself before the amazing panorama below him. The sun was melting coquettishly, sprinkling fire dust on the snow from the ridges of the Golden Horn. Atai had scarcely placed his hand on me, intending to read another chapter by crying out towards the horizons of the sombre city before night fell, when Günter exclaimed, "Tell me! Tell me, how can a city be this beautiful and why is it so beautiful? Acquaint me with it! Tell me the city's secrets one by one! Show me its districts and its villages." As he made his requests, he was not thinking of the golden statues or the miniatures or even the couplets. He was giving voice to his rapture and aesthetic delight. He felt intoxicated by the poetry he saw before his very eyes. Even I felt fondness for a man who could be reduced to such childishness when confronted with beauty.

Atai Efendi attributed Günter Kafir's requests to his interest in landscape. But soon after he took out his scrolls, the small pieces of paper began to fill up with diagrams of Istanbul's walls and waterways as much as of its landscapes. Günter placed some of these, file by file, in his bag, and concealed others inside his boots, hiding them from Atai Efendi also. This is why Atai Efendi never saw the maps of the waterways or the sketches of the city's districts.

With his usual ingenuousness and benevolence Atai Efendi went on explaining. "Around the gates of the city walls are estates and mansions belonging to the city's most affluent citizens. Beyond, you can see the odd solitary house but mostly the houses are built in clusters to form districts. For instance, if the 10,000 horses grazing in Yenibağçe here, to the southwest of Edirnekapısı, were to graze for another 200 years, building a house here wouldn't occur to anyone. Especially Ağaçayırı, between Silivrikapısı and Yedikule" – as soon as I heard the name Yedikule, I remembered Rukal and felt a pang of sorrow – "and to the south, between the Samatya and Davut Paşa districts, Bostanyerleri, Langa Garden, Kadırga Garden, Cündi Square, are all places far too deserted to go unescorted. What is more, over the past quarter-century, people have preferred to build their houses in the Byzantine forums, which is illegal, instead of building nearby."

Günter Kafir thought of the exotic life behind the domes and minarets before him. He imagined the wondrousness of watching the sun rise after a blissful night of love with a woman.

"Now look here, brother!" Atai Efendi resumed. "Inside and outside the city walls are completely different worlds. All entry and exits are monitored and recorded. The janissaries mutinied in midwinter of last year in an attempt to depose the chamberlain and Ağa. They took matters too far and brought into the city the scum and vermin from outside..." He was rubbing and breathing onto his hands which were parched from the fierce cold. "They struck a match and set fire to the books. All this happened after they hanged the Jewish woman by the name of Kira and her two sons at the Yedikuleler, the fortress of seven towers you see here."

"Why Kira hanged?" Günter asked.

"For corruption, what else? This Kira woman apparently used to go from door to door peddling textiles. During the Lawgiver's reign, she came all the way into the palace and was the first to use Şemsi Paşa's bribes to promote officials to the highest posts in the state bureaucracy. In my teenage years when I was preoccupied with pimples, rumours circulated that she had acquired significant influence in the palace through Safiye Sultan and that she procured official posts for those who sought them in exchange for bribes. Back in those days, this Kira woman, was said to secretly shuttle love letters back and forth. My father used to explain how she recited poetry and relayed messages to those afflicted with love, that she pulled trick upon trick to unite crossed lovers. She was versed in the most beautiful love poetry and knew hundreds of *gazals* by heart."

As Atai Efendi spoke, a slight breeze blew up and began to scatter the snow on the ground as though it were snowing once more. Günter Kafir counted the districts and minarets. At first, he was curious about the little hill and the houses upon it that he saw from land between the sinuous extension of the city walls. Istanbul's districts were organic units with their own unique identities, formed around a mosque, a synagogue, or a church. Each district was alive; it grew, developed and even aged over the centuries. As the district was its own guarantor, all district inhabitants monitored their own people and instilled in them a sense of civic responsibility. In this respect, the district was like an extended family or a non-governmental organisation.

Atai Efendi shook his head and hands as though tired of speaking. He took me out of his bosom once again and said in his authoritative manner, "You go on observing, I'm going to read a little." Günter had fallen silent. Now I was watching the sun set on Istanbul in Atai's hands. And the first thing I saw was the dome of the Mihrimah Sultan Mosque on the hill in Edirnekapısı catching the last light of the sun. "Mihrimah Sultan had a mosque in Üsküdar, too," I thought all of a sudden. They say that the full moon of a snowy day is bright. I had seen the full moon there and it had risen right between the two minarets of the mosque. Had Atai Efendi noticed what I had noticed, he would undoubtedly have penned verses immortalising this vision with his poetic imagining. Mihrimah meant "Moon and Sun" and now, while the sun was setting over one of the mosques that the Lawgiver's benevolent daughter had built in Istanbul, the full moon was rising over the other. Suddenly I thought of Leyla. It was as though I saw her face in the full moon. At sundown, Atai was struck dumb with enchantment by my master Fuzuli's verses, Günter Kafir from the spell of this dream city and me from Mihrimah's time-defying inspiration. We did not know how much time passed. It was as though life had stopped in this old Genoese tower. "Here, in this city!" I exclaimed. With Leyla on my mind, I felt suddenly inspired. "Leyla ought to be in this city! If the sun and moon meet here, then night and day can meet here also; my night-coloured Leyla is manifest here." I felt all my fibres shiver and thought I sensed Leyla's warmth.

I woke from my Leyla reverie to the shouts of the watchman. "Enough is enough! It's about time you came down!" Atai Efendi was slipping me back under his sash and Günter Kafir was positioning the new topographical sketches that he had completed in line with Atai Efendi's explanations in the hidden section of his leather case. In this bag were stored panoramic drawings of Istanbul's residential layout, and plans pertaining to the city's war strategy. There was geographical information as well as diagrams of its waterways, which he had drawn, all as Atai described them.

As we returned home in the twilight accompanied by the howling of stray dogs, a sense of sadness descended on the city. Again, the wind chased the snow it lifted from the hills and trees, and the red smudges of sunset disappeared one by one off the windows of the houses. When we passed the janissary checkpoint at Bahçekapısı and began climbing towards Ayasofya, it was as though the cousins had no strength left to speak. I had been swept up by melancholy. I was chewing the crumbs of sorrow of my love for Leyla. I weighed up my condition. I liked Atai Efendi. We perceived and experienced things together. There were even times when we cried together. Leyla's tragic end had inflicted wounds on both of us and I was happy to find a fellow sufferer. As I spent time in the company of this witty and plump man, I fostered within me the hope of finding a way through his sentimental and romantic side and perhaps reaching Leyla. His family, his children and home gave me a sense of belonging for the first time since Rukal. The *mesnevis* that he wanted to write were going to be replete with my memories and perhaps I would find life once again in this way. The respect that he had for my master Fuzuli had already been a source of inspiration for the books he was to write.

But for the past month someone has come between us, ruining all this beauty: Günter Kafir. I had not liked him from the first day I set eyes on him; now I feared him. I was not at all pleased with the things he did in secret from my master who is the poet son of a poet.

And you, O daughter of the desert, Leyla! I am ready to fight against those who seek to tear you from my heart with armies the likes of Nawfal's. This city is so beautiful, and you would fit it perfectly!

Ah, if only I could find a trace of you!

20
How secret Servicemen swarmed Everywhere and my Secrets drifted into deep Sleep

There is no one without anyone, everyone has someone.
I have been left forlorn, come to my rescue, O Companion of the Lonely!

Ruşeni

Atai Efendi did not go to the university to teach on Tuesdays, but instead engaged in research at the library of the Süleymaniye *medrese*. There seemed to be no one left in Istanbul who did not know that he came home late on the days when he went to the library. He regularly held protracted discussions on poetry with his poet friends Ganizade Nadiri, Kafzade Faizi, Riyazi, Sabri, Vecdi and a few others. Depending on the season, they would take place either in the dark shadows of the sycamores or in the snuff-scented corners of coffee-houses.

Many a poetry enthusiast would cover the expenses of tea, snuff and coffee to win over the hearts of the poets just to be able to attend such gatherings. The places where they met were generally considered higher academies of poetry. I know because Atai Efendi took me with him on a few occasions. Here the Turkish *gazal* poets recited verses far surpassing in sophistication those of the poets of Iran. They deliberated in depth the need for innovation in the *kaside* and *mesnevi* styles. If my master Fuzuli had been present at such gatherings, he would undoubtedly have added extraordinary poetic dimensions and depths to the love he felt towards his teacher's daughter. Atai Efendi first held and embraced the idea of writing five separate *mesnevi*s here. He even swore an oath on it with Nadiri, and sealed the pledge by mingling blood.

On the Monday night after Günter Kafir hid in his boots the panoramic pictures of Istanbul he had drawn from Takiyyüddin's windows, which were themselves impregnated with memories of space observation, Günter Kafir obtained new information from Atai Efendi regarding my master Fuzuli's miniatures. He requested that I stay with him when the time came to retire for the night. When Atai Efendi raised not the slightest objection and withdrew to his room, I realised that being left alone with Günter Kafir for the very first time gave me indescribable distress. I do not remember ever missing Leyla so much or being in need of her closeness as much as I did that night. It was worse even than that fearsome night when I heard the screams of the prisoners tortured by the priests of the Inquisition in Rome, or the time where Rukal was dropped into the sea or the slaughter on that snowy night on my way to Istanbul from Baghdad. I had never been so afraid. I concentrated my existence on the flower that Rukal had drawn on my forehead with her own blood and the point touched by her lips and began to *feel* Leyla. The deep agony of separations built up within me and just as I was envisioning reunion with Leyla in Istanbul, the nightmares of new separations engulfed my heart. That night seemed to drag on forever and time lingered like a century.

The following morning Günter Kafir gathered up his sketches and paintings and, placing them in his bag one by one, he got ready to leave the house in the usual manner. When he began collecting the important items from among his personal belongings I realised that he was going to steal me too.

Reaching the Greek physician's house in Galata took us only two hours. The three individuals waiting for us in this room were none other than Günter Kafir's Babylon Society colleagues. One of these individuals was Prince Frederick's secret service chief, Dodge Staiger from Salzburg, the second was a Coptic hieroglyphics expert brought in from Cairo and the third was a chemist from Fener. If these men had not clenched their two little fingers and placed their fists on top of one another by way of greeting, I could have easily taken them for greedy treasure hunters rather than Society members. I judged from their discussion that the Babylon Society was now after the golden idols as well. Perhaps I was mistaken, as the Egyptian Copt was a stranger to the rituals and found Günter and Staiger's enigmatic discussions odd. Perhaps the Copt was just an expert hired to examine the writings. "My mission to Constantinople is over, O great Marduk!" Günter addressed Staiger. He stood there to attention for quite some time.

In the middle of the dingy and dirty room, where the dust danced in the light, stood a table with three people seated around it. They listened intently to Günter's words. "I am honoured to inform you of His Grace's gratitude, dear Günter!" Staiger said. After linking arms, he took him up to the head of the table and indicated for him to be seated. "So tell us everything right from the very beginning," he invited. At that point, the Greek physician had extended the snuffbox to the Coptic visitor. "Can I persuade you to take a pinch?" he offered.

"Atai Efendi really looks a lot like me, in both face and build," Günter started. "And, of course, like all Mohammedans, he readily believes everything. He was very well chosen for our objective. Stirring his interest for poetry and painting was enough to convince him that I was his cousin. I must admit that I was greatly affected by his love-steeped poetry.

Especially this L&M book!" At this point he lifted me out of his bag and laid me on the table. "Our poets do not know how to write such works nor do the Turks know their worth."

As he began to spread the drawings and paintings across the table, he said, "First I needed to earn the trust of my so-called cousin. I was very careful about how I settled into his home and learned poetry so I could obtain the necessary information. After the first week, I visited the Byzantine ruins, saying that I was going to the synagogue, and studied the waterways, sewers and rat runs. A wall even collapsed on me once."

An old man entered the room carrying a wine-filled ewer and four glasses. Until this man, apparently the owner of this decrepit house, walked in, I noticed that no one uttered a single word. All eyes turned back to Günter and he began relating the rest of his story in an easier manner. As he presented the items that emerged from his bag, he explained reverently all that he had done. "I prepared for you, Sir, Chief of the Knights Hospitallers' Ottoman Surveillance Team, these drawings to be presented to Frederick, the esteemed servant of our Emperor Charles V. But that was not my true intention, of course. I am proud to present to you, respected president of the Babylon Society, Marduk XVI, the work entitled L&M, in the serene knowledge of having served humanity's most elevated ideals. My notes here include the current budget of the Ottoman state, treasury and military information as well as descriptions of the waterways, tunnels and sewers beneath Istanbul city. This is the information you requested in view of shaping the future of the Society, Marduk, Sir. I can assure you that I have prepared these diagrams and maps precisely in accordance with the instructions of Your Worship. You taught me to carry coal dust and black ink in my sash and I saw the benefit of doing so when producing the panoramic sketches. When I paint these up in the future, this will form a complete Istanbul album. Tonight, I will have a comfortable night's rest for the first time since you, venerable Marduk, charged me with producing such an album for the Society and the Knights of the Universe. I will also prepare copies for the Dutch, French, Venetian, Italian, Spanish and Genoese branches. I hope that His Holiness will bless me through you, my venerable master."

Günter spoke while performing certain rituals which enhanced the ceremonial atmosphere of the occasion. "Incidentally, I must admit that there were also times when I was very afraid. I frequently asked myself what would happen if the Ottoman secret service, whose spies are famous even in our nations, established my identity and interrogated Atai Efendi. When leaving the house for the last time today, I was very relieved at having fulfilled my mission, and I pictured to myself the bewilderment that Atai Efendi will experience tomorrow." After this, they all smiled, as though wanting to restore an air of normality to the meeting. They raised their glasses in a toast.

The chemist assumed an air of distinction and began dripping certain solvents on my miniatures and smearing my colours. I felt faint from the smell. He was checking to see whether or not there was another layer of paint beneath the colours. But this man had no respect for his own craft. He splattered the solvent on my paintings with a ferocious appetite each time and blurred with brutality the delicate memories that were the labour of many craftsmen.

Under the gaze of four pairs of ravenous eyes, one hour proved sufficient to destroy my delicate paintings and smear my make-up into the script. So much so that on the open page depicting how Leyla and I came together in our youth, during that autumn which coincided with our last days of school, first my Leyla's dress was ripped apart through the effects of the chemicals, and then my heart. At that moment, I thought that Leyla's intimacy, which even I had not seen, the nakedness of her body, would be laid bare before these four pairs of foreign eyes. Under the effect of the chemicals, each painting on my pages suffered injury in a separate place: tents, trees, horses, camels, lion and gazelles, as well as the desert – all lost their beauty.

After the chemist's fruitless probes came the turn of the Copt from Cairo. He examined my writing and held his magnifying glass over those of my master Fuzuli's marks that he was able to liken to Babylonian letters and cuneiform script. He interpreted the marks that the reed pen had left on the paper and, when he could not find a resemblance between the curves of my Arabic letters and the wedge-shaped alphabet, he pricked the paper under my writing with the tip of a needle as though perforating my stomach. He focussed most on the words that contained the letters *alif*, *kaf* and *lam*, wanting to reach a conclusion based on their wedge-like forms. He would not stop piercing my script with his pointed knife.

Like the Sufi Mansur who is famous in the East, I felt I was being skinned alive. I was weak from all this mauling and battering. I realised at one point that I looked like a spy tortured to talk by having his nails ripped out or his skin flayed with nail-toothed combs. I was like the Roman slaves whose flesh stuck to hot gridirons and who were made to inhale ether. They would pass out and then be tortured again merely for their masters' sadistic pleasure. The masters would drink their wine and put on a show of strength for the half-naked women dancing around them.

If I could have done, I would have said, "You are mistaken, gentlemen! Read my couplets instead of hurting me! What you seek is found in love, not savagery!" But then I realised that, if these men had understood love, they would not have treated poetry and painting in this way. I could see that the Babylon Society was increasingly made up of abject individuals. When compared to the venerable Marduk Arshiya Akeldan and the obliging librarian with whom my master Fuzuli had become acquainted, these people operated like beasts of prey. This would certainly cause the Society to deviate from its objective.

The desired result can be obtained from a task approached with love, but every exercise undertaken with violence is fruitless; surely they could not have been ignorant of this truth? Or rather, those who were oblivious to this truth were, at most, treasure hunting bandits, not members of the Babylon Society. I was in no doubt that the Society had ceased being a club devoted to scholarship; now it was contaminated by greed. Perhaps the world they lived in required more money for scholarship and this is why they pursued their interests with such brutalities. Just as the current membership had forgotten the way to look at things, they had also forgotten the grace and courtesy of their old masters. They developed a violent approach to the created realm and had no respect for benevolence. I, who had longed for refuge with the Babylon Society against the treasure hunters, now dreamt of being sheltered by the treasure hunters instead.

In order to conduct a final check on whether my paper bore any watermark, the Copt from Cairo pierced four of my pages and copied some of the letters onto a separate leaf.

He then superimposed them on the letters upon the papyrus that he had brought with him and held it up to the light. He was obviously an expert in his field, but I rejoiced with all my hurt and agony, that I had taken revenge and his efforts came to nothing. I could not accept that they behaved like common thieves because they were too uncivilised to appreciate platonic love or understand the meaning of my couplets. "O Lord, do not allow the lofty secret that I carry to fall into the hands of these men!" I prayed. "Reveal it to those who deem knowledge sacred!"

The last of their investigations continued until the late hours. The department chief wrapped up the session saying angrily, "Following the advice of the master priest, we now need to hand over this work to his Lordship, the Paşa at *Kubbealtı*. We will have to inform him that our labours have been fruitless. The mystery can only be solved by understanding the meaning in the connections between the couplets. This now rests with him." He stuffed me in his leather bag showing the frayed temper of a bureaucrat who has to give up his authority to his rival, or a politician who has lost an election. I would be lying if I said that I was not curious about which Paşa he was referring to, who this member was who had risen to the rank of vizier of an Imperial Council.

When he handed me over, I presumed that they must have been congratulating themselves. "The fortress will be conquered from the inside!" they might brag as nobody could remove or steal me from the Society whilst I was in a vizier's house. "Perhaps it will be better this way," I thought as I tried to soothe my dejected spirits. "I will be safe until the true knights of the universe brighten the realm of science and my wounds have healed." I was like one of those unconscious patients who has just left the operating table.

The cold solvent, iodoform and ether that had blurred my colours still chilled me. The burning I felt within did not assuage this shivering. Long afterwards it occurred to me that – thank God! – they had not touched the peony on my forehead. They had not smudged my precious flower bearing the salt of my Leyla's lips and the bloodstain of my Rukal. All my fibres ached from chemicals and needle wounds. The agony of my condition burned my heart.

"So, dear brother Günter, tell us about these waterways and sewers," invited the Department Chief as he left me to one side on the table. Günter passed his finger along the spread of drawings and began eagerly. "These blue lines indicate the old Byzantine sewers and the waterways built by Sinan the architect." Just then the door opened violently. "Finally! Finally!" I shouted with my inaudible breath. What I heard were the voices of the men I presumed to be members of the Ottoman secret service. All Istanbul's inhabitants knew the man who yelled, "Don't anyone move!" It belonged to the steward of the beggars and behind him there appeared to be his apprentices dressed in beggars' guise.

The members of this secret intelligence network in the ranks of guards and footmen obtained information by begging. As soon as they had entered, they grabbed Staiger and Günter by the arms and immobilised them. The Copt ran to jump from the window, but a fortress commander leapt through the air and caught him by his calves. The chemist from Fener began stuttering, "I'm i-i-innocent!"

At that moment, I both laughed at and pitied Günter. I would have liked to see his arms droop to his sides like a merchant gone bankrupt after all his toil and exertion over the past three months. In fact, I knew that he carried a poison pill in his sash and I thought that he would use it when necessary. But he turned out to be too much of a coward and did not dare to reach out for it.

Last to enter was Atai Efendi, carrying his large trunk. My joy made me forget the pain of my wounds. The Atai Efendi whom I had taken as a simpleton had his own plan all along. Had I been able to utter a sound, I would have cheered and shouted out to all of Istanbul, "That's him! That's my master, Atai Efendi!"

In his air and manner could be discerned the justified pride of an old member of the Ottoman *akıncı* forces who had completed a noble duty for his country with ease. When Günter saw him, he lowered his head and my kind master did not utter a single word even then, only looking at his face as if to say, "You were never able to deceive me!" This glance even managed to convey the warmth of a three-month friendship. When he came and lifted me into his hands, I hoped that my prayers would henceforth be answered. I at once thought of entreating God to find my Leyla.

O Lord! Reunite me with Leyla as soon as possible. Keep me away from adventures that end in the bottomless pit. Reunite me with my beloved. It is only Leyla's love that keeps me in this city. Reveal to me, O Lord, is Leyla close or far away? Show me, O Lord, is my fate bleak or bright! If she can hear my voice, let her know that I love her. Be my witness, O Allah, that I love her very much!

21
How Nef'i Efendi's Life came to an End and Lagari Çelebi went to Space

I am a parrot who speaks miracles not palaver,
Converse with fate I cannot, as its mirror is not pure.
I cannot call those whose breast is not pure, people of heart,
There is no justice in people of heart not knowing each other.

Nef'i

It occurred to me just now that the Istanbul I have known over the past quarter century has never before experienced such complicated years one after another and has never before seen such a power vacuum. It turns out that the day I was smuggled from the land of Atai Efendi marked the beginning of the years of great misfortune for the state, but I only realised this later. First, when Sultan Ahmet's eldest son Osman II had been sultan for four years, he was dethroned at the age of 17. The following one and a half years saw unknown hands govern the state during the insanity of Mustafa who could not even bear the sight of women. I do not know if the Babylon Society played a part, but I now thought that they had the power and the wealth to dominate all the kingdoms on earth. If Murad's anger had not been so great, perhaps the Society could have instigated another janissary revolt; the Society would then have been able to maintain its influence in the palace in the ensuing power vacuum.

Murad IV seized the throne when he was only 12 years of age and he fell foul of the janissaries who had supposedly stripped his elder brother Osman of his good fortune and conferred it upon him, for long years to come. The janissary corps took a different approach back then and came to be rivals rather than protectors of the state. Everyone associated this with the plots and intrigues of recent times. Unfortunately, no one but me knew that all this rapid transformation was being steered secretly by Babylon Society members who spent heaps of money in their efforts to overthrow the state. They even reckoned they could manipulate Murad as they had other rulers and, when the Sultan bared his teeth, they changed their target.

As Murad grew up, he was transformed from helpless caged lion to a champion of great valour. All his childhood memories became associated with the persecution of his elder brother Osman and other qualified state officials, and he demonstrated that he had never forgotten those savage days of blood. He resolved on the need to assert himself as Sultan, and began by exacting revenge on the janissary corps. For two years, he raged like a storm and left nothing standing that could be considered a threat to his sultanate.

First he shut up his mother Mahpeyker Kösem Sultan in her room so that he was left as the only powerful player. The Babylon Society's dealings with the Sultan's mother had been proceeding rather delicately and she was not as sorry as the Society for the Sultan's new stance. Murad did not realise that, by stifling the Society's political ambitions, he had made himself a target. What frightened the Society and caused them to suspend their activities in the following years was Murad's order to execute in the main square the janissary leaders whom they had formerly incited and urged on to ransack even the Topkapı Palace.

Rebels and soldiers trembled as the name of Sultan Murad reverberated throughout the land. He adopted the policy of keeping soldiers at the headquarters of their local army corps instead of at their barracks so that they did not even have time to re-sheathe their swords. Thanks to a series of victorious military expeditions, the Baghdad Campaign first and foremost, as well as those to other regions, the Ottoman state was preparing for its second spring.

My friendship with Ömer Nef'i Efendi began in the Covered Bazaar and coincided with these years. Ömer Nef'i Efendi was a little irritable, but he was also a good-hearted poet. He had all the pride of a provincial who has scaled the social ladder. There were three things that he did well: praising others, singing his own praises and swearing. All three found an outlet in Sultan Murad's Privy Council where he was put on a pedestal for the satires he composed about statesmen. These satisfied the secret spite that the Sultan felt towards these men. In the time left over from military campaign, the Sultan convened councils in the Baghdad Pavilion which he had built in the palace garden. On Fridays, he gathered together scholars, then court singers and musicians on Saturdays and poets on Sundays for pleasant days on the green. It seemed as though he was set on consuming the stocks of alcohol and tobacco that he had banned to his people.

Nef'i Efendi was like the hors d'oeuvre on these occasions; he would make the Sultan laugh, entertain him, recite satires at his request and would receive honoraria in return. Being this close to a sovereign who was most renowned for the decree, "Off with his head!" scared him from time to time. But Nef'i Efendi's motto was, "If a person is not to live in this fleeting life as they wish, then it is better that they not live at all!" As a result, his life continued to satisfy his unfettered instincts.

Nef'i Efendi's behaviour and bearing were manly and, even when reciting poetry, he exuded this gallant air of being beholden to no one. While reading my master Fuzuli's *gazals* I felt that he, like all other poets, shivered on the inside, but in contrast to the others, Nef'i Efendi did not feel any envy towards him. When reading some of my master's couplets, I was even aware of him saying to himself, "I don't think this is how it is! I wouldn't have said this, but would have raised my voice!" Perhaps purely for this reason, I had a greater respect for this child of Erzurum than for my other owners. His love was not platonic and impotent. He enjoyed sensual pleasure. It was not as if he did not resort to certain metaphors in his descriptions of love, but he attached greater importance to the eroticism he experienced in the night hours with the concubines he secretly brought to his room and enjoyed alluding to these. I learned of very different expressions of sexuality here after the sheltered family life I had led in Atai Efendi's house. The lust-laden breath, perspiration, warmth and words coming from the wiry body of this dark swarthy man in his fifties, washed over the silver skins of the girls in their twenties and crushed, kneaded and shook those tender bodies. On the days and nights that I stayed in the bedroom, I pitied the old man and the young girls who spent their lives dedicated to sensuality. They were offended by my master's attentions and he unwittingly held me witness to his private doings.

Yesterday, I saw my previous owner Atai Efendi; he was reciting one of his *gazals* in the Imperial Council in a voice grown quieter. We ran into each other often after that day, but he does not know that I am so close and that I reside in the home of his friend Nef'i Efendi. However much I wanted him to discover this, this never happened. It was clear in his every manner that he no longer lived as he used to. I heard that he had begun his projected series and was very pleased.

Atai Efendi lived through a great many misadventures after the episode with Günter Kafir. During the janissary uprising when Sultan Osman II was mounted back-to-front on a donkey – as though he alone were saddled on the seat of revenge of all the Ottoman sultans – and paraded throughout the city, Atai Efendi's home, like a great many others in Istanbul, was set alight and looted. A Cretan docker stole the gold and silverware and the dinner sets in the kitchen and then grabbed me. He passed me onto a trunk-seller who put me up for auction at the Grand Bazaar for three *tümen*. This cheap transaction reminded me once again of my slave status. I had forgotten my servitude and become accustomed to living like a sultan.

One month later, when calm had descended on the streets of Istanbul and people slowly began going out again, Ömer Nef'i Efendi from Hasankale purchased me from an auction at the Covered Bazaar for exactly 32 gold coins, purely out of reverence for my master Fuzuli's memory. There was another keen bidder who kept cursing that he had only 30 coins in his purse and he was one of those after the gold of Babylon. The two members of the Society I saw at the auction did not bid, but this did not surprise me. It was enough that Nef'i Ömer Efendi's had bought me. I questioned for a long time whether my new master was a member of the Society and was only able to conclude several months later that he knew nothing about it. There were times when the Society did not want to get hold of me, but merely to know that I was safe. It sufficed that they were on my trail.

It appeared that life for me as well as for the Babylon Society returned to normal at those times when I was in the company of poets. Maybe they expected that the poets who were my new owners would stumble upon a set of ciphers whilst roaming through my couplets, and travelling in my environs. But they never thrust out a hand in my direction. When they met every seven years, they made their evaluations, determining whether they would solve the ciphers, resolving on new strategies and courses of action and acting accordingly. World wars, the balance of power between states and internecine struggles played a pivotal role in their strategies. They did not merely seek to decode the ciphers or obtain the gold, but to dominate humanity at the same time.

It was around the time I had gone under the hammer and it had been ages since I had received any news from Atai Efendi. However, I heard it reported that, during the uprising, his daughter had been raped and enslaved and that he now expressed his terrible anguish in his couplets. He had also begun to spend his days on the five separate *mesnevis* that he had always wished to write. Now, when I saw him sporadically, I could understand the extent to which pain takes its toll on human beings. The grief of losing a child was causing this man to melt away before everyone's eyes. I was crushed by my inability to wish him a speedy recovery.

If Ömer Nef'i Efendi had known that I belonged to Atai Efendi when he purchased me at auction, he would surely have reunited me with my former master and old friend. All my masters used to write on me, in the margins of my pages, on my covers or between my lines. Sometimes they recorded the births of their children, or the money they borrowed, or else the day they met with the Sultan, among other such things. They might sign underneath and I would be angered thinking that they had invaded my privacy. Now, I deplored the fact I had no written memento belonging to Atai Efendi, that refined and meticulous poet. I thought that even those *gazals* which others had written on my pages and which I had hitherto perceived as an imposition were important. I would reap the benefits of these in the future because they would mark out the people with whom I had formed friendships and keep my memories alive accordingly.

As time passed, these kinds of memories built up and I was beginning to possess quite a collection beyond the verses of my master Fuzuli which told my tale. So much so that I could count a convoy of those who spilled watermelon juice on me, left their fingerprints, impressed their seals or left unappreciative glances amongst my miniatures. The strangest was the multitude of rental and acquisition records. There was, for instance, "Rented from Cafer Efendi for ten days, at ten *akçe*s per day. Saraç Arif. In Ramadan 1011." This is because at the onset of Ramadan, Istanbul's refined families would seek me out or one of my other copies with great determination. They would read a few of my pages each night, offer commentary and, by reaching the end of my story, they would add to the erudition of their household in a great many respects. This is why I can state that the generations that were raised under the influence of my master Fuzuli's words built a civilisation of the heart in a region well-versed in love.

And did I mention that Poet Nef'i Ömer Efendi was a good person? If I do not tell you about the day that he enabled me to experience one of the most exciting moments of my life, I will not have repaid my debt of gratitude to him. I think it was after the revolt when Sultan Murat's flesh was ripped apart by Hafız Ahmet Paşa's janissaries and forcibly sold to the people of Istanbul under the pretence that the meat was good for leprosy and joint pain. Or perhaps it was during the days of mourning after the death of Musa Çelebi, who had become the talk of the town and the darling of all with the rhythmic cycle known as the *yürük semai* composed in his name by the Sultan himself.

Sweetheart who has set forth on a journey
My Musa tarried and did not return
Or else he has taken the wrong road
My Musa tarried and did not return.

Pessimism turned to hope, an era of joy took over from earlier sorrows and festivities were held in celebration of the birth of the ruler's daughter, whom he named Kaya Sultan. Nef'i Efendi was going to finish his work at the Office of Accounting early and go to the palace. It is not known from whence the idea came, but he took me too, extracting me from the drawer of the wooden desk among the auction goods. I was very excited. I was to return after 40 years to the palace from which I had departed in the 1,000th Hijri year in Hakani Bey's bag and, recollecting Rukal's memory, was to shed tears willingly and gladly for my sweetheart.

From its very establishment, the army of the Ottoman state adhered to two basic ways of life: *bezm* and *rezm*. *Bezm* meant "recreation" and it resulted in *rezm*; *rezm* meant "battle", at the end of which came *bezm*. Over the centuries, the Ottoman military state apparatus had changed. The Ottomans regressed in terms of battle prowess and advanced in cultural expression. Losses sustained in battle and pauses between victories did not slow the appetite for recreation. I was the best observer of this. Now I saw how the people of Istanbul flocked to forms of entertainment which would have been unthinkable during the Lawgiver's reign a century earlier, without deeming these strange. In places of amusement set up in central districts like Atmeydanı and Üsküdar, it was now possible to see women on swings. What is more, there were even janissary womanisers and naked hamam scamps embracing these women under the pretext of helping them off the swings. If it were not for the Sultan's management of violence, there would not have been any security of life, property or honour on the streets. As the citizens' fondness for entertainment increased, new forms of amusement were invented and everyone with a talent was afforded the opportunity to demonstrate it. Mime artists as well as the craftsmen's guild processions, jugglers and acrobats were replaced by other forms of diversion.

When the call to the afternoon prayer ceased, the musicians of the Imperial council at Sarayburnu, the palace residents were again preparing to watch a new form of entertainment. Lagari Hasan Efendi had made a seven-winged rocket he had made by wrapping 50 okka – or about 140 pounds – of gunpowder around his body and his helpers were about to fire it. He jested with the Sovereign saying, "Dear Sultan, I entrust you to Allah! I am going to converse with Jesus!" and began shooting skyward when the rocket was fired. Those present uttered frantic cries and embraced one another. Some of them cried out with joy, some in alarm and some in fear. Such a journey to space had not been seen until that day in any part of the world. Alongside the sophisticates in the Council were those who favoured obscurantism. They asserted that this was rebellion against God and that stones would rain down upon their heads.

The only one saddened for Lagari Hasan and also perhaps the only one truly rejoicing for him was me. I knew that intergalactic travel would be possible in the future in accordance with the information contained on the Babylon Society tablets. I was sad because a great many people had heard that the priests of the Vatican had punished a scholar by the name of Galileo. By Inquisition decree, they had burnt his books. People even accused the church of allowing murder in its name. At the same time, there were still ignorant supporters of Kadızade on Istanbul's streets, expounding the religion of Islam in the most bigoted fashion. I was pleased, as Lagari put on this show merely as entertainment, but he actually studied space sciences until the early hours of dawn, and spent most nights endeavouring to observe heavenly bodies in the observatory built by Takiyyüddin, without anyone else knowing. "Why does Lagari Hasan shun poetry like those engaged with science?" I lamented inwardly. If he had liked poetry even a little, he would of course have taken kindly to me and read me. Then, perhaps, he would have deciphered the secrets that my master Fuzuli scattered amongst my pages, read the tablets of Akeldan who had reached the same stage in space research that he himself sought and would have thus continued on his way.

Whilst everyone waited for him to be ripped to shreds in the sky, I did not feel any such fear. After reaching the top of his ascent, Lagari spread out the eagle wings tied to his arms and descended slowly to the waters in front of Sinan Paşa Pavilion. He swam ashore, and came before the Sultan, drenched, to report, "My Sultan! Jesus sends his regards to Your Majesty!"

Regrettably, Murad only gave him one bag of gold and the rank of cavalryman in the Ottoman army. The first statement that I would have said, had I been able to speak at that moment, would have been, "Illustrious Sultan! It is incumbent upon you to establish an academy wherein this man can develop his studies! This man carries my fate. Do not sell it for a bag of gold or you will have it stolen by others." But I do wonder what kind of response this would have elicited from Şeyhülislam Yahya Efendi. When the sovereign consulted him about having the ruins of Takiyyüddin's observatory demolished because it was a place of evil spirits, he responded, "May it be destroyed at once!"

It took a long time before clerics and statesmen became concerned with matters of science. In Christendom, laboratories, workshops, schools of engineering and colleges were established, whilst here the *medrese* system consumed itself with infighting and waging an age-old struggle to monopolise the book. Mosque pulpits were turned into arenas of reciprocally bigoted debates between the Kadızadeli and the Sufi orders. In line with the views of Kadızade, Mehmet Efendi, who mocked the Halvetis and Mevlevis with the words, "Harrowers of the throne, whistle-blowers," Sultan Murad took an interest in banning opium and tobacco. Scholars and Sufis preferred to insult each other rather than to engage in scientific debate and sprang readily at each others' throats. Poetry was ubiquitous in this region and there were poets who immediately produced elegant chronograms to record this historic event for Lagari. Some poets vied to have their works sold to the Sultan...

When darkness set in and the curfew began, Ömer Nef'i Efendi was about to leave through the Bab-ı Hümayun. He thought of playing a prank and decided to send Sülün Muslu and Bekri Mustafa a quatrain. So he began to wait. Among those leaving the palace who addressed comments at him and received an answer were my former owner Atai Efendi, the calligrapher and *hilye* artist Cevri Çelebi, Şeyhülislam Yahya and the former Şeyhülislam Bahai Efendi. There was also the professional urban storyteller Tıfli Çelebi, the *tezkire*-writer Riyazi, *müneccim* Mehmet Çelebi, the court singer Derviş Ömer Efendi, Hezarfen Ahmet Çelebi – who later jumped off Galata Tower with wings strapped to his arms and landed in Üsküdar, Doğancılar, who sought the Sultan's favour but was later exiled to Algeria – and the famous Cerrahi Şeyh Ibrahim Efendi. Last to leave the Bab-ı Hümayun, considered the last gate of the palace, were Aziz Mahmut Hüdai Efendi from

Üsküdar, and dervish Yetmiş Kuruş Dede, the close friend of famous drunkard Bekri Mustafa.*

Nef'i Efendi learned then that Sülün Muslu was to be a guest in the palace that night. When news that Sülün Muslu's body had been stuffed in a sack and fed to the fish from Sarayburnu rippled through Istanbul's streets the following morning, he wondered what kind of fault or disrespect Sülün Muslu could have committed to deserve the death sentence. He felt a chill and could not make out the cause. The ode that he had recited to the Sultan on the previous day came to his mind. Since being struck by lightning the previous spring whilst reading *The Shafts of Doom* at Beşiktaş Palace, Sultan Murad considered satirical and abusive poems to be inauspicious. Sülün Muslu had vowed never to compose satirical poetry again, but had been unable to suppress the ode he recited which dragged Grand Vizier Bayram Paşa through the mud. This lampoon was now doing the rounds of all the notables.

Nef'i Efendi had spent his entire life taking the bull by the horns. The people of Istanbul, from the youngest to the oldest, could not escape his sharp tongue. Anything gone awry or anyone doing something inappropriate would become the talk of the town as a result of his satires. Such was the impact that they would not be able to show their faces in public. In fact, he was honoured by the satirical poets and considered an antidote to those who proclaimed that criticism was forbidden in the Empire.

---

* [Translators' note: Bekri Mustafa, known as 'the Drunkard', is reported to have encountered Sultan Murad IV during one of the Sultan's undercover visits to the marketplace when the Sultan was disguised as a commoner, and is described by historian Demetrius Cantemir as the man who introduced the Sultan to wine.]

His work, *The Shafts of Doom*, was full of derision. Glancing at the names appearing in the pages of this book, it appeared that the leading figures of Murad's era, whether state official, commoner or artist, were on parade. The response that he gave to Tahir Efendi, who referred to him in anger as "big-mouthed dog" became so etched in the public consciousness that people could no longer accuse each other of being dogs.

Tahir Efendi has called me dog
His compliment is clear.
For I am of the Maliki Legal School,
And in my creed the dog is pure.

In reply, the famed Şeyhülislam Yahya Efendi arranged for him a supposedly laudatory stanza. It was recited in poetry gatherings for a short while and provoked the laughter of collective revenge.

Among the silver-tongued speakers of our day, there is no poet like Nef'i.
His words resemble the poems of the Seven Odes and he is the Infidel Imr al-Qays himself.

Beneath the surface of this seemingly laudatory verse lay latent ridicule. To begin with, these words had come from a senior cleric. If a mufti calls someone an "Infidel", this indicated that his subject had left the folds of the faith irrespective of how much the mufti might appear to be praising them. What is more, he likened Nef'i Efendi's words to the Seven Odes which were deemed words of unbelief because they were uttered during the Age of Ignorance. When Nef'i

Efendi replied in kind, this time everyone began laughing at Şeyhülislam Yahya instead. This was his response:

The mufti has called me an unbeliever
I will call him a Muslim.
When tomorrow we reach the Day of Judgement
We will both be proved mistaken.

Nef'i Efendi here paid homage to Şeyhülislam Yahya, "Mufti Efendi, while you have referred to me as an unbeliever, you are most certainly Muslim." But then he alleged that both descriptions would be shown to be false on the Day of Judgement. Herein lay his astounding witticism.

Nef'i Efendi finished his work at the accounting office at mid-morning one day and went to the palace, taking me with him. We were deep in conversation before the brazier, which filtered out the cold of the snow enveloping Istanbul. He had wanted to pour his heart out to a concubine and fall asleep in her lap the previous night, but the girl had flung his old age in his face and slighted him. In anger, he had bolted down a few glasses of alcohol for Bekri Mustafa's sake.

So he had woken with a headache and, perhaps to rid himself of his hangover, he sought solace among my verses and began to read my master Fuzuli's lyric words describing the adventure of my being taken to the Ka'ba. A feeling of deep longing and yearning for the Ka'ba awoke within him. He regretted that his life had passed in swearing and invective and thought to make a penitential visit to the Ka'ba. He read my couplets with this sentiment for quite some time. I was greatly affected as he wept whilst reciting the *gazal* where I pray at the door of the Ka'ba. We seemed to be conducting a duet as he repented of his past with a deep sense of servitude to God, and I remembered the old days dejectedly.

O Lord, render me familiar with the affliction of love
Deprive me not of love's affliction for a moment.

I was still afflicted by my separation from Leyla because I desired love's affliction at the threshold of the Ka'ba. My earnest entreaty in that sacred precinct was of course to be accepted by God, but now it was as though trouble were awaiting this man also. He was very sincere in his expression and asked for what he sought from the depths of his heart.

A short time later, I started with fear and apprehension when the courtyard door was slammed shut and I heard violent knocking at the door. Panic ensued in the house with screams coming from every direction and the place was turned upside down.

Everyone understood that this arrival was not a good sign. Grand Vizier Bayram Paşa's men forced their way in and took Nef'i Efendi away. They knocked him about and insulted him. Like the rest of the household, the servants and the concubine who had hurt his pride that night, I too understood that I would never see his tough and weathered countenance again, and I wept.

I learned later that he was strangled by executioner Arap Osman, in the firewood store in the palace on the order of Bayram Paşa. His body was thrown into the sea from Sarayburnu after the Grand Vizier heard the following couplet repeated in Istanbul's refined circles:

A parallel fell from the heavens for his Shafts of Doom
Nef'i incurred Divine damnation because of his idiom.

I recall that there were many people in Istanbul who prayed for him and many who cursed him. A legend later circulated among the people presumably to demonstrate his attachment to satirical poetry. While Nef'i Efendi was heading for death, the Chief Eunuch said to him, "If you so wish, I can write a petition to the Sultan and save your neck!" What else could he possibly say, with his hands tied? Nef'i agreed. The Chief Eunuch brought a sheet of paper and dipped the reed pen into the inkwell. After a few lines, a drop of ink from the tip of the pen fell onto the written section and smeared the writing. Nef'i could not help himself and said in jest, "Sir, your blessed sweat has trickled!" At this, the Chief Eunuch replied, "You dog, you deserve to die!"

Nef'i Efendi used rarely to take me outside. He screened the smell of spring and the colours of the flowers from me; what is more, he never allowed me the opportunity to seek my Leyla. However, his deference for my master Fuzuli, even if he found some of his poems a little too sentimental, was enough for me to like him. The excitement I experienced the day I went to the palace when my memories of Rukal were revived, was sufficient for me to remember him with kindness. I will remember him with the following classical quatrain. It occurred to him when Bayram Paşa's men began to violently beat at the garden gate and it fell not from his lips, but from his heart:

O heart! There is no decent man in this realm.
Even if there were, he has no confidant.
Suffer not if you are an intimate knower at heart
And hold that there is no world like this realm anyway.

This is what this stanza meant and it summed him up perfectly:

> *O heart! There is no decent man especially in this world. And even if such a man existed, he would be alone. If you are a wise man do not grieve for this world because there is no such thing anyway.*

22
How I travelled the World with Evliya Çelebi and became fed up with Life in the Silistra Citadel

O Lord, happy may they be who have broken my unhappy heart.
May those who wish for my hopes to be frustrated attain satisfaction.

Naili

I am Kays – the magnificent slave of my master Fuzuli. The lover carrying within him the secret of the sages and the Babylonian deities... Just as I had become used to peace of mind, having forgotten the Babylon Society during my time with Nef'i Efendi, they strangled him in the palace firewood store. Like Rukal, they dumped him in the waters of the Bosphorus leading to the Sea of Marmara.

When I left Istanbul, a jetty was being constructed measured from the Maiden's Tower, at precisely the point where both of them had been dropped into the sea. During these chilly days when October and November nurture what is known as the Old Woman's Cold, we grew weary and desperate in our galley. We were frozen in the ice of the Danube's Wallachian coast trying to ward off the fire-spitting arrows of a regiment of treasure hunters who were, of course, after me. I do not know how many seven year intervals have passed and how many times the Babylon Society has taken decisions concerning me. I have also forgotten how many times the snow has fallen since we set off on our journey and how many times I have watched the violets blossom. Now, as I winnow time alongside Zıloğlu Evliya Çelebi, I presume that Istanbul has grown old and that most of my acquaintances have gone to their final destination. Sorrow, in its entirety, is inside me...

I travelled in the small trunk that my dear Evliya took with him wherever he went. With me were a few *mesnevi* manuscripts, some books of history in Turkish, Greek and Arabic, maps, *ahar*-coated paper and plain paper, reeds awaiting pointing, carved bone pen rests, a curved cobbler's knife, ink and containers filled with thinned sand for blotting. The trunk was sometimes at the bottom, sometimes on top and sometimes on the back of his camel, or else he packed it pillion on his mule or horse.

The Jannisary Ağa who searched Nef'i Efendi's mansion after having him asphyxiated seized me along with a few other valuable works from the household. He offered me as a gift to Sultan Murad's daughter Kaya Sultan, and she in turn wanted to present it to her husband Melek Ahmet Paşa to please him. When the Paşa said, "I have already read this story!" I entered the leather bag of Evliya Çelebi who was next to them at the time. I can say that I began the happiest

travels of my life right on that day. Whilst days slipped into months, months into years and years into lives, I stopped over in the serene lands of Mesopotamia. These were my native riverbanks, the land of the dark-haired, dark-eyed desert girl. Even the mud bricks of my Leyla's hearth-stone had crumbled into pieces.

At times, mixing my tears with the Tigris on the banks of which I was born, I wept for distant memories. I must confess that while missing the felicitous day when I had been about to touch the lips of my childhood love beside the Tigris, I counted down the years in search of her familiar gaze. I took to the road and this time saw the church where Rukal's father was bell ringer. I cursed the night we spent in the trunk of the walnut tree, and whilst searching for her distant relatives whom I imagined to look just like her, I felt like one of the seven sleepers who went to market after sleeping for exactly 300 years.

I travelled to Mosul on Evliya's lap. I went to the lands of Mesopotamia, to the cool banks of the Tigris in the footsteps of the Babylonians and Chaldeans. I accompanied Melek Ahmet Paşa's scouting detachment to gather military information. My reminiscences took me to Nebuchadnezzar's palaces and the ruins of the Temple of Ishtar containing the tablets on which the wise priests of Babylon recorded their space research. It felt as if everything that had come to pass had happened only the day before. I tried to imagine the research laboratories of the seven scientists who calculated when journeys into space would be conducted and even imagined I could see the faces of those fortunate sages around me. I must also add that knowing that there was just an inch of soil between the cartouches containing the door codes enciphered by sage Akeldan and my horse's hooves caused me unbearable pain. I even saw the enigmatic rock supplying these cartouches with energy from the sun. It had become rather henna-coloured and roughened over the centuries, but could still be seen to glisten in places.

If the Sirrush-headed dagger in the possession of the Babylon Society masters had been in my hands that day and I had known the code letters etched upon it, I would have immediately super-imposed them on the numerical values that my master Fuzuli scattered among my couplets. Or else, I would at least have wanted to help Evliya Çelebi or the commander of our detachment Melek Ahmet Paşa find the golden idols. To my regret, we did not linger on Babylonian soil. When the ruins of the Tower of Babel – now the lair of lions and jackals – were behind us, I could not help but think that I had completely lost my chance of reunion with the Leyla who had grown up playing in those lands. If I had been able to find it, I would have smelled the flowers blossoming on her grave; I would have talked with the grass growing thereabouts and perhaps offered to take its place. If there is still life there and if there is even a single person in my Leyla's land, I would want to kiss their hands because they might be of the same lineage and carry the same love in their genes.

It was a travel adventure during which I overflowed with enthusiasm and excitement. I was searching for love, for my love. Even if such youthful excitement proved too much for my worn constitution, I nonetheless wanted to be able to kiss the already scattering soil and dust of the lips which I had been unable to kiss when she plucked me from my stem as a strawberry. It was as though I was a janissary and that whole region was my own native country, the distant nation from which I had been taken. This is how I thought throughout the entire journey. I made myself believe it, but I was neither able to embrace my brethren, nor lie down on the fresh banks of my homeland and weep. I was not able to encounter anyone and had only the vision of Leyla that was forever with me. I think now that perhaps it was Evliya's romantic world that dragged me into that excitement once again, as living with Evliya, even if in the wilderness, was bliss itself.

Evliya was the son of Derviş Mehmet Zılli, descended from Ahmet Yesevi. Although originally from Germiyan, he was a child of Istanbul to the core. Everyone referred to him as Çelebi. Indeed, he possessed all the characteristics of a *çelebi*[*] – gentleness, poetic knowledge, literacy, refinement, kind-heartedness, honesty, boldness and heroism. I know that at age 19, he started exploring inch by inch the Istanbul he loved so much. He looked at what he saw with an eye to learning lessons as he made frequent mention of this. His sense of space and capacity for observation had developed to such an extent that he wanted to travel everywhere and see everything. About eight years previously, he had had a dream on the Night of Power,[†] which coincided with the August heat that year. In his dream, he was praying behind a holy person at the Ahi Çelebi Mosque at the Golden Horn, near the Yemiş İskelesi, or Fruit Pier, within a blessed congregation.

After the prayer, it was made known to him that that individual was the Prophet Muhammad and those next to him were the Four Rightly Guided Caliphs. Çelebi immediately jumped up to kiss the Prophet's hand, kneeling before him, but he became tongue-tied with excitement and while he wanted to say, "*Şefaat* (Your intercession) O Messenger of Allah!" the words "*Seyahat* (Travel) O Messenger of Allah!" fell from his lips. The Prophet then gave him glad tidings of travel. Sa'd ibn Abi Waqqas who was next to them, advised my dear Evliya to record what he saw. I am aware that he related this dream with all its particulars and interpretations in the first chapter of his work *Seyahatname*, the eighth volume of which he will start writing should he escape the rogues blockading our ship.

* [Translator's note: The title *çelebi* is more generally recognised as that belonging to the head of the Bektaşi and Mevlevi Sufi orders.]

† [Translator's note: The night, according to Muslim belief, on which the Qur'an was first revealed to the Prophet Muhammad, and thus constitutes the most blessed and meritorious night in the Islamic calendar.]

It was Çelebi's intention to travel every inch of Ottoman lands and even see the cities beyond its frontiers. What he was doing was madness. Sometimes he listened to epics narrated in caravanserai rooms and sometimes he blended into market crowds, meeting with people speaking diverse languages. I was witness to how often he was a guest at the mansions of the affluent just as he was also party to unruly gatherings around fires in derelict fortresses.

He loved lodging in port cities, pacing ruined walls and writing in his journal as he did so. When necessary, he weighed an endless number of items with his hands, or joined caravans and walks beyond his dreams. Anatolia, the Balkans, the Black Sea, South Russia, the Caucasus, my Rukal's land Mingrelia, the lands of the Chechens and Kurds, Mesopotamia, Iran and many other lands, provinces, districts and regions are among the places he patiently and lovingly travelled. For his book, he collected information pertaining to all nations and peoples on pieces of paper and then sewed and pasted them together in volumes, adding his own commentary between the lines. He related anecdotes about the people of a great many lands, their social lives and cultures. The kings and sultans who lived in these lands ages ago were treated as his friends; he gave voice to their tales and imparted the moral of their stories to all those listening to him.

It is from him that I learned about how monks emerged after the long debate about the Trinity among Roman Christians. I learned also how the relations between state and religion influence the formation of the clergy and how this affects the populace. I also learned why some people in countries subject to Rome withdrew to the mountains to live hermetic lives instead of engaging in science or trade.

Escape from the company of others was prompted by denominational schisms but this often meant they left their human attributes aside to lead brutish lives. Even dressing was deemed to show over-attachment to ego and thus many chose to live naked in mountains, creeks and other secluded places. Among these hermit monks noted for deprecating their egos was St. Simeon Stylites whose fame has immortalised him. He entered a monastery in Syria as a 13 year-old shepherd and chose to undergo unrelieved austerity. After this he chained himself to a mountain near Antioch for exactly 30 years, bowing in worship 2,222 times each day come rain, hail or shine. The saint's reputation for devotion became so widespread that a great many visitors came from as far afield as India and Europe to prostrate themselves before him. Even the Persian and Arab Kings and the Roman Emperor Theodosius visited and honoured him. Upon his death, the Patriarch of Antioch, Governor of the East, six famous bishops, 20 judges and 6,000 soldiers brought his body down from the mountains in procession and hid it for an extended period of time as they believed it would help to defeat the enemies of religion.

Whatever interesting information there was to be learned of the world, Evliya wrote about it in his *Seyahatname* so that all those who read his words were utterly amazed. For instance, he related best how Buddha, the founder of Buddhism, was born of Queen Maya, the infertile wife of King Suddhodana, leader of the Shakya clan, after years of prayer and entreaty to God. When a Himalayan recluse foretold that the boy would become a great religious scholar in the future, his father was displeased. He gathered his council of Brahmins and ordered his senior advisors to prepare his heir for the throne. Life's suffering and anguish was concealed from the boy and he was raised in pleasure and self-indulgence. But, when he saw a funeral procession, he understood the fleeting nature of youth, health and life. For seven years, he withdrew into seclusion in order to purge himself of worldly concerns and solve the mystery of life. So he underwent a compelling period of suffering and began to be called *Shakyamuni*. He sat cross-legged for two and a half months upon a tree in a state of nirvana and eventually, aged 36, whilst looking at the full moon one night on the banks of the Ganges River in a state of vigilant awareness, the veil of his heart lifted. He attained the secret he sought and developed the Buddhist doctrine. Evliya described the impact that this life, which resembled the life of Ibrahim Adham in Islamic mysticism, had on the world.

In particular, he had such a way of telling stories that one wished for the pages to keep turning so the sentences would not end. There was the account of how, when Melek Ahmet Paşa defeated the Khan of Bitlis, Abdal Khan, eight large trunks of books came out of the khan's coffers along with trunk-loads of furniture and other things. I learned in my travels with him how a hypocritical and immoral gossip from the Kadızadelis bought Firdevsi's famous *Şehname* for 1,600 *kuruş* at the imperial auction. But he butchered the human depictions in its enchanting miniatures with the peasant knife on his belt as if gouging out their eyes. Melek Ahmet Paşa had the man stoned for his bigotry. I learned how they sold over and over again the same damp log as firewood for winter to men staying as guests in one of the Black Sea towns. I learned how whilst the apples were still growing on their trees, the women of Malatya cut with scissors the couplets they wrote and glued them to the apples with beeswax so that when the apples were picked, the poems were read from the apples as though they had been divinely bestowed. I heard the tale of the loincloth between Nasreddin Hoca and Timur in the hamam, how the snow brought to Istanbul by the curative snow dogs at Uludağ was kept in snow wells to be used in sherbets in the summer, how the mentally ill were cured at Edirne's hospital, how the Paşas wrestled and competed in loosing arrows, how the arrow shafts were cut from cypress in the Domaniç forests, how the old pines in Bolu were turned into wooden pitchers and cups, how garments dyed in copperas are cleaned through burning, how cats from Divriği and Erdebil mice hunt one another, how the astounding brain surgery in Vienna had developed and how the cannonball festivities on the Dardanelles Strait were held.

Now I waited and hung on to him. We experienced touching moments amidst the tumult of the 40 or so men busy fending off the fiery arrows raining down on our galley. I could read his heart: on the one hand, he wanted to escape and save himself, while on the other, his eyes watered as he would not be able to carry the chest into which he had packed his entire life. He tried to hide his rolled-up travel notes in his sash, robe and underwear, then his gaze shifted to the books where I too was once found. He momentarily faltered between going or staying, could not choose between falling captive or sacrificing his books and then, planning to escape by sliding across the ice if the ship caught fire, he still tried to tie two pieces of timber to his boots. I wondered whether he would have given me up if he had known that this bandit scourge was befalling him because of me. He loved me, remembered my master Fuzuli with fondness and had kept me by his side for all these years on horseback, in his lodgings at night, in caravanserais and encampments, over summer and winter, by night and by day. Among the peony petals that Rukal had inscribed on my bosom with her blood were now the memories of his warm breath. His was the sixth pair of lips to kiss the peony; the memories of all these people came together on my forehead, which my dark-eyed Leyla had first etched with soot. All these lip prints had been super-imposed on top of each other and all these heartbeats had caught the same rhythm. This is what I was thinking at that moment of dread.

With a roar, the main mast that had caught fire came crashing down. At the same time, a horrifying clamour could be heard from the deck and the ship's hull, which had been stuck in the ice, was wrenched free and water began to seep into the orlop deck where we were. My dear Çelebi wanted to take me into his hands for the last time and read his fortune. He fixed his eyes on the page that he opened at random. He intended to do what my master Fuzuli said in this verse. Before turning to the companionway of the cabin opening to the deck, he read:

With no strength left in heart and spirit
He left the ship of fire like water.

He was awestruck, as the couplet was the reply to the very question he was asking.

I wept after my dear Çelebi's departure. He covered the lid of the trunk in which he had hidden me, placing me among the other books and wrapping me in oilcloth and beeswax to ensure I was not affected by water. It seemed as though the anguish in his heart was projected onto his face. He thought that at least when our galley burned the trunk could float for some time further. It might sink into the icy waters further down, in one of the stretches of the river that had not frozen over, and he hoped to find us again. I even prayed for him. I feared he would drown or else contract pneumonia if he survived. What if he had known that the galley had burned because of me...

All wrapped up and awaiting my fate, I thought that I resembled the gazelle in my master Fuzuli's tale: the gazelle that got its foot caught in a trap waiting for the hunter to arrive. Was it because I missed the warm sun and the mud brick house in which I was born as I languished in the frozen below-decks trapped between fire and water? I did not know, but once again I wished I had been able to whisper about Nebuchadnezzar's Temple of Ishtar and the Chaldeans in my dear Çelebi's ears during our travels to the land of Babylon. If my kind-hearted Çelebi was now to fall prey to the cold or the thuggery of the thieves in pursuit of the Babylonian gold, no one would ever be able to write my tale. In that case, maybe I too would merge Leyla and Rukal's love in the waters of the Danube. I would flow from here and reach the seas, then become a cloud, then rain down upon all humanity and the whole world would learn love, my love. These were the last hours I would spend bemoaning my fate. "Oh, if only I could speak, I could inspire him and permeate his heart as he makes his notes while sitting on horseback or at the camp and in the marketplace. I could relate to him my entire tale including everything about my master Fuzuli. I would reveal to him one by one all the secrets I carry and have him write all of them down." I must confess that I have never wanted to speak to anyone as much as I did to my dear Çelebi. It has been a long time since I would look enviously at the white spaces on the pages before him as he embraced the journal in which he wrote his travel notes, waiting for morning on frosty nights which echoed to the sound of sand storms. How I prayed for him to write my tale in one of the spaces he left in-between!

At that moment, as I waited for my tyrannical hunter in-between fire and water, teary-eyed and stricken, I was constantly praying for Çelebi. I have just realised that everyone loved him: everyone – friend or foe... It was he who went as an envoy to the Paşas who had turned Celali rebels and again he who brought the letters of the Celali Paşas to the palace. His name would be mentioned with deference and he would be remembered with praise in the Silk Road caravans where they told stories of wolves and bandits. His name would come up in epics and poetry and, if one encountered trouble on the road or in the mountains, one could invoke his name and be forgiven. If one happened to be homeless and desperate, one could go to the mansions of the tribal chiefs and Çelebi would set them right, feeding the hungry and dressing the unclad. His reputation had travelled far beyond him himself and more often than not, people became acquainted with his fame rather than himself. Evliya Çelebi was a legend in Ottoman lands; those who saw him would not fail to respect and honour him and those who heard his name would want to listen to his words. It looked as if he would personify the memory of the Ottoman tradition, which transcended time and space. I would refer to him as my dear Evliya or my Çelebi, while I never knew his name. In any event, no one knew or mentioned it. He was Çelebi, perhaps even Evliya.

By that stage, some of the 42 men with whom we had become familiar and who longed for Istanbul distinctive for its houses with their bay windows and lattices, and for its graceful women and iced pomegranate sherbets, were giving up their lives to the Danube. Some took lives there also. Among their last memories were the coastal villages left behind with the spring, the fringed shade of the fruit trees and the smell of fried fish.

I could hear the howls of the dogs coming from the other side of the Danube and the squeaks of the boat mill waterwheels which were in need of oiling. The mill was composed of two hulls with a waterwheel in-between and, as the rushing waters of the Danube propelled the wheels, the millstones turned to keep pace with the river. The wheat, barley and corn of the villages was ground into flour in the process.

I was covered in flour on one of these boat mills the day I was brought to the Silistra Citadel and new images began to form on my pages. I wish I had been scattered into pieces instead of witnessing that day. I had seen that the men after me were not Wallachian or Austrian treasure hunters, but a legion of rogues who had made a deal with Siyavuş Paşa, and I was shaken to the core by their betrayal. Having taken the wages to cover a few days' carousing, they spurred their horses with the images of slender-waisted Wallachian dancers already taking shape in their eyes.

Resting against high cliffs, Silistra Citadel resembled a falcon nest perched on top of a bow-shaped bend of the Danube at a point where the river flowed fiercely. All 40 of the culverin cannons and the piles of şayka and *balyemez* stone cannon balls on its bastion and ramparts were directed towards the Danube. On its gate was hung a lion's hide stuffed with cotton, with velvet sewn in its mouth for its dagger-like teeth. It was as big as one of the elephants of General Hannibal, the African. It was not known who had brought this lion or where they had hunted it, but it was treated by all as the talisman of the citadel. The lion was regularly maintained and its roughened stuffing was changed every year.

All the valuables of neighbouring towns and villages were stored in the Silistra Citadel which was very secure during the summer. But it was vulnerable to assault in the winter when the Danube froze over. The day I was sold to the citadel, ice floes broke away from Austria and smashed into the fortress wall 80 *zirai* high* where they shattered into pieces. One of the fragments shot over the fortress walls and caused the roof of the granary to cave in so that the wheat became wet. Siyavuş Paşa issued orders to remove the ice in the granary and sift out the damp wheat. Fortunately, there was no rain and the sun shone generously as on a spring day.

In the afternoon, I was in the citadel's watchtower, between the Paşa's cold hands. Along the banks of the Danube, which had all the placidity of a frozen port, children played winter games with anklebones they tied to their feet, while adolescent youths fastened ox shoulder bones to their feet. The children sanded them down and held skating races along the Danube. Some of them somersaulted over the trees they placed across the ice as hurdles and others spun about so fast as to make their faces blur. Nothing like it had ever before seen or heard of before. Further on, young girls in colourful frilled dresses made swings under the sycamores which branched out over the river. They pushed each other, trying not to fall onto the ice, and sang songs and enjoyed themselves. I could make out from the small fires burning along the banks that some of them had poked holes in the ice and caught fish with rods. The wind blew the smell of grilled fish and whetted Siyavuş Paşa's appetite. Surround-

---

* [Translator's note: Ottoman unit of measurement equivalent to 0.758m.]

ing the merrymakers stood the guards of the fortress command. It turned out that I had chanced upon the weddings organised for the sons of the citadel imam and head of the cannon corps, with the girls they had abducted from the Wallachian villages when they took advantage of the freezing of the Danube. All the residents of the citadel's 20 houses came down to the icy river for the celebration. This was why the fortress guards were standing watch on the shore.

On that day, I understood that Siyavuş Paşa sought not a tale but a clue among my pages. As the afternoon sun dipped between the leaves of the sycamores, he released three pigeons with three messages tied to their claws and two weeks later I was laid upon the operating table of the Babylon Society once again. I realised that one of the pigeons had reached Wallachian Voivode Matei Basarab's vizier Şerban, one had been sent to the chief architect of Czar Peter the Great, Alexander Dimitrov, and the third was conveyed to Johann Jakob Froberger, imperial organist of Emperor Leopold I of Habsburg, considered the last stronghold of the Catholic world.

That day, I noticed that these four men, seated on the sofas of the vizier's princely suite in the bastion from which the walls of the Silistra Citadel could be viewed from the highest point, had certain things in common. Siyavuş Paşa and Şerban Mihali had come from a background of slavery and had served as commanders of their respective Royal Guards. As with all slaves, they seemed to harbour secret spite for people other than themselves. Both were brave, but this bravery merely fed their tyranny and was not able to strip away their slave characteristics and elevate them to gentlemen. Like all slaves, they were not to be trusted. The pain of repression, ill treatment and being shoved about from a young age brought them together and led them to produce excuses to justify their schemes.

Johann Jakob Froberger and Alexander Dimitrov, however, shared the artisan's personality. The former was respected for expressing divine powers through his musical gifts at a time when Austria stood at the heart of music in all the Catholic world, while the latter was considered one of the masters of the classical architectural style in Russia.

All four were seated around a high table with a brazier placed underneath and were keeping themselves warm with the shawl tablecloth with which they covered their knees. They had each earned the trust of their own monarch on whose fate their future hopes were set. Siyavuş expected to become a vizier after serving as a fortress commander. Şerban believed that the Wallachian Voivodeship belonged to him. J.J. Froberger ruled like King Leopold's confidant and head advisor, while Alexander gathered state secrets by sleeping around with the women of the palace. They did not regard the other three Babylon Society members as so important. One of these was a priest of the Church of Rome, one a lecturer at the French Academy in Paris and the third was the tailor of the king of Spain.

Judging from their discussions, they planned to form a single state in Europe and were going to rule the world from the Babylon Space Research Centre they would build in Transylvania after wiping out the Hungarians and Slovaks from the face of the earth. They were after the gold buried in the Chaldean temple as much as the tablets. They spoke of their plans to spend the gold in order to foment rebellion in some of the European states and then seize power. They hid all the information of the secret intelligence service they set up with the earnings of the Society's merchant ships plying the Mediterranean in the library of Notre Dame and directed all of Europe's political developments using countless spies in addition to their pigeons.

My pages were handled one by one beneath the watchful gaze of four formidable faces. They had in their possession the ciphers decoded by previous masters in Rome. They even had records of the conversations between the painter Elsheimer and the Austrian merchant and their debates on the topic of love. They all knew by heart my couplets numbered 607, 617 and 687 and juxtaposed the terms pertaining to love and concealment within them. I could not help but think that they had prepared themselves well and that they would even find with ease my other couplets and the cipher numbers in them. I worried for my future.

"Yes, we are at the beginning of the moment where history will be rewritten," Şerban Mihali said, framing his words in a solemn manner. He drew a circle on the stone floor of the room with a piece of terracotta tile. They gathered around its circumference, closed the two fingers of their hands in a fist for the sacred oath of the Babylon Society and placed their hands on top of one another right at the centre, chanting together in Chaldean as though singing a hymn. This Society caused me added amazement each time and appeared to have invented a different ritual on each occasion. I had never seen a master conducting a ceremony like this before. It would seem that when people's ambitions begin to stifle science, rules rather than reality come to the fore and the truth goes astray.

Siyavuş Paşa read and Şerban translated into German and Russian. In fact, even if the Society's members knew certain inscriptions in Chaldean, this was not enough for them to agree. They enciphered simple expressions in their communications and corresponded using such words as, "come, I have it, I found it, alright, send it, help, protect". The language and script they used when sending messages with the homing pigeons was for this reason always the language of the cuneiform script of the Chaldean era.

"We know that the words relating to love and mystery in the first three couplets are common," Siyavuş said. "Now let's continue by reading, if you like, and comment on the couplets in which these two words come side by side." The others agreed and my tale was read from my school days onwards, very slowly and thoughtfully, or perhaps I ought to have said searchingly. My story faded off into the darkness through the nights when the whistling of the fierce winds breaking against the battlements caused the banks of the Danube to tremble. On those long nights spent reading, which seemed to last longer than I can remember, I was overjoyed on the one hand and suffered deeply on the other. I was happy because my tale was being read once again whilst I was burning with longing for my Leyla. I felt myself grow afresh, I felt myself falling in love and reuniting with my beloved. I remembered taking to the wilderness and becoming enchained, I remembered my old friends the gazelles and pigeons and, finally, I remembered how my heart had filled with Leyla in these strange lands. Although it was not like a poet or a lover's recital, it was still enough by way of solace for days which were so long and bad as to be irksome.

As Siyavuş read, J.J. Froberger became increasingly affected by my story and to listen with ever more attention. I could sense that his interest in me was not in deciphering a certain code, but in genuinely understanding the love in my tale. He was the one who found my next cipher couplet. The couplet was positioned right underneath the miniature illustrating the scene of my meeting with Leyla in the wilderness and included my utterance when I went to the desert for the first time after fainting.

Adoration made black my day
Love took from me the reins of my will.

After reading, Siyavus translated the couplet to those present. "Let's stop here," said Froberger at that point. "A person's day being darkened implies nightfall. Love likes the night most, as does the lover... This is because lovers remain alone together with their love only at night. In this case, the night is to be filled with the secrets of love. Indeed, the night is referred to in all sacred texts as that which veils secrets. Fuzuli was of course well versed in the Qur'an. And, by the way, we must not forget the fact that all secret affairs are carried out at night." – "Just like you are doing now!" I felt like interjecting. – "Perhaps Hilleli Fuzuli understood the veil of night as the best place of refuge, a fortress in which secrets can easily be protected. Is this not possible?"

"Of course it is and indeed has been!" interjected Dimitrov.

"In that case, allow me to calculate its numerological equivalent," continued Siyavuş, then writing the word "black" in Ottoman Turkish under the careful and curious eyes of all those present, adding up in turn 60 under the letter *sin*, 10 under the *ya* and 5 under the *ha*: 75. "Indeed, the number seven has emerged here, just like the number of Babylonian gods, the seven planets, the seven days' fast or the seven herb wine. I don't know if it means anything, but this seven appears to me to be of some significance," he said.

The articulation of the number seven on this frosty night in this dark council made me feel as though something had fallen away from within me. For some reason, I realised that I did not like the Babylon Society as much as I had done before. How unrefined these people were, especially when compared with Arshiya Akeldan or the librarian who gave his secret to my master Fuzuli. What is more, none of them had a scientific background; they had joined forces using their diplomatic or political authority to assert the secret power of the Society and behave like the Knights of the Universe. Although these men knew exactly how to operate and were expert spies, they appeared sceptical about re-forming the Research Council. I personally knew that some of them had no desire to advance the Society's research work and were only after the gold.

Şerban Mihali was lost in thought with his hands resting against his temples. "Friends!" he exclaimed. "What if there's a cipher in the line numbers of the couplets with the number seven! Let's take a look at the order of the previous couplets, what do you think?"

They started scanning my pages from the beginning in order to ascertain the line numbers of the couplets they had formerly identified. They ascertained the line numbers of these couplets and discovered that these were located on lines 607, 617 and 687. They continued to count and two nights later, Siyavuş Paşa let out a yelp that tore the silence of the dark. He said that he had identified a key couplet at line 872. "Yes! Our predecessors were never as close to the golden idols of the Babylonian gods as we are at this very moment. I suspect that if we number in sequence the couplets to follow and examine only the couplets containing the figure seven, we will save time." To celebrate his triumph, he took a pinch from his snuffbox and, covering his left nostril, took a deep snort. Then he raised his napkin the size of a tablecloth to his nose and began sneezing.

Architect Dimitrov undertook the task of writing the line numbers of my couplets on the edge of the page as he was most well versed in the cuneiform system of numbers. In this way, first three and then four digit numbers began to line up beside each of my couplets. Of these, those featuring the number seven were written in red while the others were written in black ink. Any reader might have mistaken these for the doodles of a child. The reason why they had chosen not to write in Roman or Arabic numerals was because they did not want my secret to fall into foreign hands. Beside my last couplet was written 3,098 in cuneiform digits. It was then that I discovered the dimensions of my existence and the breadth of my love. So my master Fuzuli had composed exactly 3,098 couplets for my tale, each more beautiful than the other. May the Lord judge my master!

The nights passed with the same monotony. Every half an hour the watchmen shouted in turn, "One! God is One!" As their calls blended with the call to dawn prayer recited by the muezzin from the wooden minaret, the four grew weary from work. The smell of snuff and aniseed hung heavily in the room and the temperature of the brazier had fallen. As Siyavuş Paşa would make his ablutions and head for the mosque, the other three would drift off into deep sleep. They would sleep until noon, watching the Danube from the bastions until nightfall, sometimes leaving the citadel for fishing or for walks.

On that last night, snacks consisting of roasted grains, raisins, almonds, walnuts, roasted chickpeas and fruits bought from pedlars plying the Danube were placed on the table heaped upon silver platters. Two pitchers of wine had again been prepared for Siyavuş Paşa's guests, as was customary. This was to be the last night when I felt like I was performing the role of an aperitif to a drinking spree.

The first words were the same as those spoken to my master Fuzuli by the blind librarian of the Baghdad Academy of Sciences. "There are seven true secrets for one who knows love and one who possesses them gains mastery over the world." My couplets which contained the figure seven in their numbering and words denoting both love and concealment revealed themselves one by one. All my couplets coinciding with the number seven were now being interpreted in sequence. Towards midnight, when the sleet dissolved into the thunderous roar of the Danube, Siyavuş Paşa read my 1,117th couplet.

Free me of mental disquiet O Lord
Render me forever familiar with love.

This couplet was in the chapter describing the time I was sent to the Ka'ba to pray for recovery, when word got out in the nomad household of the Banu 'Amir that I had lost my mind. My father had taken me to the Sanctuary believing that all supplications made at the Ka'ba, the Sacred House, would be accepted. I had placed my head on the threshold of that blessed door and prayed.

"My Lord! Render me free of all worry and make me forever intimate with love!" Whilst Siyavuş Paşa qualified my behaviour as madness and translated it thus to his colleagues, I was beginning to experience with a sense of ultimate hopelessness the rapture of my entreaty to remain in love at the Ka'ba to which I had been taken to pray for liberation from love. That day, the Sacred House appeared before me in all its glory. What distinguished me from other people and other lovers throughout history was this contrary behaviour I exhibited. That is what made me *me*, what first drove me mad and then made thousands of sane people pursue me with envy for centuries. What made my name resound with reverence was this most gallant statement of mine. I still remember like yesterday my tears flowing and streaming forth on the threshold of the Ka'ba. Leyla's image was right between my eyes and there, within this vision, I found divine beauty.

"What is implied by 'concern'?" Froberger asked Siyavuş in a calm voice.

"Idea and thought," came the reply.

Froberger seemed dissatisfied, "This word has to have another meaning. Love coincides with the figure seven, but there is no secret in sight. This is why it must have another meaning!"

"Yes, it does!" replied Siyavuş jeeringly. "Sorrow, grief, worry, misgiving, curiosity, doubt... Shall I keep going?"

"Enough, my friend! This is enough. I have found what I was looking for, as both misgiving and doubt are hidden. Moreover, the sorrow and grief of lovers must also be hidden."

It became clear that the palace organist knew love and was rather experienced in this matter. I had trouble describing the feeling overwhelming me at that moment. My secrets were being lost on the one hand and on the other hand, a lover was discovering my secret. "For one who knows love," the blind librarian had said. Due to the fact that this man understood the secret love within me, he appeared different to all the other masters and Babylon Society members. I began to feel a hidden admiration and affinity towards him.

I presumed that the astronomical secrets of the Chaldean priests would not be abused in this man's hands. Rebellions could be staged with the money from the golden idols to reshape the world anew, the lives of innocent people across various nations of the European continent could be destroyed, and wars could even be contrived and armies kept, but the refined spirit of this man who had excelled at music, could never sacrifice the tablets for mere gold. As I considered this, I felt ashamed of myself for the accusations I had levelled at all of them together just before. Maybe things would not go as badly as I had imagined. I felt a slight sense of relief.

Not long after my change of opinion, I felt anxiety overwhelm J.J. Froberger. While he appeared to be listening to the discussions as the others endeavoured to compute the numerological equivalents of the meaning and cipher of the couplets, he was undergoing a process of questioning. He had a secret apprehension that the three others who were bouncing questions off each other could not know. "Had the Babylon Society done well to turn away from science and go in pursuit of money?"Yes, perhaps good things also remained for me in this world. The same concern that had gnawed away at me since the day I was brought to the Silistra Citadel like a political prisoner had now begun to pound and pulsate in his heart also. The identity and personality of former Society members now took shape together in Froberger's mind. Should this great secret, hidden in only one heart in each era and entrusted at the last moment from a single source to only one reliable scholar, now lie with the men in this room? Were they really qualified to keep this lofty secret?

From the time I had been smuggled from Rome, no member of the Society in the Vatican had sacrificed the Society's interests to those of the papacy. Assuredly, the four people in this room had been given this secret in different lands, by masters who had acted with the same honesty and integrity. "What kind of age do we live in that the oath of allegiance into which evil thoughts were unable to penetrate for 4,000 or so years is now crumbling?" he lamented to himself and delved into deep thought. The world was truly changing, yes, but should the lives of innocent people be jeopardised for the sake of reshaping it anew? Was the new shape of the world going to make people happy? Were the herds of lovers turned into beasts on Circe's farm going to want to be human once again? With what power were Society members going to use their authority to decide on the happiness or misery of others? Which mortal could desire the authority to change Divine destiny? And was this right? What kind of power did the other three present at the Silistra Citadel right at this moment envisage procuring upon obtaining the cipher? How could the oaths of allegiance renewed in the council, which had convened seven years earlier, be changed so soon? Were the wars waged over the past seven years the reason for this or the changing balance of income in the world? Perhaps it was down to increasing human population? But none of these warranted or should have warran-

ted that the doors opening to space should be used to rule humanity.

The intergalactic space research conducted by Chaldean priests was designed to save all humanity and the world in its entirety. So, was the solving of these mysteries going to hearten human beings or make them miserable? And had we come to the world to weep or to laugh? The words, "O God! What are we doing?" were the last to emerge from the lips of musician Johann Jakob Froberger.

The next day, the guards of Silistra Citadel removed the mangled body of a man who had jumped from the highest bastion into the Danube. He was had nothing on him except, in his sash, he carried the musical notation for a poem he was composing.

Oh Leyla, should I have patiently endured all this pain in your absence? Would my master Fuzuli have wanted me to shoulder all this pain for the sake of protecting his secret? While I was a lover who risked his whole life for the sake of his undying love, of what consequence was gold and science? I miss you so much Leylaaa! Where are you my beloved!

23
How I travelled North and beheld stupefying Sorcery

We have so removed our physical existence, O Neşati
That we are now hidden in the gleaming mirror.

Neşati

Mullah Mehmet – in the third pocket of whose dirty donkey-load reeking of raw meat I had been tossed about from city to city and from land to land for a long time by then – knelt before the Paşa, as was his custom everywhere. He bowed and sought permission for the show he would put on, saying grandly: "By your leave, O vizier of the age and unique light of our times! Great vizier!"

The slim, tall, dark man in his fifties who had been nicknamed the Handsome Caller to Prayer by his troops was Baltacı Mehmet Paşa. He had grown weary of the gossip put about after the agreement reached with the Russian Tsarina Catherine where he lost out at the treaty table despite the fact that he had defeated the army of her husband, Peter the Mad, and left behind troops piled up like mountains in Prut.

On his way back to the capital, he was forced to extend his journey and travel from the East of the Black Sea in order to remove from office the Arab and Kurdish Beys who during that period had revolted frequently against the administration and stirred up trouble. Despite wanting to experience the relief every individual with a sense of responsibility feels after fulfilling their mission, the rumours that were spread regarding him and the Tsarina Catherine doomed him to woeful nights. He was not even able to enjoy that gorgeous autumn in Aleppo. He stayed in the provincial palace with a commanding view of the city. On that September evening, he delved into distant memories. In the tired twilight, he looked down upon his army, which was encamped outside the city walls. It was as though his heart was contracting and he felt suffocated. This was a grave trial for a Paşa: his own army was speaking ill of him. This army now before his eyes caused him pride. The lined-up tents, training grounds, leaders' procession, barns, stables, archers and targets had all been organised by him and he had personally taken pains with and raised a great many of the soldiers as his own children. It was to be regretted that now all of them frowned on him, and levelled an accusation that he in no way deserved. He felt himself betrayed. He did not expect those within the army who were jealous of him to be so influential and for them to be able to turn practically half of the soldiers against him. He was a little angry with himself for his heedlessness and cursed himself for granting those heads that needed to roll the right to life.

The people next to him and the tables prepared for banquet, the lively and unreserved jokes and the velvety sounds of the court singers were not enough to shake off this fatigue. Usually, the rhythmic shuttling of hundreds of looms which resonated from every corner of the city gave him a sense of poetic harmony. But that night, it seemed to pound his brain and beat against his skull like the pendulum of a clock dealing small blows as it swung.

He was distracted from his unease by the arrival of a homing pigeon. He stroked the bird, read the message written personally for him that had been sent from Istanbul and came to himself with a sense of bitter-sweet joy. All he wanted was a little smile and to forget the whispers of his troops. "First he placed the tsarina on beds of silk and then he took bribes!" they grumbled. "Were it not for this, we would have removed the Russian flag from the face of the earth!" The relief he felt whilst stroking the pigeon was due to this hope for deliverance. According to the imperial edict that was currently on its way, the city's most prominent citizen, the *beylerbeyilik,* was to gather the gossip-riddled army and dispatch the men and their whispers to Istanbul. On top of that, the family that he had missed so much and the new administrative staff he himself was to designate would be setting off towards Aleppo around the same time.

When my current owner, Mullah Mehmet, sought permission from Vizier Baltacı in the wide courtyard of the *beylerbeyilik* walled palace, the army's leading commanders, Aleppo's statesmen and notables as well as court singers, musicians and poets were all present, but Baltacı did not seem to be there. Mullah Mehmet recited his flowery greeting in a kneeling position. At first, the Paşa recoiled. "What is the meaning of this?" he demanded. Then he nodded to show that he had granted permission to Mullah Mehmet. Virtually everyone in the assembly ascribed his absent-mindedness to the depression he was suffering at the time. Even I thought this inattentiveness showed the usual distraction of a Paşa after signing a peace treaty when he feels a combination of pleasure at a humanitarian level but also 1,000 regrets in political terms. I later realised that the Baltacı vizier was lost in delightful reverie. After stroking the pigeon for the last time and releasing it, he shook himself out of his solemnity. "Alright! Now for a bit of fun!" he exclaimed, smiling at Mullah Mehmet and even clapping his hands with joy. He called for the real hosts of the assembly, the *beylerbeyi* servants, to come to him and ordered them to collect the round copper trays in the centre, the dessert plates and the tablecloths. It was he who had summoned Mullah Mehmet to this assembly in any case, wanting to cheer up the Grand Vizier a little during these difficult times.

I had been together with Mullah Mehmet for a long time now. He himself was a Kurd in his sixties who was familiar with the finest details of alchemy. He had come to prominence through 1,001 feats of sorcery in a great many provinces and countries. His preoccupation with the occult sciences began while he was studying at the *medrese*. Thanks to his curiosity for all things strange, he spent his whole life in sand divination and fortune-telling, thus turning his profession into sorcery. Since conjuration was prohibited in Ottoman lands at that time and he could not practise his art, he travelled to Crimea, Lechia, Wallachia, Moldova, all over Germany and Sweden. Eventually, when his fame had spread far and wide, he returned and made Aleppo his home.

The night before Froberger committed suicide at Silistra Citadel, he entrusted me to the renegade Pole, Sergeant Gustaf. "For goodness' sake, dear fellow," he had said. "Protect this book with your life and deliver it to Lützen, to

Queen Christina. She will reward you generously." They knew Gustaf as Mustafa at the Silistra Citadel. Gustaf could not have realised of course, when on his way to Sweden to find the great master of the Babylon Society Marduk and chancing upon Mullah Mehmet at Brandenburg instead, that his life would change. In fact, the day they met, Mullah Mehmet affected Gustaf and they became friends. As Gustaf found magic, which was more in line with his nature, more congenial than delivering a book to a queen of the cold countries of the north, they travelled without a care in the world from Pomerania to Moscow, Ochakiv to Kraków, Bukhara to Kabul, passing through desolate inns, halls ringing with applause, circuses, fairs, mansions, palaces. Sometimes they were hungry and thirsty, and every so often they wore embroidered outfits.

Of course, they dragged me with them everywhere they went. Perhaps I should be grateful for this. Thanks to them, I visited a great many parts of the world and better understood the plans of the Babylon Society. I cannot forget the time they were as close to Vladislas VI of Lechia and Michael I of Russia as to be their guests of honour, or the days they played chess with Shah Safi of Iran, being on such friendly terms they could allow themselves to beat him in a game. I was afraid of the Babylon Society as well as excited by the interesting adventures I had through them.

The two cronies saw the greatest generosity from the Uzbek Khan Imam Kuhadır and spent their happiest times there. In Samarkand and Buhkara, I was kept waiting in pitch-black barns for 40 to 50 days. I watched horses being wrestled before great crowds who had yielded to the jubilation of the Nevruz Spring festival. We spent eight years there, during which I watched slant-eyed beauties celebrate Nevruz beyond the Altai range, and missed my Leyla repeatedly. I had the opportunity of becoming acquainted with a simple existence in Central Asia and I came to know people from the Bayat clans who were my master Fuzuli's ancestors, but could no longer liken any of them to him.

During our nomadic life, my binding became completely worn and Kuli Khan died. The *beylerbeyi* of Aleppo invited us to his city thanks to his interest in mysterious happenings. It was then that the smouldering embers of love were reignited and the ashes began to scatter away from me. I remembered the Babylon Society and the Babylonian thieves. I realised that I could neither be with them nor without them. "Dear friend! Had I not left Silistra, then I might have been able to set up a life for myself in a Muslim country. However, after sinking into worldly sin and reaching the age of 60, and especially with my ailing body, I cannot bear the hypocrisy of living as a Muslim again!" said Gustaf as he made his farewells and gave me as a memento to Mullah Mehmet.

We have since been in Aleppo for a few months. The year they met in Brandenburg and became friends, Gustaf was wearing not the Muslim turban, but the tall padded *barata* hat of the Poles. The night he hid me in his bosom and fled upstream from Silistra, he smeared the blood of a rabbit he had hunted for food onto his inner shirt, short coat and *serpuş* head-dress, and left them in the Danube. So, as he approached the Wallachian villages, he stripped himself of his Muslimness and ensured that those finding his short jacket would assume, like in the story of Joseph, that Mustafa Çavuş had been devoured by a wolf and they would never set off to find him.

In the second month of their ripening friendship, he showed me to Mullah Mehmet and related my story as well as describing Froberger. Mullah Mehmet did not believe this tale at all and deemed Froberger an imaginary figure so he never pursued the idea of going to the Swedish queen. For Mullah, encountering a Turkish book in these foreign provinces was more exciting than any tale of intrigue. In later years, when Gustaf abandoned himself to opium and sorcery, he preferred being Mullah Mehmet's assistant over being a nobleman in the Swedish palace. Whenever he remembered Froberger, he sighed in the hope of perhaps one day putting on a show with Mullah Mehmet in the Swedish palace. However, he never raised this with his master. "My master!" was what he now called Mullah Mehmet.

When the two were together, they lived contentedly. I must admit that I too, experiencing thrilling adventures for the first time in a simple life, was happy. Sometimes the two of them walked the tightrope together and sometimes they had swordfights. There were times when one cut the other in half and the other placed the former in a barrel and rolled him off a cliff. They made each other swallow living rats and made themselves targets for the venomous fangs of snakes. Sometimes they would somersault over piles of bottles and sometimes they would look down on their audience from stilts. In the magicians' and acrobats' fair held once every five years in Isfahan, they competed against their colleagues, and each carried a lamb on his back across ropes tied over a chasm wearing felt skins on his feet. Then they ran among the spectators bearing wine-filled jugs hung on poles they carried between their teeth and turned the place upside-down. After the show ended amidst applause, they feasted on lamb meat, rice with ginger and various types of sweets with the money collected in the beggar's cup made of coconut shell in their hands. By nightfall, they were exhausted and covered in sweat after performing acrobatic sword fights suspended in mid-air from the reels they attached to their hair hanging from the rope tied across the chasm, or likewise after the magic show where one made the other invisible. Then Gustaf would rest, placing his wine glass and drugs box between the breasts of a bawd, while Mullah Mehmet found repose on his prayer mat after making his ritual ablution in preparation.

No resentment or division on the basis of religion ever came between them, or was allowed to do so. One studied Arabic and Persian at the *medrese*, the other had learned Polish, German and Russian as a child. When alone, they spoke only Turkish and the other languages enabled them to find work in the places they visited. They spent a vagrant life together lasting 35 years.

When Mullah Mehmet felt himself doomed to perform solo before the Ottoman Vizier Baltacı Mehmet Paşa, he burned for the very first time with the pain of separation from his bosom friend Gustaf. "I told him countless times that he had to give up alcohol and opium; maybe right now, he's dying after swallowing opium in a barn reeking of urine in Bukhara's filthiest inn!" he thought to himself and decided to put on this show in his cherished memory. A show performed in his honour deserved to be grand so he resolved to demonstrate his greatest alchemical skills. He was hoping to make himself accepted by the Baltacı vizier. If he could dispel the cloud of gloom hanging over the vizier, then he might even become his sycophantic protégé. This is why he had to do his job very well.

First he knelt before the vizier, greeted everyone and prayed. "Come and join me in prayer! May the hospitality of the vizier be everlasting, may Baltacı Paşa remain, may the soul of Pythagoras be accursed and the souls of Ibn Sina and Abu Harith pleased!" He stood up and remained with his eyes shut, repeating certain sentences as though mumbling for a few minutes. On cue, the *beylerbeyi* musicians began beating their small drums. As the bell and the drum beats rose in the *zirgule makam* rhythm, he warned his audience as was his usual practice: "Faithful friends! Be wary and on your guard! If you are brave and undaunted, then fear and flee not as you watch. If you are afraid, then leave the arena now!"

Not a single person budged from among the crowds filling the courtyard to the palace belonging to the Beylerbeyi, and all began to feel excitement on hearing Mullah Mehmet's words. Mullah immediately removed his garments, down to the very last item. When he was completely naked, the crowd started making a booming sound. Mullah Mehmet began: "Esteemed Ağas and Beys! Brothers! As you can see, I am a man with neither penis nor testicles. I don't even have a backside for that matter. Consider it thus and no matter!"

His spectators saw that Mullah Mehmet's front and back consisted of flat skin and thought, "What kind of a person is this? Does he never eat, with his front and back being pieces of leather like wood?" Mullah Mehmet circled the arena three times. Then, from the dirty sack in which he had carried me from Samarkand all the way to Aleppo, he took out a finely woven Yemeni towel, wrapped it around his waist and, like a cormorant walking on water, began to flap and fly with his feet completely lifted off the ground. He made laps, flying at the level of the courtyard's high walls and calling out the names of those present, individually greeting all of them. "O clever ones, O heedless ones, O son of So-and-so, O So-and-so, father of Such-and-such!"

I had watched this show many times before, and now beheld the astonishment of the people gathered in the courtyard seeing a flying man for the first time. I looked as their stupefied faces took on different expressions. The awe and thrill they manifested as this master of magic flew like a bird on the one hand while simultaneously calling their names correctly as he touched their heads with his feet, as if bringing good luck, was truly something worth seeing.

The courtyard was suddenly filled with violent uproar when he removed his towel from his waist after greeting nearly everyone. Amidst such utterances as, "Shame on you!" "Have some modesty!" "Cover the scoundrel!" "I thought he had no penis!" Mullah Mehmet grabbed his member of two hand-spans in length and began urinating on the confounded people so that they scattered helter-skelter. Remembering Mullah Mehmet's performance of this same show before the noblewomen at the Russian palace, I thought that they had acted in a much bolder fashion than the men here. Soon after, most of those gathered in the courtyard wanted to escape under the *eyvan*, the vaulted hall opening onto the courtyard, in which the Paşa and Beylerbeyi were seated on kilim-fitted couches and watching in laughter their commander and the people of Aleppo. The courtyard soon turned into a sea of mud with the water Mullah Mehmet sprinkled from above. The people were so drenched that only their armpits remained dry.

While those exclaiming, "I thought he had no penis, so what's that in his hand and what is now raining upon us?" increased in number, Mullah Mehmet turned to the Paşa. "Your exalted Highness, please instruct them to shut the gates of the courtyard tightly and even cover the keyholes and gaps." So saying, he shook his member in the direction of the Paşa, as if threatening to wet him also if the order was not fulfilled. The Paşa managed to raise a laugh while saying, "Shoot this scoundrel!" but not a soul obeyed or even heard him. Finally, the Paşa ordered the holes in the courtyard to be covered. Mullah Mehmet continued urinating, chasing the people fleeing in confusion, like a cloud hovering over them. When the water in the courtyard started rising, everyone feared for their lives. Those who knew how to swim tried to keep their heads above water while those who could not began climbing the walls and gates. Soon after, those swimming in the courtyard started to resemble the victims of a shipwreck in the middle of the ocean trying to cling on to each other to survive. Everyone began fighting for their lives as if the Tigris had flooded over. The screams and cries for help, the wailing and lamentation were indescribable.

As the water level rose, the Paşa seated in his elevated position was also uneasy. "Have these doors opened, my men are going to perish!" The *Beylerbeyi* tried to assuage him with the words, "Fret not, Your Excellency, this is a stunt and no harm will be sustained. Please bear with us!" When Mullah Mehmet saw the Paşa's apprehension, he thought that it was time to end the spectacle and landed on the water like a seagull. He flicked the ceramic bowl that he took out of his sack with his index finger. Such a ringing sound reverberated throughout the courtyard that all those present froze like the people of Sodom and Gomorrah. Mullah Mehmet came up to the Paşa without his frontals and backside, as before, and kissed the hem of his garment saying, "May my trespass be pardoned and evil be averted; may my lips be silent and what I have poured be sweet water!"

As he clothed himself, he pointed at the men, some climbing the gates and some the walls like bats and others stuck in swimming positions on the ground or reciting the Declaration of Faith while drowning. When the Paşa, startled by this state, ordered, "Save these men at once!" he flicked the bowl in his hand once more and everyone came to their senses. The courtyard was now filled with a procession of people covering their private parts, cowering in corners from shame at their nakedness, the result of removing everything they were wearing to avoid drowning, or else screaming, "Where are my clothes?" "Where is my dagger?" "Did you take my short sword?"

The Paşa liked the spectacle, but had taken offence at seeing illustrious commanders being humiliated among lawless townsmen. Turning to the *Kollukçu* officers at his disposal, he indicated Mullah Mehmet. "Seize this scoundrel and dangle him from this door at once!" The *Beylerbeyi* intervened and asked for mercy. "Alas!" I said to myself, "They're going to kill the poor man!"

Mullah Mehmet pleaded. "Your Excellency! If you are to hang me, then may my blood be lawful to you. Come what may, I have one last wish. Allow me to perform two units of prayer and have me hung with my own rope."

The Paşa spat out his dismissal angrily. "Mullah Mehmet! You deserved to die long ago, but you can have your last wish!"

I had grown very used to him. What was going to happen to me now? In the lands I travelled with him, I had lived with memories of Rukal and Leyla, had walked in their footsteps and breathed the fragrance of the flowers upon their mountains. What hopes we had brought when coming to Aleppo! He was to settle here and repent for his sorcery and alchemy. He was to seek peace and repose among either the Baykara assemblies or among the wide-skirted dervishes of the Aleppo Mevlevihane. What is more, the next day he was due to meet with the famous poet Nabi Efendi of Urfa to talk about poetry, me and my master Fuzuli.

As I pondered all this and lamented the abrupt reversal of my fortune, Mullah Mehmet performed his ablution in the middle of the courtyard and observed two units of prayer. He offered his last supplication in tears. He wiped his hands over his face and walked over to his sack. He felt for the bag woven in silk thread in which he kept me without anybody noticing. When he took me out and began to wind the thread of the bag around his hand, I realised that he was up to something again and felt a sense of relief. The warp of the bag became unwound as it came out of the sack and, as it did so, it transformed into waxed English tether

and grew longer, skein-by-skein, in Mullah Mehmet's hand. Mullah handed to the Paşa's officers the rope of about ten cubits in length that he obtained from the bag and said valiantly, "Come, do as you must!" This time, everyone took pity on Mullah Mehmet. When those requesting his pardon and aspiring to intercede on his behalf saw the look of dread on the Paşa's face, they stepped back. The eyes of the Aleppo *Beylerbeyi* filled with tears. Those who just before had been deceived and watched him with revenge-filled gazes had now begun to pray. Mullah Mehmet had of course said at the very beginning and invited those who could not withstand what they were to see to leave the courtyard. He was not to blame here. Eventually, an old man in his seventies who had been watching the unfolding events from the *eyvan* alongside the Paşa stepped in. "Illustrious vizier, please forgive this poor servant. It is said that forgiveness is the purifying alms of victory. Deem what you have seen a mere diversion!"

"Poet," the Paşa replied, "I will not have the honour of my commanders trampled on! Do not interfere!" At his words, all the commanders whose honour he was defending shrank back into separate corners and huddled together in shame. The Baltacı vizier knew that two of his commanders were not in fact men of great virtue and that they even included the ringleaders of those who had spread gossip against him. First, he said, "The soldier is the soldier of my illustrious Sultan!" Then he attempted to break the ice between himself and the army with which he had fallen out.

Mullah Mehmet looked at the Paşa for the last time as he walked towards the noose suspended on the upper hooks of the courtyard gate. He made his final entreaty. "My dear Paşa, I leave you to the Almighty. May prayers forever be said in your favour and may you play in the sand and no thorn ever prick you for as long as you live!" He stuck his head through the noose and began reciting the Declaration of Faith. At that stage, none of the officers approached to tighten the noose. Everyone stood gaping for a few minutes. In the end, the rope around Mullah Mehmet's neck suddenly changed shape and began transforming itself into a large snake with colourful skin. Mullah embraced the snake, wrapping himself around its back as though mounting a horse. The snake kept growing. The people began fleeing once again. Within half a minute, the snake turned into a seven-headed dragon, reared up on its feet and went out the door in front of everyone, kicking up dust in its wake and taking flight towards the mountain.

Everyone, the Paşa first and foremost, fumbled as though having woken up from a dream, while some pinched those next to them, wanting to be woken up. This time the Paşa felt embarrassed. "Bring the scoundrel's sack!" he cried out. Opening the sack in fear, the Janissary Ağa began to take out its contents one item at a time. All sorts of chemicals which had made me faint for many a long year, the dried scorpion and centipedes, snake skins, sheep and goat's heads, vinegar, wine and tar bottles were revealed. Out came piebald threads of camel wool, old pieces of cloth, pig and mule feet, multicoloured beeswax, live ants and cockroaches in boxes, a roll of paper, a carved shoemaker's knife and a pair of scissors, binding covers, miniature plates filled with battle scenes, a bejewelled dagger, the *Şehname* epic by that magnificent liar Firdevsi of Tuş and finally me. We were all made public, one by one.

The Paşa asked, "Is this man an unbeliever that he carries wine and spirit?" and the *Beylerbeyi* answered: "By God, he has been with us for two weeks. He is a man who fasts during the day and prays at night. These are all instruments of alchemy and sorcery. If you were to sell all of them, they would not make two Abbasi gold coins. You saw for yourselves, he conjured a spell by smearing oil over his body, showing himself to us without buttocks or frontal appendages and, when he smeared glaze from a small bottle, his appendages reappeared. He poured water from a small jug upon your men and everyone thought he was urinating. He made us laugh, but he wasn't a bad man, to be fair."

The Baltacı vizier displayed the satisfaction of already having reached his objective in his manner of responding to these events. Looking at those around him, he agreed. "You are right, sir!"

"He turned one thread into a dragon, like the miracle of Moses, and disappeared from sight. May God protect him. Let him amuse himself in his own way and assume a state in accordance with his faith. In any case, Mullah Mehmet seems to have been an avid reader and had an appreciation of beauty. Pay particular attention to the charm in the script and binding of this *Şehname*, the likes of which I have not seen even in the palace treasury. And what can be said of the beauty of these pictures! Here, you too have a look. And this book is the *mesnevi Leyla and Mecnun* of master Fuzuli from Baghdad. And this behoves only one who possesses the *Hayriyye of Nabi*. Here, master!"

The old man in his seventies to whom he gave me was the "poet" who had bravely asked for Mullah Mehmet to be forgiven. Whilst thanking the Paşa, he tried to make sense of the cuneiform numbers written before each of my lines and pondered the reasons behind these being written in a *mesnevi* such as this. He tried to imagine Fuzuli writing seated before a book-stand and mumbled, "What a great poet you are, O Hilleli! If all the world's books were to burn and if all libraries were to face that which befell the Royal Library of Alexandria, this book of yours would be sufficient to show the summit which humanity has reached in literature and poetry! May God bless your soul!"

My gazelle-eyed, hyacinth-perfumed, beloved Leyla! I saw Mullah Mehmet for the last time that day. Even if not in the way I miss you, I will miss him also as there was friendship between us. I can easily say that, as he left his instruments of alchemy in the Aleppo mansion and disappeared towards the mountains, he was smiling and at peace with himself. Who knows the Sufi lodge where in all likelihood he lives as Mehmet Dede? And who knows which land of love you now preside over as sultana, O Leyla? Oh how I have missed you! I beg of you, send me your scent with the dawn breeze, so that I may at least know how you are.

24
How I was happy listening to the Poets in Aleppo and found Leyla at a Moment I sought her not

Such mastery human beings have attained in intrigue
That Satan's fame in this has long been forgotten

Nabi

Aleppo's *Beylerbeyi* Baltacı Mehmet Paşa had addressed him as "Poet". Later, I learned from the conversations about poetry held in his home that others called him "the most perfect of Anatolian poets". This olive-skinned man in his seventies on whose countenance could be discerned the map of his soul, said for a long time with experience what my master Fuzuli had said with love. The journey of poetry that my master undertook towards his heart was in this man undertaken to reach the mind. My master used to speak by feeling, while he spoke through thought. While my master drew the word towards the axis, he spread it towards the periphery; my master described the volcano of emotion within him, while this man described the volcano without. While my master positioned the human being at the centre, he took society as the basis. The inner profundity of Divan poetry spread to the people with his pen. He held up a mirror to the facets, long since manifest, of an increasingly regressive society. Anatolian poetry was being kneaded into shape and a brand new form was emerging. Every caravan travelling to Aleppo, each Procession of the Purse, all the groups of Hajj pilgrims brought him bundles of newly-penned poetry from Istanbul. After reading and criticising them, he would return them to their poets with notes and provide some of my couplets in the *gazals* articulating my conversations with Leyla as examples. He was a teacher of poetry and he taught with artistic flair and reminded me of Zati Efendi, who instructed the young poets in meter and mode at the geomancy shop in the courtyard of Bayezit Mosque. How many poets seem to have been raised in Ottoman lands whilst I was smuggled from the Silistra Citadel with Froberger's help and travelled through snowy northern nations instead of Ottoman territ ory!

While thinking on these lines, I remembered the Babylon Society once again. "If I had been in Marduk's hands or in the hands of one of the masters, I could I have learned all this not by hearing but by seeing," I thought to myself. It seemed to me at that moment, that there was a secret compact between poetry and the Society. When escaping from one, I wanted to fall into the lap of the other, but regrettably it too would instantly desert me.

Why was the Babylon Society not looking for or inquiring after me all this time? Or, if they were making inquiries, then why could they not find me? This astonished me. Was something amiss with their plans? Or had the gold statues of the Babylonian gods fallen into their hands? Worst of all, did they not need me anymore? But I had not even been able to disclose my secrets to them; there were still couplets woven with love and mystery that they were yet to read. My master Fuzuli had composed these, positioned them and written them on my bosom with painstaking effort. Was all this effort to go to waste?

And why were the Babylon Society masters and not the poets after my secret anyway? Could the poets have discovered the black hole if they had been interested in space? In Ottoman territory, poets unfortunately did not view space like the Babylonian sages. They thought that the sun sultan reigned over the skies and imagined it ruling over them like an Eastern sovereign. What Babylon referred to as gods, they treated as servants. For instance, the Moon was like the sultan's vizier, Mercury his scribe, Mars his commander-in-chief, Jupiter his judge, Saturn his warden and Venus his musician. Nef'i, the last poet with whom I was acquainted, knew them very well and mentioned their names often in his poetry.

It appears that, after he was killed, a great many poets came to prominence in Ottoman lands who often repeated the theme of the sultanate of the sun in the skies. Naturally they remained quite oblivious to the hierarchy waiting beneath the Great Ziggurat of Babylon in the form of the golden statues symbolising the Babylonian gods. A great many of them were held in high esteem by all *saraylıs*, paşas, the affluent and the noble. One positive element about this was that while I lived in need of warm attention in snowy cities, even from women more interested in watching alchemy, poetry continued improving in the warmer climates to which I felt I belonged.

Masters of eloquence, each more expert than the other, lived therein. Tales of lovers the likes of me were written in the lands where I travelled under the name of novels and in prose, but here the subjects of novels were compressed into couplets. These included the refined couplets being sent to Aleppo. At times their authors squabbled and at times they engaged in one-upmanship. Mustafa Naili made a name for himself with his delicate fancies, Uncuzade Fehim with the *kaside*s he wrote which did not take aim at anyone, composer Nazim who was known for his *naat* poems, Osmanzade Taib who attained the greatest favour of the palace, Sünbülzade Vehbi who wrote a *mesnevi* of counsel to resemble the *Hayriyye*, dedicated to his son Lütfullah Çelebi and entitled *Lütfiye*, Sabit Efendi who could not fit into his shell and many others besides...

"The aim of art is innovation and beauty," said this man whom I admired a little more each day, who produced such beauty as would have made the oases along the Hijaz envious. He derived immense pleasure from hosting gatherings each day at sunset in his stately home overlooking Aleppo's white-washed, roofless houses set in rows like the foamy waves of an ocean sprawled out at its feet, and conversing about poetry with the city's gentry and notables. On this hill the local Arabs referred to as Bagh al-Nabi, Aleppo's first king Yarim-Lim I once lived. A few centuries before wise priest Arshiya Akeldan, the foundations carrying the walls of this manor were put into place by the king of the Hittites, Suppiluliuma I, and here he had his famous palace constructed. The nobility lived at Bagh al-Nabi for generations during which it was famed for its beauty and goodness. In music, speech, mind and vision...

When the sun had already begun to singe the crops of the Mesopotamian plains, the musical assembly at Bagh al-Nabi opened with songs in the *Rehavi* musical style sung by the smooth voices of the fresh court singers. So hearts began to blossom. Yusuf Nabi Efendi of Urfa left Istanbul during a plague epidemic and set off for this city, the air and water of which he loved so much. The praise of Sultan Mehmet the Hunter followed and the latter bestowed this manor to him as a state-owned country estate.

Since the day Mullah Mehmet had mounted the dragon converted from the threads of his bag and disappeared, Baltacı Mehmet Paşa, Aleppo's *Beylerbeyi*, sat here most frequently, deriving the greatest delight from Nabi Efendi's conversations. He frequently smothered him with compliments and assisted him in meeting the manor's expenses as well as contributing towards the poetry gatherings. The esteemed Paşa was at the gathering again one day and the court singers sang his favourite songs and recited Nabi Efendi's new *gazals*. As Caucasian concubines served the guests, a new ode was dedicated and recited by the host poet to his Paşa, the guest of honour. Nabi Efendi recited the couplets with a harmony evoking the impression that they came from a single note. He added excitement to the stanzas with gestures and mimics befitting the meaning of the couplet and the Paşa looked as though he could not be contained by the cushion on which he was seated and thanked God for the blessing of being in the company of such a poet in Aleppo. The praise-laden couplets seemed to have intoxicated him. "Master!" said the Paşa after listening to the final prayer section of the ode, "May your language be as sweet as sugar. Allow me to fill your mouth with diamonds, ask of me what you will!"

"Oh, Your Highness embarrasses me. It is sufficient that you grant your friendship."

"And who, O Sir, could not be friend to you? You must have some request. Speak that I may make it my command!"

"In that case, your Highness!" said Nabi Efendi without further show of reluctance, "If you may confer upon me a female servant with a beautiful voice, who is also able to write, that I may dictate to her my poems which wait in bundles."

"I will do better than this! Let me send you a concubine tomorrow!"

"Very well, sir! All the better!"

The gathering livened up even more after sundown. Readings from the divan of Hafız, the *manzume* poems of Ali Şir and verses by Yesevi's Hikmet were recited. The degrees of the poets were debated and joy was brought to the gathering with Arabic and Persian couplets. "If I may," began Abdusselam Ağa from the Aleppo notables who wrote poetry. He sought permission to speak from the Paşa and turned to Nabi, "Would you talk a little of the Anatolian poets and demonstrate how poetry developed in those fortunate lands?"

This suggestion excited me most. I was to learn when such a discussion arose what had happened in the Istanbul where I had lived for almost half a century, in that magnificent city in which I lost my Rukal, in the houses of my residence and the land of the poets with whom I had been acquainted.

"In Anatolia, just as in Arabia, poets are in constant pursuit of innovation in order to attain beauty," began Nabi Efendi. He sipped from the date sherbet he poured from the jug by his knee into his ornate goblet. "Nowadays, they are in constant search of fresh ideas for original meaning and original imagery. Until the age of the King of Kings Süleyman the Lawgiver, Anatolia's masters of speech deemed Persian poetry beautiful and inclined to imitation. This is because at that time, these poems were to us new. This search for beauty and fresh meaning, which started with Edirneli Necati Bey and Sultan Mehmet II the Conqueror's vizier Ahmet Paşa, found new form in the Lawgiver's era with the words of such masters as Zati, Yahya Bey, Baki and Hayali being distilled still more. But above all, our master Fuzuli of Baghdad brought a new love to art. Now, an Anatolian poetry with its profound feeling, delicate dreams, ordered ideas, rich harmony, masterful utterance and individual style enveloped the whole Ottoman world. Books dedicated to poetry alone were composed. Sehi Bey, Aşık Çelebi, Hasan Çelebi, Kastamonulu Latifi Efendi and others cropped up one or two at a time. They wrote of poetry and poets over hundreds of pages. Poetry became a noun and poet a title. Before being introduced by their names, protagonists were referred to by their nicknames. It was as if babies were growing up with their pen-cases and inkwells in their nappies. Former poets had tried to imitate their masters, now they were competing with each other. In the preceding generation, they surpassed Persian poetry to a state of satiety. Nef'i's *kaside*s and Şeyhülislam Yahya's *gazals* were increasingly imaginative. Language became more and more beautiful and refined. Formerly, poets would say 'beloved as beautiful as the moon', or 'lips as red as ruby'. For those who followed, it sufficed to say 'moon beloved' or 'ruby lips'. Now, all ears familiar with poetry began to take 'moon' to mean the beloved and 'ruby' to mean her lips. Why should today's poets say 'as tall as a cypress' when everyone associates 'cypress' to the beloved's height in any case? Language treated with the meticulousness of a goldsmith ensured that verses were woven like lace. There was no longer any need for favouring the Persian models. As you can see, the Anatolian poets endeavoured to surpass one another and Turkish poetry is now competing with itself."

"So, how can they achieve this when they are living far apart and removed from each others' voices?" asked the Ağa this time.

"Both an easy and a difficult question!" said Nabi, spinning his hand in the air. "It is easy as, while poetry is not taught in Ottoman *medrese*s as a separate subject, it has permeated the walls of the schools. Students study prosody, but they become acquainted with Iranian poetry whilst learning Persian. Outside class, poetry is both their entertainment and their common language. As they dip their spoons into their soup or study algebra and geometry in their cubicles, poetry

waits beneath their tongues. There are those among them that are so embedded in poetry that they snore in rhymes and turn in their sleep in prosodic meter. Those showing promise and a poetic disposition cannot stop at reading while they are still students and must begin writing. Those with a poetic disposition will manifest themselves in a very short time and will have their names written in the biographical compendia of poets. The difficult part of your question is that there can be no poetry without knowledge. It is by means of extensive knowledge and culture that beautiful poetry is written. Otherwise, you would not be able to renew yourself. Now, if a person has a poetic disposition and possesses knowledge, then the only thing he needs is style. If you will, let us call this self-hood and creativity. The greatest among the greats are precisely those who possess this style. Our master Baki and our master Fuzuli are both distinguished from the rest with the *rindane* or joyous style of the former and the *aşıkane* or amatory style of the latter. Anyone can write a *kaside* devotional poem, but it is precisely because they cannot write as valorously as Nef'i that we must be fond of him."

"Do not be unfair to yourself, dear master!" said Baltacı Paşa, "Your *kaside*s and in particular your erudite style are unmatched across the Ottoman world."

"Until reaching me, your Excellency, the rapture of Sufism, majesty of the state, prosperity of victory and the blessing of the poets have exalted this poetry to such a degree that my task has become both easier and more difficult. It has become easy as the examples stand before me. It became difficult as it is as though my predecessors have already said everything. And composing in the Indian style did not quite seem becoming to me. The political and societal turbulence of the ages through which we have passed has frequently led me to seek solutions, so that my style developed as a matter of course. I was plunged into deep reflection and strove to express this succinctly, taking great pains and tying myself in knots... And this is precisely the secret filling my nights. Contentment and trust in God, journeying to one's inner world, years spent fluttering in an intellectual world replete with whys and wherefores, contemplating the solution to all injustice, corruption, bribery, rebellion, defeat. How often the sultanates change hands, factors driving brothers to turn Celali and such like, all want to pour forth onto paper from my bosom in the form of an ache or pain. Besides, what is it that you call wisdom, your Excellency, other than a deep anguish?"

When Nabi reached this point in his words, he was shaking his head mournfully. Whether he was troubled for his own life or his youth, or the predicament of the increasingly weakening state, nobody could tell. It was as if melancholy fell upon the gathering. The poetry recited thereafter took flight upon these wings of sorrow. Before long, each sensed a somewhat astringent taste about the dire situation of the state. The Paşa sensed it most intensely, followed by all the poetry enthusiasts who left the gathering, one by one.

The next day, Nabi Efendi woke up early and was having his breakfast, which consisted of cheese, milk and date jam as befitted his dietary regime, in his pergola. He heard horses neighing outside and was all ears, followed by the round clap of the knocker on the courtyard gate. The gate was opened by the steward and three couriers entered and dismounted from their horses. These were the guards of the caravan taking the Procession of the Purse to the Hijaz that year. They wore sad expressions on their faces and were tense in their demeanour. "This visit bodes no good. Let's hope for the best!" Nabi mumbled to himself and invited the three to the table. First came the greetings. Then, one of the messengers handed the stamped imperial cylindrical pencase he took from his bosom, to Nabi Efendi. Nabi Efendi removed the decree contained within it and read:

> *It has been decreed to Urfalı Yusuf Nabi Efendi domiciled in Aleppo that, owing to the transfer of the manor appropriated for your residence at present to the Privy Purse being fixed upon, pursuant to the new austerity measures executed in the state treasury, it is the decree of our felicitous Sultan that the key to the vacated premises be surrendered within a period of seven days to the esteemed Beylerbeyi.*
>
> *In Recebü'l-mürecceb, Year 1122.*
> *Grand Vizier Ali Paşa*

Shaken by the gravity of what he read, Nabi Efendi knew full well that this decree was sent not by Sultan Ahmet III, but by Çorlulu Ali Paşa, who used his seal. This was because when he himself resided in Istanbul, he gave a letter of goodwill to Sultan Mehmet the Hunter for the Grand Vizierate of Musahip Mustafa Paşa, who was his patron at the time. When he later became aware of this action, his rival Çorlulu Ali Paşa deemed it treachery and repressed it saying, "I'll show you, O poet! May fate grant me opportunity at once!" Moreover, so as to intimate his pique, insult him and exact revenge, he asked Nabi to write a special stanza, or chronogram based on numerological calculations for the lavatory he had built in Üsküdar where he had formerly served as judge. As it was not customary to record the date of completion of a lavatory, Nabi drew the intended lesson. In the stanza he produced, he composed an adroit epigram – registered and reply paid – and made his own riposte. The stanza became legendary in those days.

My judge made a lavatory
So that waste remained not on skin.
Said O Nabi record the date
I'll crap on such benefaction!

After this, the paths of Nabi Efendi and Çorlulu Ali Paşa separated and their enmity began. Now that Çorlulu was Grand Vizier in Istanbul, he was exacting revenge for that unsettled account.

Even if Nabi Efendi tried not to show his sadness to the messengers bringing the decree, he could not put out the flames he felt within. He was to vacate the manor in a desperate hurry but where would he go now that he was well into his seventies? It would be one thing if he was on his own, but all these men worked for him and he provided the means of livelihood for all their families as well. He knew that Baltacı Paşa would boil over with rage when he came to hear of it, but he would be unable to oppose the Grand Vizier's command.

When the knocker of the courtyard gate was beaten once again towards evening, Nabi Efendi was on the verge of completing a *gazal* in his room.

> *We have seen both autumn and spring in the orchard of this world*
> *We have beheld the winds of both jubilation and sorrow.*

"We have seen both autumn and spring in the orchard of the world. This is why we know very well that both sorrow and joy blow like the wind." In his *gazal* beginning thus, he related the fleeting nature of Çorlulu Ali Paşa's intoxication with power and position, and reflected how those incurring the curse of the aggrieved would surely not prosper. In this arena many a fast rider was knocked to the ground by a single arrow loosed by the curse of the wronged and those overcome by pride one day fall flat. The cup from which they drink the wine of purpose turns into a beggar's tin. He wrote with the experience that 70 years of life had given him and with the *hikemi* philosophical form that he spoke best.

When he heard knocking on the manor house door, he was left baffled. He hastened to hide the paper on which he wrote the gazal, the ink of which had not even dried. Taking me from the table and placing his trembling hand on the frontispiece of my first page, he slipped the paper inside my threadbare cover. "Come in!" he said.

❦❦❦

My God! What an unspeakable moment that was! It was so real that it did not resemble any of the dreams and reveries into which I had delved over the years. Here she was right before me! The beloved I sought for close to 200 years, in every place that I went, whom I missed more with every quest and with whom I fell in love more with each yearning, the one I loved, the one with whom I dissolved in my spirit and froze in my mind. My beloved was right before me. This was Leyla! This was Leyla herself. This was my dark-haired, dark-eyed, hapless beloved who plucked me with her delicate fingers from the Tigris banks while I was still a strawberry and then threw me between the date fibres boiling in a cauldron instead of taking me to her lips. The scribe girl that Baltacı Mehmet Paşa had the night before promised to send Nabi Efendi was Leyla, my Leyla. My Leyla whom I had sought for years and years since leaving Hilla, travelling from region to region and land to land.

I, my master Fuzuli's magnificent slave Kays... Found my Leyla at a time I did not remotely seek her. I rejoiced at a time when I had lost all hope. The Kays living inside my tale had never been this close to Leyla when chancing upon her in the country or in the desert. And here she was right beside me. Between her heart and mine was only Nabi Efendi's breath. Poor old man! Like me, he too was dumbfounded and his tired heart began pounding with excitement before such beauty. How could it not pound, when he had never before had such a beautiful concubine. And what is more, a concubine who knew how to write, was versed in poetry and had a beautiful voice... He thought about the place in which this girl had been brought up in seclusion and where she was raised. "She must have been raised in the bosom of a dark rose!" he later said and then immediately changed his opinion. "No, no! Allah must have kneaded the dough of this girl with the fragrance of rose." The things that were going through his mind at that moment! At one point, I even sensed him lament, "Why am I not young, or where was this girl when I was a youth?" and then this couplet fell from his lips:

Fate's taster pottered about so much that
When the serving came the appetite left.

Of course my Leyla knew what this couplet was about. "When you dither and fuss too much over your fate, you will have lost all your appetite by the time the meal to be consumed comes to table." This was the reason for her blushing, in any event. She first cast her eyes to the ground and then directed her gaze to me in the hands of old Nabi Efendi. He was in a state of perplexity having first received bad and then good news and, what is more, he was flabbergasted by her beauty. It was as though she felt it... I spoke in place of Nabi Efendi's speechless tongue: "Yes, it is me, the Mecnun who lost his mind with your love and pronounced your name to the whole world. It is me, Kays... You know, we went to school together and remember how we read one another like a book. Remember how once upon a time you would send your messages to me on clouds and your smell wafting in the early morning breeze? You know, how wars were waged in your name and how the gallant heroes of the Nawfal, who had wanted you to be mine, and the Ibn Salam, who wanted you for themselves shed blood on the scorching sands. Remember, how you made an appointment with me in a deserted place, and covered yourself with a shroud, and I reached your side before your body grew cold? Remember how lovers began to make their vows in our name? That is me, Kays, your mecnun, the Kays who went mad in your name! Throughout the centuries that passed in your absence, I said:

If I am me, then who are you, O love?
And if you are you, then who is poor me?

I kept you alive inside me. I knew that you would live for me, that you would stay alive for me and that you would one day come to me. Welcome, the light of my eye! Welcome, my happiness, my spring! My love, my soul and my tears, welcome!"

She reached out and took me from Nabi Efendi's lap. As soon as she opened my cover, she cried, "Kaaays!" and placed her lips once again on the forehead which she had first kissed in the hut on the banks of the Tigris and had then covered with charcoal. She renewed her kiss, took a whiff of my scent which transcended the centuries and, with an instinct that showed her humanity, recognised her own scent after so many generations and embraced me. I realised that she recognised me while reading my name that she had written once in charcoal. I sensed this from her excitement, the beating of her heart and the shaking of her hands. Yes, I was in the hands of my Leyla. How many generations had she hidden herself in all the ages that had passed, how many cells had she changed and through how many gene chains was she filtered, and from how many lifelines had she descended, I could not make out, but my Leyla's lips had touched the most ancient mark of her lips. The blood-coloured peony blending with soot and my Rukal's flower of innocence found new colour from her lips. I realised that this minute marked the ultimate union of a whole expectation which gave meaning to my entire life, and that this moment was a re-birth carrying the mystery of all my anticipation. At that moment, when half of my life was complete, I screamed, "Leylaaa!" just as I had done before when sacrificing my life for her. Just like my master Fuzuli had written, I wanted to give my life once again, 1,000 times in a single moment, and to come back to life 1,000 times to cry out her name in my last breath and to thus rise to the heavens. The world faded from my vision, life became blurred around me, existence annihilated itself and consciousness took flight. "Leylaaa!" I shouted and the last image remaining in my eye was the vision of me that I saw in Leyla's dark eyes...

I remembered nothing else, I know not for how long, I forgot how to remember. I slept and erased waking from my lexicon.

Ahh, reunion! Remind me that I have forgotten!

25
How I kissed Leyla on moonlit Nights and fell into the Hands of Thieves at Sadabad

Who is it to preclude us from the gardens of Paradise?
'Tis bequeathed by our father and we will enter the house that is ours.

Nabi

A hidden affliction I knew was love
An adventure stricken with grief was love.

"The sixth cipher is before my very eyes!" rejoiced İbrahim Paşa, clapping his hands with delight. "The 1,375th couplet... In it is contained the love and the secret and the mystery. Good news, my friends, Arshiya Akeldan's secret as well as the golden statues of the Babylonian gods are about to fall at your feet, good news!"

Ibrahim Paşa was one of the most interesting men I had ever seen or been acquainted with. He was the son of Izdin Voivode Ali Ağa and had come to Istanbul aged 14 to work as an assistant to a halva-maker. His acumen was visionary and his efforts were rewarded with success. He advanced one step at a time, beginning in the palace *helvahane*, one of the three domed halls of the kitchens, and had reached the heights of his ascent 12 years prior as Grand Vizier. In the early years of his vizierate, he had greatly impressed the Sultan with his refined, innovative and luminary personality. Having earned his trust he had begun to gradually hold the administration in the palm of his hand. When he would reassure the Sultan, saying, "We are obliged to protect your state in your name!" he actually spoke in the name of the Babylon Society and matched the Sultan's interests with those of the Society. He began to put officials at the service of the Society and transformed his power into a kind of oppression. He would get his way in everything from diplomacy to war, from treaty agreements to economic measures, job appointments and the distribution of salaries to the janissaries. He was even in charge of ceremonies and organising entertainment. Many of the individuals he promoted to state administration were his friends and acquaintances. In addition, the spies that the Ottomans maintained abroad would leak highly classified information to him personally, over and above their official duties, and he in turn used this intelligence against the Sultan, the administration and the state.

He exercised influence over the sovereign to such a degree that the year he turned 55, whilst he had a Kaptanıderya son-in-law and two grandchildren from him, he sought Fatma Sultan, the 14 year-old daughter of the Sultan, who was himself only just 44 years-old, as a wife. The powerless sovereign was not able to refuse his vizier.

I was only just beginning to understand the real power of vizier Ibrahim Paşa as he sat in splendour glorying in the title of "son-in-law", in the ornate hall of Kağıthane's legendary Sadabad Palace. He was with Prince Rakoczi of Transylvania, next in line for the Hungarian throne, the Austrian ruler Eugen's favourite general Stefan and Afshar shepherd Nadir Ali known as Tahmasp Kuli Khan. With them were the Russian Tsar's Jewish secret service chief, Levian, Louis XV of France's *charge d'affaires* to Istanbul and former Duke of Bourbon Martel Clovis, and Bektaşi Baba Şeyh Abdülhay Efendi famed for his sway over the Janissaries. They sat around him reverently and none spoke without his permission. This summer palace was constructed as a magnificent work of art entirely for entertainment and the stately pool was decorated with waterworks and fountains. The Grand Vizier looked like a true Marduk in this setting.

As the radiant September sun glinted on the windows of the male quarters, the assembled men were served white wine in crystal glasses. Some came in disguise and some graced the gathering as the frequent guests of Ibrahim Paşa's famous salon. Just as the priests of Babylon had done with sage Akeldan, they greeted him by clenching the two fingers of their right hands.

I was witnessing a full-member meeting of the Babylon Society for the first time. These seven people, all well versed in politics and diplomacy as much as in literature, art and music, first debated at length the state of world affairs. I became more and more amazed as I heard their words. They talked in great detail of how fear of the Turk might cease to haunt the European imagination since the Treaty of Karlovac that the Ottomans had been forced to sign after 16 years of war. Thanks to the Treaty of Pasarofça which was then being negotiated, they saw that territory could be taken from the Ottomans and that the Ottomans could even be defeated. One by one, the now-scattered Mediterranean city-states could be captured and Christianised. Ways of weakening the Ottoman state with a view to promoting this course needed to be sought. At the same time, the army still waiting in Üsküdar to advance upon Iran had to be delayed as much as possible so as to demoralise the troops and enhance the influence of Russia over Iran. Greek convert Paşas needed to be assigned posts in senior state positions in order for Greeks on the Mediterranean islands to be given more active roles. In addition, they needed to repatriate the Swedish King, Charles XII, who had spent three and a half years displaced in Bender and this meant coming to an agreement with his formidable foe, Russian monarch Peter I. They would also need to boost Nadir Ali's reputation in the eyes of Tahmasp Han so that the Safavids took more efficient measures in Afghan and Khorasan territory in the East, which would also ensure he prevailed over Ashraf Khan. They would encourage the Ottoman palace to ostentation and fashion, opening the taps of corruption and allowing the palace women in particular to indulge in extravagance and luxury. European fashions were quickly popularised by these women who picked them up via envoys, travellers and diplomats and in turn influenced the wider population. The men discussed how *medrese*-taught subjects could be secularised as much as possible and how grand buildings in the better suburbs of European states could be built. This would pave the way for new embassies. At the same time, the printer-merchants would be provoked and they would interfere with the Ottoman printing house established by Ibrahim Müteferrika. The world would be prepared for Vatican-based governance through the success of the Babylon Society.

The current aims of the Society frightened me. Whilst I had been travelling in the icy nations of the north, the Society had changed its entire approach. Ideas, administration and philosophies of management had all changed. I could see how time flowed inexorably and consumed the weak ruthlessly.

The afternoon sunbeams began splitting into shafts through the windows of the men's quarters and projecting different colours into the hall. Some of the Society members were watching children as they played in groups whilst washing their feet in the cool waters of the Kağıthane brook. Further out, the eye roved on the generous flirtatiousness of the embassy women aboard the *pereme* boats, or the suggestive dimples and flippant languor revealed by the disarranged yashmaks of the seductive belles flashing through the windows of landaus drawn by silver-harnessed horses. Or again, the eye alighted on graceful women getting on swings with their tailored dresses made entirely of guipure lace. Meanwhile, servants entered the hall and began setting the tables abundantly. Before long, the court musicians took their places. All hearts seemed to flutter with delectable excitement brought on by the sight of the various kinds of jam in crystal bowls, cheeses, appetisers, thin sheets of sun-dried mulberry and plum pulp, walnuts on a string dipped in starch, grape molasses arranged on round brass trays, bejewelled trays on which were piled flat breads with pheasant meat alongside fish soups, pastries, grilled cutlets brought upon trays inlaid with amber, rice with pine nuts in large deep copper dishes, olive oil dishes, sherbets, different halvas, rose jams in porcelain bowls and various wines cooled in ceramic jugs.

They had just done away with ceremony and posturing with the intention of passing the night in the arms of pleasure, when Ibrahim Paşa repeated the previous couplet and indicated me. "Esteemed friends! By virtue of the treasure we thought was lost to us, we now have the world in the palm of our hands. The stars will shine upon us and the celestial strength of the Babylonian gods will be ours to command." In so saying, he included not just the seven planets worshipped by the Chaldeans, but also the information contained in the tablets, as well as the golden idols waiting in the treasury of Babylon, and he laughed.

It is strange but, being amidst all these intelligent men who were engaged in determining the course of the world's future by discovering the secrets hidden among my couplets, who wanted to govern time through the ciphers decoded from between my lines and who were not content with mere aspiration, but who closed ranks with one another to achieve the same end, gave me a bitter delight impossible to describe. This was a pleasure distinct even from the ambling of Baltacı Mehmet Paşa's horses carrying us when we set off for Istanbul with Leyla, with whom I was reunited after ages long enough to be measured in close to five human lifetimes. I thought back to Nabi's manor house in Aleppo, Leyla's sorry tears throughout the journey, and the drunken sensation of sleeping in a tight embrace after kisses witnessed by the moonlight on Leyla's jasmine-perfumed chest. Following the 12 poor but elated years that passed in travelling with Leyla from lodging to lodging after the death of Nabi Efendi the year after our arrival in Istanbul, we now spent a sorrowful life apart. Yet we could still sense one another in the

Grand Vizier's palaces on the banks of the Kağıthane brook. After Nabi Efendi died, Leyla was sold to the mansion of Ibrahim Paşa who was then grand vizierate steward and he in turn presented her to his daughter Huri, whom he had given in marriage two years prior to Kaptanıderya Kaymak Mustafa Paşa. At the time, Leyla was only just 23 and Huri was 12 years of age. The power of my love had never separated me from Leyla. Moreover, there were two things that she prized and cherished in the world: one was me and the other was the needle lace kerchief she wore when she was brought to Aleppo as a slave. I offered her the memories of the lands which she loved and the kerchief reminded her of her mother. Her happiest times were those in which she read me and my happiest moments were those when I could feel her hand. I was so intoxicated by her touch that it made me feel anguish alongside elation. My joy was due to reunion, while my anguish stemmed from the thought of separation. At times, I could not even savour the taste of union due to this fear of separation and my torment chased away my happiness. This is what love meant. A lover desiring union had to be prepared for separation. That is why I thought that the most felicitous lover was the one who always sought union, but could never achieve it. It was possible to live until the end of time hearing the footsteps of the approaching beloved, but one could have died immediately after ultimate union. A separation whose end is union transformed even affliction into pleasure, but a union ending in separation smothered joy with suffering.

To my mind, all of the days spent with Leyla, all the way from Aleppo to Istanbul, were valuable and all were granted by Divine favour. How can I explain what unbearable bliss it was to sleep listening to the heartbeat of the Leyla with whom I could not unite in my story? Even on the happiest day of the wild life I spent apart from Leyla in the Najd desert, I had not felt myself this fortunate. I, who lived the same life as the gazelles and lions of the desert, could now caress my beloved like I caressed the gazelles. I dreaded her withdrawal as much as I feared the lions. I cannot express, for this reason, my suffering at the thought of her perhaps one day deserting me somewhere. What is more, the possibility that someone in pursuit of me would tear me away from her harrowed my mind at every moment. In these last years, after nearly seven quarter-centuries in which I experienced what separation from her truly meant, I remembered the first days I closed my eyes to all but her. That was when I opened my heart to her alone. I recalled that first flush of love when I was strung together in verses by my master Fuzuli. I wanted to send separation far away from me and continue my union for at least as long as I had waited.

The memories rendering Leyla's sleep of a single lifetime as fragile as a spider's web melted in crucibles my love that had endured over the centuries. They distilled and separated it into threads, wove it like steel mesh armour and clothed me with it. In this way, the only thing remaining unchanged in a world in which time rapidly changed everything was my love. At each turning of the page of history, which then remained closed forever more, the sole element saving from the clutches of death was my love. After having lived thus for seven quarter-centuries, I could not explain my finding Leyla in any way other than as an act of Divine grace. I prayed ceaselessly for Him not to deprive me of this blessing and shivered like a willow leaf caught in the wind. This is why the happiness and suffering I experienced were equal. I was suffering and knew that the Arabic word denoting torment and anguish derived from the trilateral root meaning "sweet". My delight was magnificent even in suffering. Was I not with Leyla after all? What would it matter if what I endured was torment? Who could grant me a greater happiness after I had sought sanctuary through her during my suffering? I do not know whether I could bear the torment of happiness without her. May God grant me the torment of death with her in place of happiness without her!

The happiest times of the days we spent together were undoubtedly when we conversed tête-à-tête. There were times where she related our adventure at length to the Paşa's daughter Huri. Where did I stand in such an adventure, where did our paths cross with Kays, the hero of L&M, and where did they diverge? I could not guess. He is neither separate from me, nor am I unlike him. My agony knew his agony and I rejoiced in his happiness. And God is witness to my wishing insanity upon him. I cannot remember the number of times I concurred with his prayer, "O Lord, render me familiar with the affliction of love / Deprive me not of love's affliction for but a moment," and how much I dwelt on these words. This is why I could not consider Kays and myself as different individuals. Sometimes I even reckoned that he had as great a share in love as me. But then I deemed this an injustice and felt ashamed of myself: he confined his love to Leyla, the hapless daughter of the Banu ‹Amir clan, whereas I had fallen in love once again with a Leyla on the cool banks of the Tigris. I had come to smell one rose upon another and, what is more, had been favoured with a brand new blessing after all the centuries that had passed. Leyla had appeared before me after all this time. I knew that she was descended from a bloodline distilled from the Banu ‹Amir and shaped by the Tigris, that she smiled in the same manner in the light of love that the genes, which had remained unchanged for six generations after the Leyla I knew on the Tigris, transmitted onto her heart, and that the coolness unique to the Tigris shaped her manner and temperament. This is why Leyla lived thrice in my love and I fell in love with her over again each and every time. And now, in the happy life we lived in Istanbul, if she knew how joyful I was whilst excitedly describing our old adventure to Huri as though feeling and living the love between us amidst my pages, I suspect that she would perhaps not want to read me. With the contentedness of the beloved bestowing the pleasure of union upon her lover, she would instead wish to hold me close to her heart and carry me thus.

When Huri married the Kaptan Paşa, she took Leyla and me with her to her home. And when she moved to the apartment next to her father's palace the night the Sadabad season opened in Kağıthane for this year's Hidrellez festival, she requested me from Leyla. She read out certain sections of mine to her husband who did not understand much about love, in an attempt to say, "What lovers there are in the world!" Perhaps she had formed passionate fancies of a romantic night at the beginning of summer. Regrettably, only the moonlight saw me on that night and Huri, with eyes closed in crude lust, had to make do once more with dreamy musings.

All that happened took place on the following day. When Ibrahim Paşa, who resided in the apartment adjacent to the Sadabad Palace, entered his son-in-law's room in haste for an urgent meeting, he noticed me upon the *elibelinde* motif woven into the rug, which was reserved for the candelabra. At first, he turned a few of my pages as though I was an ordinary book. He understood poetry, knew about eloquence and envied my master Fuzuli's *rana* style. He had actually seemed to me to be a good person. The bags under his eyes, sunken cheeks and grizzled beard gave him a handsome air for someone of his age. A great many poets and artists around him received support and everyone knew that he praised their art.

At first I thought that what surprised him while reading me was finding such a fine book of poetry in his son-in-law's room, as he knew very well that his son-in-law was not acquainted with poetry. But when he got to my numbered pages from the 607th couplet onwards, I thought that his heart would stop with excitement. He recognised cuneiform script and, forgetting the urgent meeting he was to have with his son-in-law, seized me and went directly to his own room. I have not heard from my Leyla since that day.

My fears had come true. I was not mistaken in supposing that he was a member of the Babylon Society. At least the great Grand Vizier of the Ottoman state with treasure at his command could not be a bounty hunter in pursuit of the Babylonian idols. All that had happened to me was my unavoidable destiny; when we left Aleppo for Istanbul, I had suspected as much and had even prepared myself for this. But my real worry now was the predicament of my Leyla, to whom I could not even bid farewell before leaving. Who knows how she is in a fluster to find me too!

According to what I learned while under house arrest with Ibrahim Paşa, the Babylon Society had assumed my ink was completely washed away when I was plunged into the waters of the Danube carried by Froberger who leapt to his death from the Silistra Citadel. The Society had then focussed all its efforts on the dagger still in its possession. Meanwhile the bounty hunters had made my master Fuzuli's flask strap with its pattern of numbers and letters look like an authentic decorative item and sold it for a measly price at the covered bazaar, thus trading their hopes for a few pieces of Venetian gold.

Evliya Çelebi's son, who was a baby when we set off together, was now an old man with grandchildren. I had lived a solitary life all this time and had occupied myself solely with my longing for Leyla. Those were the years when both the Babylon Society and the treasure hunters remained in the past, the years in which no one was aware of my existence and the years when I was sifted through time in Mullah Mehmet's sack of alchemical preparations. I wonder if those years were a good slice of time for me. To be honest, I never asked myself this question. And I do not think that I can find an answer to this question now. I had been forgotten and had begun to feel anguish and joy simultaneously. This was a strange contradiction. No longer was vitriol spread onto my fibres in order to uncover the secret of the Chaldean priests. The sages running after me like lovers were not around me. My tale continued sparking passions, but my secret was as though lost along with me. I was trying to distil life, sometimes in the seclusion of a hamam, sometimes inside the ox-cart of a melon seller, or accompanying the call of a fried liver seller which reverberated in alleyways. I had grown tired of the butchers thrusting me in their bags with their greasy hands and taking me home. Tired too of the imams who examined my lines before instructing the children about my story at the endowment house of the town mosque. I had had enough of the coarse behaviour of the neighbourhood merchants hiring me out after the *teravih* prayer in Ramadan. The simple and sometimes meaningless couplets written in my margins, the dates of reading on my last page and the readers' names, as well as the signatures of semi-luminary know-it-alls who derived pleasure from stamping their signet rings on my frontispiece increased in number during these years. These were the times I felt like a strumpet and sought a man of rank. I sought a gentleman who would love me with delicacy, who would be propelled into sweet dreams as he read my lines and who would shed tears and not watermelon juice upon me.

In Ibrahim Paşa's hands, I felt as helpless as the drops splashing from the dragon-headed fountains of the artificial pools made by the Kağıthane brook. I can even say that I was pleased that the Babylon Society had found me. Despair had obstructed my path, forcing me into a life of adventures filled with mystery instead of a life of love. Now I was sad because I was separated from my beloved and deprived of love. Nonetheless, I had one consolation and that was that Leyla lived and breathed somewhere near me. Even if I did not see her face or hear her voice, the same sun warmed her skin and my binding and the same night fell on us both. My beloved, who was engraved on my centuries-old being by my master Fuzuli as an adornment, was here; my Leyla, the *raison d'être* of my love was here and was to grow old right beside me. So I trust that our paths will most certainly cross one day. Perhaps it was this consolation that made me want to share with others this great secret that I carry. Did I have an inflated sense of my own self-worth? Had I become arrogant? I do not know, but I thought if the treasure remained unknown, then it would have no value. Kays too had fallen in love from the very beginning, had gone mad and had thus become famous. Since I bore the same love, then I was also entitled to fame. Love was a matter of the heart and where it existed there was no room for reason. Love could not enter the heart until reason was left behind. Love began when emotions held sway over thoughts. There could be no such falsehood as speaking of love when thoughts were directing emotions.

My heart longed for Leyla, which was all well and good, but why then was my mind saying that the road to reunion with her involved divulging my secrets? Perhaps this is where I went wrong. I spent the rest of my life in anguish and suffering because I coveted Kays' fame and wanted to be famous myself. But what could I have done when no one would know until the end of time that I was a greater lover than Kays? They would read me and, as they did so, they would be dazzled by Kays' love and fail to recognise me. Whereas if I were to disclose the secret I carried within, I suspected my fame would increase as much as Kays'. And then Leyla would love me more. Fame functions as a natural magnet to love. If I cannot explain to anyone that the passion within me is oriented not towards fame but towards love, and if, at the very least, I cannot tell Leyla that I am her lover, than what would be the value of all the pain and suffering I have endured in her name? This is why I decided that revealing the treasures within me to the Society members was not such a bad thing after all. At any rate, carrying two treasures at the same time was now as difficult for me as living two separate lives. While the poetic verses describing my love had been strung on my pages like diamonds on a necklace, the threads strung by the treasures of the Babylonian sages had long since begun to rouse within me merely a sense of connectedness and captivity. I wanted someone to come after me and take the secret from inside me. In this way, I could return to my Leyla, share her love, dry the tears falling from her eyes and share the anguish settling in her heart. If I gave away my secret, then Leyla could return and I could be by her side long enough to see her grow old. No one can reprove me for wishing to see, on my own, her very first strand of grey hair.

I think that I wanted to chase rather than flee and be seen instead of going into hiding. Moreover, even in these few hours, I had greatly missed my Leyla's radiant cheek, her flowing locks and her ruby-pink lips. She appeared before me wherever I looked. This is why I loved Sadabad so much, because it always presented me with memories laden with Leyla... And also Ahmet Nedim Efendi... It was as though he described Leyla in all his poems, my Leyla!

On this night, when September's sadness began to fall on Sadabad along with the leaves of autumn, I felt as jubilant as the colours of the Bohemian chandeliers illuminating the hall and perhaps just as fortunate to be at the septennial meeting of the Babylon Society. That night, I felt myself ready to disclose all my secrets. On the morrow I hoped to start a life filled only with love, freed of all secrets. If the masters who searched for my secret by candlelight in gloomy rooms in the past had seen the colours reflected from the hundreds of oil lamps of this radiant hall onto the countenances around me, they would surely have investigated not just my secret, but my love also. I am afraid to say that there were then present only three people in this hall who could read and understand me: the Grand Vizier, Şeyh Abdülhay Efendi and Nadir Ali. The remaining four spoke the languages of Christendom.

When the last servant clearing the tablecloths, ewers and napkins, left the room, Ibrahim Paşa raised his glass. "In honour of wise priest Akeldan and his faithful friends!" Moses Levian, the secret service chief of the Russian Tsar, removed a cloak from the small trunk he carried with him and placed it upon Ibrahim Paşa's shoulders in a mystic ritual. I had never before seen such a cloak upon the previous masters. He said with religious rapture that this was a cloak like those worn by the Chaldean priests. He had had it sewn based on the illustrations he obtained from old Egyptian treasures. Wearing it at this sitting wherein he presumed the secret would be revealed was a spiritual offering to the Chaldean gods and the gods would, in turn, help them solve the mystery.

The other members – holding I know not which council – gathered around the master to exchange greetings once again. That Sirrush-headed bejewelled dagger upon the table with which we shared the same fate, the worn flask strap that enabled me to experience once again my master Fuzuli's warmth, a rolled-up leather panel two spans in width which I could not make out and I, waited together helplessly like the four children that Nebuchadnezzar brought from the four corners of his empire to be sacrificed during his last ceremony.

When they sat at the table, having performed the ceremony of greeting upon great Marduk's shoulder, Martel Clovis first unfurled the leather scroll. On this piece of leather was a depiction consisting of seven triangles of equal size from the centre outwards. In the acute angle of each triangle was one of the seven planets representing the Chaldean deities and, in their angles of expansion were, respectively, the cuneiform counterparts of the numerological equivalents obtained from my couplets and finally the texts of the same couplets. Each triangle was painted a different colour. The gold-coloured triangle pertained to the Sun and the silver one to the Moon. Nebo's blue and Ishtar's white followed one another. The red triangle contained Nergal's name and Marduk was in the purple and Ninib in the black triangle. Beside these were Pisces, Virgo and Leo motifs, among other symbols of the gods. Each triangle was separated into quadrants and divided into 360 degrees to the millimetre and centimetre.

"The Society has made a good deal of headway since I roamed the snow-covered cities of the north!" I thought to myself. While Şeyh Abdülhay Efendi was busy writing each of the five couplets identified in earlier meetings on a separate sheet of paper, General Stefan was trying to memorise the sixth couplet, the meaning of which he did not understand at all, though he was affected by its harmony. He thought about the rise and fall, rhythmic accent and cutting points of the syllables, the sounds of the syllables matching exactly the first verse and how they roused within him a sense of the beauty of the poem though he did not always understand its meaning. What he admired was the musicality of its structure, surpassing the meaning. Tapping his index finger on the table at regular intervals as though rendering the meter, he parsed the couplet loudly:

"A hid-den af-flic-tion I knew was love
An ad-ven-ture strick-en with grief was love."

Şeyh Abdülhay Efendi, I suspect to increase General Stefan's admiration, requested Rakoczi of Transylvania to translate and explain his words: "I knew love to be a hidden affliction... And that love was a painful adventure..." He then continued excitedly, "Our condition resembles that which the love master Fuzuli describes in this couplet. The astronomical secrets of the Chaldean masters are woven into a love story for all of us – as hidden and calamitous as all loves must be. Even the way we hide our work from everyone corresponds exactly with lovers hiding their loved ones. Our adventures in pursuit of the tablets transcend the centuries and are filled with the affliction of love. Concealing is as dangerous as revealing. It is such a painful adventure that even the tears that our mystics shed with love for God remain as ingenuous as the words of a novice. Of course love needed to be hidden. Otherwise it could not have lasted. God veils Himself and wakens within the servant an endless quest. Like a mystic seeking God in everything he sees, the concept of intergalactic travel within the boundlessness of space, has oriented us towards the Chaldean mystics. Our eyes are now like those of a lover who sees no one save his beloved. Wherever we turn, we want to see the ciphers of the old masters. In the same way that the greatest worldly blessing and most exalted pleasure for a lover is to reunite with his beloved, we too continue to connect the accumulated love of the centuries to one another to attain that love. The suffering and hardship, wretchedness and anguish we have endured together in this way with all our former members, is of course as extreme as the joy of a lover attaining his objective. However exalted the emotion, the lover is always doomed to suffer the longing and pain of separation to the same degree. The love of a lover increases in proportion to his anguish and suffering. It is the magnitude of the pain of separation that increases the joy of ultimate union. The rapture of ultimate union is proportional to the peaking pain of separation. We are now very close to feeling the joy of union of the 5,000 year loves our former masters carried forward to our day."

He walked to the window ledge and directed everyone's attention to Venus. "On this night when Ishtar shines in all her whiteness, when she is illuminated by the red light of the Sun, world domination will be ours, along with knowledge and gold. The secret the librarian referred to when he said, 'There are seven true secrets for one who knows love and one who possesses it, gains mastery over the world,' will reveal all its mystery on this night and present the world like an apple in the palm of the hand."

"The place from which we observe objects in the universe is important," began Stefan, sanguinely. "Ishtar winks at us tonight. You all know that there is constant progression and expansion in the universe. It is as if Ishtar reigned over time tonight, from the peak of her radiance. You know how volume, temperature and density each became a separate dimension and how height, depth, width and breadth emerged. God then placed an ether, or quintessence, in the cosmic universe. Just as this liquid gas prevents the co-mingling of the different layers of the firmament, it also enables each one of these layers to rotate within the other, in different directions. Time, which passed from the early universe to the ancient universe and to the current one, was able to complete its rotation by means of this liquid. Setting the universe in motion with a radiation independent of a sense of direction, night and day, God created the galaxies consisting of hundreds of billions of star clusters and separate systems. Great Marduk, Nebo and Ishtar then each came to a decision and designed destinies for mortals. There is no doubt that more than this is written on Arshiya Akeldan's tablets. Therein are calculations for heat and light years, as well as mass and volume. Given the differing mass indices and diameters of each galaxy, we at the Babylon Space Research Centre will soon be able to measure the time required for travel to the nearest heavenly body on the basis of the ciphers we will discover tonight."

"Then let's send you first, Stefan, if you wish!" joked Ibrahim Paşa. "You speak of the seven layers of the firmament as though they were right here!" he added with astonishment.

"Indeed!" retorted General Stefan. "Galaxies cluster in varying dimensions like villages, towns and cities. We will encounter innumerable villages and cities in innumerable systems over there. If I am the first to go, then I'll tell you all about it on my return."

"Of course!" said Abdülhay Efendi. "After all, Lagari Hasan Çelebi conveyed Jesus' greetings to Sultan Murat. But he didn't travel far at all!"

Even if Nadir Ali and Levian tried hard to understand all that was being discussed, they were at a loss after a few sentences. Levian even kept saying that they had blasphemed and that they needed to repent for speaking of God in a mocking manner. At that point, I thought, "If these people obtain Akeldan's tablets and read the electron, proton and neutron calculations therein, if they learn that that which they call quintessence is composed of 75 per cent hydrogen and 25 per cent helium, see the formulae for a thermal doomsday in the event of the depletion of the world's energy-producing reserves and then realise that they could reach the heavenly body in the nearest galaxy via space travel only after travelling a distance of 10 to the power of six light years, they would probably go out of their minds."

However much information they possessed in relation to the enormities of space, they kept relating what they knew as if wanting to outdo one another. Some of them went on about Eastern mysticism, some about atheistic theories, others spoke of the old Greek philosophers whilst formulating theories justifying the Babylonian sages. Each asserted that he alone possessed accurate knowledge. When their knowledge on these subjects was exhausted, the topic of discussion was steered towards the future and they began to imagine the new face of the world. As far as I could understand from the ambitions concealed behind their words, important decisions had been taken at the Babylon Society meeting convened seven years earlier. I realised from their discussions that all of them were present at that meeting also.

As Ibrahim Paşa and Nadir Ali Han searched for a cipher among my pages, Şeyh Abdülhay Efendi lit his pipe, and the others drank wine as though sipping the elixir of life at a sacred Babylonian sacrificial ceremony. They discussed and debated what they were going to do. The subject shifted to the political transformations in Europe and Martel Clovis took the floor. "I can now send a messenger to His Majesty Louis XV to tell him to terminate the viceroyalty of Philippe I, Duke of Orléans, and warn him not to trust Cardinal Fleury, who secretly spent the gold coming from his colonies. With the power of the secret that we solve tonight, and on my return to France, I can become a vizier and, as the world assumes its new shape, protect the exalted interests of France in the name of the sanctity of our Society."

"Certainly, your Excellency ambassador extraordinary and plenipotentiary!" agreed Nadir Ali Han, turning his face away from my pages, "Certainly! The dream of one day being freed of Tahmasp's yoke and establishing the Afshar State enchants me. And when we send Count Rakoczi to Transylvania and General Stefan to Austria, then we can initiate a long era of peace in Eurasia. From this day forth, we can redirect all the effort and money which would otherwise be spent on war on space research instead. When we use Abdülhay Efendi's influence over the janissaries to discourage voguish talk of revolution, and prevail upon the Ottoman troops for peace, then our task will become easy. The Balkans and Babylon Space Research Centre: here we come! Maybe we will even establish the Research Centre in Mosul, where our secret is buried. We will gather the scientists in our respective countries and urge them to work for the common interest of humanity, placing before them heaps of gold and the tablets bearing sage Akeldan's fingerprints."

"Friends!" interposed Ibrahim Paşa authoritatively. "Let us postpone our plans for the time being and return to our couplet. The numerological sum of the words denoting 'secrecy' and 'love' is 576 and our couplet is the 1,375th couplet. Now, we need to find the relationship between these two numbers. After subtracting the common numeral seven, the number of Babylonian deities, then the total of the remaining numbers in the sequence is 11 in the first (i.e. 5+6) and 9 in the second (1+3+5). The question now is: Are we going to add 11 and 9, or subtract the lesser from the greater?"

"You will do neither! You will add the figures in the number 1,375 and divide the number 16 that you will obtain from seven, such that the remainder which is the number 2, is your sixth cipher," I felt like saying, as I wanted them to find all my ciphers before sunrise and return me to my Leyla.

By the time the resplendent sconces on the decorated walls of Sadabad palace met with daylight, the tired eyes and wine-clouded minds of those present were buried in deep silence. The morning wind of the last days of September blew up wildly, bringing with it the sound of drums beating from

Istanbul, but by then they had all at once drifted into such a deep sleep that they did not hear these sounds.

Within Istanbul's city walls, hamam attendant Halil, nicknamed "Patrona" in honour of his prior career as a seaman, and Muslu Beşe formerly of the mounted *Zağarcı* corps, had raised the flag of rebellion with 17 others they had gathered around them. They were shouting, "We have issue with evil! Let all those from the community of Muhammad unite under our banner!" Thus they marched from near Bayezid Mosque all the way to Atmeydanı at Sultanahmet, bringing hundreds of Istanbulites to the point of repeating this same slogan under their banner. The army was in Üsküdar so the city was defenceless. In alarm, Sultan Ahmet III sent for Ibrahim Paşa.

The massed crowds were shouting. "Ibrahim Paşa issued a secret order for Tabriz to be surrendered to the Shah. This is why he is stalling the army. We demand the shari'a!" Implied in the call for shari'a was the desire that all offenders be punished and the law be upheld. The majority of the populace rose against the extravagance of the Grand Vizier's lifestyle. They resented him for appropriating their taxes for his own personal interests, using revenue to build pavilions for entertainment. They believed he was ruining the state by spending on entertainment on a scale never before witnessed by the people of Istanbul. They held him responsible for bringing about a corrupt order where the poor grew even poorer and the rich grew richer.

While Ibrahim Paşa was in a drunken slumber in Sadabad Palace, the people of Istanbul ran riot and prepared to take control of the city. Heads were sure to roll. The number of rioters had reached the thousands towards noon but the ringleaders were actually observant Muslims and had mutinied because they could not stomach the state's maladministration. In the main, the demonstrators were discontents who privately hankered after a bigger slice of pie. When inmates from the Baba Cafer, Galata, Rumelihisarı and Tersane prisons joined the fray, trouble started and looting and murders began rocking the city.

The members who had participated in the secret meeting with Ibrahim Paşa were woken around noon with news of mutiny. The damage had been done. Handing the six couplets that Şeyh Abdülhay Efendi wrote out on separate sheets of paper to each of the members, Ibrahim Paşa instructed, "Protect these and bring them with you when we next meet in order to carry the world's future to space."

After each of them dispersed to leave the city in disguise, travelling in different directions and taking differing routes, the agents of the Ottoman secret service realised that they had come too late. In the large hall of Sadabad Palace, only dirty drinking glasses and the overpowering smell of aniseed remained.

Martel Clovis took the dagger and General Stefan took my master Fuzuli's water bottle strap with him. The Chaldean-cut cloak and leather cartouche on which was written the names of the Babylonian gods, Bektaşi Baba Abdülhay Efendi hid beneath his coat before making his way to the Sufi lodge.

Before Ibrahim Paşa left Sadabad Palace, he called for his son-in-law Kaymak Mustafa Paşa, entrusted me to him and enjoined, "Give this book to city boy Nedim and tell him to hide it well. We will take back our trust once we weather this storm!" He reckoned that Nedim Efendi was the most popular poet in those parts and I could easily be hidden amongst his thousands of books.

I saw my Leyla for the last time that day, from a distance. She was crying and afraid. If she had known my love and sensed that I wished she would drop a single drop of the tears she now shed upon the tapered stain of the peony image on my bosom, she would certainly have stopped everything, made every effort and would be searching for me right now. If the peony that Rukal drew on my bosom with her blood had been watered with her tears, it would surely not have faded until the end of time. When she first saw me, she kissed me in the same place, on the picture of the peony, and the marks of her lips blended with those of Leyla, her mother from numberless generations earlier.

Unfortunately, she did not kiss me on the same spot. I dreamt of my life on the cool banks of the Tigris and thought of touching the lips of my beloved Leyla whom I left in the desert centuries ago, but I experienced over again the pain I felt the day I was thrown into the boiling cauldron with the date fibres. Now, this beautiful girl, whom I believed was created anew for me, from her progeny and descendants, this black-browed, dark-haired belle, was putting me through the same pain for the second time. When she saw me in the hands of her master Kaymak Paşa, she ran to grab me. But the Paşa had given me not to her, but to Ahmet Nedim Efendi.

As I drew away from Sadabad Palace in Nedim's hands that had begun to shake from the effects of alcohol, I realised that I would never again see my Leyla. Like her hair, her luck was dark, and my innards burned once more with the pain of previous generations. I had returned to the identity I possessed in my story. It was as though I were re-living the day I saw Leyla for the last time in the wilderness when I headed for the bleak desert to experience my love alone and increase my devotion. My life was attached to my tale and my fate was sorrow again.

I waited in Nedim Efendi's house in Beşiktaş for eight days. These were eight days filled with poetry. Used to reciting lewd poems, Nedim Efendi was now living in a state of fear and he had come to derive great pleasure from reading among my master Fuzuli's verses befitting his own state. One night, he even penned poems similar to some of my master's. Amazingly, he uttered verses as beautiful as the verses of my master and adorned the latter's platonic love with the sensations that he dreamt of or actually experienced in night-time embraces, or in sensual pleasures with boys. I was quick to realise that he was taken with the Albanian boy who worked as a gardener in his mansion. He would occasionally call him on the pretext of asking a few questions and seek to offer himself to him, but the young man did not fall for the play of this wizened degenerate in his fifties. There were even times, in the few gazals he wrote after he let this young man slip through his fingers, where he surpassed the lyricism of my master Fuzuli. My master was in love with love itself. In contrast, Nedim Efendi wanted to take the object of his adoration into his arms and allow him to feel the pinnacle of pleasure through his verses of love. You could feel the imaginary beloved of Divan poetry living in flesh and bone through his language. He spoke of touching rather than imagining and wrote of kissing the private parts of his beloved in lieu of describing his love. His way of representing sexuality was completely in accord with elite attitudes to entertainment peculiar to the era in which he lived.

Whilst reading my story, he was in constant astonishment before the greatness of my love. How was it possible that I did not possess Leyla during our encounters, that I did not make love to her, if only once? Why had my master Fuzuli not written in such a scene? His love found life on the strings of the lutes enlivening the Sadabad gaieties and the songs he wrote became fashionable on the lips of loose Istanbul women. Young men making passes at young women recited his couplets and lovers declared their love to their sweethearts with his verses.

The noble love that had filled the skies of Istanbul since the time of my master Fuzuli had given way to carnality and Nedim had assumed the role of its spokesman. But he was uttering all this so beautifully... Not a single mortal can be found in this world who can read Nedim Efendi's poetry and deny love. If you were to instruct the chief eunuchs in his words, their hearts would certainly burn with ardour.

For eight days, I watched Ahmet Nedim Efendi reading poetry from certain divans and heaving a sigh. In some of the new poems he wrote in his book, he burned constantly with longing for those old days. He knew that blood was being shed on the city streets but, as he reached the dregs of his glass, he could not stop himself missing the gardener boy and so could not evaluate rationally what was happening. I did not blame him for his behaviour as the city's uprising concerned me only in so far as it affected Leyla. Who knew what had become of her? Had she fallen into the hands of an irresponsible janissary or been raped by a fugitive? Perhaps death was very close to her and I was floundering helplessly, incapable of doing anything for my beloved.

Nedim Efendi, however, burned as he recalled his sins, but he was unable to bring himself to repent, just as the Pharaoh could not bring himself to acknowledge his own faith. He thought that he would appear before the Creator with a blackened countenance, but could not bring himself to do what was needed to clear it. As I looked at him, I thought I saw a genius who would come to be understood centuries later – a genius who had gone to waste. Here was the prodigy of Istanbul Turkish, the prodigy of life turning into pleasure in Istanbul, the prodigy of an art milieu kneaded with subtle pleasures. As debonair as his surroundings, this man had lived in a debonair space with debonair pleasures. However bad the social life in his time, his artistic milieu remained agreeable and pleasant. The arts enjoyed in the tulip gardens were highly sophisticated and in Sadabad, great heights were reached in poetry, urban design, architecture, music, visual arts as well as in the crafts of glass and fabric, marble and water design. It was a time of high aesthetics in thought and vision, and this screened the repugnance of social life. The life of a state is marked by the span of its art. When the age of its downfall begins, meridians in art reveal themselves. It had been quite some time since the Ottoman state started encountering internal and external setbacks, but the arts were still flourishing. The contemporaries of Ahmet Nedim, Ibrahim Paşa and Ahmet III were the children of precisely such dynamics.

It was a Monday. The gunshots coming from the city and the cries of the rebels could be heard coming nearer and nearer. By mid-morning, Nedim Efendi had guzzled down the contents of the last *rakı* bottle in his house, but had still not overcome his fear of death. The opium paste that he carried in his sash was also finished and he was harassing his servants to find him some tablets. Just then, there was beating upon the courtyard door and jarring voices shouted, "Hey, Ibrahim, you self-seeker! Get ready to make your last prayer!" He had wrapped me and the book in which he wrote his own poetry in two layers of oil cloth and hid us in the secret compartment of the flooring of the hall upstairs, between the floorboards, where he had formerly stashed his opium and hashish. When the rioters entered the house, I heard Nedim Efendi's last moans filtering from the garden between the roof tiles. Even if the arrivals said that he had fallen while jumping across to the neighbour's roof in an attempt to escape, I realised that he had committed suicide, believing that his honour and dignity would be violated in the event of his being captured alive.

A concubine came to the house after a three-day silence and took a few items of clothing, Nedim Efendi's divan and me from the ransacked mansion and headed for the disorderly houses by the high city walls at Surdibi. While crossing the wooden bridge at Karaköy, I saw Kaymak Mustafa Paşa's mansion upon the Süleymaniye hillsides, in which we spent many a night in each other's arms. Smoke was still billowing out of its roof, but it was no longer the old mansion. If was clear that the city's chief bandits had settled inside, looted its property and turned it into bachelors' quarters.

As the reign of Sultan Ahmet III, known as the Age of the Tulip, was coming to a complete close, this beautiful city was a living hell. There were no more potteries and paper factories, no fabric or broadcloth mills. The Sadabad summer palaces, pavilions, pools and tulip gardens were no more and Müteferrika's printing house as well as the newly opened schools were reduced to rubble. While the mob ransacked the city, I feared that my couplets and pages would be looted as well. For a few days, it felt as though my miniatures were trampled on. My pearls, verse by verse, were strewn about and the innocence of my story was violated.

These were days filled with anguish for everyone. Istanbul had not seen such a calamity since the Byzantines and such fear and terror had not been experienced in the city that people called *Dersaadet*, meaning "Abode of Felicity" or "Land of Safety". I never heard from Leyla again. Was she alive, into whose hands had she fallen, which grubby hands touched her golden hair? I knew not. How much had the dirty hands that touched all those who were lonely and vulnerable touched her also? I did not know. The pain of not being with her when she shed tears of blood was never going to leave me – this is what I felt.

26
Concerning the Night of Dervishes at Galata and the puzzling Puzzle of Love

Such a flame has the candle of the spirit
That the dome of the skies cannot contain it.

Şeyh Galib

Gazing upon the redness of the sunset reflected on Üsküdar's windows from the linden scented pergola of the Galata Mevlevihane, I pondered how many centuries it had taken for mysticism to become such a vital part of the refined cultural life of Istanbul. I, who had made all the cells of my existence readily available to poetry, could have lived happily until the end of time in this mystical place, where wood and marble meet. One side of this complex possesses Istanbul's most splendid view and the other leans against the cemetery and faces death. Days filter in the union of earth and love around the magnolia tree in the middle of the cobbled courtyard. The visitor entering from the arched door joining the annexe – the top floor of which was used as a library and the ground level as a public fountain and time-keeper's office – and the stone walls of the tomb is greeted with the celestial splash of the drinking fountain to the right and the çilehane* to the left. The construction of the cemetery – the dervishes here refer to their dead as the quiet ones, and describe burying as "glazing" – gives the impression of life merging with death in this stony place right where the pleasures of life wink at poetry across the arbour of the well and meet with harmonious strains of music.

After entering the three-storey wooden Mevlevihane fitted with marble steps, the visitor is struck by the squeaking stairs, lattices, *sema* floor, Şeyh chamber and the musicians' gallery. Centuries-old melodies permeate each and every ornament here. The melodies find their own harmony in the wide whirling skirts of the dervishes gyrating on the floor and spread to the far horizons of all Istanbul.

The Mevlevihane in which I entered as a glorious guest represented the smiling countenance of Islam to the embassies and churches in Galata in those days. The Sufi lodge had two types of guests distinct from its regular visitors: foreign embassy staff wishing to satisfy their curiosity and those fallen on hard times who were living on Istanbul's streets. The former would leave after filling their hearts and the latter their stomachs. The lodge saw its most refined activity during the rare times the Sultan visited, when state protocol would be added to the spiritual protocol to which it was already accustomed. During such times, I would draw aesthetic delight from every movement and sound within the

---

* [Translator's note: Retreat room where the dervishes spent periods of solitude and worship.]

Sufi lodge and think that these people were not living, but merely playing the roles cast for them.

From the bawdy houses in Surdibi until I fell before Galib Dede, I was ceaselessly tossed around Istanbul's dingler living quarters. While being carried from Yedikule to Ayvansaray, from Galata to Eyüp, sometimes in a rowing boat and sometimes in an ox-driven cart, I became acquainted with men whose minds functioned beneath their belts.

Even now I cannot estimate how much time passed in Eyüp's halva shops and in the rooms of whores in Sulukule, reeking of human flesh, listening to the crude and abusive voices of I don't know how many ruffians and bandits. People living in those times could have assumed that Istanbul was being tested with unemployment, hunger, anarchy and lust. Fortunately, nobody recognised me and there had been no shady characters hovering about me for a long time by then.

More and more often, I drifted off into sleep shouldering the sorrow of a trollop's unrequited love and woke from nightmares where I saw myself in Leyla's arms. I longed to see my Leyla but I also dreaded finding her in such surroundings. Much later, when I had given up all hope of finding her, I lamented, "She probably grew old and died without me!" It was even a source of bitter solace that I had not run into her.

At a time when I was most preoccupied with the thought that my essence was created out of love and when I felt the greatest yearning for love, I happened upon this lodge, as though the hand of al-Khidr* had touched my heart. At

* [Translator's note: A spiritual personality and a man of wisdom in the Islamic tradition who lives in a saintly way, serving God to carry out divine commands and succouring people in difficult circumstances.]

sundown one day, when the icicles on the eaves turned into swords, between snow and storm, Üvendire Veyis got a foot in the door of the Mevlevihane and said to Sebilci Dede, "I have a word for the Shaykh!" Üvendire Veyis knew that, after the call to evening prayer, the doors to the Sufi lodge were shut and no one was allowed to leave or enter. His intention was to rest his dark legs that had been battling with the frost, by sleeping whilst wrapped in a warm fleece and he also wanted to line his stomach with hot soup. He had had a fight with his lover Rastıklı Anush and so, to teach her a lesson, he grabbed her most prized possession – me – telling her that he would palm me off on a second-hand bookseller.

However, Üvendire Veyis did not want to venture all the way to Bayezid from Zindanarkası in this cold, so he went to Beyoğlu in the hope of running into an acquaintance in one of Galata's taverns and attaching himself to him. After hovering about for quite some time, he failed to find a familiar face and thought to seek sanctuary in the lodge. Despite Sebilci Dede telling him that it was not possible for the Shaykh to see him and that he ought to come back on the following day, he insisted that he had come on important business and that he would stir up trouble if the Shaykh refused to see him.

As a matter of fact, Üvendire Veyis was a brave fellow. In Kastamonu, a young man from a neighbouring district had his eye on the girl next door, whom he himself also loved, and had composed the following folk song for her:

Rose comes of nightingale's advent
The forelock from the tress ensemble.
Travel not by a place of worship
You will annul a great many prayers.

Üvendire Veyis set upon him and got blood on his hands. After that, he fled to Istanbul in no time and disappeared without a trace. He began wandering idly in disorderly houses and dens. He was young and assiduous enough to collect salt on his brow and walk with his eyelashes, so he felt crushed inside and pained at heart that fortune had led him here.

When he came across Anush, he was lonely and helpless, seeking a shoulder to cry on. As for Anush, she was the floozy, market-hopping mistress of an Andalusian Jew who sold perfumes in the Grand Bazaar, and after drawing the attention of this gardener from Kastamonu who worked in the mansion in Balat, she began to frequent the mansion more often. Two months had not even passed before Anush and Veyis began meeting for assignations. They turned this into a game and squirmed out of their responsibilities to blatantly spend time together. On one occasion, after a night Anush had spent with the perfume merchant, she announced she would go to the hamam and left the house arm-in-arm with him. Veyis followed them. Their intention was to get rid of the man and meet up later. However, after Anush went into the hamam, her master set to waiting for her in the coffee house right across the road. This threw Veyis into a panic. Scarcely a few minutes had passed when a woman left the hamam and approached Veyis directly. Taking him by the arm, she said, "Hey handsome, come with me!" It was none other than Anush, who had gone into the hamam and swapped her clothes with those in the spare bag she left there. Now she came out looking completely different, swung right past her Andalusian Jew and thrust Veyis into a house around the corner. On re-entering the hamam an hour later, she put on her former outfit and returned to the lover waiting for her outside. Then she plodded wearily on their return to the mansion as if she had worn herself out at the public baths. This same plan was repeated for several more weeks by always leaving a bundle of spare clothes at the hamam. Üvendire Veyis no longer wanted to share her with her Andalusian master so he rented a house and brought her to live with him. But he soon found he could not keep up with her expenses and realised it would be more profitable to work as her procurer. Thus he threw himself into a rough and wretched life.

The dervish taking Sebilci Dede's news to the Shaykh swiftly came down the lodge stairs and returned among them. Then they ascended the stone stairs together. They heard the sound of two knocks indicating permission to enter from inside as they waited at the door of the Shaykh's upper chamber. Like the dervish, Veyis also touched the door frame lightly with his lips and entered.

He had tried to conceal me in his sash, but the rosette of my binding was exposed. On top of that, it was not just him who was feeling the cold that day; I had absorbed so much moisture that my script had smeared. I could not hide the happiness that the warmth of Shaykh Efendi's chamber gave me. When I saw that the Shaykh reading upon the cedar chair was Galib Dede whose name I had heard frequently, I was more excited than Veyis. This was a gentleman in his thirties, of medium height and sparse beard, whose face radiated serenity. To the dervishes seated on the floor listening to him, he read sections of the *Beauty and Love mesnevi* that he had then started writing in a challenge, and sought their opinions. The "Soft-hearted Shaykh" by whom the sister of

Sultan Selim III, Beyhan Sultan, was struck, and who had established this Sufi lodge as the centre of poetry, was right before me.

Perhaps because he thought it was almost sundown, Galib Dede asked immediately, "How can we be of service to you, sir?"

Joining his hands before him, Veyis lifted his head and looked first at the Shaykh Efendi and then at the dervishes around him. Then he blushed a beetroot red and instead of asking whether he could spend the night which he felt was beneath his manliness, made a request in the Sufi formulation, "Esteemed Shaykh, I ask that you grant me permission to disrobe!" In the special language of the Mevlevi Sufi order, this meant, "I intend to enter your order, affiliate myself with you, make do with a single Mevlevi garment and become intoxicated with the wine of Divine love." However, Galib Dede deduced from the arrival of this half-naked man on this freezing evening right at this time that his real aim was to lounge about and sponge food off the lodge. He tried hard not to laugh. First he thought for a while, then he scanned the faces of those around him. "Sir," he said. "Dis-

robing is no matter, but let us dress you first!" Then, looking at the dervish with whom we had entered together, he added: "Take this, dervish. Give him something to wear and prepare somewhere for him to sleep tonight."

I spent my first night at the Mevlevihane on the bottom floor, in one of the cubicles opening onto the hall, beneath the pillow of Üvendire Veyis who was lying on a goatskin and covered himself with a woollen blanket. Veyis spent the whole night thinking about what he had said in the presence of the Shaykh and he struggled with his carnal self. At times, he cursed himself for abasing himself by lying purely to gain one night's rest and planned how he would sidle away the next day. Occasionally he thought about how he needed to put an end to the bad life he had led for a long time now. But he consoled himself saying, "God made me say these words. There must be good in it!"

As for me, I pretty much prayed the whole night for Veyis to settle there. I cannot even decide whether I wanted this for him or for myself.

Life began early on the morrow. Everyone stood by a ewer and basin for the morning prayer. After the *ocak* officer brought the last of the full ewers and emptied the dirty water from the basins, prayer was observed in congregation. Later I learned that the imam, the leader of the prayer, was the famous musician Ḥammamizade Ismail Dede Efendi and that, like Veyis, he had spent the night in the Sufi lodge as a guest. There was no doubt that the *müezzin*s were students of the previous Shaykh of the place, the musician Ali Nutki Dede.

The devoted reverence and nobility of their worship that I felt and observed from the open door of my cell affected me deeply. I suddenly remembered the morning prayers observed in the palace during the Lawgiver's reign. Imams with beautiful voices, *muezzins* with a knowledge of music, the prayer performed with the *ilahis* sung in-between and the proclamations of God's greatness, took me to memories of the tears that Rukal shed with her prayers.

Veyis returned to his cell as affected by the morning prayer as I was and, while the *tekke* dervishes completed their morning invocations and then slept through till mid-morning, he wept ceaselessly. That he had seen a dream that would change his whole life was clear from his every manner. Along with washing him, his tears also washed away the profanities and impurities of a cheap life that had also penetrated me. When we were called for late-morning breakfast, both of us were purified and prepared. We had surrendered.

Despite the fact that the outer door of the *tekke* had been opened and the path outside been shown to him without causing him any embarrassment, Veyis volunteered to kneel at the place known as *Saka Postu* or the floor fleece in the kitchen to observe the goings-on and to put himself to the test. I can say that, in his big-boned hands, I learned Mevlevi teachings and practices for exactly 18 days. They called him *muhip*, or *nevniyaz,* meaning "young initiate" and everyone treated him as though he were not there.

Since he could not read me and used to take me with him to have people read me to earn his drinking money, he would occasionally look at my pictures and sometimes lament. "I wish I had sold it!" Sometimes he was resigned to his fate saying, "If I had sold it, I would not have ended up here!" He tried to discover my tale from the second-hand story he had heard as a child, as though wanting to understand what I was. This is what all those seeing me from Nedim Efendi onwards, on the outskirts of Istanbul, had done in any case, limiting themselves to expressing admiration for my pictures, rather than understanding my language.

The *Matbah-ı şerif* was comprised of a kitchen where the food was cooked, but it was also the heart of the Sufi lodge and an administrative headquarters of some sort. In the kitchen under the supervision of Aşçı Dede, the most senior authority after the Shaykh, served dervishes known as *ocak zabitan*. They conducted their daily affairs and chores without speaking to the initiates, sometimes going to market and sometimes reading the *Mesnevi*. Veyis really wanted to read me when he saw the refined grace that they possessed. "The manner of a learned person is different indeed," he would say to himself.

This 18 day period of excommunication was a true ordeal. No one showed any interest in Üvendire Veyis's presence and, when the time came, a small amount of food and a jugful of water were brought before him. He spent his entire day either in prayer or self-reckoning or in supplication and entreaty. Only a few days earlier, if someone had told him to shut up next to Anush in his house in Zindanarkası, he would have drawn his short sword. If he had been instructed, "You're going to sit here and leave only for your physical requirements and even then with permission," he would have considered this a slur on his honour and on his reputation for rowdiness. The result would have been murder; but here in this atmosphere of love, he was silent and seated of his own accord. I observed life moving very slowly here. I thought that the inner peace that Veyis had sought for years on end could perhaps be found here. People here lived oscillating between having and not having. They were quiet, peaceful, cheerful, pleased and contented. Whether they were present physically with their self-hood elsewhere, or did not possess a carnal self at all, it was difficult to tell. The most cheerful times in the kitchen were the gatherings in which the head *kudümzen* managing the *mutrip* octet of musicians and the *neyzenbaşı* dervishes had the *cans* observe *sema* or whirling ceremonies and practise whirling themselves. These were entirely unlike the drinking bouts to which Veyis was accustomed.

On the eighteenth day, Veyis earned the rank of *muhip* and the Shaykh placed a *sikke* upon his head. A dervish was appointed to him to instruct him in spiritual initiation and journeying. In future, he would receive instruction in how to perform the *sema*. He would also learn how to play the reed flute or read the *Mesnevi* depending on his ability. He would spend 40 days in retreat and then be granted the rank of dervish. After that, he could serve in the *Matbah-ı şerif*, settle in one of the 18 dervish cells and, after participating in the İsm-i Celal invocation following the morning prayer, pray on the rosary beads containing 1,001 beads, each the size of an egg.

"Love is the essence of existence!" the dervish had declared in the first lesson and I felt my small room expanding, growing too large for the world. This dervish spoke of the Divine dimension of metaphorical love, so I focussed all my attention on his words. "Our spirits, like everything coming into being in this world, come from God, the Absolute Existent One, and ultimately they return again to Him," he was saying. He continued, "When God became manifest with His knowledge, He first created light and to it said, ‹Be, O Muhammad!' This was the first intellect that was created and comprised the essence of all created things. Before this address, light exuded love and exalted the True Beloved saying, ‹There is no god but Allah!' This Beloved, the source of all beauty and the Absolute Beauty, favoured these eloquent words with the response, ‹Muhammad is His Messenger.' Then our spirits were created, gathered together and asked: *'Alastu bi-Rabbikum*?' This meant, 'Am I not your Lord?' *'Qalu bala*,' or 'Yes, You are our Lord!' the spirits proclaimed in unison. When our spirits made such a covenant, they became enraptured before that beauty and lost themselves. From that light, the galaxies and universe were created as Divine manifestation. The nine layers of the firmaments and the celestial bodies and stars contained within them, all came into being in a whirl. In order for you to understand this alternating rotation, it is sufficient for you to observe the whirling of the dervishes in our Sufi lodge." At this juncture, the dervish made a turning gesture with his hand and shook the cup containing the coffee, the fresh aroma of which had permeated the room.

I set to wondering about the secret I carried, about the Babylon Society's ideals and how they overlapped with what the dervish was explaining. Was this the first sign that I would meet the Babylon Society from whom I had been estranged for so long? The dervish quickly passed on. "Then Allah adorned the universe with four central elements. These are earth, air, water and fire. From these four mothers, three offspring were born. Plants such as trees and vegetables, inanimate beings such as minerals and metals, and animates granted the ability of movement. Only one group of animates was granted reason and these were called human beings. And so, these elements are present in every human being who is conceived and they come from the seven layers of the firmaments. In this tiny world, just one of billions of heavenly bodies in the billions of galaxies contained within creation, each of the billions of human beings over the billions of ages assumes the form of an embryo from the loins of a mother and a father, nourished with the plant, animal or mineral nutrients composed with the aid of earth, air, water and fire. This is our separation from God and our assuming humanity in various stages. When the foetus is three months old, our spirits, which were entranced with the beauty of eternity without beginning, are blown into the physical being in order to be reunited with their beloved and to be put to trial as to whether they will honour the covenant they made with their Lord on that day. The point at which the human being is furthest away from God is this moment of birth. This is the stage when the human being who, in the Qur'anic expression, is the noblest of creation, is as at its lowliest.

To enable every human being reaching adolescence to scale this vast distance anew, this time in the reverse and again in stages, each Sufi teaching developed a separate method of thought and endeavoured to find different paths. From the Prophets to the philosophers, from Buddhism to Sufism, that which Ptolemy, Aristotle, Gautama Buddha, Geylani and our Mevlana of Anatolia sought, was perpetually that sole, unique Beloved. Everything in this Sufi lodge has been tied to rules that pertain to facilitating this return journey. The first step is annihilation of the carnal self, or ego. The *saka postu* on which you waited for 18 days was the first example of this. Now, you will advance with knowledge and the day you completely annihilate your carnal soul in the çilehane will mark your first step on the path of the true Beloved, as the beloved is reached with love, with the heart. The carnal self, however, desires reason and the world. Just as a journey of the heart is not possible without abandonment of reason, the spirit's purification and elevation is not possible without first annihilating the ego. Death is necessary for us to find life. Let us annihilate the carnal soul so that we can subsist in the Beloved and let us thus abandon everything that pulls us away from the Beloved. And this is realised step by step. Years go by. This path cannot be trodden unless the traveller is enraptured with love. Be enraptured with love so that you may either shout out like Mansur, ‹I am Truth!' or say like Bistami, ‹There is nothing save God under my cloak!' It matters not which."

The dervish explained excitedly and Üvendire Veyis listened in astonishment and awe. There was no doubt that his every sentence caused storms to rage in Veyis's spirit. Had Anush seen this previously treacherous and drunken man thus subdued and resigned, she too would have forgotten herself, thrown herself at his feet and devoted herself to him.

The dervish provided a case in point so as to make his meaning clearer. "Now look, Veyis *can*, you know taverns. You know well the tavern-keeper – the *pir-i mugan* – the bartender, the goblet, the wine, the opiate, drunkenness, inebriation; consider our lodge also thus. Consider our master Galib Dede to be the tavern-keeper, his lips the goblet and the elevated words therefrom to be the wine. You know how the wine at the tavern makes a person drunk..." Veyis indicated with his two hands the dede should stop and concluded the rest of the sentence himself. "Yes, I understand. Here, those words of love intoxicate a person, enrapture them, first emptying and then filling them with love. The drunkenness of love and ecstasy of the goblet was this."

"Think of the loves you have experienced," began the dede while mixing the coals of the brazier in the centre. Veyis's thoughts turned to his sweetheart in Kastamonu for whose sake he had shed blood. Veyis felt his heart sear and the dervish formed his sentences in haste, as though he felt his anguish. "Your beloved carried only an iota of the Divine beauty. Now, the journey of reaching the essence of that iota will begin, the drop will merge with the ocean, you will find yourself in love and return to your essence. Our bodies came from the soil and will return to it; our spirits came from Allah and will return again to Him. Lures have been set along this journey to deceive you, as well as fleeting loves to try you. The philosopher by name of Plato expressed this by means of his conception of Forms, where he explored man's preoccupation with the shadows of existence rather than with its essence or truth. The true lover can complete this journey not with their reason, but with their heart. Your mind is merely a vehicle. Whether you make your carnal soul or your heart subservient to it is up to you: give it to all other than Allah or to Allah alone. Following one path, pitfalls will forever await you, while the other path will always be open. Do not be deceived by the world; do not be carried away by its embellishments. The world is like the shadow of a human being. If you turn your back to it, it will pursue you and if you chase after it, it will always run away from you."

In truth, I too was rather affected by what the dede explained, while Veyis was completely confused. My master Fuzuli had known all this, to be sure, but had placed my love somewhere between humanity and God, by way of Platonic thought. I had never been able to understand the reason behind my rejecting Leyla when we came across one another in the desert. I was never able to get at what my master Fuzuli was trying to express through this rejection, which I always regretted. Now I grasped it. Yes, for me, becoming one with Leyla at that time and feeling both of us united within one body implied union with God to some degree. When Leyla appeared before me in all her beauty and caused me to lose my senses, he had made me say:

If I am me, then who are you O love?
And if you are you, then who is poor I?

and had protected me from the perils of the world. By hiding my love in the most sublime way, my master had ensured I would be remembered and my name would echo through time. It seems that my master had found the truth then. He found it and made me repeat it, making me live his destiny. By continuing the adventure, which had begun on the "Day of the Covenant", he had wanted me to be cleansed, purified in his name. "So the road that I have trodden for all these years through filthy valleys was for this trial!" I thought to myself as I searched for the truth. "In all this time spent looking for my Leyla, was I actually seeking my Lord?" What an onerous question this was, what an unbearable burden! I had to examine my entire existence, my past and myself and I was now doubting my own self and my love.

I began to spend all my days and nights to-ing and froing between Leyla and *Mawla,* the Lord. Whilst listening to the sound the gusts made when battering the *kündekari* bay windows on the side of the Galata Mevlevihane facing the south-westerly winds, I began questioning the reality of life. Were the Babylonian sages set on determining the fate of humanity, or the love that this dervish talked about? The sages had relied on reason and this strange dervish spoke of the heart. This unendurable conflict had driven thousands of minds to distraction in the mental exertions of Sufis and philosophers and had granted thousands of hearts the inspiration of truth. I felt like a sentence that had lost its meaning or a verse whose era had passed. Did carrying the secrets of the sages, which overcame the millennia, confer greater peace? Or was it conferred by what this dervish described? I could not decide. Or again, would I have been happier if I had undertaken a journey of the heart instead of boasting of the secret of the Babylon Society all this time? The road forked before me: one path was outward oriented and the other led toward the interior. I had a feeling that things would never be the same again.

⁂

Üvendire Veyis presented me to Shaykh Galib Dede when he was conferred the high brown cap or *külah* of the Mevlevi order, the symbol that he had attained the spiritual maturity needed for changing his life. My spirit was more tired than it had ever felt before. This was perhaps not so much tiredness as intoxication – an intoxication that enveloped my entire being. I had felt myself in a space wherein I could find repose for the first time since my days with master Fuzuli. His name was often mentioned under this roof and a great many of his poems were on the lips of the dedes here. As I was being presented into Galib Dede's hands, I felt myself fortunate, thinking that in that case, they would understand me, read all that occurred to my heart and weep as they learned of my adventure with Leyla. Thus, perhaps it would be more appropriate to say I entered into service, rather than being presented in homage.

Galib Dede was considered the greatest representative of the Indian style which had become much more influential on the poetry of his age. Everyone read his poetry with reverence, musicians made harmonious compositions to accompany his verses, the *kudüm* drums and *ney* reed flute played along with his poems in gatherings and inscribers and embroiderers distilled their inspirations from his couplets and put them to paper. The Divine love that he described with rich imagination was as magnificent as he had related to Üvendire Veyis. A lyricism as exuberant as that of my master Fuzuli was present in his verses. Even while describing his dense Sufi thinking, he embraced the reader with the ivy-like arms of his associations.

My master Fuzuli penned his poetry for love; he described not the lover but love itself and embodied in his works a poet who was a lover in love with love. Galib Dede, however, had a mission and he subordinated his poetry to his ideals, repeatedly making reference to this, just like Mevlana whose hat he was proud of wearing. The objective for one was a means to the other. And who knows how many centuries the poems he intoned as a means would live on among couplets, the more beautiful of which were not spoken. Now he represented the aspect of Ottoman poetry which looked to Sufism and again he exhausted the treasure that he himself discovered. There was no one who did not know that the poems he wrote after his discussions with his dear friend Esrar, a few years his elder, and following the spiritual retreat with his friend Yusuf Sineçak who lived in Sütlüce, were a further treasury of meaning. They brought his readers to the edge of a cliff top, blindfolded them then and there, and then let them go. To turn or to leap? To fall when leaping, or to take flight and soar?

When he first took me into his hands, he was sitting facing Esrar, discussing Greek history about which he had been reading from books in Italian and Latin. Listening to their words, I can say that I felt I had come close to the

Babylon Society. So be it. If the Society was close to such a love, then it was incumbent upon me to be sacrificed for it. But unfortunately, this refined man to whom I had been presented was not even curious as to what I was and did not open my front cover for quite some time.

They spoke at length of the exhaustion of the state, the successive battles and moral degeneration brought on by defeat, internal revolt and economic woes, the new taxation system that Selim III had put into effect the previous year, the war erupting in and around Muscovy and the military situation. They also discussed whether or not the new army to be formed under the name of *Nizam-ı Cedit* would avail in solving the problems at hand. They reviewed Hatice Sultan's wasteful spending which came of her wish to keep up with fashion, the Grand Vizier's struggles in the harem, how another poet writing in the philosophical form who could erase Urfalı Nabi's impact on poetry had not emerged. They touched on the Mevlevihanes' want of care, the French and English instructors at the newly opened Berr-i Hümayun and Bahr Hümayun engineering faculties impressing irreligion upon the minds of students, the janissaries' transformation into city bandits, moral corruption and a great many other scourges of the day. I thought of what had happened as I had travelled about the cheap Surdibi districts and the current predicament of the Ottoman state! What a great pity!

When the *ney* and *kudüm* sounds began to be heard from the music room, Galib Dede grabbed me from the woollen mattress on which I had plunged into old memories, with a view to changing the subject. For a while he examined my binding, moved his fingers above my tattered rosette and then he addressed Esrar. "Dede! There's no respect for books any more. It's clear that this binding is a work of the palace, but does such an old and battered garment suit a palace resident and is it fitting for a former boiler room boy like Veyis? Even this is enough to show how degenerate our people have become."

Esrar fixed his gaze upon me and asked, "What is that, my dear Shaykh?" I felt myself as restless and troubled as a *medrese* student entering an exam. I thought about not paying attention to the first impressions that the Shaykh would share upon opening me. "What if he does not like me?" I feared all of a sudden. Happily, that is not what happened. First, the Shaykh looked at the inside of my front cover, my marbling, illumination, and the *ahar* coating of my paper, as though I were any old book. A few minutes were enough for him to become a little more amazed with each page of mine that he turned. He began to feel the thrill of anticipation of the next one. He examined some of my couplets and illustrations for a while and then jumped up, exclaiming, "This is a treasure, Esrar, a veritable treasure!" At that moment, I praised God for my existence. I can say that I felt a sense of pride in my master Fuzuli.

"There are many treasures to be found in ruins, dear Shaykh!" replied Esrar in veiled reference to Üvendire Veyis's former life. There was no one else in the Shaykh's quarters and we were unable to tell how the hours passed, when the music in the music room stopped, when the devoted friends at the Galata Mevlevihane retired, when the embers in the brazier turned to charcoal and when the snow began to fall more heavily. When the lodge lamps were lit for the morning prayer, my mind was about to seize up from hearing so many beautiful words. So many tears were shed about my story, awe-filled utterances were made pertaining to my and my master Fuzuli's manner and many prayers and entreaties were recited. In all my centuries-old lifetime, I had not felt this much pride in myself. I felt and experienced to my core that night, my master Fuzuli's verse, "I am a servant like a sovereign, a magnificent slave!"

When I was left alone in the room with the warmth of these two men upon me, on my forehead and upon every inch of my body, the caller to prayer was reciting the *temcit* in the *hüseyni* rhythmic cycles. While I tried to remember some of what had been discussed that night so as to engrave it on my memory, I realised I could recall a few conversational climaxes.

On the first night, Galib Dede had said with that initial excitement of his, "This is the most magnificent *mesnevi* and I am jealous. Never mind, Esrar, the *Hüsn ü Aşk* that I am currently writing, which I penned just to spite Nabi's *Hayrabad*. It is this book that I would really like to surpass! The fear in my heart that I might not succeed eats away at me each night and I never articulate this secret ardour of mine. I never voice the thought that perhaps I will be defeated by master Fuzuli's verses. I can never even bring *Hüsn ü Aşk* and this book side by side. For this book, from beginning to end, describes suffering. L&M also represents the summit of Islamic poetry. A great many poets attempted to write this tale, but very few succeeded in writing it as beautifully as master Fuzuli. Had I presumed to write L&M, then perhaps that jealousy of outdoing the Türkmen master would have impeded me. This is why I am endeavouring to offer my *mesnevi* on a new subject, a tale that no one has hitherto conceived. At least *Hüsn ü Aşk* will not remain in the shadow of L&M with respect to subject matter."

"Oh, for goodness' sake, sir!" interrupted Esrar. "There are certain couplets in *Hüsn ü Aşk* with a degree of delicate imagining not found in L&M. Do not do yourself such a disservice! In particular that chapter in which you describe the tribe of the Sons of Love, where you mention Love's crossing the seas of fire with ships made of wax, and especially that intricate discourse on the land of Love... No, no, you have blazed such a trail in this subject that the spirits of those who came before will envy you. You have enveloped love with symbols and adorned it with allegory, while they tried to understand love with their bare feelings and were only able to describe it to the extent of their love. Fuzuli was a waterfall of emotion, Nabi spoke with wisdom, but you feel, dear dede, you live. Where and how the poet sees beauty and the beautiful is important. Baki saw it in Istanbul, Fuzuli in his imagination, Nedim on the street and Nabi in the intricacy of thought. You found it in your heart and were able to say,

'Such a flame has the candle of the spirit
That the dome of the skies cannot contain it.'

Do not do yourself an injustice. And while you approach your thirtieth year, consider that Fuzuli wrote L&M when he was over 55 and, when Nabi put *Hayrabad* to paper, he was in his sixties. Think how many more great works you will write and what magnificent necklaces of words you will string together."

"God willing!" I said to myself at that point.

"Dear Esrar!" Galib Dede had interposed at one stage, as he indicated my first few pages. "And what are these number-like jottings beside the couplets?"

"I don't know, dear Shaykh. It seems as though someone numbered them in a script foreign to us. Only Halet would know this, let's ask him when he gets here."

The following day, the Galata Mevlevihane woke from its slumber with the cries, "Fire! Fire!" The alarm call of the fire brigade and children had become a most familiar sound for Istanbulites that year as the Balat, Samatya and Hasköy fires occurred just one month apart. But this time the flames set all of Istanbul's outskirts alight. I had escaped from the Balat fire by accident in Rastıklı Anush's bag. She had taken me with her to be sold to I do not know which owner, coincidentally putting me in her bundle whilst fleeing.

This time, the fire began in Cibali. The brazier tipped over and a blanket caught fire as greengrocer Kirkor Efendi guzzled down the *rakı*. He was at a loss as to what to do and, when his wife thought to take the swaddled baby outside, the flames spread and the wooden partitions, which had lost their clay cladding, caught fire within a matter of minutes, just like kindling. Non-Muslims were the majority on both sides of the Golden Horn and their houses were constructed in terraced fashion, so the fire swept through the neighbouring eaves in a short time. Thanks to a strong north-easterly, the Golden Horn's foothills turned into a sea of fire at one stroke.

At Galata, we could easily follow the course of the flames and could almost hear the screams of the neighbourhood communities. The multicoloured smoke engulfed the sky like a rainbow and even the city's gushing waters began to vaporise. That day, we saw that the sky could ignite. The flames rose above the city's obelisks and towers and grew in height over the day. At night, the stars were replaced by sparks. The following day and the next, many a fire-cheeked beauty, lovers burning with the fire of love, some young, others intrepid, perished in the flames. On the third day, the whole city, from the Golden Horn to Yedikule, Kocamustafapaşa to Bayezit, Topkapısı to Silivrikapısı, was reduced to ashes and nothing remained of houses and dwellings save the domes and minarets whose lead finials had melted. Those who knew something of the past said that Istanbul had not burned thus since the days of Byzantium.

After that day, Galib Dede always referred to fire and touched his poetry with fire. So many words, imaginings and emotions were associated with fire in his couplets that it might have been said of him, "This man has become fire and burns from head to toe!" This was the fire of love, love's scorching and flaming. Upon the completion of the *Hüsn ü Aşk mesnevi*, I could not help thinking that the fires of Istanbul had erupted with such frequency purely so they could become the subject of this book. This is why flames rained upon the tribe of the Sons of Love, why the people there donned the sun as a garment and drank flames as water, sowed sparks like seeds and reaped seared hearts.

After this fire, my days in Galata passed in a fiery dimension. The fire of my love for my Leyla and that for my Lord embraced one another. In the same way that the fire burns the egos of the dervishes in the kitchen and purifies them, the fire in the *semahane* purified me of the filth of the city which had penetrated my being for more than half a century. Even on the day when Üvendire Veyis first received instruction in how to perform the *sema*, it burnt and annihilated his impurities. I realised that day that both the one burning and the one being burned, the one causing to burn and the one doing the burning are forever one. Everyone lived their destiny on their own and this was comprised of a lifetime of burning. After all, had not all lovers proclaimed in response, "Yes!" on that day in pre-eternity?[87] Now they would assuredly be tested with afflictions and singe their hearts in the flames in order to elevate their love further.

After a few years, this fire would kindle the life of Galib Dede, who resembled my master Fuzuli in heart and feeling. The time in Galata was still productive and that fire paved the way for my being burned; my verses became wet with the tears from the smouldering flames. As I witnessed the singular love spells of each dervish, Leyla's love within me ignited anew and I was made to burn once again.

Leylaaaa! You ought to know that all my fires in this Sufi lodge came from you and my eyes forever shed tears to extinguish them. As my ships of beeswax, which I loaded with your love on the passage leading to you, plummeted to the ocean depths, I kept crying and melting... My life thread burned. The flames upon your head kept setting the city aflame Leylaaa!

27
How the World met with Revolutions and my Pages intermixed

(Due to their difficult nature) they did not find repose nor let others rest
They departed from the world in ruin, may those in the Hereafter now endure (if they are so able)!

Laedri

"There are seven true secrets for one who knows love," the steward of the imperial court Mehmet Raşit Efendi had said whilst breathing his last, adding, "One who possesses it gains mastery over the world. Seek that love in L&M, son, and translator Kalimaki Efendi will relate the rest to you."

Mehmet Sait Efendi says that his life changed after seeing the Jewish physician Kalimaki Efendi. In those days, he worked as the assistant to the mansion's Keeper of the Seal and used the pseudonym Halet in some of the poetry he wrote. This handsome man, whose real name everyone later forgot so they all called him Halet Efendi, liked to dress well. He was eloquent in speech and in writing and thirsted after new reading. So it was that we took off for Paris. He had all the maturity of a 40 year-old man, an accomplished Ottoman intellectual and an ambassador for Sultan Selim III. Accompanying our delegation of embassy officials was Valentin Efendi, one of the clerks of the French *chargé d'affaires* in Istanbul.

During the journey, which took 72 days on horseback, I saw different lands and provinces more prosperous than those in the Ottoman state. This was unlike my former travels in Rome. It turned out that the revolutions that had engulfed the continent in the 15 years following the happy times at Galata, had engendered a different world view here. Everything had changed and was much altered. The stream of life had suddenly gathered pace. In contrast to the Northern provinces to which I went after setting off with Evliya Çelebi, I was able to see how the transformation of the medieval regimes and feudal structure of the Western European lands had shifted the axis of human history. Popular movements and revolutions in America, Ireland and England brought forth dissatisfaction with the governments in the Low Countries, in Geneva, in Poland as well as Belgium, Germany and Italy. These forces had been strongest in France where they had erupted in the destruction of the Bastille and the subsequent execution of King Louis XVI and his Queen, Marie-Antoinette. The leaders of the French Revolution championed the power of reason against the authority of church and state. The symbol of the monarchy was removed when the royal family was forced to leave Versailles and made to settle in the Louvre in Paris, where they were kept under secret house arrest. In this way, the first seeds of participatory democracy began to spread from Paris to the rest of France and from there to the whole world.

The day Halet Efendi settled in the consulate in Paris, he behaved like a bureaucrat who feels the power of the Ottoman state behind him. He internalised world politics thanks to his experience of having occupied important government positions. He rebuked Talleyrand, whom he referred to as a so-called priest for not receiving him correctly. I was struck by his capacities as a diplomat and realised that this man, whose personality was like a monument to ambition, possessed a character that would never be satisfied with trifles. I had a feeling that he valued his own interests as highly as the splendour of the state and that he viewed the years he was to spend in Paris as a time of harvest when he would reap his reward.

Just as soon as he arrived in Paris, he drew the attention of Napoleon, the country's most powerful man, and soon reached a position of greater influence than the ambassadors of other nations. On the other hand, he was always hard-pressed financially through having to support large numbers of embassy staff and also needing to send gifts that friends in Istanbul requested so frequently. The routes to which he had to resort troubled me.

In those years, all kinds of illegal activity was taking place in a France the traditions of which had been turned upside down. Here was a people that had only recently believed they were created to serve their masters. Now they rejected feudal serfdom and began engaging in influence peddling. They sought out a set of ready formulae. What Montesquieu called "honour" amounted to a spider's web; little flies were trapped but large flies broke right through. Villagers who until yesterday were barely deemed human by their masters, were today treading with great carelessness in their raw-hide sandals upon city pavements laid for the nobility. Church squares in which the sick had formerly gathered in the belief that they would regain their health with the monarch's mere touch, now teemed with angry crowds clamouring that the king's hand no longer hold any healing power.

Seeing murder on the streets and orators in the squares each day made life very difficult for Halet Efendi. There was also no order or regularity in the gifts coming from Napoleon or the salaries sent from Istanbul. Embassy staff expected everything from him. The debt accumulated from the clothing, furniture and jewellery that his wife demanded of him, and her envy of Parisian noblewomen, grew with each passing day. His only solace was a love affair that had begun in an unaccustomed way. He had become enamoured of Countess Laurent who caught his eye in her revealing dress when he had kissed her hand with a genteel bow on one of the receptions hosted by Talleyrand. He observed that love, which grew secretly and slowly in Istanbul, here drew a person into its waves with hurricane-like force. When he first set eyes on the Countess, he lamented, "This rose was created for me, but blossomed in other gardens! What a shame!" Then she called upon him suddenly one week later at the embassy and he lost his head, promptly sending his private clerk on leave.

On the day Galib Dede was interred in the reserved burial area of the Galata Mevlevihane, Halet Efendi sneaked into the Shaykh's chamber and slipped my binding into his bosom. I recall feeling a sense of delight that he had selected me as a memento of his friendship with the Shaykh. I also felt a shade of pride that he manifested his sentimentality in this manner. But I soon realised how mistaken I was.

At the end of the night when he had held lengthy discussions with Esrar and read me from cover to cover, after Galib Dede first showed me to him in order to make sense of the number-like markings on my pages, he had replied saying, "I don't know, dear sir!" However, on each visit to the lodge, he would become lost in reverie among my vignettes so as to read a little more of my story. I never realised how well he acted his part. It was as though the man I saw now was not the tender-hearted Halet Efendi who joked with Galib Dede at the Sufi lodge, brought presents for him and established cordial links between him and Selim III. I no longer recognised him. It was like young lovers who dress up their darlings in an identity and personality that is unlike anything they have ever really been by thinking the best of them and then, when they confront the true face of their beloved, say, "You are not the person I fell in love with!" This was the feeling that I was experiencing in this European land.

Halet Efendi was like a crescent in my eyes, a crescent I had transformed into a full moon by constantly thinking well of him. However, as I saw from his behaviour in Paris, I began to feel the full moon within me wane and turn into the former faint crescent once more. I dreaded the day when this crescent would become completely invisible. In the four years which had passed since Galib Dede's death, I sensed that Halet Efendi had not retained a single shred of the Mevlevi discipline and that he had peddled all his higher feelings in return for diabolical passions. This was no longer the man who read my love with so much fervour as to make his eyes water each time. Before me now was a monument to greed who only lost sleep to worry about the Babylon Society's scientific secrets and the golden idols. This happened to coincide with the time when the seventh couplet to which my master Fuzuli had entrusted his secret was revealing its meaning to the Babylon Society.

Paris had started as a settlement on a small island of the Seine. It had then become the capital city of the kings in the Middle Ages and later the centre of the revolutionary spirit. Now it assumed the position of the world's most important city. The new order that Sultan Selim had named *Nizam-ı Cedit* had long since taken over this country of chateaux, where peasants had previously been bought and sold along with the land. Now, thought and writing, which had been the exclusive province of a handful of clergy for centuries, had become accessible to all. The Rue de Rivoli opened by Napoleon Bonaparte, the Place de l'Etoile and the neoclassical monuments of the architect Fontaine were visible from the three-storey embassy building in which we sat. The Arc de Triomphe, too, demonstrated the city had adopted a new approach to life. Despite the city's careful social and architectural arrangements, it was also possible to see Paris as a gigantic village in which half a million people longing for a lost paradise were jumbled together.

Just as there was no record of those coming in from the outside, certain checks were also not in force at the city gates. I concluded that the six other Babylon Society members had entered the city in disguise, taking advantage of this lack of checks and controls, in order to convene. I could not make out their identities but, judging from their demeanour, I guessed they were influential persons in their own countries. They greeted Halet Efendi with those familiar rituals, in the hall which was illuminated with gas lighting channelled through a strange pipe in a manner unknown in Istanbul. I had the sense that the Society had formally assembled to exploit the political turmoil in Europe and the Balkans. They were poised to play a game of chess that would position anew all the pieces in the world order to their advantage.

Within the 250 years during which I had grown weary of playing hide and seek with the Babylon Society, I had almost invariably known the identities of the members. But this time they gave each other code names. They addressed Halet Efendi as "Master Marduk". The one resembling an Egyptian was Shaykh of Love and the one whom I presumed to be Parisian they called Mr Knowing. Mr Knowing possessed a nobility that seemed to distil the greatness of Voltaire, Rousseau and Diderot put together. The man who acted as freely as the seamen in the Italian armada was "Mr Somebody". The bulky man they referred to as "Mr Seven" had to be one of the generals of Catherine II; maybe this was the general who sent the writer Radishchev into exile in Siberia because he spoke of socialism in his work. The clothing of the small man they called "Mr Reality" indicated that he was a Polish Jew and presumably a poet or a scientist. To my great surprise, I saw a woman among the members for the very first time, a blonde, beautiful woman. They called her "Countess Secret" and she spoke English.

The code names had a familiar ring to them. I remembered the statement that the Assyrian librarian at the Baghdad Academy of Sciences had uttered once upon a time to my master Fuzuli. "For one who knows love..." I thought that, this time, the Society was nearing the end of the road and concluded that the level of scientific development had reached a point warranting the re-establishment of the Research Centre. It was clear they attached great importance to their work.

I did not want to perish in embassy halls lying between these grubby-looking terraced blocks which those accustomed to living in the wooden houses set on gardened grounds in Istanbul, would find most uncongenial. Far from the poetic life to which I had grown used, removed from gatherings where poetry was discussed, I suffered from boredom. I was weary of the people around me who travelled about with their embassy staff. "And precisely what about carrying a bejewelled dagger with silver inlay denotes refinement?" I kept asking myself. They called this fashion and, in Paris, that which is called fashion is not a passing fad, but a matter of nobility. How pleasant my life at the Galata Mevlevihane seemed; how pure and refined in contrast.

My insides burned in those days as I was suddenly struck down with gloom and desolation. I strove to find consolation in my couplets filled with pain and tears. I realised that my hopes when setting off for Paris were in vain. "Perhaps my Leyla, of whom I have lost all trace, is in the lands of Europe!" I had told myself. But my feelings of admiration for Halet Efendi had deceived me. I think that what I truly deplored was the possibility that the secret with which my master Fuzuli had entrusted me would be unravelled in these foreign lands. I was troubled by how scientific advancement had slowed down in the lands to which I belonged so that their potential to dominate the world had diminished and they were at risk of being completely ignored. What had happened to the Islam which was open to science? Where were the Ibn Sina's, Ghazali's and the Ibn Khaldun's, the writers of those books embroidered in gold? How had scientists who could fathom the space travels to which the Babylon Society aspired been replaced by close-minded men? These regressive types even deemed thinking on such lines to be blasphemy. How did ninnies come to power when they did not understand that the world cannot be controlled by turning one's back on the sciences? It was the Eastern world's decline in science that pained me most. As I travelled to Paris, it saddened me to see that the space research of the Chaldean sages would be more welcome here. The only consolation left to me here where I waited for seven pairs of eyes to lose sleep poring over my pages was that the secret I carried belonged to science, and that this knowledge was the property of the whole world. After all, one aspect of me was living outside myself and in a universal dimension. But this was not enough to dress the wound that the sentences and discussions in French rebounding off the walls at this very moment, describing the culture of my land with hatred and rancour, opened in my heart. In none of the other meetings of the Babylon Society do I remember the people being as tense as they were here. These seven people did not look like a single side, but rather like adversaries. They were all marked by the restlessness of planned and plotted calculations for self-interest. It was certain that this meeting was to be a very strategic one.

"I can almost see the gates of the universe from the observatory that we will build in the Bois de Boulogne," began Mr Knowing whilst surveying the distant woods from the window and opening his hands towards the sky. "This is not just our triumph, but the triumph of all humanity," he added. From his gestures and his tone of voice, it might easily be supposed that he was a hero of the revolution and had assumed the role of supreme leader.

"What if this man were Robespierre?" I thought to myself, picturing the master of discourse who, with his speeches, had provoked all Parisians to revolt.

"Not so fast, Mr Knowing!" interjected Countess Secret. "Maybe the sky can be seen with much more clarity in Scotland than in Paris!"

"Those wanting to control the skies have always wanted to drink water from the Nile," said Love. "Luxor or the pyramids are as serviceable for our research as to render telescopes redundant." I noticed Mr Seven look derisively at the Shaykh of Love at that point. This was the attitude the different regions had had towards each other since time immemorial. It encapsulated the Occidental attitude to the Orient. This was why he assumed a mocking manner while he chose to explain at greater length what was running through his mind. "The world has entered a new era. Regionalism and nationalism have gained prominence. Until today, wars of religion determined the fate of nations, while from now on national sovereignty will do so. On no account can permission for a research centre be granted to Egypt while it remains an Ottoman province."

I noticed that Halet Efendi reddened to his ears, but waited patiently to hear the rest of the speech. "For a long time, the Ottoman central administration has been unable to exert authority over the provinces. They are fighting on four separate fronts. In particular, the Balkan Orthodox tribes, the Wallachians living under the Voivodeships of Wallachia and Moldova and the Karabakh Catholic groups are uneasy under Ottoman rule. Samuel Klein said that the Wallachians were of Roman origin and we would ignore him at our peril. With the support of young priests coming into contact with the Church of Rome, a new state will very soon be established in the region and they too will begin ripping the Ottoman state to shreds. Russia is currently carrying out the necessary promotion and propaganda. Austria has even already accepted that they are Romans. And the Slavs and Teutons are sure to be pleased with such a development. If the Turks are weakened in this region and if we support one another for their defeat on these fronts, then there is no reason for us not to build our observatory in Roman lands, in Montenegro, the region closest to the sky, the realm beneath the moon. We would be laying it before Nebo."

"Then what will you get out of all this, as a nation?" asked master Halet Efendi. "It seems the Muscovite tsarina intends to expand southward. What I mean is, she is moving down to the warm seas. I dare say this is why you accepted bishop Osep Aragotyan's Ararat Kingdom Project, eh! What do you think? Do you suppose that they do not know in Istanbul how you have been encouraging the Bulgar and mountain brigands of Rumelia to revolt? Do you think they are unaware that you have allowed the spread of Abd al-Wahhab's fanatical religious ideas in the Arabian Peninsula, that you have incited the Ta'if blockade and offered the sultanate to Tepedelenli Ali Paşa in Egypt? They are also aware of how Napoleon stowed operating printing machines in the ships transporting his men to Egypt and that they have been printing Arabic treatises, leaflets and brochures to conduct subversive propaganda against Islam in the Hijaz region. And what is more, your intrigues against the Turks..." Halet Efendi's voice was getting louder and louder when Countess Secret suddenly interrupted in a manner no Society member had ever before displayed towards the master.

"Mr Seven is right, honourable master! Forget Europe, Christendom will never be able to find peace as long as the Turks remain in any part of Anatolia. Until we construct anew the Eastern and Western Roman Empires, and revive the philosophy of Athens and the culture of Rome once more in these lands, we will not give your Sultan a peaceful night's rest. You have to accept that power is now in our hands. Sooner or later, the Great Greek Project and the Megali Idea will be realised with the support of the Istanbul Greek Patriarch. The anthem that poet Rigas dedicated to the Hellenes as the Greek imitation of *La Marseillaise*, the anthem of French revolutionaries, is being sung in the Balkans also."

Mr Seven, who had earlier shrunk back from Halet Efendi's sudden outburst, was emboldened by these statements. He raised his head and started reciting the anthem just to spite him:

"Sons of Greeks, arise! The glorious hour is here,
And, worthy of such ties, display who gave us birth.
Sons of Greeks! Let us rise in arms against the foe,
Till his hated blood flows in rivers past our feet."

I felt a cold current of air envelop the hall and wondered if Halet Efendi had felt the same chill as me. The silence was broken by Mr Reality who had until then waited without saying a word. "In Istanbul, they say to people in such situations, 'Don't count your chickens before they're hatched!' This is what your situation resembles, esteemed members. Let us first find the key unlocking the door."

I realised that Halet Efendi was angered because I could feel the sweat on his hand moistening the rosette on my binding. Had I remained in his palm a little longer, I would have perished and turned into papier-maché. I judged from the way he tossed me on the table, almost throwing me, that the old scientific ideals of the Society were finished and that these had been replaced by national interests. The pigeons that the master released every seven full moons no longer seemed to carry the ideal of world peace on their wings and the members who met once every seven years without me no longer thought about the possibilities of space travel. Now, flames of ambition burned within all of them. The feelings of nationalism that the French Revolution had spread throughout the world were partly to blame. Were the people gathered in this hall the respected members of the Babylon Society or wretched bounty hunters after the treasures of Babylon? I could no longer decide. "These men are not worthy of the lofty secret I carry!" I said to myself.

Mr Reality was a conciliatory man who gave a positive speech and reduced the rising blood pressure of those in the hall. He referred to the human ideal, the world's future, universal peace, the greatness of their objective and reminded them that they were supranational individuals. He stressed how what needed debating was an ideal of humanity, rather than a set of identities. Their mission, he said, was not sycophancy to king so-and-so or duke such-and-such. They were devotees of the universe and needed to act with their reason and not with their emotions. So saying, he poured high quality Marseille wine into their glasses and presented each of them them with a warm smile.

None of the previous Society meetings had been conducted in such a restless manner and with this much formality. Three quarter-centuries had passed since the tulip-scented Kağıthane meeting where I lost my Leyla and I was rather curious about what the members had discussed in the 10 meetings held in my absence and what they had begun to think in relation to the space research of the Babylonian scholars. But here, neither the dagger bearing the fingerprints of my master Fuzuli that Martel Clovis had taken nor the flask strap that General Stefan had slipped into his pocket, and not even the leather cartouche that Bektaşi baba Abdülhay Efendi took with him, were anywhere to be seen. Halet Efendi was not wearing the cloak that Master Marduk had always worn. Who knows, perhaps in all the time that had passed, certain greedy acquaintances of Babylon Society members had auctioned them off, or placed them as decoration in an ordinary church or Sufi lodge.

When they came to the page where the numbers in cuneiform allocated to my couplets finished, they took out couplets, some from their bosom and others from under their hats and placed them on the table. These were the couplets that Abdülhay Efendi had written at Kağıthane. While these seven pieces of paper that had borne close witness to the last 75 years of European history were being arranged on this night, Halet Efendi continued reading my lines and numbering the remainder of my couplets with a view to seeking my seventh and final couplet. I knew that he had read me over and over again and that he more often than not sank into deep thought as if looking for something. Now I realised that he did not as yet know what he was looking for.

By looking at the couplets in their hands, the members knew that the cipher they sought was formulated upon the juxtaposition of love and secrecy, but they could not progress as they had lost possession of me. As for Halet Efendi, he did not know, when taking me from the Mevlevihane the day Şeyh Galib had died, that the words love and secrecy were the key to solving the cipher. I realised that, if someone holding the post of Marduk remained unaware of this, then the Society no longer shared the same information: they all hid information from one another or leaked it selectively. This was the common disease of all secret societies. As ideas began diverging, information too diverged so that weapons and swords became directed at each other.

They wrote the number 1,375 on the edge of the page containing the sixth couplet they had identified and these seven individuals pored over my story, deliberating for hours on end in a tense atmosphere, for my seventh couplet. "If only I had learned the love and secrecy principle earlier!" muttered Halet Efendi constantly to himself whilst reading and simultaneously translating into French. In no way did my master Fuzuli rush in writing the final cipher, placing it right at the very end of my tale, in the chapter where Leyla visited me in the desert and subsequently perished. It is possible that he wanted the competent individuals seeking the secret of the Society to learn my story completely and had tried to explain that the universe actually vibrated with love. The members paid close attention as Halet Efendi read, striving to find the common denominator of concealment and love whilst also being awe-struck by my sorrowful tale of love.

When their tired eyes began to close after many long hours, Halet Efendi read my 2,723rd couplet with great excitement.

A speck of dust on the path of love I am
All the world knows that pure of heart I am

This was his translation. He suddenly thought about the word denoting "heart" as signifying the locus of the inner world, soul and spirituality and automatically reiterated the prosodic metre, "*maf'ulu mafa'ilun fa'ulun*". All of this corresponded to secrecy. The things within a person, the love in their heart and the belief in their spirit was hidden. Yes, this could be the couplet they were looking for. It was just as well that he had translated the word in the original, "*derun*" as "heart". In actual fact, he did not want these people to sense that he had found it.

However, Mr Somebody became suspicious from his repeating the couplet's metre and said, "Let's consider this couplet for a while!"

Master Halet Efendi felt obliged to explain what had occurred to him. He could mislead them in regard to numbers anyhow and keep this secret to himself. The world's future could not be entrusted to these victims of ambition after all!

"Let us suppose that this is the couplet we are looking for. The 2,723rd couplet. It contains the number seven and love. However, to derive secrecy from the word '*derun*' seems somewhat weak. When its numerological value is calculated, it makes 260 and an indivisible numerical value cannot be obtained upon its division by seven. While the words indicating secrecy and concealment in the numbers of the other couplets can all be divided without a remainder, the way this couplet is flawed in this regard makes me suspicious, to be honest." Such were the explanations he offered. In fact, the former masters had not made such a calculation, but as there was no one present who knew about *ebced* numerology, he had no difficulty convincing them with the exception of Countess Secret. She appeared convinced but was wary that something was being kept from her.

It took two hours for them to read the rest of my story. Our last correspondence with Leyla, her mother finding me in the desert and informing me of Leyla's last will, Leyla's death, Zayd bringing this news to me and my visit to her grave, a shrine for lovers eventually being constructed upon our grave and finally the life in Paradise. None of these scenes softened the ambition for power in the stony hearts of these men. I thought about people who do not believe in love ruling the world and shuddered. If people had no capacity for shivering and trembling with emotion, then how could they be merciful to others? Rulers who have not received their share of love would only contribute violence to the world's future. Over all these years, the only Society members who read the entirety of the love that led to my death and learned of my sad end were these seven individuals, but they had not imbibed a single drop of water from love's wellspring of mercy. At that moment I realised that previous members who had read my story were never curious as to my end when their work was finished.

When the first rays of the sun began streaming into Halet Efendi's drawing room, six people left with the couplets they each carried in their pockets and dispersed into the streets of Paris, having agreed to meet again the following night. None trusted the other and so could not entrust the couplet to be used for decoding the cipher and the calculations upon it to another. Clearly, other calculations were running through the minds of all of them. Only Mr Seven showed that he had been affected by my touching story: as he was going out of the door, he tried to hide the tears slipping down his cheeks. He was remembering the sweetheart he had loved in his youth who had been snatched away by death.

On the following night, guns fired around me and I was splattered with blood. The Society was after blood. Finding the best future for the world, working for global peace and pursuing scientific research into space travels were mere talk. The conflict at hand was important enough to shape the world's immediate future, but greed and revenge was guiding the knights of the universe once more. The blood of Countess Secret and the Shaykh of Love dribbled onto Rukal's peony on my frontispiece. I was right in the middle of the commotion. In none of my travels, whether when coming from Baghdad to Istanbul with Alacaatlı Mustafa and Gökçe Ali and being attacked by the Celali men of the Bey of Erciş on that snowy night, or indeed when I heard Murat Reis's voice during the sea battle on the waters off Crete, had I ever felt this much loss and privation around me.

I now questioned the integrity of these members whose hands thrust out at my binding, picked apart my leaves and plucked out my head and tailbands. These men made their former masters and predecessors look like saints. A copy of one of my couplets remained in the pockets of each of them. They had drawn their weapons, each wanting me for themselves and threatening one another. I had seen much violence in my time, but I had never witnessed such savagery in supposed scholars. "The world must be coming to an end," I thought to myself. If this were so, the defensive plans prepared by the Babylon Society priests several millennia earlier against assaults coming from space as well as the means of using the gates opening to space were all in vain. Each of the current members was an aggressor. That is to say, I felt I had hidden my secrets from past scholars in vain and had actually deceived them. Had they witnessed this bloody scene, they would surely have thought their own ideals of humanity were merely a dream. They would have supposed the world would end not because of some outer forcer from space but from the competition among themselves. They would not have endured all the dangers they put themselves through. At the very least, they would have freed the pigeons they released every year.

The groom informed Halet Efendi that the embassy phaetons were ready and Countess Secret and the Shaykh of Love were sent out on stretchers. My binding had been split into two and my pages into exactly seven pieces. Mr Knowing and Mr Seven had demonstrated the extent of their resolve to seize me by firing their guns but, because they disagreed amongst themselves, only two wounded had emerged from the hall. The blast of the guns brought all the embassy staff rushing to Halet Efendi's drawing room. With his usual equanimity Mr Reality tried to placate the other members. In fact, this duty was incumbent upon Halet Efendi who held the post of Marduk, but this too demonstrated that the balance of power had indeed changed. Bearing the title and wielding the power were quite different matters.

Halet Efendi ordered his men to gather all my components together and, by the time he had collected my binding, my envelope flap and even my crumbling tailband, the guns of Mr Knowing, Mr Somebody and Mr Seven had long since been seized. Mr Reality never carried a weapon anyway. Halet had all the embassy staff leave the hall. Then he cautioned his fellow members sternly. "Now, gentlemen, go along with the couplets in your hands. Neither the French Government nor any future members of the Society are to know what happened here. I hope that when we meet again in seven years, you will have learned how to behave as esteemed members of this Society are expected to behave. By then, I trust that your motives will not be dictated by national interest, and that your ideals will have been nourished by the lessons of human history. Only then will we be able to resume our meetings. L&M will remain with me for the time being. I will have the volume re-bound and will protect it. In protest at what you have done, I will not accept your farewells. Do not forget that, though you may have entered this hall as honourable members of the Babylon Society, you leave personifying all the failings of ordinary human beings."

At dusk, Halet Efendi was still feeling shaken and suffocated by all that he had experienced. In order to rest his spirit, he left secretly for Countess Laurent's villa on the Seine. I, whose colours had been melted by the March winds blowing on his bag, my master Fuzuli's slave Kays, was far away from Leyla, my homeland, poetry and smiling faces. I was shattered and forlorn. I died again every day in Paris, the city of revolutions. After my experiences over the previous two days, I believed that the Declaration of the Rights of Man and of the Citizens of the Estates-General which supposedly defended liberties was actually a lie. I thought the citizens of Paris who died for human dignity had perished in vain. So my despair deepened and I trembled with fear for the future of the world.

And I have no strength left to endure my longing for you, Leyla! Come, wherever you may be...

28
A Memory on the Paris-London Line and the Decree of Tanzimat in Istanbul

The meaning herein is as apparent as the sun
If a lifetime lasted a thousand years it would still be short as a day

Arif

A young man opened the door saying, "Welcome, Madame," just as we were about to walk into the bookshop facing the Gare de Lyon train station. He emanated a sense of thrill and complicity which I had been awaiting for so many years. With his bushy black eyebrows, moustache and paisley necktie under his frock coat, he looked like a handsome Oriental. He even seemed a little familiar. In my half century of living in Paris, during which I grew ever more impoverished alongside Countess Laurent, I had never felt this excited before. This young man was to become acquainted with me and I already felt this within me in some strange way. If

I could have moved, I would have leapt out of the Countess' bag and thrown myself in front of him. I wanted him to know me but, like him, now my garb too was different and maybe this was why he could not recognise me.

"My darling!" Halet Efendi had said the night he thrust me into the Countess' hands so that the other Society members would lose track of me. "I give you this book so that you can remember the timelessness of our love each time you look at its paintings." So it was that, in the seven years that followed, it did not occur to anyone to search for me in Countess Laurent's waterside mansion. It was evident from Halet Efendi's facial expressions during his visits to his Countess that unknown hands periodically rummaged through the drawers, bookshelves and even bedrooms of the embassy. But who would ever find a book that was unknowingly hidden by a secret lover?

After Halet Efendi returned to Istanbul from Paris, I spent years in a distraught state like a chronic consumptive: my pages were meddled with and the integrity of my tale was ruined. Whenever she missed Halet Efendi's warmth of an evening, the Countess would indulge in exotic fantasies and look at me so I remained in her bedroom most of the time. One day I began to fall apart completely. The tailor to whom she sent me removed my gazelle hide kaftan and dressed me in a rough buffalo hide coat. This marked out these sad times for me. In place of the varicoloured undergarment on the inside of my cover was a shirt of gilded cloth and instead of the rosette on my frontispiece was a printed illustration resembling one of my miniatures. I could no longer make out whether I was Eastern or Western.

The years ate into the profits of her Bordeaux vineyards and wore away the Countess' beauty. We moved from the waterside residence, first to a three-storey mansion on Boulevard Saint Marcel and then to a tiny apartment near Saint Germain. On the Countess' seventy-seventh birthday, she left the building in which she was wont to remain shut up for months on end to walk along the streets decorated for the International Exhibition which Sultan Abdülaziz would attend as guest of honour. She wanted to talk of the days of her youth with her bookseller friend next to the Gare de Lyon, and took me with her in her bag for the first time, as a possible conversation piece.

I realised long afterwards that we entered the bookstore accompanied by the tolling of the bells of Notre Dame. We headed directly to the back of the counter, whilst the young man I had seen before was wandering between the shelves. I was more interested in his conduct than in what the Countess and bookseller were talking about. I could observe his every movement from above the counter. Watching him look at works of literature and scan sections of poetry as he stood between the stacks increased my excitement. At a certain point, I saw him take out a fob watch from his vest pocket and then I realised that he could only be an Istanbulite. When he approached the counter and said in his accented French that he wanted to purchase the book, I was convinced. The bookseller realised that he was a foreigner, asked him where he was from and what he was busy with in Paris.

His name was Namık Kemal and he had come to Paris from Istanbul under the patronage of Mustafa Fazıl Paşa. He was to leave for London on the train that was departing a short time later. Countess Laurent felt a flurry of excitement when hearing mention of Istanbul. The speech of this young and handsome man reminded her of Halet Efendi. After a few minutes' conversation, the exact thing that I wanted to happen happened and she said, "What is this book, my dear? Please tell me if you indeed know."

I felt the delight of a warm Istanbul night in the hands of Namık Kemal Bey. He had read my tale when just 10 years of age and spoke of my master Fuzuli when turning my pages. Then he looked at my binding and was astonished, saying that my page numbers were wrong. Showing the miniatures of the scene of my meeting with Leyla in the countryside, he read a few couplets from my story and translated them. It was precisely then that tears began to flow from the Countess' eyes. I was afraid that my heart could not bear it, as she had remained faithful to Halet Efendi's love for all these years and had turned down a great many proposals of marriage. Namık Kemal Bey sensed that this was a sensitive issue and gave up the idea of asking whether I was up for sale. After speaking to him for a while, the Countess made mention of Halet Efendi and the conditions under which he had entrusted this book to her. She wanted to turn to the young man and ask, "Do you know Halet Bey?" but felt a secret shame and dared not. Namık Kemal found it unnecessary to tell her that he had been executed in Istanbul many years before.

It was then that the Countess uttered that sentence that would change the course of my life once more. "Please allow me to present this book to you, young man!" she blurted out. She was prompted by the thought that, if I returned to Istanbul, she would perhaps reach the memory of her beloved. She hoped to remind him that there was still a heart in Paris which loved him dearly. "I have never seen Istanbul, but I have never wanted anything as much as to see it. Seeing it is no more than a dream for me now, but perhaps I will be happy if this book does," she explained. I felt how important

I was to the Countess from the pounding of her heart. I represented Halet Efendi for her, her own beloved. Now, as she headed towards the land to which she felt herself belong, she wanted to reunite me with the land to which I belonged.

"Dear Countess," I said to myself. "You hid me in your bedroom, protected me from the ill-intentioned members of the Babylon Society and embraced me each night as your beloved. I will never forget you. Perhaps you were my most outstanding Leyla and I was not able to see this before."

I came to know Namık Kemal Bey on the way to London. He had an interesting character. In his youth, he had first studied theology as well as Arab and Iranian literature. Then he had spent his twenties frequenting the Poets' Association among such masters as Galib of Leskofça, Arif Hikmet of Hersek and Kazım Paşa of Koniçe, reading *gazals* and *münacat*s. He had attended the underground meetings of the secret organisation known as the Young Ottomans Society and become embroiled in political activities. Having come under state surveillance, he had boarded the Bosphorus ferry and travelled to Paris in secret upon the appeal of Egyptian Prince Fazıl Paşa.

Since Sultan Aziz was coming as a guest of honour to the Paris exhibition and it would be the first occasion when an Ottoman ruler entered Europe without coming on horseback, the French government had sent Namık Kemal a letter requesting that he leave the country for a while in order to avoid any unpleasantness. He was to board the train heading for London from Paris and I was about to set off with him.

I became acquainted with Namık Kemal along with other members of the Young Ottomans – who were called the Young Turks in England – as well as with Ziya Paşa, in London. The most adventurous among them were these two and they both read a great deal on every subject and talked a lot. Namık Kemal wrote fiery pieces attacking the Ottoman state and these were later reproduced by a machine they called the printing press, then being secretly sent to Istanbul. How easy everything had become while I was living shut off from the world in the Countess' house! The parchments upon which strings of scribes had previously written, straining their eyes for days on end, had grown into sheets which could be reproduced by a single machine into hundreds and even thousands of copies. These were sold to people in the form of newspapers. I thought about my own copies. I estimated that I had been copied close to 600 times. Librarians in the future will come to know this better. My tale was known to at least 600 people who had each set pen to paper, whereas now there was no need for the pen in making copies of books. Furthermore, poetry had lost its old value. As a matter of fact, I could not make sense of why Namık Kemal and Ziya Paşa were so preoccupied with prose despite each being a poet. I was baffled as to why they piled up the newspaper they called *Hürriyet* in bundles and sold it for a trifling price to certain selected customers. Why should anyone write prose when there was poetry anyway?

I realised why poetry allowed prose to express ideas and dreams when I returned to Istanbul with Kemal Bey. After Halet Efendi left me in Paris and returned to Turkey, a great many things had changed. The life that I knew no longer carried on in Istanbul. Like the city, the poets and people had also altered and Istanbul's face had become foreign to its old friends. Following the decree that Reşit Paşa had read in Gülhane Square, state institutions had also been restructured. In the more than 300 years to which I bore witness, the teeth of the cogwheels keeping the machine of state working had worn away. They had been ruined and rendered ineffectual by the rapidly advancing thought and technology of the West. When the state lost all power, it had even begun to borrow from other nations for the first time. It had emerged from battles defeated and had all but become accustomed to loss of territory.

Although my poets and my master Fuzuli were still admired in Namık Kemal's time, they had been pushed to one side. Traditional subjects were no longer taught at the *medreses* where the old poets studied and the news was brought by a machine called the telegraph instead of the Tartar courier corps.

More recently, the poets visiting Kemal Bey in the evenings had shown less interest in reading the old poems than in discussing the series of changes made under the Ottoman reform edict. They argued whether it addressed true freedoms and spoke of the absolute need for constitutionalism. How much they seemed to know when compared to the old poets and how much they were occupied in politics! Even if I was not able to accurately estimate the nature of what they called constitutionalism, I was always thinking that they would do good things. My heart only took offence when they spoke ill of former poets, to whom we owed a great deal. Almost all of them said that they were very fond of Baki Efendi, Atai, Nef'i', Nabi and Nedim, and especially Galib Dede, but asserted that their writings now needed to be cast out. This caused me embarrassment towards my former masters.

I was now in frequent dispute with myself. According to the present poets the novel, play and article were the forms to be followed. I had listened to many works of French literature when I was with Countess Laurent and had become acquainted with the plays of Molière and Shakespeare. All of these had seemed to me to be mere exposure and I had criticised them. They related, with a relentless loquacity, the fall of unfortunates without displaying the slightest sense of privacy. What they gained from exposing them to the bourgeois I do not know! If that which is called novel or play is a narrative of events, then here is my tale! Or the tales of *Hüsrev and Şirin, Yusuf and Zeliha, Beauty and Love, The Rose and the Nightingale, The Candle and the Moth, Vamık and Azra, Kerem and Aslı* and many more... The old poets related fictions at length in the form of *mesnevis* or they could tell the subject of a novel in a single couplet, concisely but profoundly. Their novels and plays existed to describe the immortality of warriors or heroes, or for narrating morality tales; they did not indulge in mischief making and looking through people's rooftops into their personal lives. I was unable to grasp how base humanity could be preferred to the celestial. I could not tolerate being trapped by matter when the spirit could be free in the abstract. To my mind, all tangibles should only be used for tangible purpose and all objects should only be used for the sake of meaning. In any case, this was how my master Fuzuli and former masters acted. They would relate abstract topics but select their examples from the concrete. In this way, the life lived and the tangible world were a means to understanding palpable emotion and non-visible thought.

Sometimes I wondered whether these thoughts of mine might be mistaken and I laughed at myself. I needed to laugh again as society and people's entire way of life had changed. People were even more heartless and their emotions were slowly being replaced by their appetites and lusts. I had been able to see this much more clearly when I was in Paris and London. Istanbulites now resembled them, so they were going to be transformed whether they liked it or not. However, did not this transformation need to be an example as opposed to a submission? The poetry of a state whose establishments and institutions had changed, was sure to change also, this I understood. But I could not accept that the forefathers would be cursed by their own children and grandchildren. "Europe will not recognise the East!" Namık Kemal Bey said frequently. It seemed to me that they did not know Europe, for they believed in evolution rather than the refutation of heritage.

While Kemal Bey and his friends reviled the poets who compiled their poems in books they called divans and wrote articles and editions against them, they were actually writing the last will and testament of poetry, just as had already happened with the state. The death throes of a man who had lived for 600 years would of course last for 50 years and they did not give the patient a single dose of medication for 50 years. In the meantime, they did not realise that they were still in need of him and were not able to give up writing poems in the *aruz* metre. The *gazal* had gone and the sonnet had come, but they could not see that a civilisational accumulation was on its way out along with the *gazals*.

I travelled Christendom and saw towns and mansions
I roamed the Muslim world and saw complete ruins

Thus said Ziya Paşa, with his eyes shut; he was turning his back on the accumulated civilisation. I knew that because, during the very same years, Western ambassadors and travellers portrayed Istanbul as a dream city.

Had my master Fuzuli known that his grandchildren would deny him, he would no doubt have turned in his grave. And Galib Dede had certainly not written *Hüsn ü Aşk* for it to be celebrated for a mere 100 years.

The poem's form may change and its structure could alter; if a life in conflict with *kaside* and *mesnevi* prevailed then surely *kaside* and *mesnevi* ought to have moved aside, but their spirit could continue in the new poetic form, cultural continuity could be preserved and compromise be reached without degeneration. When we reached the newspaper era, when novels and plays began to be written, I felt myself aged in my present state anyhow, and thought that my death had drawn near. When I saw that ink no longer flowed from the inkwell but from the roller, I could see that the printers of old as well as their writings were to change and I was ready to retreat into a corner or to sacrifice myself for the Babylon Society. But I could not bear being imprisoned on dusty shelves. I would have liked my tale to be written anew, to be the subject of plays, for my story to be read in newspaper serials, so as to meet with everyone, both young and old, like before, and to make the strings of love in everyone's heart vibrate. I wanted to be produced over again and for young poets and writers to unite the new generations with the forebears. Perhaps for this reason, I thought that the Babylon Society would one day provide me with all this, and fell into reverie thinking about those sweet times to come.

As Namık Kemal Bey and his friends fell under the influence of Western literature, I had begun feeling completely excluded in their company. I was wounded and had difficulty breathing. One night I ended up in Mustafa Reşit Paşa's room. It was a rainy February night when Namık Kemal Bey placed me in the inner pocket of his frock coat and after a

longish journey in the phaeton, he climbed the squeaky stairs which he probed with his walking stick and arrived in the drawing room of the Emirgan pavilion.

Reşit Paşa was wearing his dressing gown and gazing upon the Bosphorus from between the branches of the large chestnut trees. "Come on in, Kemal Bey!" he said when we entered. "Bring this brazier a little closer to me: the weather has cooled quite a lot. Come and sit here next to me. It has been a long time! I have missed you."

Noting his intermittent cough and looking at his face, the lines of which indicated the anguish in his soul, Namık

Kemal Bey thought that he was looking at the face of death and did not know what to say.

"Dear Sir! I have brought you Fuzuli's L&M as you instructed. I was surprised, to be honest, at your wanting to read this in your illness. While we seek the newest of everything, why is it that you wanted a musty old tale like this?"

"Sit down, Kemal Bey, sit down!" he said in an unsteady voice and continued after a few broken coughs. "My concern is not to re-read L&M. Now repeat what I tell you."

As Kemal Bey strove to overcome his astonishment, he repeated clearly and distinctly: "There are seven true secrets for one who knows love. One who possesses this secret gains mastery over the world."

For around two hours, Reşit Paşa relayed information about the Babylon Society to Namık Kemal Bey and spoke for a considerable time about its objectives, the duties of a knight of humanity, the demands of humanism, the space research of the Chaldean sages, Arshiya Akeldan and intergalactic travel, the current locations and identities of the seven members, the date of the next meeting and how the couplets to be brought to the meeting would be assembled, the new structuring of the world, the orientation of the industrial age, how certain states would be wiped off the world map in the near future with new ones being established in their place, how power would be exercised to this end, and the like. He then added: "I spoke with Sultan Abdülhamid today about your future and ensured that authorisation be prepared for your appointment to the Council of State. I have completed my journey in this world and fulfilled my duty in the name of the Babylon Society in the best possible way. From now on, this sacred Sirrush-headed dagger will remain in your possession. Don't forget that the ciphers with each of the members can only be confirmed on this dagger. For that reason, cherish and protect this dagger with your life. When you sense death approaching or are faced with such a threat, remember this day and give this trust to the person you trust most. Along with our secret of course."

Namik Kemal was about to drop me in his bewilderment, when Reşit Paşa reached out and remarked, "Yeees! Let us have Countess Laurent's trust!"

Namık Kemal's confusion increased even more. "How do you know Countess Laurent?" he was able to say in a low voice.

"Come on, Kemal Bey! It was I who protected this book for the entire time it remained with her. Or rather, I felt myself obliged to protect L&M. Why do you think I went to France and stayed there for so many years? It was because of this book."

"I see, Sir. But how did you know that I had it?"

"For goodness' sake, Kemal Bey, don't be so naive! Do you think that you found this book at the Gare de Lyon by chance when you were leaving Paris? You were not the only one who bought a book from the storefront of the bookshop that day. Why do you suppose they call me Great Reşit Paşa, Kemal Bey? It is the secret contained within this book that gives us this power. It will give you the same strength henceforth. From now on you must be careful as wretched treasure hunters will follow your trail in their search for the golden idols of Babylon. You know what is to be done of course."

I was just as astonished as Namık Kemal Bey at what I heard. So I had waited in the Countess' room for all these years for the sake of the Babylon Society. And Namık Kemal Bey had made the journey to Paris for the sake of the Young Turks.

"Let me see this book that I have followed from a distance for all this time!" exclaimed Reşit Paşa and he began turning my pages. "What a beautiful *ta'lik* script it has!" he commented. As he traversed my pages, he stopped to read my couplets, admire my miniatures or examine my numbers in cuneiform script. "Do you know how many Babylon Society masters have left their fingerprints and the sweat of their labour on these pages, Kemal Bey? For how many centuries this book has carried the future of humanity! Here's the treasure you now possess:

A speck of dust on the path of love I am
All the world knows that pure of heart I am.

The 2723rd couplet. The sum of the numbers is 14. It is divisible by seven with a remainder of zero. This zero is the last cipher on the hilt of the dagger that I gave you. It is the seventh of the codes which will open the door of the Tower of Babel. The other codes are with the other members of the Society. A door that can be opened when seven people come together. This door is the portal that opens to space. Just think, Kemal Bey, can you imagine what sort of journeys spaceships will make? This is very exciting to be sure! Hundreds of masters wishing to see this moment never managed to see it. But this old world turns so slowly and scientists are so lazy that I and perhaps even you will not live to see that time. Only when the world's end nears will there come a scientist who can open the doors of space and enable travel to another planet. Perhaps we will seek room for ourselves in outer space when the world becomes too small for humanity. Provided, of course, that extra-terrestrials do not invade our world before that."

Reşit Paşa kept on explaining…

And my beloved Leyla! Where she was at that very moment and with whom I did not know…

29
How my Secrets were scattered and the Ishtar Gate in Babylon was opened

Cast your voice loud in this world like the Prophet David.
For what endures beneath this dome, they say, is but a pleasant echo.

Baki

In the report dated 1 April 1896 that Robert Koldewey of Blankenburg sent to officials of the Royal Berlin Museum, he stated: "Most of what I will discover here will date to the times of Nebuchadnezzar. I have been excavating for two weeks. Everything went very well and I unearthed a mud-brick wall seven metres in length." What Koldewey was apparently looking for was the Library of Ashurbanipal, but what he hoped to find beneath the inner walls of the fortification built from baked clay with 360 turrets and as thick as to allow four-horse chariot races to be conducted around the top, were the seven tablets and the golden statues of the Babylonian gods. He wanted the tablets on behalf of the Babylon Society and the gold on his own account. He kept repeating that he had read about the precise location of the mountain, where he began excavating with 200 Bedouins after setting off from Germany disguised as a traveller, in the books of the historian Herodotus and the physician Ctesias. Strictly speaking, however, had I not been in his bag and had he not seen my master Fuzuli's couplets, then he would never have travelled to sage Akeldan's former land. In that case, not a soul would have known what lay behind those walls washed by the yellow waters of the Euphrates.

From the day he engineered my theft from among Namık Kemal's books at Magosa and added me to his own collection, Koldewey hid me well and acted very patiently. After finding the dagger in Paris and studying it for days, he tested the ciphers held by the different members at various times and always with his eyes closed. He had more or less succeeded in deciphering the codes of the cartouche that Akeldan's servant had placed at the entrance to the Temple of Ishtar. He knew how to act calmly so as to avoid suspicion and continued his work without paying heed to the pressure exerted by the other members in their various nations.

In the seventh year since starting the excavations, he had learned Arabic, Chaldean, Sumerian and Coptic and read to his fellow Society members the writing on an inscription he found on the city walls. He translated from Chaldean into German and English, "I, king of kings, Nebuchadnezzar, have encircled Babylon with a giant wall from the east. I dug its trench and constructed its escarpments with asphalt and bricks. Along its edges I built a great wall as high as a mountain. I constructed wide gates opening on to it, on which I hung doors of cedar adorned with bronze. So that sinister enemies do not beset Babylon from the sides, I girdled it with giant city walls in the same way that the sea surrounds the land with waves. Passage through these is exactly like passage across the sea, across salt water. To prevent them from penetrating the walls, I had soil piled in front of them and surrounded by quay walls made of brick. I reinforced the outer fortification with art and turned the city of Babylon into a fortress."

Of the Society members I saw that day, three were Jewish and four Christian. They were determined to exploit the waning power of the Ottoman state and, at the very least, convey the tablets beyond these borders. This caused me pain. I felt as though I was betraying myself and my former masters.

"Knights of the Universe, esteemed masters!" Marduk Koldewey had said. "We are face to face with the greatest of all cities to be crafted by the hands of man. In order to locate the ruins of the Tower of Babylon that we will find along with Arshiya Akeldan's bones, I will have to dig for another seven years. For this, I am in need of 50,000 Ottoman gold coins to include the cost of daily wages for my workers who are coming from Hilla. And, of course, to pay for a certain number of disturbances to draw their attention elsewhere.

I hope that when we convene again in seven years' time, I can bring with me the reliefs on the gate to the

Temple of Ishtar. By placing the ciphers that each of you possess upon it, we can together unlock the door of our world which opens on to outer space."

When Koldewey returned with eight mules, four horses and six guards to the sinful city of Babylon, he carried in his saddlebags the travel chronicles of Strabo and Diodorus, 50,000 gold coins, the Torah and me. When we reached the city's outer walls from the remnants of the Euphrates Bridge, I had a strong sense of belonging here. I felt as joyous as one who returns to his homeland from foreign lands. No, this did not stem from my master Fuzuli having lived right over yonder, just ten minutes away as the crow flies, or from the possibility that one of his descendants was among those coming to excavate the temple each day. On the contrary, this feeling came from being overwhelmed by memories of a rich history dating back to the Great Flood. I could imagine the compassionate voice of Noah calling his son Shem from above this very wall or the cry of Gilgamesh, the footprints of the Prophet Daniel on this street lined with colossal columns or the codes of Hammurabi. Further on, I might even encounter fragments of the idols smashed by the Prophet Abraham or butterflies fluttering about the hanging gardens of the mystifying queen Semiramis. I could picture the Prophet Jonah's trial of patience or Ashurbanipal taming the lions. Thousands and thousands of years... People upon people... Temples, sacrifices, banquets, victories... The history of humanity continued being winnowed out amidst the mud-brick and fired brick complex that Koldewey unearthed. If these walls, onto which the sweat of who knew how many millions of slaves had fallen, could speak, I wondered what they would say! Babylon! The rebelliousness of humanity. As related by a sacred scripture: "And they said to one another,

'Come, let us make bricks and fire them thoroughly'; so the bricks were to them as stones, and the clay was to them as mortar. And they said, 'Come, let us build ourselves a city and a tower with its top in the heavens, and let us make ourselves a name, lest we be scattered over the face of the entire earth.'"

The Babylon Society wanted to reduce the influence of the Ottomans in Mesopotamia in order to facilitate Koldewey's work. In line with their objectives, they saw fit to incite ethnic factionalism in all the southern states, especially in the Arabian Peninsula. This was the reason behind the gunfire I heard during the years I spent inside the walls of Babylon. And there were two subjects about which I heard often: Lawrence of Arabia and Wahhabism.

When Koldewey found the wide ceremonial avenue that Nebuchadnezzar constructed for the sacrifice of offerings to Marduk, he gave his workers a week's holiday, double wages as well as a bonus. He wanted to examine this place undistracted and alone. Sometimes he worked for 20 hours a day, paying no mind to the aches in his aged knees and enjoying his intellectual existence amidst the mysteries. He had grown so used to this place through the close to 10 years he had spent there that he did not care too much about finding the tablets or the gold. He lived in the arms of history and had befriended the ancients. Sometimes he would talk to them. He would carry on friendships and bear grudges, rejoicing and repining. The new street he discovered, for instance, set him wondering... Who knew how many millennia earlier it had resounded with torchlight processions and displays of jubilation by thousands of people at the same time? Neither the scientific findings of the Babylon Society, nor the glimmer of the golden idols brought him the delight of re-living these scenes centuries later. He was now almost in the position of re-discovering even Akeldan's footsteps and he could not think of anything as electrifying as attaining the secrets of ancient cultures. "Given that I have discovered this street," he remarked, "the Tower of Babel, which was at its most spectacular at the beginning of spring each year for the Nevruz festivities, cannot be far away."

When the days were not long enough to decipher the inscriptions on the slabs along the thoroughfare, Koldewey armed himself with torches and continued reading into the night. Whilst watching him, I recall thinking, "I never met another human being as determined as this man." Finally, on the sixth day of holiday he had given to his workers, he came upon this sentence: "Aibur-shabu, the street of Babylon, I filled for the procession of the great Lord Marduk, and with Turminabanda stones and Shadu stones, I made this Aibur-shabu from the holy gate to Ishtar-saki-patebisha, fit for the procession of his godliness. Nebuchadnezzar, King of Babylon son of Nebuchadnezzar king of Babylon, am I." This was exactly what was inscribed on it and he read it twice, three times, just to be certain. "Yes!" he said hundreds of times. "Yes! Yes!" He was unable to contain himself. The first voice to resound across the desert from stones, walls and monuments tens of thousands of years old, became Koldewey's cry. He cupped his mouth and shouted: "Yeees! Yeeees! Yeeeeees!"

Just as the galloping thunder of Alexander the Great's armies went unrecorded by history, his voice went unheard. But his were cries of triumph. Ishtar meant the mysterious temple of Akeldan. And Ishtar's gate was the gate which contained the ciphers that my master Fuzuli had scattered through my pages.

Koldewey did not sleep that night and studied the slabs on the street one by one. The stones brought from Turminabanda and Shadu were still ruby red and extended in the form of two lines to the street's southern side all the way to the place where the workers' digging tools were kept. Upon the Shadu stones was the sacred lion of the storm god and on the Turminabanda, or breccia, stones were the breasts of the god of fertility. On top of that was a snake relief decorated with scales on its long neck and showing a forked tongue. As they gradually borrowed more and more motifs from each other, these two figures eventually combined. Every 10 metres along the street, the ornamentations of these two figures became enmeshed and both the lion and the snake underwent transformation.

As the first rays of dawn lit up sparkles on the waters of the Euphrates, Koldewey said, "One motif from here, the lion and snake will become Sirrush the Babylonian dragon and 10 metres after that, I will be able to place my hand on the door of the Ishtar Gate." Before drifting off into sleep for at least half an hour, two pigeons took flight from his palm. They both bore pieces of paper containing the words, "Our bride awaits the groom for a night of love!"

The labourers from Hilla came back to work and I felt my patience was all but spent. I really wanted to see the fabulously old treasury whose secrets I had kept hidden for these 350 years. I noticed that some of the workers Koldewey had sent on leave had changed and a few scrawny fellows had replaced the well-built men, but he did not pick up on this. I think there were five of these newcomers. They acted as though they were working and gathered together to whisper to each other during the breaks or when Koldewey withdrew to eat or to meet his other needs. They would indicate the different sections of the temple using facial expressions and then continue pretending to work. They did not look the same as the Bedouin living in those parts. Perhaps they were descended from Turkmen people that had inhabited that area during the time of my master Fuzuli of Hilla. When I was born and raised in Hilla and later began my travels, those parts were richer and more prosperous and its natives better educated. Koldewey was also struck by the shabbiness of these men. "My God!" he exclaimed, "Are these men really born of the great civilisation which made these temples before my eyes?" The man was right. I too was witness to how the quality and wisdom of the people had been debased since the time of my master Fuzuli.

Koldewey gathered all his workers in one place and had them excavate a mound just 50 metres before the Ishtar gate to bring to light the famous Tower of Babylon. To those who asked, he described the Tower of Babylon as being an ancient observatory used for tracing the cosmography of the planets and stars as well as relating the ziggurat legends mentioned in the Old Testament and books of history. Thus he diverted them from his true purpose. He spoke of the great significance of unravelling the history of this place for understanding the prophets as well as science. He explained that the meridian passing right over this region divided the land and seas into two equal parts, that a number called 'pi' could be found upon dividing the perimeter of this temple by twice its height, that the total weight of the earth was recorded somewhere within the temple. He also explained that the temple was constructed with a total of 2,500,000 stones placed on top of each other and that if, with extraordinary effort, 10,000 workers laid 10 slabs on top of the other each day, it could only be completed in 250,000 days, that is in

664 years, whereas the tower was completed in just 20 years. As he baffled the small minds of his labourers with all this information and raised himself to the level of wise king, Koldewey slowed down the momentum of work in the comfort of having finally directed everyone's interest to this new mound. He smoked his pipe twice a day and watched the labouring workers. On the inside, he was reciting prayers for the great masters to come without delay. Over the following days, I could not see a single worker in front of the three metre thick layer of earth remaining sandwiched between life and the Ishtar Gate.

As the workers dug, the shiny bricks remaining from the splendour of the Tower of Babylon reminiscent of a seven-storey terrace were slowly emerging. I could make out cracked walls, doors covered in sculptures of animals and humans and the adjoining arches leading to Semiramis' hanging gardens. I surveyed the Ziggurat and arches and imagined its splendour in Babylonian times. It suddenly occurred to me that, if my master Fuzuli had lived to see this sight, he would most certainly have penned poems for these arches and this tower also.

The sun beat down on the bare, sweaty shoulders and chests of the workers from Hilla. Some of them were maybe even descended from my master Fuzuli. Koldewey tried to join together the cylinder seals which had been broken on impact during excavation. He studied the stamps on the baked clay used as currency and the decorations on the pieces of pottery and earthenware. He spent his days making sure the sound archaeological artefacts were stored safely while also monitoring the guards set to watch them. Sometimes he changed the guards or increased their number. In addition, he took pride in showing the artefacts he had discovered to local Bedouin chieftains who came to visit him. He derived pleasure from their astonishment and enjoyed guiding them around the streets of the city he had unearthed. He brought them to the point of total amazement when he explained how God separated the languages of those constructing the Tower of Babylon. He related how those people built a city for themselves so as to avoid being scattered across the globe and how they wanted to rise to fame by building a tower the apex of which reached the firmament. He spoke of the fleeting nature of life and, referring to the desert animals, how wild dogs and ostrich chicks reigned for longer in this city than the Babylonian magicians, space scholars and the calendar-making priests who had measured time. He formed friendships with them through conversing about daily affairs, gleaned their thoughts about the Ottoman state, followed news about Lawrence and occasionally offered their chieftains bags filled with gold.

One night, when he was re-reading the works of Strabo and Diodorus in search of new information and other facts relevant to the objects and walls he found, six guests at once paid a visit to his tent. These were the Babylon Society members I had met in Baghdad two years previously. I saw they were all as impatient and excited as I was. They mentioned the universities of Paris, London and Rome and said that, after inviting seven separate scientists and archaeologists to come from these institutions to examine the tablets and decipher the engravings on them, they would begin work at the Research Centre, which was to be established in Brussels or Geneva. But there was one problem: how would they remove the tablets without the workers realising and how would they take them beyond the border?

"Honourable knights," said Koldewey. "Do not fret thus in regards to the tablets! These men think of nothing and desire nothing but gold. The tablets are of no interest to them whatsoever." And to the question, "Then how will we take the golden idols?" he responded: "They will not know about the gold at all, esteemed master! In three days' time is the festival of sacrifice for the Muslims. We will send all the workers to Hilla. Whilst they read the poems that Fuzuli dedicated to the Prophet Muhammad, we will be reading his L&M and having the treasures read." He placed handfuls of cheese produced in goatskin, as well as cured beef, dates and peanuts on the ancient Babylonian altar positioned in the middle of the tent and continued. "As long as you are prepared to grab the pick-axe and shovels in three days' time!" he smiled. He then instructed his servant waiting at the tent entrance to bring the jug of wine that he had placed to cool by the roots of the palm trees springing up along the Euphrates.

That night, they held a religious ritual like the priest scholars and offered sacrifices to their Babylonian gods. Then they collapsed like so many wretched drunks.

As the calls to prayer and glorifications to God could be heard from a distance from the minarets of the surrounding villages, the Babylon Society members began digging to reach the Ishtar Gate, certain that no one was around. For two days, lyrical yarns and digging sounds accompanied each other. I was always next to them and wanted them to raise their heads from their work and notice the five people eyeing them from the top of those walls. Finally, on the third day, the ornate gate of Ishtar resembling a chess piece began to surface. On the marble arch at the top was a relief of the same Sirrush as was featured on the pommel of the dagger that my master Fuzuli obtained from the blind librarian of the Baghdad Academy of Sciences and buried beneath the mulberry tree in the *medrese*.

Leaving the picks and shovels aside, they cleaned the gate completely with brooms, rags, iron chisels and metal rods. A square grid was inscribed upon the gate. Inside the grid were 7x7 disassembled palm-sized cartouches and from the first line onwards was written: "Akeldan – Trusted-in Ishta-r and Mar-duk. In th-e love of - Sirrush."

A	K	E	L	D	A	N
T	R	US	S	T	EL	D
I	N	I	S	H	T	A
R	A	N	D	M	A	R
D	U	K	I	N	T	H
E	L	O	V	E	O	F
S	I	R	R	U	S	H

"Beloved Leyla!" I said to myself upon seeing that the numbers etched into the temple gate by Akeldan's servant to whom he had entrusted his secret were like those written between my pages at different times and with different inks. I was convinced that the end of the road had been reached. "A new life in which I will live solely with your love will begin soon! Open your arms to me and console me in a world sunk in deep barbarity!"

On the morning of the fourth day, Koldewey requested the ciphers that each of the members held. He placed the pieces of paper he obtained from each of them sequentially upon the stone altar at the gate's entrance. These were the new numbers obtained from the cuneiform figures indicating the line numbers of the couplets on love and secrecy that my master Fuzuli sprinkled among my pages increased by seven and its multiples. As he was reading them one by one and calculating their numerological values once more, I was blissful. I hoped to begin to experience the love of my Leyla all over again.

The old days had even begun coming to life before my very eyes. Our school days, the beginning of our love, how Leyla's mother scolded her and I took to the desert where I lost my mind. I re-visited my journey to the Ka'ba with my father, the gathering of gazelles and lions around me and our life far from the people, Leyla coming to visit me in the desert, how I learnt of her last will from her mother and threw myself on her grave weeping. All these memories remained fresh.

As Koldewey turned my pages on the stone altar, I suddenly saw myself in one of Nebuchadnezzar's ceremonies of sacrifice in which he was making an offering to Marduk. I felt like Kays' forebear from numberless generations earlier, and the Great Ziggurat of Babylon presented itself before me in all its majesty. Thousands of people, completely unclothed, had filled the square and ziggurat terraces. Their hands were open facing the sky and they were all shouting. When Nebuchadnezzar appeared on the seventh terrace with an eagle head-dress fitted out with jewels, I thought that the very walls would collapse from the screams of joy. Next to him were seven scholar-priests and immediately to his right I saw Arshiya Akeldan. He was smiling at me and it seemed as though they had gathered to behold the knowledge to which they had dedicated their whole lives to producing to envelop the world once more, so many millennia later. I suddenly felt those seven sage priests next to me. Koldewey and the other Babylon Society members were no longer there. Now, at the Ishtar Gate, stood seven wise priests in their silver-embroidered cassocks greeting each other with their felt headpieces and it was as if no time had passed and they had come together in the morning to re-open the gate that they had locked just the night before. I did not even want to think that the hand reaching out to the gate belonged to Koldewey; it was as if the door's keys resembled a chessboard and each was the width of a palm. It seemed they were being pressed by Akeldan himself and he was doing this as though it was something he knew by heart, as if he wanted to show himself to us. Each key he pressed moved inward after some seconds and a few handfuls of fine sand started trickling onto the threshold. Akeldan's fingers successively touched the numbers and letters on the cartouches in exactly the same order as on the wrapping of my master Fuzuli's flask strap around the hilt of the Sirrush-headed dagger. As the cartouches containing the letters were touched, the timbres of the seven musical notes pervaded the shadowy corridors. I realised after hearing those seven notes in order that the Babylon Society members had deciphered the code system and that Koldewey had pressed the keys correctly. I had never imagined that Akeldan was also a musician and that musical notes, even if they were to be named later, were known in those times. While Koldewey pressed the name AKELDAN horizontally, he pressed vertical keys according to the numbers that my master Fuzuli had placed in my couplets. Thus, when he pressed twelve cartouches (my master Fuzuli had encoded two figures with zero) a sound giving all the Babylon Society members a chill blended with a clamour raising clouds of dust and the age-old marble gate opened with a great roar.

The Babylon Society members seemed stupefied. It was not easy; it was the door of a world tens of thousands of years old that was opening.

I sensed that the five people waiting on the walls were also excited by the grinding of the gate. "Wedding night!" exclaimed Koldewey to demonstrate his glee to his friends who were looking at one another curiously and waiting for the dust to disperse. I wondered how many mortals had experienced such a thrill in this world. "No surprise could be as exciting as this marble gate opening to the mystery of thousands of years!" I thought to myself.

A door which had absorbed all the damage of history required the toil of seven people for exactly three hours to be opened as far as to allow a single person to pass through. There was of course, the wreckage of thousands of years, but there was also all the mystery of the past. Inside was dark and cold. They lit the torches they had brought with them and entered the antechamber with timid steps and saw a wide vestibule with seven doors opening to a hall. This was the ceremonial hall of the Temple of Ishtar and the doors opened successively to the rooms of the seven priests. But none of the doors would budge. By the time they were convinced that it was not possible to open the doors with the picks and shovels they carried, it was already deep night and all of them were about to collapse from exhaustion. But then they reflected that they were short of time and the Hillan workers would return the following day. They realised that they had no time to rest and their panic increased even more. It was Koldewey who was the archaeologist and everyone waited for him to come up with a solution. Adding oil and bitumen to their torches in the late hours of the night, they began working again. This time, they checked for any kind of mark or sign upon the doors and tried to gauge whether or not there were hollow spaces by striking them with hammers. Their jubilation turned into a demoralising battle of nerves. They all felt increasingly frustrated. They had only just begun raising their voices at each other when the impact of one of the hammers brought the plaster on the third door crumbling to the ground. There was a small hollow in the void which emerged. This was a recess into which the Sirrush-headed dagger could enter. When they cleaned the recess with the rags they held and placed the dagger in the chamber, the door opened mechanically.

The Babylon Society members first thanked God as they believed that their centuries-old work, the mystical objects relayed from hand to hand and the ideals transferred from mind to mind were about to bear fruit. The future of science and the world was to be shaped by the tablets behind this door. And what would these tablets they had learned of from previous members look like? What were their weights, volumes and shapes?

"Great Marduk! The honour of lifting the veil of our bride must belong to you, please!" said Koldewey, showing the way. This Jew who now bore his torch aloft, was the one among the seven people trying to keep his nerves most steady. He spoke least and thought most. His shrewdness was evident in his eyes.

Everything in Arshiya Akeldan's room, the door to which had been opened, was in its proper place. The centuries had first destroyed this temple and then covered it in layers of grit, but had not changed it inside. The headpiece and cloak he used during the ritual, the silver-gilt girdle and cartridge cord he wore around his waist, the depictions of deities on the walls in the form of dragons, lions, eagles and winged infants, the silver knobbed staff and a great many other items gave those present the sense that this room had only just been vacated the day before. They looked at each object they saw with amazement, but the eyes of these seven men were also seeking out the cuneiform tablets. They did not come across anything resembling a tablet in the visible section of the room. When they opened one of two cupboards on the sidewall, they discovered a secret passage. This must have been Akeldan's private room wherein he dressed for ritual. The ground of the room measured 3x3 metres and its shelves were filled with hundreds of statues large and small. I have been in palaces, the private quarters of kings and in their special treasuries, but I had never before seen in one place a treasure as valuable as the statues in this little room. These were the idols that I had heard about over and over again from the members of the Babylon Society. This was the most magnificent treasure which would be used for the re-establishment of the Research Centre! Amidst the statues half a metre in length was a lion of solid gold which must have been the depiction of the deity Samash. The great mirror made of silver must have been Sin, the dragon sculpted of blue turquoise, Nebo. Nergal was represented with chinks of pink ruby, the golden idol inlaid with purple stones was Marduk and the snake head carved from a solid pitch black diamond must have been the portrayal of Ninib. And the human-headed horse with amber incised into its milk coloured body had to be the representation of the deity Ishtar on Earth.

The members of the Babylon Society were on the verge of swooning before all these treasures. They would leave one and pick up another, caressing each individually, rejoicing, joking and losing themselves.

"Dear friends," the master said. "We must carry these out before daybreak. Otherwise, we will not only lose them tomorrow, but we will also lose our lives and our dreams for the Babylon Space Research Centre. Let us leave the search for the tablets until later. The tablets won't be of any use to the Bedouins anyway." On hearing these words, I was truly petrified. What is more, none of these seven men objected. They were all unfaithful to their oath to consider the tablets before the gold.

The final image reflected in the eyes of the first member to leave the temple at dawn was the voracious look in the eyes of a man wrapped up like a mummy. After thousands of years in darkness, the Babylonian gods were greeted with foreign bullets and daylight. And while the workers coming from Hilla the following day were most curious as to why Koldewey had killed his two visitors, where the other four guests had gone and why he himself was wounded, they did not dare ask. They merely listened to a lecture about the need to keep the news from the regional governor. If the police came here, Koldewey explained, they would have to close the dig and they would be out of work.

I, Kays, my master Fuzuli's slave, saw everything. The only thing I could not make out was the identity of the secret service organisation that stole the idols of Babylon and which country the idols went to. That is all. If the love journey of my Leyla does not end, if I am not rumpled in some place like the treasure whose secret I carry and if I happen to visit once again the palaces of kings or museums, then I will one day certainly recognise the statues I saw in the Temple of Ishtar and relieve you of your curiosity.

It was when the governor of the Ottoman state came and seized everything during Koldewey's convalescence. The first person to enter the Temple of Ishtar was the guard appointed to prevent anyone else from entering. After him came his friends, a bunch of bribe-giving locals and finally a gang of self-interested bandits that the workers formed within a matter of days. Since the Sirrush-headed dagger and the idols belonging to the treasure had been snatched from Koldewey by secret service agents, he had been thinking of ways to open the other doors once he recovered. He believed that, so long as the Sirrush-headed dagger's barrels remained empty, none of the other six doors could be opened. "The tablets are more important than the treasure!" he said to himself. At any rate, the long arm of the Babylon Society would punish the thieves and take back the statues. And even if he did not recover the treasure, money was not that important to the Society. The reins of the twentieth century world would be in the hands of the Society anyhow. Directing political powers and using secret intelligence was sufficient for this. His responsibility was to match the brides with the most suitable grooms.

He was able to get up after a week. Then he saw how all the thoughts that had invaded his mind were groundless. The rooms of the Temple of Ishtar had been smashed with a sledgehammer and their contents plundered. He found the tablets broken into pieces in the middle chamber. They were broken in such small pieces that it did not seem possible for them to be put back together again. On each piece, he could make out a star point, a diagram, a sign, a letter, a number, but which was part of which and which the continuation of another, he could not tell. I saw the Society's tears for the very first time then. Here was a man who assumed authority over every corner of the globe falling flat on the ground and wailing and weeping like a hurt child. The sight affected me greatly.

If I had the power of speech, I would have told him that the guard he trusted had betrayed him and what the man had then gone on to do to his accomplices out of his greed for gold. I would have explained that the thieves who made off with the artefacts were robbed along the way by other gangs, that these vicious *fellahs* had paid no mind to danger as they tunnelled into dark rooms and began quarrelling even while still inside the temple. The items belonging to the Babylonian sages and Arshiya Akeldan's clothing were bought and sold among the thieves for paltry prices. I would have lamented how love, memory, history sometimes dating back thousands of years can be cheapened. These ignorant ruffians, who had virtually vied with each other to leave succeeding generations mind-boggling puzzles, could not be among my master Fuzuli's descendants. The first man to find the tablets had claimed that they concealed jewels, diamonds, and rubies. He had smashed them into smithereens by throwing them against the wall and beating them with hammers and so the efforts of the Babylon Society dating back thousands of years were sacrificed for a few pieces of gold. There was more besides. I knew that Leyla meant as much to me as the tablets did to this man. The only difference was that my love gushed forth from my heart and his from his mind. My love had grown within me to save a human being while his had grown to save the world. For me, there was nothing more real than Leyla; for him, it was the Babylon Space Research Centre. I am heartbroken that I cannot find Leyla...

Leylaaa!

30
About the Tear in my Eye and the "L&M" in my Heart

Attaining lofty stations through scientific study turned out to be wishful fancy... Everything in the world was composed of love, knowledge was merely idle hearsay...

Fuzuli

I know not who gave me the name Kays. Nor do I know who taught me love. I am my master Fuzuli's slave and, from my four hundred and fiftieth birthday onwards, I have been waiting in the same place with my feet in fetters. Outwardly, they placed me right in the times of my birth, within the memories of the Lawgiver and Rukal to protect me from wearing away, withering and being annihilated. But in reality they threw me in dark and airless cells like a captive whose lungs are gnawed away by maggots and whose wounds are blistered. I dreamt with longing of Istanbul, which bedazzled all with its golden glitter, overshadowing the Scandinavia of misty colds, the Russia of frozen rivers, the Italy and France of half-lit musty chateaux, even the Baghdad deserts of starry nights, all the way to the lodges beyond the sacred lands. I do not know whether I resent my current imprisonment. When I strolled around Istanbul's streets for the last time, I saw that not a trace remained of the city's former refinement. The Russian princes from Kiev, the doges of Venice, the priests of Notre Dame, the Kings of Sicily, the Spanish seamen, the Portuguese merchants – none of these miss this city like I do, but I can't help it. I cannot go out and breathe its air! I am right in the bosom of the land, but absence from my home is a pain which grows all the time within me. Perhaps you cannot know what longing for this city while being within it is like. This is how I yearn for this city. This city has something of Rukal for me, as it is voluptuously beautiful... But it also represents Leyla... It means Leyla a thousand times...

I realised that this city was for me, Leyla, when I was placed on the cold shelf in the cell where I reside. This is why I felt myself to belong here despite all the pain, all the suffering. Hilla is the small town of my distant memories, but Istanbul is the city in which I nurtured my loves.

Istanbul was for me my beloved from eternity without beginning; it still is. Now I perch on one of its seven hills, in the Süleymaniye library. I carry on my margins a raft of useless and futile notes on everything from disasters, fires, dates deemed important by my owners, memoirs of births and deaths, to medicinal cures for stomach aches and impotence as well as exercises recommended to young brides wanting to give birth to boys. On my forehead is the inventory number which serves as my name to distinguish me from tens of thousands of other captives on a vast array of topics from folk tales, Kesikbaş epics, the *Arabian Nights*, allegorical love *mesnevis* to Sufi and science treatises, *medrese* textbooks, Qur'anic commentaries, Islamic jurisprudence and hadith collections among others. I am not waiting for the visit of a friend on my cold, damp and lonely days. No one comes to visit me. There is no longer anyone who remembers my master Fuzuli, the Babylon Space Research Centre or Arshiya Akeldan. Even the note on the inside of my back cover is indecipherable. It reads: "This book was hired out by Takkeci Hüseyin Çelebi residing in the vicinity of Şengül Hamam, in the Ramadan of year 1055, for 15 days, in return for three gold coins. May those souls reading this henceforth not omit to mention him in their prayers." I wonder if I went wrong, or whether my master's descendants were disloyal. I do not understand.

I am Kays. Leyla's primordial lover. I am the Mecnun envied by all lovers. I am my master Fuzuli's slave, Mecnun...

I could not find my Leyla. Moreover, not a soul will know of my love or about Leyla for as long as I remain here. People nowadays know Leyla's name and they have even heard about me, but they have no interest in my tale whatsoever. Every so often, a young man is said to dress up as me, a young woman assumes the identity of Leyla, and they call it a stage play.

I am Kays, my master Fuzuli's slave. There may be some who will tell my tale every now and then...